SWORD OF VENGEANCE

BOOK 4 IN THE SAXON WARRIOR SERIES

PETER GIBBONS

Boldwood

First published in Great Britain in 2024 by Boldwood Books Ltd.

Copyright © Peter Gibbons, 2024

Cover Design by Head Design Ltd.

Cover Photography: Shutterstock

The moral right of Peter Gibbons to be identified as the author of this work has been asserted in accordance with the Copyright, Designs and Patents Act 1988.

A CIP catalogue record for this book is available from the British Library.

Paperback ISBN 978-1-80483-485-5

Large Print ISBN 978-1-80483-486-2

Hardback ISBN 978-1-80483-487-9

Ebook ISBN 978-1-80483-483-1

Kindle ISBN 978-1-80483-484-8

Audio CD ISBN 978-1-80483-492-3

MP3 CD ISBN 978-1-80483-491-6

Digital audio download ISBN 978-1-80483-489-3

Boldwood Books Ltd
23 Bowerdean Street
London SW6 3TN
www.boldwoodbooks.com

For my family. Love and support is everything.

Ūs Godriċ hæfð,
earh Oddan bearn, ealle beswicene.
Wēnde þæs formoni man, þā hē on mēare rād
lancan þām wicge, þæt wǣre hit ūre hlāford;
forþan wearð hēr on felda folc totwǣmed,
scyldburh tōbrocen. Ābrēoðe his anġin,
þæt hē hēr swā maniġne man āflȳmde!

Godric, cowardly son of Odda, has betrayed us all.
Many men supposed, when he rode off on the
    horse,
On the proud steed, that it was our prince who fled,
And so the people in the field were divided
And the shield wall was broken. May all his
    enterprises fail,
That he caused so many men to flee.

— AN EXCERPT FROM 'THE BATTLE OF
MALDON', AN ANGLO-SAXON POEM
WRITTEN TO CELEBRATE THE BATTLE
FOUGHT AT MALDON IN 991 AD

GLOSSARY

Aesc spear – A large, two-handed, long-bladed spear.

Burh – A fortification designed by Alfred the Great to protect against Viking incursions.

Byrnie – Saxon word for a coat of chain mail.

Danelaw – The part of England ruled by the Vikings from 865 AD.

Drakkar – A type of Viking warship.

Ealdorman – The leader of a shire of the English kingdom, second in rank only to the king.

Einherjar – Vikings who have died in battle and have ascended to Valhalla.

Euton – A supernatural being, like a troll or a giant.

Gafol – The Danegeld, or tax raised to pay tribute to Viking raiders to save a land from being ravaged.

Heriot – The weapons, land and trappings of a thegn or other noble person, granted to him by his lord and which becomes his will or inheritance.

Hide – An area of land large enough to support one family. A measure used for assessing areas of land.

Holmgang – A ritualised duel common amongst Viking peoples.

Jomsvikings – Viking mercenaries based at their stronghold at Jomsburg who followed a strict warriors' code.

Njorth – The Viking sea god.

Norns – Norse goddesses of fate. Three sisters who live beneath the world tree Yggdrasil and weave the tapestry of fate.

Odin – The father of the Viking gods.

Ragnarök – The end-of-days battle where the Viking gods will battle Loki and his monster brood.

Reeve – Administer of justice ranking below a thegn.

Seax – A short, single-edged sword with the blade angled towards the point.

Thegn – Owner of five hides of land, a church and kitchen, a bell house and a castle gate, who is obligated to fight for his lord when called upon.

Thor – The Viking thunder god.

Týr – The Viking war god.

Valhalla – Odin's great hall where he gathers dead warriors to fight for him at Ragnarök.

Vik – Part of Viking Age Norway.

Whale Road – The sea.

Wyrd – Anglo-Saxon concept of fate or destiny.

Yggdrasil – A giant ash tree which supports the universe, the nine worlds including our world Midgard.

1

Beornoth clung to life, although many had tried to rip it from him with sharp blades, treachery and bloodthirsty malice. He was a Saxon warrior, a thegn, and all his friends, his brothers of the sword, were dead. Beornoth stared up at a shifting sky the blue-grey colour of rotten meat, and a spiteful rain spat across the war-torn land. Tiny droplets whipped and twisted by the wind soaked his face, washing away rivulets of blood from his bruised, tattered flesh.

He lay beneath a sycamore tree, staring up through the dark green leaves and veined seeds at the broiling clouds. The tree curled from the top of a hunchbacked hillside a half-day's ride from the battlefield at Maldon. The battle had been fought and lost that day and Beornoth saw faces in the shifting clouds, the faces of brave men he had loved like brothers, and who had died on a blood-soaked riverbank. A stab of pain took his breath away and Beornoth coughed up another gout of dark bloody ooze, the iron taste of it thick on his tongue. His stomach burned like fire where a Viking blade had stabbed and ripped at his insides. It was as though a serpent twisted and gnawed at Beornoth's guts, devouring him from the inside out. His hip throbbed where a spear had stabbed through the meat above his hip bone. Cuts and gashes littered his face and arms so that there was barely a hand-breadth of flesh free from wounds.

'Steady now,' said Brand Thorkilsson as his face appeared above Beornoth. The raven tattoo on his neck shifted as Brand worked at Beornoth's clothing, cutting away his jerkin and peeling the blood-soaked cloth away from his torso. Brand grimaced and tossed the cloth onto the coiled chain-mail byrnie, which lay on the grass like the shed skin of a war-monster from legend. It was Beornoth's coat of mail and Brand unhooked the smashed links from the flaps of Beornoth's wounds. It was slow, grim work as Brand painstakingly peeled the armour from Beornoth's body. Beornoth bit down on a sycamore twig, gnashing at the foul, bitter wood as Brand prised the tiny hooks of metal from the lips of his wounds. Both Brand and the byrnie had saved Beornoth's life. The small, interlocked links of iron had deflected more blows than Beornoth could remember, and its strength had lessened the wounds which penetrated beneath it. A byrnie was the symbol of a thegn and a warrior. The mail coat, sword, horse, spear and lands granted in return for a thegn's oath to fight for his lord whenever required, that was Beornoth's heriot, his inheritance, the thing that defined him as a thegn: the weapons and land granted to him by the ealdorman, which would pass to the next thegn upon Beornoth's death.

Beornoth sucked in a gasp as Brand wrapped a strip of clean cloth around his stomach wound and tied it off with his teeth. Brand Thorkilsson shook his head and wiped sweat from his brow with the back of his hand.

'You should be dead,' Brand said, and smiled. 'But you are too stubborn for death, even Fenris Wolf and the rest of the Loki brood fear taking you beyond the gates of hell.' Brand spoke Norse, and

Beornoth understood. Beornoth was from north of Watling Street, born to a Saxon thegn of the Danelaw, where they spoke Norse as widely as the Saxon tongue.

Brand ran a hand through his golden hair to wipe rain-soaked strands away from his face and Beornoth was too exhausted to speak, too horrified from defeat in battle to form words. The Viking warlord Olaf Tryggvason had brought his fleet of dragon ships, his drakkar warships, as sleek and deadly as the blade of a seax, to the shores of the River Blackwater at Maldon in the shire of Essex. Olaf and the Danish King Sweyn Forkbeard had crossed the tidal causeway at Northey Island and laid waste to the army of Ealdorman Byrhtnoth in a great slaughter. Byrhtnoth. The greatest man Beornoth had ever known, imperious warrior, noble lord, the *dux bellorum* of King Æthelred of England. Byrhtnoth had been the king's chief warlord tasked with holding back the Viking advance and protecting the East Saxon people from Viking slavery, brutality and murder.

A memory scythed into Beornoth's consciousness, unwanted and unwelcome. The great ealdorman's golden-hilted sword crashing into the churned foulness, the mud, blood, piss and shit-soaked earth beneath the shield wall. Olaf and his Jomsviking drengrs had come for the ealdorman. Olaf's picked champions had formed a swine-head wedge and encircled Ealdorman Byrhtnoth and cut him down in a welter of blades and fury. Beornoth cursed the foul vision and cast it back to the depths of his mind.

'Warriors, lord,' said Brand. He did Beornoth a courtesy refer-ring to him as his lord. Beornoth was not even sure he could call himself a thegn any more. Olaf and his warriors had laid waste and burned Beornoth's lands at Branoc's Tree. The Vikings had put Beornoth's people to the sword and hung their corpses from the great oak tree, which gave the place its name. Beornoth's heriot was gone, sword, spear, helmet and horse all lost in the battle. All that made Beornoth who he was, and what he was, lay crushed, stabbed and trampled on the field at the Battle of Maldon.

Beornoth tilted his head, and three Saxon warriors emerged from the treeline. They strode towards where Beornoth and Brand sat at the top of a small rise beneath the sycamore tree. The three men must have followed their trail away from the battle and through the forest. Beornoth coughed, but his pain-wracked body now exuded hate instead of self-pity. The three warriors were his own people, Saxon warriors of King Æthelred's realm. But they shamed Beornoth and the king, for they came unscathed in hard-baked leather breastplates and carried spears with shining leaf-shaped tips. They had not seen battle that day. Their armour was clean and the spear points unsullied by the blood of the dead.

'Traitors,' Beornoth wheezed through gritted teeth. He wriggled and shuffled, trying desperately to rise from his supine position and strike at the three men. He raged and spat and bled and sank back, too injured and exhausted to rise. Ealdorman Byrhtnoth had lost the Battle of Maldon because the core of his army, the fyrd, or levy of common men duty-bound to fight in time of need, had run from the fight. The cowardly Godric and a handful of Byrhtnoth's thegns, terrified by the sight of Olaf, Sweyn and their feared Viking horde, had led the fyrd away from the battle. Those thegns turned from the fight and took the fyrd men with them, leaving Byrhtnoth with only his hearth troop of East Saxon warriors, and a handful of brave men from Wessex and Cheshire, to stand alone, outnumbered against the heathen.

The three men levelled their spears and spread out, wolfish grins on their bearded faces. They saw two men spattered in blood, one on death's threshold, and the other surely unable to stand against three. Beornoth despised them, cowards and turncloaks, men who had left Beornoth and his friends to die. He wanted to rise and strike at them, to cut them down and scream his defiance in their dying faces. Brand understood. He laid a calloused hand on Beornoth's forearm and squeezed. Brand stood and slid his axe from its belt loop. It was a Viking bearded axe, still crusted with blood from the battle. With his left hand, Brand pulled his long knife free of its sheath and rolled his shoulders to loosen the stiffness which had settled in from a day of hard fighting.

Brand Thorkilsson was a Viking. Born and raised on the shores of a fjord in Hålogaland, Norway. His parents had raised him to follow the ways of Odin, Thor, Týr and Frey. His father had taught Brand to fight from the time he could first walk. He was a professional Viking warrior, a raider, and he was Beornoth's friend. Brand had dragged Beornoth away from the horror at Maldon just as death's terrible embrace tried to smother him in darkness. He had pulled Beornoth away from the clutches of Ragnar the Heimnar and had forsaken his own people to drag Beornoth to freedom. Brand owed Beornoth a debt of honour, for Beornoth had once saved Brand's life, and now the mighty Viking had repaid that debt, for had Ragnar and Olaf captured Beornoth they would have subjected him to the worst tortures imaginable.

'Kill them, kill them, kill them,' Beornoth hissed through clenched teeth stained with his own blood. He rocked back and forth, lying on his back and desperate for Brand to send the three shirkers to hell.

The warrior on the left-hand side paused. He was young, with chestnut hair scraped back from his thin face by a strip of leather. He glanced at the bigger, older man at the centre. That man came on confidently, with a round face and heavy paunch pushing at his breastplate. The man on the right faltered, his large eyes fixed on Brand's weapons, and his tongue darted out between missing front teeth.

'He looks dangerous,' said missing teeth.

'Let's go,' said the man with the chestnut hair. 'There are easier prey, wounded men in the forest like the bastard we just robbed.'

'Shut up,' barked the big man in the middle. 'This one's a Northman and the other is dying. There's three of us. Look at his byrnie and his axe. If we kill this bastard, we'll be rich. Enough ale and whores to last us a lifetime.'

Beornoth raged inside the cage of his battered body. He longed to charge into the three Saxons, to make them pay for leaving the battlefield. He seethed with impotent rage, wanting them to understand what they had done by running from battle, of the suffering of his most honourable friends. Beornoth wanted them to feel what Byrhtnoth had felt as Viking axes hacked into his body. The cowards must feel the brutal, icy bite of steel just like Beornoth's oathman, Wulfhere, who had died holding a causeway beneath the ebb-tide as swords and spears carved his body to ruin. Aelfwine of Foxfield, Leofsunu of Sturmer, all noble warriors, and Beornoth's blood brothers hacked to bloody pieces by the victorious heathens. Even worse, Saxon cowards now preyed on the few survivors who limped from the field of battle, setting upon those who had fought bravely for their ealdorman and king. Beornoth was ashamed to call those three men his countrymen.

Brand advanced on the big man, axe in his right hand and knife in his left. Brand wore a byrnie chain-mail coat which protected him from neck to thigh, his long blonde hair was tied in two thick braids, and his beard neatly trimmed and threaded with small iron trinkets, symbols which honoured his gods. The big man paused as he noticed that his two friends hung back. They saw a Norseman with blood-crusted weapons. A brave man who strode into a fight against three armed warriors. Brand showed no fear because he relished the prospect of combat. That separated Vikings from Saxons and other folk who worshipped the one true God. For a Viking warrior, death in battle was the ultimate honour.

He lived his life to please Odin All-Father; he fought to burnish his reputation as bright as the shiniest blade; and on the day of his death, he longed to die in combat with his weapon in hand. A Viking yearned for that day, when upon being slain by his enemies, Valkyrie shield maidens descended from Asgard to carry his soul to Valhalla and join the ranks of Odin's einherjar. In Valhalla, the warrior spent an eternity fighting and dying each day, then rising again to feast and swive by night until the day of Ragnarök, when the einherjar, Odin's army, would do battle at the end of days against Loki and his monster brood.

So, Brand advanced on the three men with fearless Viking confidence, and Beornoth felt no guilt as the Northman set about the Saxons with savagery and war skill. Brand feinted with his knife, and the big man braced his spear shaft to deflect the blow. He moved slowly and clumsily, and Beornoth snarled with contempt at the coward's lack of skill. Brand's axe blade whipped around like a darting serpent. Its bearded blade cracked the big man's knee like an egg and he stumbled, kneeling on the other leg and staring at Brand with open-mouthed terror. Without hesitation, Brand stepped forward and plunged the length of his knife into the man's eye and twisted the wicked blade. He yanked it free, and with it came a slop of grey, gluttonous filth.

The big man's body quivered in its death throes, and Brand kicked him contemptuously down the hill. The Saxon with the missing teeth held up his hands as if to say he surrendered, as though that would spare him from a Viking warrior's wrath. Brand spat at his feet and plunged his axe blade into where the man's shoulder met his neck. The gap-toothed man held up a hand and turned away from the blow, but Brand's axe sliced through two fingers and chopped into his shoulder with the sound of a cleaver slapping into a side of beef. The gap-toothed man howled in agony and terror. His fingers dangled from his hand by tendrils of skin and Brand yanked his blade free to send the man sprawling to the grass.

The third man turned and ran. He risked a glance over his shoulder to see if Brand followed and tripped over his own feet. He tumbled down the hillside, past where Brand's horse chewed lazily at the wild grass. Brand sheathed his weapons and picked up a fallen Saxon spear. He hefted it in his right hand, assessing the balance of the aesc spear and its polled ash shaft. Brand took two quick steps forward and threw the spear in a low, flat arc. The blade took the running man between the shoulder blades, bursting his heart and killing him instantly.

'If only all of you Saxons fought like those dogs,' said Brand, grinning as he knelt beside Beornoth. 'England would be a Viking kingdom already and I would be a great lord, ruling over your people and drinking your ale.' He laughed and pulled Beornoth gently to his feet. He hooked Beornoth's arm across his shoulders and they moved gingerly down the slope.

'What now?' said Beornoth, the effort of whispering the two simple words dragging any remaining energy from him.

'I'll take you north, to your wife and friends. Then, my debt to you is paid.'

Brand searched the dead men and returned with a half-empty purse of battered coins and a handful of hacksilver. They would need coin to buy food and ale for their journey north to Cheshire, for Beornoth's wife Eawynn waited for him there, and he had one remaining friend who would welcome him, if he could survive the long journey through a country burning with the flames of war. Fleeing Saxons littered the Essex countryside, and the victorious Vikings could raid and plunder the land unopposed because Ealdorman Byrhtnoth and his band of brave warriors were all dead.

2

Brand Thorkilsson carried Beornoth north. They spent the first night under the stars, in the bowl of an upturned oak tree where Brand made a small fire between roots thick with black soil. On the second day, they found an upturned cart in a meadow littered with the remnants of a family's possessions. Carved wooden bowls, a horse's harness and a threadbare jerkin. The scene told of a family desperate to escape the war, fleeing with their possessions but finding only the cruelty of fighting men. Now that Ealdorman Byrhtnoth and his forces were dead, Essex was a war-ravaged place of lawless marauders. Saxon warriors who had fled Maldon formed bands of scavengers, looting for food and silver to take home and have at least something to show for their time away from field or forge. Viking bands also roamed farms and villages, taking slaves to sell at their great markets in Dublin and Hedeby.

Beornoth lay at the side of the road as Brand righted the cart and harnessed his horse to it. Brand lifted Beornoth and laid him in the back on his horse blanket and they picked their way north, keeping away from roads and villages. They traversed pastures and crop-heavy fields, making camp in forests, on high crags or deep caves. For the first three days, the sunlight jabbed at Beornoth's eyes. He rolled in the cart, catching glimpses of rolling clouds and malevolent skies. His breath scraped at his nose and throat; every intake of air tore at his belly wound like a fresh blade. Beornoth twisted, groaned, suffered and survived. Two words kept him alive, Eawynn and vengeance. He repeated them through the long sleepless nights, clinging to life as the demons and wraiths of the dark shifted and crept in the undergrowth with glittering eyes and mean spirits.

Brand made Beornoth wear the lice-ridden jerkin they had found in the field for warmth now that he had no byrnie or its leather liner, and the tiny creatures shifted in Beornoth's beard. They itched and writhed in his chest hair. The battle at Maldon had been a visceral welter of the best and worst of humanity. As he lay in the cart, Beornoth recalled scenes of heroism beyond compare. There had been mindless slaughter and unforgiveable cowardice. But Beornoth had watched the lowliest man of the fyrd, armed only with a wooden club, defend the body of a fallen warrior as though it were the corpse of the king himself. He saw brave men fight with broken swords against the Viking shield wall, and the bravery of it, the sheer magnificence of those men who had perished on the battlefield, made Beornoth weep. His tears stung the rips and gashes on his nose and face, and Brand fed him ale and oatcakes bought on the road, and every day he sniffed Beornoth's wounds to check for the rot that kills a man as sure as a war axe.

Beornoth's body was battered and broken. He had been slashed, stabbed, punched, kicked, clubbed and battered with the force of a hundred forge hammers. On the third day, Brand led them to a babbling brook. Its water danced over shining rocks as it wound its way towards a great river and on to the vastness of the sea. The proud Viking warrior carried Beornoth into the shallows and the cool water kissed his skin and washed his wounds in its chill embrace. Brand held Beornoth like he was the baby of a great euton, a giant from legend. Beornoth was a huge man, a head taller and broader at the shoulder than most, but Brand cradled him like a child so that the water flowed over his chest and stomach. Flakes of crimson swept into the leaping ripples and Beornoth wondered at the honour and kindness.

The dance and leap of fresh water masked the creaking and crackling of Beornoth's ragged breath and some strength returned to his arms and legs. Brand carried Beornoth back to the cart and loaded him in. Beornoth tried to thank Brand with his eyes, the warrior who had once been a hostage in Beornoth's home. Brand had lived with Beornoth for a summer, his life offered by Olaf Tryggvason in warranty against his empty promise of peace. Beornoth should have killed Brand when the peace was inevitably broken. That was the exchange, the life of Olaf's trusted warrior in exchange for his oath. But Beornoth had not killed him. Perhaps it had been God who had stayed Beornoth's hand, or fate itself.

They travelled out of Essex and always north. Brand used coin to buy food and ale, and on the fifth day Beornoth ate some bread and cheese, and Brand sniffed at Beornoth's torn guts again for any smell of the food escaping the wound, but still there was none.

'Odin favours you,' Brand had said, with wonder in his fjord-blue eyes. 'He is the bale worker, the lord of frenzy, lover of warriors, but also betrayer of the brave.'

'I live by God's will,' Beornoth croaked. 'For Eawynn, and vengeance.'

His weakened state embarrassed Beornoth. He felt like a child humbled and driven before an enemy. Every day of the journey was torture, a relentless battle to suffer the pain of his myriad injuries and cling to life. Before leaving Eawynn in Cheshire, at the home of his friend, the Ealdorman Alfgar, Beornoth had taken

Eawynn's red scarf. He clutched it tight in his right fist. His nails, broken and ripped from battle, gripped it and its softness kept her close to him. It gave Beornoth a reason to live, to defy death, and so he did.

On the seventh day, Beornoth's scabs became a hardened, itching shell across his body, cuts knitted together. Beornoth could sit up in the cart for small periods until the pain became too much. He could speak by then, and asked folk in the hills for any wise women who could help tend his wounds. He could seek an abbey or church, and the monks would surely help him heal, but they would rail and protest at the sight of Brand and his heathen pendant and worship of the Norse gods. So, he sought something ancient instead, the deep knowledge of the simple folk. All knew of the Volvas, or witches, of the high places. The women who kept alive the old knowing of herb, plant and poultice. Folk called them to come down into towns and villages when a woman's baby would not come, or a child became possessed by devils.

They found such a woman, a brown-toothed hag with crooked fingers and rancid hair in glistening ropes. She cackled at Brand and touched his raven tattoo. The wise woman brought forth a blackened staff, marked with ancient words and magic. She made an old sign with her fingers to ward off the evil of Brand's neck pendant and cackled, pointing at strange idols dotted about her hovel. A figure of a woman's body with bloated belly and pendulous breasts, a writhing serpent eating its own tail. She took Brand's hacksilver and sewed Beornoth's stomach and hip wounds together with a greased twine made of Beornoth knew not what. The woman danced and sang in the old words, those which were only remembered in the high places. There were things kept hidden in the dark corners of England, more common in the kingdoms of Wales and north of the Roman wall, in the wild lands of the Picts. It was an ancient knowledge of forest lore, or plant and branch and spell, passed down by word of mouth from the time when the world was young. From before the Rome folk came to Britannia with roads, aqueducts, law, order and God. She applied a stinking poultice to Beornoth's many cuts and covered them in what she said were spiderwebs, the tears of a fox, and the spit of a badger. Beornoth wasn't sure about that, but the stuff worked and on the ninth day, even though the stitches itched worse than the lice, he felt closer to life than death.

When Beornoth slept, nightmares plagued him. Dead friends with mutilated corpses begged him to avenge their cruel fate. Godric's crooked smirk haunted him. Godric had led the traitors from the field at Maldon, he who was of the blood brotherhood sworn to fight for Ealdorman Byrhtnoth to the last. Beornoth would wake soaked in sweat, and Brand told him he shook and raged in his sleep. That he emitted terrible cries, jagged sounds from the depths of his soul, the madness and despair for his dead brothers, animal sobs of horror and hate. For Beornoth hated Godric and the traitors with a spite which helped him cling to life.

On the twelfth day, Beornoth tried to stand on stiff limbs, but the pain in his gut and the weakness in his legs made him vomit. The surrounding land lurched, a thorny briar upended, and the sky came towards Beornoth as he fell and Brand caught him and forced him back into the wagon. Beornoth had been aware of weapons clashing and men screaming at various points on their arduous journey north. Brand would not answer his questions about those fights and told Beornoth not to worry. On some days, Beornoth would wake from fitful sleep to find a fresh spear or axe lying next to him, or tattered cloak or woollen trews for him to wear. The leavings of the dead. Brigands and masterless men who had tried to attack Brand on the road, thinking him a merchant or vulnerable traveller, but instead they had found a ruthless killer who ripped away their lives and everything they owned as brutal payment for their mistake.

Brand sold the weapons or exchanged them for food and on the eighteenth day since the Battle of Maldon, Brand led the cart along a road for the first time and they saw Mameceaster's mighty gates. Brand clicked his tongue and his horse carried the cart up a slope; its tracings jangled and Beornoth held on to the cart's side as it bounced on the Roman-built road. They reached a strip of rocky headland and below the forest sloped down towards the River Medlock, and to the west, in a great sweeping hook of that river, perched Mameceaster. Her walls shone like a red sunset on a bright afternoon, and shafts of light shot through the cloud to bathe her gateway in warm sunlight. It was late summer, and hedgerows grew thick with blackberries and Beornoth felt a sense of excitement at the sight of the great old Roman city. Eawynn had fled there following the fall of Branoc's Tree, so that Alfgar could keep her safe behind his high walls and his warriors' spears.

'You were born around here, were you not?' asked Brand, taking the opportunity of the high ground to stare at the surrounding country. It was a rich land of winding rivers, bountiful farms and rolling pastures.

'I was,' said Beornoth. He was growing stronger with each day, and his speech had restored. 'South of here. This was once a borderland between shires, cursed by raids and border disputes. It sits between Northumbria, the Danelaw, the kingdom of York, Mercia and, out of those borders, King Edgar forged Cheshire.'

'The place looks very grand, but it's a backwater. I never heard mention of it until I came to England.'

'It was a city of the Rome folk, and we lost their building skills in the smoke of time. They hammered these places from cut stone and brick. Old and hard. Built to keep out the ancient folk, the Britons who lived here before my people came across the sea.'

Mameceaster sat on a broad hill and was a square of high brick walls. Four great gates opened the walls to the north, south, east and west, and the River Medlock's meander protected it on three sides. The main gate faced to the south, where a cobbled path led into a high turreted barbican with two arched gateways below. Straight pathways cut the fortress into four sections, and timber-built turrets dotted around the walls. Alfgar's great hall stood at the centre where the pathways crossed. It was a town and a fortress, and Beornoth remembered riding into it on Ealdorbana, his old warhorse, to free Eawynn from Alfgar's predecessor, a wicked ealdorman who had taken her hostage to punish Beornoth.

The sight of the city, and the knowledge that Eawynn was inside, swelled Beornoth's heart. After so much suffering, and the arduous journey, there was finally a glimmer of hope for a sliver of happiness, and perhaps a chance to put the horror of Maldon behind him.

3

Alfgar was not at home when Beornoth arrived at the walled burh of Mameceaster, but there were warriors there who recognised Beornoth from the fight at Folkestone. The men of Cheshire had supported Ealdorman Byrhtnoth in that fight against the Vikings, and they remembered Beornoth's bravery in the battle. They escorted Beornoth and Brand through the gate but scowled at Brand, for although the north of England was thick with descendants of Viking settlers, many were now Christians, and Brand's obvious paganism rose their hackles. They showed concern at Beornoth's wasted appearance, for his injuries had taken much of his former strength, and ushered the cart inside the bustling city.

The guards led Beornoth and Brand to Alfgar's hall and the ealdorman's living quarters at the centre of the old Roman fortifications. Servants provided clean clothes, food and drink. A thin man with a face marked by childhood disease led Beornoth to a chamber large enough for man and wife, and Brand to a smaller room adjoining Beornoth's with a single pallet bed. The thin man helped Beornoth clamber onto the bed and then left him in peace. The room was airy and clean, with fresh rushes scattered on the floor and clutches of wildflowers on a small table and hanging above a small hearth. Those flowers spoke of Eawynn's touch, for she was ever a lover of the garden.

Two young girls brought bread, ale and cheese and a bowl of water to wash away the dirt of the road, and Beornoth stood awkwardly, still not able to walk properly as the wounds in his stomach and hip continued to heal. The girls left him alone, and Beornoth grabbed a bedpost to steady himself, wincing at the pain in his guts. Beads of sweat broke out on his brow, and just as he was about to let himself collapse on the bed, the door burst open, swinging back on its leather hinges to bang against the rear wall.

'Beo!' said the woman who filled the opening, and Beornoth sighed with happiness at the sight of his wife. Light shone in from a half-open shutter; her once lustrous hair was tinged with grey, and as the late summer sun bathed her face and the curve of her neck, he smiled at her beauty. She dashed to him, and then flinched as she took in the state of his appearance, taking in the scabs and marks from the myriad cuts and scrapes.

'My God,' she whispered, and made the sign of the cross. 'What have they done to you, my love?'

She sat carefully beside him and ran her soft fingers across his face. A single tear escaped from the corner of her left eye and ran down her cheek. She touched the scabs across his nose, forehead and cheeks. Eawynn bit her lip as she gently caressed the gash which traversed his mouth and split his chin. Half of his right ear was cut away, and he had lost the tips of two fingers on his left hand. Beornoth was a ruin, a smashed and hacked-up memorial to the bravery on Maldon's shore. He searched for words, but none came. So, he stared into her eyes and the knowledge of what he had endured passed between them, as it does between a husband and wife who have lived and loved together for most of their adult lives.

Eawynn nodded and wiped her tears. She set her jaw and moved to the table. She wrung the excess water from a cloth and dabbed at the dust and grime on his hands and face. Beornoth longed to kiss her long, swan-like neck, even the scars left there by Viking raiders long ago. Eawynn cushioned his head with a shining fur blanket, and she tore a chunk of bread from a loaf on a small table and handed Beornoth a bite. She dragged her fingers through his ragged beard and smoothed his hair, tutting at the lice. She reached for the water jug and a comb and wordlessly made him clean.

After she had finished, Eawynn lay next to Beornoth, holding his huge, calloused paw in her small white hand. Beornoth drifted off to sleep, the first without nightmares since the battle. The fight for life, the endless days of bleeding, coughing and unconscious drifting between the realms of living and dead, had been worth it. This was the reason Beornoth had clung to life.

On the following morning, Eawynn helped Beornoth into Alfgar's hall, and Brand joined them. Eawynn and Brand knew each other from the summer Brand had spent as Beornoth's hostage, and whilst Beornoth rested in front of a summer fire, she questioned Brand on the events at Maldon. Every so often she would bring a hand to her mouth in horror, and although Beornoth could not hear their words, he knew she would mourn for the losses of Wulfhere, Ealdorman Byrhtnoth, Leofsunu, Aelfwine, Cwicca, and the rest of their friends who had perished at the hands of Brand's countrymen.

Alfgar arrived late in the afternoon, bustling into his hall before a retinue of mailed warriors and clad in an expensive byrnie coat of chain mail, and a light blue cloak, a bright sword belted at his waist.

'Beornoth,' he said, his voice echoing around the smoke-darkened rafters. 'I was told, I am sorry...' Alfgar stopped in his tracks as his eyes took in Beornoth's appearance. Beornoth sat hunched on a feasting bench. He wore a black jerkin and a long cloak with the hood thrown back. 'My friend,' Alfgar said. He strode to Beornoth, and even though he was an ealdorman, one of the highest-ranking men in all of England, he knelt before Beornoth in the floor rushes and took Beornoth's hand into his own. Beornoth's head sank into his broad shoulders and Alfgar pulled him close with a warm embrace.

'Streonwold,' said Beornoth. 'Fought bravely, but he fell, as did the warriors you sent south with him.'

'He was the captain of my warriors, and he was your friend. We will miss his sword and his experience, but he died a warrior's death and we shall remember and honour him.' Alfgar had sent Streonwold south with a company of his warriors to help Beornoth and Byrhtnoth in the fight against the Vikings, and they had fought courageously and perished in the slaughter.

No more words of pity needed to be spoken between the two men. Alfgar just held him close and kept him there, the big man's shoulders shuddering with anger and sorrow.

Alfgar made them welcome in his home, and despite the unthinkable desolation the battle had left inside Beornoth, there was peace and stability in Cheshire. Alfgar had the respect of all in his burh, warriors and nobles alike. He had grown a beard and looked every bit the ealdorman he never thought he could become. That night, Alfgar invited Beornoth, Brand and Eawynn to a small meal in a room behind his hall. It held only a long table for eight people, a shining oak sideboard for candles and enough food and drink for a feast. Alfgar brought guests, including his wife, Wynflaed, beaming with her flame-red hair. She entered the room with a tiny baby swaddled in soft blankets, and Eawynn's heart melted as she held the small pink child. She kissed its wrinkled forehead and showed it to Beornoth, and he smiled, happy for

Alfgar and the prosperity he had found. Alfgar had been destined
for the Church, but had not felt its true calling. His father had
passed the callow youth into Beornoth's care, entrusting his son's
development to Beornoth and his harsh ways. The lad had grown
from a fearful and pious boy into a stout fighter and leader of men.

Alfgar spoke of masterless men abroad in the north, supporters
from the dead Ealdorman Oslac of Northumbria, outcasts who
roamed the countryside as brigands, raiding and killing.

'Wicked men, every bit as brutal as the Vikings,' grumbled
Oswine, the new captain of Alfgar's household troops. 'But these
are our own people, grandsons of Danes perhaps, but people born
of these lands. Killing their own.'

'Those northern lands are cursed because of the heathens who
settled there,' Lady Wynflaed said. She was young and fresh-faced
and wore a silver crucifix over a blue dress. She cast a sullen frown
in Brand's direction, but the Viking didn't notice because he was
too busy supping ale and stuffing his mouth with roast pork. 'We
could fight forever and there would never be peace. It's futile.'

'But yet we must. That is our duty,' said Oswine. His blue eyes
glinted as he spoke. He was a short man, but broad across the
shoulder, and spoke slowly. Beornoth had heard Streonwold talk of
Oswine, and the old warrior told of a fierce warrior of reputation
and skill.

'Thank you for your hospitality,' said Beornoth, breaking the
tension. 'You have been most generous to keep Eawynn here, and
for extending that generosity to Brand and I.'

'You are welcome to stay as long as you wish,' said Alfgar,
inclining his head. 'Please, consider Cheshire your home. There
will always be a place for you here, Beo.'

Beornoth listened to the group make small talk, but though
they spoke of small raids from Welsh cattle thieves, and of the
wildness of Northumbria, he felt their eyes upon him. His every

living moment was haunted by the battle, a horror that he could not escape from. In the clatter of knives and ale jugs, Beornoth heard the clash of sword and spear. In the scrape of a wooden plate on the tabletop, Beornoth heard a shield split by a Viking war axe. Every time he closed his eyes, he saw men's bodies hacked to bloody ruin, and the faces of his friends dead on the battlefield.

'I will tell you of the battle, if you wish to hear it,' Beornoth said softly, keeping his eyes on his plate. They all longed for the news, and Beornoth knew that if he didn't give voice to his tale, then it would follow him around like a ghost. So, he told them of Olaf and his dragon ships, of Sweyn Forkbeard and his war-Danes. They wept at the tale of Byrhtnoth's fall, and of how Wulfhere held the causeway against overwhelming numbers, and of Streonwold's death.

'Did the king not ride to war?' asked Oswine.

'He sent a force of his household troops,' said Beornoth. 'But the king himself could not fight. His bishops believe that Olaf and Sweyn should be paid to leave our shores, not fought, and the king is ever cautious to heed the advice of the Church.'

'Christ will protect King Æthelred and our people from the godless heathen,' said Wynflaed.

'He did not protect us at Maldon,' said Beornoth, and he spoke more harshly than perhaps he should. Eawynn placed her hand on Beornoth's arm.

Wynflaed fussed with the cross upon her chest and fidgeted in her chair. She opened her mouth, but Alfgar coughed and raised a finger to catch his wife before she challenged Beornoth on the power and glory of God.

'So what will happen in the south?' asked Oswine to fill the awkward silence. 'If there is a Viking army marauding over Essex, the king will have to ride to war?'

'Forkbeard does not want war,' said Beornoth, recalling the

cleverness of the king of Denmark and their challenge of riddles last year. 'He is only here for silver and will probably return to Denmark before the summer ends. Olaf, however, is here for reputation and war. He is the son of a usurped kingdom in Norway, and he would rule there rather than here in England.'

'So why fight your ealdorman then if he doesn't want to own land here?' asked Wynflaed.

'Olaf needs to burnish his name so that he can attract ships and warriors to his cause. He has that now. So, the bishops will offer him cartloads of silver, and Olaf will give an oath of peace. He will sail away rich enough to build a mighty army and win back his father's kingdom.'

'So, the battle was for nothing?'

'No, lady. Olaf had to be fought. Though he won the battle, he lost many of his warriors. Vikings fear those losses. To replenish their numbers, they must either return across the sea, or wait for fresh ships to arrive, and that could take a year or more. We had to fight Olaf to stop his raiding and force him to the parlay table.'

'Could you have won?' asked Alfgar.

'We could,' said Beornoth. His hand curled into a fist, and he had to take deep breaths to still the tense shudder that ran through his body. 'But we were betrayed.'

'How?' asked Oswine, dropping a glistening chicken leg onto his plate.

'Cowards led the fyrd away from the field of battle. They saw the Viking numbers and fled the field, and left us all to die.'

'Do you mean Byrhtnoth's own men fled with the fyrd?'

'They did. The thegn Godric and his brother led the retreat, and he was an oathsworn member of the ealdorman's hearth troop.'

Alfgar wagged a finger and stared at Beornoth with hard intensity. 'Then they shall be punished; the king must hear of this, and he must act.'

'And what of your... friend, here? What role did he play in the battle?' asked Wynflaed. She flicked her hand at Brand as though he were a dog in the street.

'This is Brand Thorkilsson, and I owe him my life. He pulled me from the battlefield when I was wounded and fallen beneath the axes of our enemies. Had he not, then Ragnar the Heimnar would have subjected me to unthinkable torture.'

'Then I thank you, and you are welcome, Brand,' said Alfgar, and he raised his cup of ale to honour Brand. The Norseman spoke only a spattering of Saxon, and that was only because the two tongues were close enough for a basic understanding to pass between men who spoke carefully.

'What is a heimnar?' asked Wynflaed, and Brand laughed at the sound of the word coming from her pretty mouth. She blushed and scowled at him in return.

'Ragnar the Heimnar was once known as The Flayer, my lady,' said Beornoth. 'He was a slaver, and I caught him in his camp full of our captured people. He used the flayed skins of our folk to cover his men's shields. So, I took his legs and arms and left him alive. That is a heimnar, a stump of a man completely reliant on the care and charity of others. Unable to feed himself, or take himself off to void his bowels, and yet able to see and hear the revulsion of others when they look upon him.'

'Such cruelty.' Wynflaed shook her head and made the sign of the cross again.

Beornoth's world was full of cruelty and war. He fought like the Vikings, and to match them, a man must be both brutal and savage. The guests ate and drank and talked of gentler things for the rest of the evening. Eawynn tended a fine garden and curated beehives, which Alfgar swore produced the finest honey in

Cheshire. The baby cried, and Wynflaed let a maid usher him off to bed. Beornoth remained silent, brooding again on events in the south. He thought of Ragnar, and what it meant to be a heimnar, and the irony of it wasn't lost on Beornoth. Branoc's Tree was gone, and Ealdorman Byrhtnoth was dead. Beornoth had neither land, lord nor heriot. He, too, was now dependent on the care and charity of others.

Beornoth slept beside Eawynn that night, and though he was content and happy to be in her company, he did not experience the peace he had hoped for. Still, the events at Maldon nagged at him, the faces of his slaughtered brotherhood coming to Beornoth in the darkness. They whispered the names of Godric the traitor and others who had fled the battlefield.

The days passed in quiet reflection. Beornoth visited Mameceaster's church with Eawynn and Alfgar. He lit candles for the dead and even prayed for their souls, finding solace in the words. Brand spent his time riding in the forests and fields around Mameceaster, or at axe and spear. He practised with Alfgar's men, who complained to Oswine of Brand's ferocity. More than one man suffered a broken wrist or arm under his fury. The priests tended Beornoth's wounds, but his face and body would forever bear the scars of Olaf's war.

Summer turned to autumn, and as leaves changed to bronze and copper, Beornoth grew stronger. He could walk again and take short rides. He helped Eawynn with her garden and spoke to Alfgar about the affairs of his shire. The young ealdorman asked for advice, which Beornoth provided. He kept away from the training fields, and whenever he heard the clash of practice weapons, Beornoth would go indoors. The sounds evoked the ghosts who lived inside his head, and he could not bear the ring of steel or the clash of linden wood shields.

On a day of blue skies and low sun, when dew left the grass wet with gleaming pearls, Beornoth rode south, taking Brand with him to a ford across the River Mersey, and to a fortified holding he knew well. He and Brand took a rest on the river's edge, where the horses could drink from the river and they could eat some of the bread and cheese brought along for the journey.

'Do you know this place, lord?' asked Brand through a mouthful of cheese.

'I am not a lord any longer, so call me something else,' said Beornoth. He wasn't a thegn any more, and not deserving of the title. 'I know all of it. I was once thegn here, long ago. I was born and raised here. My father and his father were thegns here.'

'So this was your home?'

'It was. And what of your home, will Olaf and your people take you back? Men will have seen you drag me away from battle. Ragnar saw you, and he will hate you for denying him the chance to torture me.'

'Ragnar will be furious, but Olaf respects debts of honour and he is a drengr. My family would welcome me home, I have not betrayed anyone. I merely paid my debt. But for now, I will remain with you and we shall see what the Norns have in store for my destiny.'

Beornoth walked to a small wood of trees blown bare of their orange leaves, which rose at the centre of a field recently harvested. The wood perched upon a hillock of green grass and thick, twisting roots, its lower edge ringed with grey rock. He closed his eyes and inhaled the air, fresh and thick with memories. Birds chirped from the clutch of trees, and the breeze was cool upon his skin. In his head, he heard children laughing. Beornoth smiled. He remembered two little girls running through that same field when it was waist high with golden wheat. He remembered chasing them, playing hide-and-seek amongst the high crops. Beornoth reached the copse and put his hand on a cold slab of stone which jutted from the twisting roots like a huge tooth. Its rough coolness brought back a memory of sitting in that small wood, hidden from the folk beyond the palisade and buildings beyond. He and Eawynn would sit there for hours, talking and laughing. Planning their lives together, holding and kissing each other. Beornoth was young then, and Eawynn had been so beautiful, so carefree, but sure of herself. She had run the burh with confidence as the lady to Beornoth's thegn.

Beornoth sighed. His children were dead, buried behind the burh, and he had been away fighting for Alfgar's father, Aethelhelm, when Vikings had come up the river to burn this place to the ground, slashing, rending and tearing with their spears and axes. Beornoth had found his girls' bodies burned, shrunken and blackened in the ruin of his own hall. Beornoth's hand trembled. He swallowed at a hard lump in his throat and felt the impossible weight of the cloak of grief and sadness weigh him down. He looked up to the sky, wondering, as he had countless times, why his God had forsaken him, in those days; why had God punished him by taking their precious lives? His breath was ragged and caught in his chest. God had deserted him and allowed his family, good, pure and innocent, to be slaughtered and brutalised by raiders. They had died, whilst the ravagers went unpunished. What sort of God allowed that to happen? How could God allow Olaf and Sweyn to win at Maldon, and good men to fall to heathen swords? In his time as thegn and in the darker years as a reeve, Beornoth had seen and dispensed justice on murderers and thieves, and yet God had let Olaf and Sweyn live without punishment. Beornoth did not understand how the Almighty could take so much away.

Beornoth closed his eyes, trying to recall the faces of his two dead daughters. He searched the depths of his memory for the detail of their small faces, of which side of her face Ashwig had a dimple, which of Cwen's ears had a deep red birthmark at the bottom corner. All he could remember now was their joy, their soft hair, and their laughter. The savage men who had ripped their warmth from him had taken that away, and left Beornoth hollow, just a vessel of violence, justice and vengeance.

The pain of his past was thick in the place, memories so vivid he could almost touch them. For years Beornoth had wallowed in drunken anger at what he'd lost in those dark days. That had passed, and Beornoth had built a new life, but hate burned inside him like the red fiery pit of a smith's forge. It was a hungry thing of blood and iron, which could never be sated. If Beornoth paused to think of all his pain, it overwhelmed him, sending him into a spiral of malevolent thoughts and feelings. So, he fought a constant battle to keep that hatred at bay, to master himself. Beornoth had accepted Alfgar's hospitality. He would turn his back on war and death. He would be a man of peace now. Beornoth had come to his childhood home to search in the ruins of his past for a way to live the rest of his life. He told himself he must bury his hate and hear his lost children's laughter in the leafy boughs and ripple of river water. Perhaps there was a chance for peace in Beornoth's life, maybe it was time for him to hang up his sword.

But fate laughs at the hopes and dreams of men, because as autumn turned to winter, the king's man came.

4

Frost touched the grass like a dusting of flour. Nights drew in and people brought animals down from high pastures to stay close to their steadings. A roaring fire burned day and night at the centre of Alfgar's hall. Folk prepared for the long winter ahead, storing food, checking roof thatch, and repairing window shutters and doors. Stores were full of harvested wheat and barley, logs chopped and stacked, and fresh ale brewed to last through the long months of short days and frosty nights.

Winter was a time of fireside gatherings and storytelling, of close living huddled in furs and waiting for the first green shoots of spring to appear. But it was only the beginning of winter when the king's man arrived on his white horse. Beornoth sat by the fire with Brand, and the two men worked on Brand's Saxon words. Eawynn paced the long hall with Alfgar and Wynflaed's baby, shushing and singing to the infant boy, who would scream the rafters down until he released the tiniest of burps.

The thin-faced steward and head of Alfgar's household servants came bustling through the hall doors. He leaned into the heavy oak and barked at two female servants to push them closed after him.

'A man approaches,' said Wynstann, the thin-faced man. He spoke quickly, and his long fingers turned over themselves, hands wringing like a butter churn. 'Says he is come from the king, no less.'

Beornoth stood and winced in discomfort and he clasped a hand to his stomach wound. The outside of the stab wound was now a red, puckered scar, but the insides still ached and throbbed if he made any sudden movements. Now that colder weather had set in, the spear thrust he had taken in the hip had also stiffened, to join his already painful shoulder and the other aches and pains his body had suffered during a lifetime of warfare.

'What is his name?' asked Beornoth.

'Lord Hrodgar of Defnascir. King Æthelred's man, come to visit with you, lord, and Ealdorman Alfgar.'

Beornoth nodded and then peered down at himself. He had worn neither weapons nor mail since Maldon, and for the first time he felt less than his former self. A pang of shame made him glance around the hall, wondering if there was an axe, spear or seax that he could grab and keep by him to show a semblance of his status as a warrior.

'Do not worry,' said Brand in Norse, sensing Beornoth's concern, of how his warrior's pride needed the visitor to know that he was a fighter of renown, a member of the warrior caste of Saxon society. He rose and clapped Beornoth on the shoulder. 'Though you do not wear your armour or carry a sword, your scars tell the truth of your reputation.'

Beornoth nodded and brushed down his woollen tunic. Eawynn came to stand alongside him, Alfgar's child sleeping soundly in her arms. Wynstann ordered the servants to fetch bread, cheese and ale and set an eating bench to welcome their guest. He peered out of a window shutter and ran to pull the hall doors open. Alfgar strode in, clad in his fine byrnie and with his sword strapped to his waist. The man beside him walked confidently. He was of average height and build, with the narrow face of a monk or cleric rather than that of a warrior. His left hand was missing, the wrist covered by a leather cap tied around his forearm. He wore byrnie chain mail, whose links were a dark black over a black leather jerkin, and his hair was closely cropped to his scalp.

'Beornoth, allow me to introduce Lord Hrodgar of Defnascir,' said Alfgar, gesturing to the man in black. 'This is Beornoth, thegn of Branoc's Tree.'

'Lord Hrodgar,' said Beornoth, and he bowed his head. Defnascir was a shire to the south-west of King Æthelred's realm, and to be addressed as a lord of that place, Hrodgar had to be a son of the shire's ealdorman.

'Beornoth, tales of your bravery are told across the country, and I am honoured to meet you,' said Hrodgar. He spoke quickly and had clever eyes, deep set and ringed by dark shadows. 'I come from King Æthelred.'

'How is the king?'

'His heart is broken at the loss of Ealdorman Byrhtnoth, and your fellow warriors at Maldon. He bitterly regrets what happened there and sent me here to talk to you.'

'Beornoth is lucky to be alive,' said Alfgar. 'His friend here dragged him from the battlefield when his life hung by the slightest of threads.'

Hrodgar glared at Brand, eyes flitting from the hammer pendant around his neck to the axe at his belt and the raven tattoo upon his neck. Brand returned his stare, and the enmity between the two men was palpable, even though they had met but moments earlier.

'News came to the court of your survival,' said Hrodgar, tearing his eyes away from Brand. 'King Æthelred does me the honour of presenting you with the heriot due to a king's thegn.'

'A great honour,' said Alfgar, beaming with pride. 'Only the king has jurisdiction over a king's thegn. There can be few men in the kingdom as worthy of the honour as you, Beornoth.'

Beornoth struggled to find the words to respond. It was indeed a great honour, placing Beornoth on the same rank as an ealdorman. But where an ealdorman held power through the swathes of land he owned as the leading man of an entire shire, a thegn usually served an ealdorman. A thegn protected and brought order to a collection of hides, or farms, in his hundred, and all the collective hundreds formed an ealdorman's shire. Each thegn was oathsworn to serve and fight for his ealdorman when required. A king's thegn served no ealdorman and took orders only from the king himself, and Beornoth was nervous about what the king expected in return for such high honour from a man who had been a thegn of the East Saxons.

Hrodgar inclined his head, and a stout lad with ruddy cheeks and a mop of sandy hair bustled into the hall carrying a sack over one shoulder.

'The king presents you with sword, spear, seax, byrnie, warhorse and helmet to own as your heriot. You owe your fealty to the king himself,' said Hrodgar, 'and the heriot of this war gear passes to him in the event of your death.'

The lad bustled forward and hefted the sack from his back, and the heavy iron and steel clanked on the floor as he set it down. The lad left it at Beornoth's feet and stepped away nervously.

'I am thankful for the king's generous gift,' said Beornoth. But he was not thankful. It was a gift born of guilt. Æthelred should have summoned an army to fight Olaf and Sweyn, they could have outnumbered the Vikings five to one, but the kingdom was too fragile for it, too brittle under the yolk of the Church, the bitterness of the Danelaw, and the in-fighting of the powerful shire ealdormen. 'Does he ask something of me in return?'

'Only that you serve him with the ferocity and loyalty with which you served Ealdorman Byrhtnoth.'

'We shall celebrate the king's kindness and grace,' said Alfgar. 'Wynstann, prepare a feast for our guest. Show our friend Hrodgar to some quarters where he can rest, and we shall eat before sunset.'

Hrodgar stepped forward and offered his good hand to Beornoth, who took it in the warrior's grip. Hrodgar pulled Beornoth in close.

'I too am a king's thegn,' Hrodgar spoke softly into Beornoth's ear. 'The king is aware of how events unfolded at Maldon. He would see that things are set aright. That those who drove Byrhtnoth to his grave are punished for it. He gives you this ring, as a mark of your authority, should you need it.'

Beornoth stared down at the shorter man as Hrodgar pulled a gold ring from a pouch at his belt. The band was deep yellow gold, inlaid with a green stone etched with the dragon banner of Wessex. 'Æthelred is the king; he can strike down whoever he wishes,' said Beornoth. He held the cold metal ring in his hand but did not slide it onto a finger.

'If only things were that simple. We shall talk more this evening. But the king has set me a task, and revenge is at the core of it. He said that there is no finer warrior in all England than Beornoth of Branoc's Tree, and no man fiercer or more capable of laying down vengeance on those who must face a reckoning.' Hrodgar smiled and followed Wynstann towards the back of the hall, his lad trailing after him with his eyes fixed on the floor.

'What's in the sack?' asked Brand. The quizzical look on the Northman's face showed he understood little of the previous exchange. He knelt and opened the hemp rope and pulled the sack open. Brand whistled as he drew out the leather-bound hilt of a sword. He examined the craftmanship of its hilt and crosspiece and ran his hand down the fleece-lined leather scabbard. Brand handed the weapon to Beornoth, and the leather was supple and warm in his fist. He slid three fingers of the blade free, and a smoky pattern gleamed on shining steel. Beornoth slid it back in and rested the sword against the bench. A sword was a tool he had learned to wield as a child, taught the strokes by his brutish father. But it felt wrong in his hand, its touch an unwelcome reminder of the bloodletting and slaughter on an East Saxon riverbank.

'This helmet is worthy of a king himself,' said Brand. He held a shining helmet, its nasal the shape of a boar with curved tusks. It was full faced, cheek guards forged of strong iron. It rose into a conical shape and was crested with flowing black horsehair. Brand cradled the magnificent piece of armour in his hand and passed it to Beornoth, who placed it on the bench without even looking at it.

Brand didn't notice. He examined the seax, as long as a man's forearm with a single edge and a broken-backed blade. The hilt was carved from antler, and a groove ran along the blade's centre, above which the smith had carved a writhing beast on the back edge. The spear point was wide and leaf shaped, but needed a polled staff for its shaft.

'You are as wealthy as a jarl,' said Brand, grinning. A jarl was a Viking earl, a leader of men and warlord. 'Any man who kills you in battle becomes instantly wealthy when he strips this war gear from your corpse.'

'You keep it,' said Beornoth bitterly. 'I have no use for it any longer.'

A red sun dipped beyond where the meander of the River Medlock carved its path through a rolling valley of dark forest and high pasture. Wynstann busied himself with preparations in the great hall, scolding serving girls for improper place settings, sipping at soup and shouting for more onion, and directing the serving men on how to properly cast fresh reeds on the hard-packed earth.

Beornoth lay on his bed, one hand moving over the jagged scar on his stomach.

'The king honours you, Beo; you cannot throw that back in his face,' said Eawynn. She held up two sets of earrings for him to choose from. One pair was silver wire twisted around a small shell the colour of milk, the second pair were twin birds carved from ivory. Beornoth pointed at the shells.

'I'm not throwing it back in his face. My place is here now, with you,' said Beornoth. He stared at the high rafters, concentrating hard to force away the darkness in his mind.

'Alfgar suffers us to live with him. This is not our home.' She sat on the edge of the bed and pulled on a pair of doeskin slippers.

'It was my home, once.'

She turned to him with a raised eyebrow. 'When you were a boy. We left here to make our home when we were young, and that was taken from us. Then we found a new home in Essex, and that was also taken from us. We are guests here; we do not live here.'

'Alfgar will grant us a house and some small landholding in Cheshire, and we can live out our days in peace. Together.'

'And what will we do on those days? Spin yarn? Plant wheat? Milk cows?'

'Is that not what the simple folk do?'

'Do you know how to milk a cow or plough a field? You are a warrior; it is all you have ever known. I can spin yarn, for that is the bane of all women, but I have no idea how to tend to goats, sheep, and pigs.'

'How did you fill your days at the nunnery?' Beornoth wanted to pull those words back the moment they escaped from his lips. Her hard words tugged at the edges of his dream of a simple, peaceful life. They pulled away the cloak of wish and hope and revealed the reality, which was a shit pot of foolishness.

Eawynn stood, hands on hips and with a scowl fierce enough to send the moon running back beyond the horizon. 'Are you really bringing up the years I spent under the care of nuns after Vikings raped and beat me and butchered our daughters? The years where you left me to rot whilst you lost your heriot and disappeared into an ale jug?'

'I didn't mean that...' Beornoth sat up and reached out for her, but Eawynn slapped his hand away.

'If you must know, I spent my days lost in madness. I don't recall much of those years, other than the pain of my slit throat and the crushing loss of my children.' Eawynn's hand went to the scar around her neck, where the raiders had slashed a knife and left her for dead.

'I am sorry, my love. I should not have said that.' He didn't know what else to say. His words had been cruel, slipping out during a moment of thoughtlessness. Beornoth knew well enough how he had failed Eawynn, but she had recovered tenfold since the burning of Branoc's Tree. She was restored to her old self, but stronger in mind and wiser in counsel.

'You need to think about the future, Beo. Do you think you could be happy living subject to Alfgar's whim, and reliant on his charity? Will he pay you silver? What happens if you fall out with him, or one of his hearth troop takes a dislike to you? What do we do if, God forbid, Alfgar dies? And what of your Viking friend? What will the pagan murderer do now, help you cut wheat and weave baskets in Cheshire?'

Beornoth moved to where the king's gifts were stacked in a corner. The pommel of the blade shone, three balls set into the iron tang, and supple leather so comfortable to hold. He had not thought about his future as deeply as Eawynn; he had considered nothing beyond the now. Brand would surely return to his people now that his debt to Beornoth was repaid; whether or not they would welcome him was a different question. All Beornoth wanted was peace, or rather, no more bloodshed. He rinsed his hands in water ten times a day and still could not wash the blood from them. All he could see were his dead blood brothers, and a house above a soft meadow in Cheshire with Eawynn at his side seemed like heaven.

'So, you think I should accept the king's offer?' he said.

Eawynn came to him and cupped his face in her hand. 'Æthelred is the king, he does not make an offer. You are a king's thegn now, and he expects you to do his bidding. I know you are hurting. What happened at Maldon was terrible, and the slaughter will echo through history like the great battles of our forefathers. But we must live, Beo. Life goes on. A king's thegn takes orders only from the king; with your ring and your sword you can ride into any hall in England and demand respect from any ealdorman. Do not the lives of your friends need avenging?'

'Do not talk of that,' Beornoth said. He moved away from Eawynn, teeth grinding, the muscles in his face working like a blacksmith's bellows.

'Why not? Who can avenge their deaths but you? Don't you see it? That is why the king has sent Hrodgar. He cannot take action personally. Those who must be punished are some of the most powerful men in the kingdom. If the king openly kills or apprehends them, then his place as king could be snatched away as easily as it was from his murdered brother, who was king before him. So, the king asks you to do it for him. Godric, Archbishop Sigeric, the East Anglian nobles, are all warm by their fires. Untouched by Viking blades, they plot and scheme to take benefit and enrich themselves now that Byrhtnoth is dead. Those men who left the field laugh at you and your friends. Why let the Vikings cross the causeway? Why fight at all when the Vikings will be paid to leave our shores? Can you live with that, Beo?'

'Stop it!' Beornoth shouted. He clasped his head in his hands and paced the room. On the journey north, lying in the back of the cart, his lifeblood sloshing in its corners like sea water in a fisherman's coracle, he had thought of nothing but revenge. But he had been gut stabbed and ripped to pieces. Beornoth couldn't touch a blade now without the horror of Maldon flashing before his eyes. 'Let other men seek vengeance for the dead. I was almost dead myself. I will not spend the time I have left in this world surrounded by death. Have I not earned some peace?'

Eawynn came to Beornoth and pulled him into a deep embrace. 'You have,' she whispered. 'We both have. But don't forget who you are, and what you are. I love you, husband, and I will stand by you, whatever you decide to do.'

Beornoth kissed her soft hair and held her close. 'I am sorry for what I said about the nunnery.'

'I know. Come, let's join the feast.'

The fire roared, and Alfgar's table overflowed with freshly baked bread, honey, roasted duck, salted pork and platters of vegetables. Ale flowed generously, but Beornoth drank only water. Hrodgar took a seat of honour next to Alfgar, and around the table were Wynflaed, Eawynn, Bishop Wictred of Cheshire, Oswine and Brand. As they ate, a bard sang a song of long-ago heroes, dragons and monsters who had once lived in the mountains and lakes of Britain. His voice was clear and bright, and he played a flute between verses which delighted Wynflaed. She clapped and urged the bard on to new songs and tales of old.

Brand sat next to Oswine, but kept to himself, unable to understand much of what was said around the table. The Northman stuffed his face with duck and pork until his beard ran wet with the juices, and he drank as much ale as the rest of the guests put together.

Alfgar made toasts to Beornoth, and to the king, and Hrodgar spoke of events in the south. He told of how Archbishop Sigeric had sent emissaries to Olaf Tryggvason to sue for peace and that those discussions were ongoing. He told of his own lands in Defnascir where he was the third son of the ealdorman and had gone into the king's service as a warrior, rising to the position of king's thegn through deeds he had performed for the king. Beornoth kept silent. He ate and listened. He wondered why, if Hrodgar was such an important warrior for King Æthelred, he had not met the man before. Beornoth had fought many times in England's southern shires, at Watchet, Folkestone, Maldon and countless skirmishes.

Wynstann and his fellow servants removed the wooden plates and platters once the guests had eaten their fill, and the guests moved about the hall, talking and warming themselves by the fire. Wynflaed and Eawynn looked to settle the baby down for the night, and Beornoth sat on a bench with Brand. They shared the last remaining chunks of bread and watched the fire dance in the hearth, its smoke running away though the smoke hole cut into the thatched roof.

'The food is good,' said Brand, in between mouthfuls of meat, bread and ale.

'Do you like it here, in Alfgar's shire?'

Brand shrugged his muscled shoulders. 'There are too many Saxons here,' he said, and laughed. 'Further east there are Danes and Norsemen, around York. There would be better.'

'What's wrong with Saxons?'

'You don't eat enough fish, and there is too much talk of your nailed god. It's all you talk about. It's like a sickness.'

'You can stay here, with Eawynn and I. There is a place for you here if you want it?'

'Ha!' Brand scoffed. 'Your priests and women would force me to let a bishop wash me and make me forsake my gods. The women here are pretty enough, but I could never pray to a god who let his own son die on a cross, or that son who let his enemies crucify him. I will always follow Odin, Thor, Njorth and Týr. When I die, I do not want to go to a heaven where a God will judge me for living my life, where I must be pious and pray for eternity. I will go to Valhalla. I will feast and drink with the men I have killed and fight all day with great heroes. That is my destiny.'

'So, you will return to Olaf?'

'Yes, or I will go home. Olaf might not welcome me after I saved you from Ragnar's spite. But he will enjoy the story of your survival, for he is ever amused by bravery and tales of courage and battle.'

'Lord Beornoth,' said Hrodgar, appearing beside the fire. 'Might I talk with you?'

Beornoth stood, hiding his grimace at the stabbing pain in his stomach.

'Of course, Lord Hrodgar.'

Hrodgar led Beornoth towards one of the hall's supporting timbers, as thick around as Beornoth's waist and carved with flowers, racing hares and prancing deer. Hrodgar leaned into the post, took a pull at his horn of ale and smiled at Beornoth.

'There are only ten king's thegns in the kingdom, Beornoth, so welcome to our small brotherhood,' he said.

'Thank you. What services do you provide for the king?'

'We do the things that men cannot. We move between the kingdom's rich tapestry of Church, king, ealdormen, and merchants. We dispense justice, carry the king's word, and provide aid to those who are granted it by the king.'

'My days of fighting in the shield wall are behind me, Lord Hrodgar. So, I doubt I can be of much service to King Æthelred. Perhaps the honour would be better granted to another man.' Beornoth held up his left hand to show the missing tips of two fingers.

'Do you think I can stand in the shield wall with this?' Hrodgar held up the stump of his missing hand and waved the leather cover as though he carried an invisible shield. 'We do not fight on the battlefield. We do our fighting in the wild, on the road, or in halls like this. I may have failed to mention that the king will make a payment to you each year in silver, enough to make sure your wife is well cared for. You will be a wealthy man, Beornoth.'

'I came north in search of peace. I have no desire to return to a life of combat.'

'I mentioned the king's desire for vengeance today. Have you thought about that?'

'I have thought of little else since the slaughter. But I am not the man to seek it out.'

'The king's hands are tied. The Church is too powerful, and they would pay the Vikings off. To raise his army, the king would need money from the deep Church coffers, and the blessing of the archbishop. His inevitable war tax would fall most heavily on abbeys and church lands across the kingdom. War is an expensive business. Then there are those who are not loyal to the throne, like the bastard Aethelric you punished at Bocking. Men who descended from Viking fathers or grandfathers, the powerful men of the old Danelaw who yearn for a return to Viking rule. They are sick of the king's taxes, and of the land they must yield to the Church. Delicate threads hold together the kingdom, like a spiderweb in a thunderstorm. But the king has not forgotten Ealdorman Byrhtnoth, nor his own men, Wiglaf and Wigstan, the Wessex twins who perished in the shield wall at Maldon. Despite the mire through which he must rule his kingdom, he would have us strike back at those who conspired to cause the deaths of men Æthelred loved and admired.'

'And you will go after the men who led the retreat from the battlefield?'

'I will, and I will teach Godric what it means to incur the king's displeasure. For I am his hammer, his sword and his executioner.'

'Then I wish you well on your journey, and hope that those responsible suffer for what they have done.'

Hrodgar stood straight and stared up at Beornoth, his eyes flickering as he peered into Beornoth's soul. 'You will not ride, then?'

'I cannot.'

'Did you know that the Vikings have Byrhtnoth's corpse? That his head is displayed on a spike before their camp?'

Beornoth shook his head and turned to leave, but Hrodgar pressed the stump of his missing hand into Beornoth's arm to stop him.

'There was another survivor. Thered, who was of your brotherhood. He is now the ealdorman of Northumbria and one of the most powerful men in England. He would support any move against the betrayers at Maldon.'

'Thered lives?' The young Northumbrian had fought like a bear at Maldon, and Beornoth had been sure the lad had perished in the battle.

'Did you know that the entire Viking army pissed on the bodies of your old hearth troop? Are you aware that the coward Godric, son of Odda, has claimed land in Essex belonging to Ealdorman Byrhtnoth? That he and his brother enrich themselves whilst Byrhtnoth's widow mourns for her husband with no sword to defend her?'

Beornoth snarled and dragged his arm free. 'You have my

answer,' he said and stalked away. He wanted to vomit and thought he would throw up his meal there in the floor rushes. Could all that Hrodgar had said be true? Beornoth's head spun, anger, fear, rage and sorrow swirling around his mind, confusing him, ripping at his very being.

'The king gave you a warhorse. She is in Alfgar's stable,' Hrodgar shouted after him. 'If you change your mind, I travel south in the morning.'

5

Beornoth heaved the hall doors open, leaning into the heavy oak. He strode out onto the timber walkway and sucked in gulps of chill night air. His breath steamed around him, and Beornoth reeled from the words that had spilled out of Hrodgar's mouth like arrows falling on an advancing army. He leant upon the balustrade which ran around the front of Alfgar's hall and the sounds of Maldon pulsed through his thought cage and banged at his skull like Viking war drums. Beornoth's head ached. He retched and coughed up a sliver of stinking bile.

'Are you all right?' said Eawynn, emerging from the hall with soft steps. She placed her hand on his back and peered around at his face.

'No,' he croaked. He wanted peace, but it was not within his reach. Beornoth was done with war and blood and pain, but it was not done with him.

'Can I help you?'

Beornoth turned to look into her beautiful eyes, dark and deep as mountain pools. His mouth opened and closed, words unformed, thoughts clouded and impossible to wrangle into something coherent. Could they run, become unknowns? Could he find work labouring for some lord in a distant land? No, that was fool's talk. The thoughts of a child and a coward. There could be no running away from his fate. He felt it chasing him, hunting him. The ghosts of Maldon lived inside him, and they wanted something from him.

Eawynn kissed Beornoth on the cheek and returned to the hall, but as she closed the door, another figure slipped through. The doors creaked closed, and Beornoth stared into the black night, interrupted only by the gentle glow of a rushlight or torch in a window in Mameceaster's winding streets. Beyond the city was nothing. Thick night, vast and unforgiving like death's embrace. A sliver of moon fought to wink through the smothering cloud, but the darkness won and enveloped it.

'They want you to fight again?' said Brand in Norse. He leant on his elbows next to Beornoth, staring out into the void.

'Yes.'

'The man with the wolf-joint is a killer, is he not?'

'He is. Wolf-joint?'

'When the great wolf Fenris was loosed upon the world, the offspring of Loki, monstrous and savage, the gods had to find a way to stop him. They tried to chain him, but Fenris broke through each of their bindings with ease. The gods played a trick on the great wolf, telling him that the chains were a test of his strength. Each chain was stronger than the last, and the gods whooped and clapped as Fenris broke each one as though they celebrated his prowess and strength. Finally, a mighty fetter was forged for the wolf. The gods journeyed to Svartalfheim, the home of the dwarves, greatest of smiths. The dwarves formed a fetter named Gleipnir, made of the sound of cats' footsteps, the beard of a woman, the breath of a fish and the spittle of a bird...'

'This is a nonsense; those things don't exist.'

'Exactly, my Saxon friend. So, it was impossible for the wolf to escape from a fetter made from such deep cunning. Anyway, Fenris suspected trickery was afoot, and he refused this ultimate test of strength unless one of the gods would place their hand in his maw whilst he tried to break the chain. None of the gods would consent, none but Týr. For it would mean the loss of a hand and a breaking of an oath, but Týr agreed to do it for the sake of the world and to avoid the onset of Ragnarök. When Fenris Wolf discovered that he could not break free of Gleipnir's links, he bit off Týr's hand. So, we say any man who is missing a hand is wolf-jointed.'

'The king sent Hrodgar to make me his man. He wants me to seek those who fled the field at Maldon and punish them.'

Brand stood and frowned at Beornoth. 'So why are you so sullen? Those men should die, and you should be proud to be the man to do it.'

'I just... don't think I can...'

'I sailed with a man once, a Dane from Jutland...'

'I am in no mood for another story.'

'Stories help us see things more clearly sometimes. I once sailed with a man who was injured in battle, and he believed that the blood that leaked out from his body took away his bravery. He could not and would not fight any longer, even though he had once been a warrior of reputation and skill.'

'And?'

'What?'

'What happened to this man?'

'We left him in Frankia, because he was no use to a raiding crew.'

'So why tell me the tale?'

'Because it was all in his head. Our Godi, the ship's holy man, tried to explain that to him, to cure him with foul drinks, but he would not understand. Your strength is in your heart and your arm; they did not take it from you in the battle.'

'They have Byrhtnoth's head on a spike.'

'Just so. He is a defeated lord, a famous warrior whose death does Olaf great honour.'

'They pissed on the corpses of my friends. Olaf has Byrhtnoth's body, and men come to look upon it. It's not right, and there is no honour in that.'

Brand smiled. 'He was a great warrior; men will want to see it. His spirit has already left the corpse; it's just flesh and bone.'

'The men who fled the field, Godric and his brothers, are stealing land from Byrhtnoth's widow, and the bishops conspire to pay Olaf his gafol payment.'

'So, are you going to do something about it, or just complain about it?'

Beornoth stared into the Northman's pale blue eyes, and Brand held his gaze. A dog barked in a distant lane, and the sound of chatter from Alfgar's hall was muffled by the closed doors.

'If I ride with Hrodgar, I'll kill them all.' Beornoth spoke quietly, his hands curled into fists. 'Every man who led the retreat from Maldon, everyone who conspired with the Vikings, the men who stopped the king from raising his army. All of them.'

A grin split Brand's face. 'Now that would be worthy of a song. There is reputation in such an undertaking. If you ride, I go with you.'

'Even if it means fighting your countrymen?'

'I fight who I want.'

'How many men did you kill in the days after the battle when you brought me north?'

Brand looked out into the night sky and sighed, a plume of smoke bursting from his mouth and drifting upwards to disappear into the blackness. 'Three on the first day, two Danes the next day, and two more Saxons on that same day. More on the road north. The land around the battlefield was thick with Forkbeard's men, and roving bands of Saxons who had fled the battle. They saw you on the back of my horse and thought we were two men easy to rob. And they died for it.'

'You saved my life.'

'So, let's use that life to punish the men who brought about Byrhtnoth's defeat.'

When the feast was over, Beornoth and Eawynn retired to their room. Eawynn was exhausted and fell asleep in moments. But the decision to ride or stay kept Beornoth's mind working, churning around the problem like a river in spate. He tossed and turned and fought with his head and heart.

'What is it, Beo?' Eawynn said eventually, looking at him with bleary eyes in the darkness.

'I have to go. I must ride with Hrodgar,' he said.

Eawynn sat up in bed and rubbed the sleep from her eyes. 'Then we had better get you ready,' she said simply, as though she had known that would be the case all along. By the light of the small hearth in their bedroom, Beornoth pulled on his trews and boots. He tied a leather jerkin about his torso, and gingerly rose his arms. Eawynn stood on the bed and slid the chain-mail byrnie over his hands and shoulders. Beornoth shrugged it down over his chest, the iron rings cold against his neck. It fit well, and the craftsmanship in the king's gift was extraordinary. Beornoth had not worn mail since Maldon, and the coat of armour was heavy upon his shoulders. He cinched the byrnie with a thick leather belt around his waist, upon which he hung the king's sword. The dragon of Wessex was stitched into the red scabbard, but Beornoth refrained from drawing the blade. He fastened the seax in its sheath on the back of his belt with two leather thongs, and suddenly he was a warrior again.

Eawynn brushed his hair in silence and tied it at the nape of his neck. She trimmed his beard, polished the full-faced helmet with a cloth.

'I'll wait for Hrodgar in the hall,' said Beornoth. He couldn't summon the words to tell Eawynn how much he would miss her, how much she meant to him, and he hoped he would see her again. He just smiled at her, and she began to cry. 'Thank Alfgar for his kindness. He is a good man.'

'Come back to me, Beo,' was all she said, as tears streamed down her face.

Beornoth left the room with a lump in his throat and strode along the corridor, his boots heavy on the timber floor. The hall was empty save for a boy who sat beside the great fire. It had died down to a small blaze, and it was the boy's job to keep the thing lit all night. The flames cast dancing shadows across the rafters and Beornoth sat on a bench beside the boy.

'Lord,' said the lad, springing to his feet in shock. He had been half-asleep and had not noticed Beornoth's approach.

'At sunrise, have my horse saddled and find someone to add a shaft to this,' said Beornoth, and he handed the boy the aesc spear blade.

The boy left Beornoth in peace, opening the hall door to reveal a tinge of buttercup yellow in the early morning sky. The door creaked closed and Beornoth warmed his hands in front of the fire. Its flames crackled and spat, and he fed the hungry fire another log which it devoured in its creeping but inevitable grasp. The longer he wore the mail and weapons, the more Beornoth felt like his old self. The emotion of leaving Eawynn crept backwards, like a night spirit frightened away by sunrise. The desire for peace burned and shrank like the log in the fire and was replaced by the hunger for vengeance for his slaughtered brothers in arms. It blossomed in Beornoth like the rising tongues of flame, licking at his heart, forging his resolve. He welcomed it, letting the softness in him die, the want for a gentler life drowning in the sea of rage.

In the empty hall, Beornoth steeled his mind towards those who had to pay for Maldon. Godric and his brother, who led the retreat from the battlefield. Wictred of East Anglia, and his father, the bedridden Ealdorman Leofric, who had promised the support of East Anglia's swords but failed to march. Archbishop Sigeric and his coterie of churchmen who sought to bargain with Olaf and Sweyn, and therefore forced the king to hold his army back or face their displeasure. There were others, thegns, who fled the field with Godric, men who broke their oaths to Byrhtnoth and left him to die.

Servants awoke and busied themselves with the morning meal which Alfgar and his household would consume once they finished morning prayers. Hrodgar entered the hall in his byrnie and war gear, ready to ride out early on his journey south. Beornoth stood and walked to him, and the warrior smiled as he took in Beornoth's gear from the king.

'You look like a king's thegn this morning,' said Hrodgar.

'That's because I'm coming with you,' said Beornoth.

'The king will be pleased.' Hrodgar clapped Beornoth on the shoulder. A wracking cough echoed around the hall and both men turned to watch Brand stumble from the rear door and hawk a gobbet of spit into the floor rushes. He grabbed a jug of ale from a tabletop, leftover from the feast, and took a long pull. Beads of golden liquid poured into his beard and he slammed the jug back onto the table and let out a monstrous burp. Brand wore his byrnie, axe and long knife along with a thick woollen cloak.

'I need a shit,' he barked, and chuckled to himself as he approached the two Saxons.

'Why is this Viking dressed for the road?' asked Hrodgar, looking Brand up and down as though he were pig droppings.

'What did the Saxon sheep-humper say?' asked Brand in Norse. He closed one eye and returned Hrodgar's withering stare. Brand reeked of old ale and sweat. He belched again and blew the foul stink in Hrodgar's direction.

'He asks why you are dressed to ride.'

'Tell him I must go and visit his mother for some warmth on this cold day.'

'He says he is eager to help us punish those responsible for Ealdorman Byrhtnoth's death,' Beornoth lied.

'This man is a Viking. He is our enemy, a slaver, a defiler, and a heathen.'

'He is my friend. He saved my life and killed ten men to do it. Brand is a Viking, but if I ride, then he comes with me.'

Hrodgar tightened his sword belt and shook his green cloak closer about his neck. 'Very well then, but he must learn our tongue. And I won't abide any prayer to his foul gods.'

'His gods do not demand worship or prayer. They ask only that a man lives with honour, that he fights with fury, and if he wants to go to their heaven, then he must die with a blade in his hand. We will need his axe if it comes to a fight. Which it will.'

'Very well.'

'But we do it my way. Everyone must die.'

Hrodgar laughed and took Beornoth's hand in the warrior's grip. Beornoth was not yet healed, still burdened by pain, and even to ride would be difficult. But it was time for vengeance, and Beornoth would bring fire and sword to betrayers, turncloaks and cowards.

6

Beornoth, Brand, Hrodgar and his servant Tata rode south through a land in winter's grip. They kept to the old Roman roads, so that the travellers could spend nights in roadside taverns rather than camp in the wild. The roan mare the king had gifted to Beornoth had been trained for war in the king's own stables. She was not as large or vicious as Beornoth's old warhorses, Ealdorbana and Hrid, but she was fast and strong. Her name was Virtus, which Hrodgar said meant courage and strength in Latin, the tongue of the Church and of old Rome. It was a good name, and the animal responded well to Beornoth's ride: his unhealed wounds made riding uncomfortable, but the mare was gentle and he bonded with her quickly. He fed her oatcakes and brushed her down himself each evening. Beornoth had always felt a closeness to horses. He enjoyed their company. There was a bond between a warrior and his mount, the care and respect of the rider in exchange for the horse's strength and willingness to carry his burden.

They arrived in East Anglia after fifteen nights, to find that Sweyn Forkbeard had left England's shores before winter. The talk

in the taverns was that Sweyn had grown too rich, that he had
plundered so much silver from England that he could not take it
all back to Denmark, because his dragon boats would sink under
the weight of so much silver. Such taverns were the waypoints
along the merchant and trade routes across the country. Beornoth
listened to the drunken men in the tavern talk of Forkbeard as
though they knew him, as though he were a rogue or a legendary
figure, to be respected for his bravery and guile. That tavern was
far enough away from East Anglia for those men not to have felt
the touch of Forkbeard's malice. The men who slopped ale, ate
smoked fish and talked of Forkbeard would not have sisters,
cousins or mothers snatched by his crews to be raped and
enslaved. They would not have brothers, fathers or uncles slaugh-
tered in foraging raids or in Forkbeard's bloody search for silver
and wealth. Beornoth wished the Danish king had stayed in
Gippeswic, which he had taken in summer and used its mint to
create coins for himself. Beornoth remembered the exchange of
riddles in Forkbeard's hall, and how he had not the face or the
bearing of a warrior, but then how Forkbeard had emerged
snarling from the River Blackwater and fought like a demon. He
was gone now, across the sea and beyond Beornoth's reach. Fork-
beard had won. He had enriched himself with silver and reputa-
tion and returned to his kingdom a hero. That was a dark thing, a
knot in Beornoth's gullet, that the king of the Danes had trampled
his way to glory over the corpses of those Beornoth had loved like
brothers.

The four riders followed the old Roman roads, cut straight and
true as the crow flies. Even in winter, evenings in a road tavern
were busy affairs of crackling fires, flowing ale and gossip. Taverns
were places where news was exchanged between men of different
shires. Merchants from London brought carts filled with horn
cups, ivory combs, lumps of amber and iron from Frankia. They

had news of battles in Frankia and the Holy Roman Empire, which they told in exchange for other stories from tin traders from Cornwall, or a mercenary band from Northumbria.

Beornoth and Hrodgar listened to such tales but kept their own affairs private. Tavern keepers honoured the three warriors in chain mail, and the folk who supped bowed their heads and kept their eyes away from the warriors. Tata fetched them ale and food and cared for the horses. The lad kept to himself, quiet but respectful. Talk of Maldon increased the further south they travelled and Beornoth held his tongue as men with grubby hands and stained woollen clothes spoke of the shame in Byrhtnoth's defeat. They laughed at how he had allowed the Vikings to cross the tidal causeway when they were trapped on an island. Men with missing teeth and bulging stomachs roared with laughter at how the Vikings had tricked the ealdorman in allowing them to cross, and how he and his foolish men were slaughtered because of Byrhtnoth's pride. Such talk kept Beornoth awake at night, but those men were not worthy of his wrath. They were the sheep, whom men like Byrhtnoth protected from the seaborne wolves, and it was shameful that Byrhtnoth's name was spoken of with such disrespect. It all added fuel to the fire, building up the roar inside of Beornoth which he contained and allowed to burn in his heart.

'So, Sweyn's gone back home to Denmark,' said Brand on a blustery day. The three riders crossed a babbling brook outside Celmersford, only a half-day's ride from Maldon. 'He's a cunning bastard that Forkbeard. Bled enough riches here in England to keep his warriors rich and happy, and back in Denmark with enough plunder to secure the kingdom he stole from his own father.'

'So, there's only one Viking army in England now,' said Beornoth. 'And it's winter, so Olaf is holed up in Maldon's burh, unopposed and growing fat off Saxon stores.'

'I wish you wouldn't talk in his filthy tongue,' grumbled Hrodgar for the dozenth time since they had left Mameceaster.

'We are talking about Olaf Tryggvason.'

'I am still not convinced about this plan of yours. Surely, if we ride into his camp, the Viking bastard will cut us down, or worse, torture us and then kill us.'

'I have met Olaf before, and although he is a Norseman and a pagan, he has a sense of honour and respects the warrior code.'

'And you think he will simply hand over Ealdorman Byrhtnoth's body?'

'He will let me take the body, but it will not be simple.' Beornoth knew Olaf, had fought the man and spoken with him before. He was hungry for power and glory, and there was no doubt that he was the callous murderer of innocent Saxons. But he was a Viking and a drengr. That was the Norse word for warrior, but to be referred to by that honorific a man must follow the ways of drengskapr, the way of the warrior. If Beornoth asked for his lord's body back so that he could honour his corpse and soul with a proper burial, he believed Olaf would respect that.

'Well, you surely know these pirates better than I.'

'But you have fought the Vikings?'

'Many times.' Hrodgar stiffened in the saddle. 'Part of the bidding I do for the king is to ride to places where raiders strike and assist local thegns to fend them off.'

'And how is it you came into the king's service?'

'Let us save that tale for another day. So, you will do the talking when we meet Olaf?'

'Aye.' A fox scampered across the foot of a hedgerow. It paused and turned to look at Beornoth with glinting eyes and lolling tongue and then disappeared. Olaf would grant Beornoth an audience, but the Viking leader hated Beornoth. Beornoth had killed warriors close to Olaf, and one who had been as a father to the

Viking warlord. Bravery amused Norsemen. The tales of their gods spoke of such things, and they would admire an enemy with the sheer fearlessness to ride into their camp after a defeat to make a request. But there was always a price for such an audience, usually a challenge. With Forkbeard, it had been a challenge of riddles, but more often than not, it involved a fight with one of their champions. Vikings loved to see armed combat or wrestling. It was cultural for them, the battle for supremacy between two men trained to fight, and Beornoth supposed that his own people would have been much the same before they gave up the old gods in favour of the one true God. Beornoth loosened his grip on the horse's reins after noticing that he clutched the leather so tight that his knuckles had turned white. Olaf's challenge would be a fight. It was inevitable, and Beornoth had not fought since Maldon. He was not fully healed, and not even sure he could bring himself to face another man in combat. The defeat had left Beornoth with scars inside as well as out, as though Viking blades had scored the inside of his skull and damaged his mind.

They reached Maldon amidst a driving rain so dense that Beornoth's head hunched between his shoulders and the chill, sheeting wetness soaked through cloak, mail and jerkin alike to coat his body in misery. The horses plodded slowly along the banks of the wide River Blackwater as it swept around a deserted fishing village, once home to a thriving Saxon community, now little more than a huddle of charred posts and tattered wicker. Olaf had spent much of the previous year sailing his fleet of fifty warships around England's south coast, raiding and plundering, before coming to rest at Folkestone. Since the slaughter at Maldon, Olaf had made the burh his home. Burhs were the invention of King Alfred: a network of fortresses constructed to his design, stout and positioned at strategic locations across the old Wessex and Mercian kingdom to allow people to flee within their palisades in

the event of a Viking incursion along rivers from the sea. The
thegns of such burhs were duty-bound to keep the ditches and
palisades in good order, and to make sure men were ready to guard
their walls in times of need. Now, the burh at Maldon was the
fortress home of a Viking warlord, and provided a perfect port for
his fleet in the tidal estuary in and around Northey Island.

The builders of the fortress had chosen its location wisely, with
wide views across the estuary and its surrounding valleys. It sat
atop a hill, dominating the approaches from the river and from
land to the south and west. It stood sentinel over a bend in the
River Blackwater, which began its journey deep within Essex as the
freshwater River Pant. Where the river turned into salt water and
became subject to the tide, it emptied into the Blackwater Estuary
and then on to the heaving mass of the grey-green sea. The rain
pounded the earth and churned the river water. Beornoth tore his
eyes away from where the land curled away towards Northey
Island, and the causeway battlefield where he had lost so much.

'Lord God preserve us,' gasped Tata. Beornoth turned on his
horse, so shocked was he to hear the boy utter a word. He had been
as quiet as a field mouse for the entire journey. His ruddy cheeks
ran pale under his hood, and he pointed a shaking finger along the
road towards Maldon's burh. The breath caught in Beornoth's
throat as he noticed what had so horrified the lad. Rotting heads
on spear points marked the edges of the road, set ten paces apart.
Saxon heads. Beornoth clicked his tongue and Virtus plodded
forwards, snorting at the foul weather. The heads were gaping
spheres of green flesh, empty eyes and crooked yawns. Ravens and
crows had long since picked the tongues, eyeballs and ears from
the grisly waymarkers and each one was a Saxon warrior who had
fallen to a Viking blade at Maldon. They were unrecognisable,
scraps of skin and wisps of hair on yellowed skulls, but each was a
man who had stood in the shield wall and traded blows with the

professional Viking warriors of Norway and Denmark. They were brave men who had stood their ground and not fled in the face of so fearsome an enemy. They had been denied a Christian burial to have their severed heads gawked at by passers-by.

The heads closest to the burh were draped with smashed and slashed scraps of chain mail. These were the thegns, Beornoth's friends. He could not recognise them, but they were undoubtedly the heads of Wulfhere, Cwicca, Leofsunu, Aelfwine, Streonwold, Wigstan and Wiglaf. Men Beornoth had fought beside, shed blood for, and who had bled in turn for him. At the end of the line was a head on its own, the skull draped with a gold chain and set into the rain-spattered mud before Maldon's gate.

'Byrhtnoth,' said Brand. Anger flared in Beornoth. He could barely control himself, fighting the urge to charge his horse into the burh and lay about with sword and seax until the streets ran with Viking blood. Beornoth clenched his shaking hands around Virtus' leather reins, and asked God to care for the souls of the brave dead, to send his angels to search for the brave men of Maldon if they walked in hell unable to ascend without their bodies being whole. The gates to the fortress were wide open, but the rainfall was so heavy that the road leading in was deserted save the four riders. Beornoth closed his eyes. He tapped the fingers of his left hand onto his thigh, those whose tips were cut away on the battlefield, repeating the names of his friends over and over again, whispering and remembering their faces, the way they had laughed and how bravely they had fought.

'Are you coming in or not?' shouted a voice in Norse. Beornoth scrunched his eyes to stare into the relentless downpour, but could see nobody at the gate. 'Up here, you stupid Saxon bastard.'

Beornoth looked up to where a fat-faced man with a bulbous nose leered down at him from the rampart. Beornoth took down the cloak of his hood so that every man on the wall could see his

face. He was more than aware of who and what he was. Beornoth
had been amongst this nest of Vikings before and had fought them
before. They knew his face and his reputation as a Viking killer.
Beornoth crossed his arms over the pommel of the saddle and
leaned forward.

'I am Beornoth Reiði,' he shouted, using the name the Vikings
called him. It meant wrath or anger, and he had earned it.

'So what?' the man shouted back, and laughter pealed out
across the walls. More faces appeared, bearded and curious. 'My
name is Bjarki Goathumper.' More laughter.

'I am here to speak to Olaf Tryggvason.'

'So come in and speak. Why are you shouting at me like an
angry whore?'

'Careful, Goathumper. Or I might come up there and cut your
ugly head off and mount it on a spear. Though I doubt even the
ravens would want to peck at your ugly face.' That at least earned
Beornoth a few laughs.

'Come in, Lord Beornoth,' said a man who stood a head taller
than Bjarki on the palisade. He clipped Bjarki around the head
and the smaller man slunk away to the jeers of his shipmates.
'You have safe passage into the fort. I will tell Olaf that you are
here.'

Beornoth raised his hand in thanks and urged Virtus towards
the gate. He wondered if Olaf would be enraged to see him, or if he
would mock Beornoth for the defeat. Inside the fortress was a mess
of discarded baskets, smashed pots and scrawny chickens. Men
lined the street which ran from the gate to the centre of the burh,
and they were the hard men of the north. Beady eyes peered at
him through the rain. Cold killer's eyes, which had seen furious
seas to the north and south, which were whipped narrow by the
Whale Road's wind. A big man with a mashed nose looked
Beornoth up and down, and a stocky warrior with a tattooed faced

smiled like a man looking at meat roasting on a spit. Tata moaned in fear, and Hrodgar hushed him.

The Vikings pressed in close so that Beornoth's boots brushed past broad chests and fat bellies. A man with a missing ear spat across Beornoth's path, and a warrior with bushy red hair and beard snarled through gritted teeth. A thin man held up the stump of a missing arm and shouted something at Beornoth, and he wondered if he had cut the limb from the bastard in the battle. Once that first shout went up, the rest of Olaf's army followed. They roared and banged weapons on the mud-slick earth. Rain dripped into gaping maws as cruel faces bellowed and spat hatred at Beornoth and his riders. A pink pig whined and ran across Beornoth's path, chased by a small boy with a stick. Even in the rain the place stank of piss and shit, too many men closed up in too small a fortress. Olaf's fifty ships had carried a long two thousand men across the sea from Norway, but Olaf had been in England for two years, and he had fought through two summers. The fight at Maldon had been vicious, and though the Saxons lost, Olaf must have suffered at least three hundred dead, and more injured. With the previous fights at Watchet and Folkestone, Beornoth thought Olaf would be lucky to have a thousand men left. Even a thousand men holed up for winter in a burh would mean rampant disease before winter's end, regardless of access to fresh water.

Beornoth patted Virtus' neck to calm her as the Vikings shouted and roared in the riders' faces. He met their stares, locking eyes with a blue-eyed man on one side, and then a one-eyed growler on the other. Beornoth did not fear them, and that realisation stoked his soul. He had believed Maldon had drained the fight from him like ale from a broken barrel but now Beornoth felt his reluctance to fight ebb away, and it strengthened him. He had fought and killed bastards just like them his entire life.

The hall came into view ahead, rising above the throng of

warriors with dirty, rain-soaked thatch above a high gable. The hall had once held a cross above its door, but that had been replaced now with two huge crossed war-axes.

Men came from the hall; they carried shields and wore helmets. Beornoth's jaw tightened as he recognised the Jomsvikings, the famed warriors from Jomsburg. They were a professional company of warriors who sold their services across the Whale Road. Their skill was famed and expensive, and Olaf had been raised amongst their ranks. In their midst strolled Olaf Tryggvason. He wore a green jerkin and a long fur cloak. Olaf glanced up at the rain and muttered something to himself, shrugging his cloak closer about his shoulders. Olaf smiled at Beornoth, the hard planes of his sharp face shifting like shards of broken ice. Beornoth reined in before him and hefted himself from the saddle. He kept his face still, even though his stomach wound pulsed with agony at the twisting movement.

'Well, well,' said Olaf, putting his fists to his hips. 'I had hoped you were dead, but I couldn't find your corpse when I was mounting the heads of your warriors along my road.'

'Greetings, Lord Olaf,' said Beornoth.

'I would have boiled your skull, I think, and used it as a drinking cup.'

'Or a pisspot,' growled a second man, looming behind Olaf. He was large and baleful, with a bald head and a face even more scarred than Beornoth's.

'Have you come to congratulate and honour me for my great victory over your warriors?' said Olaf, tucking his thumbs into his belt and smiling broadly at Beornoth.

Beornoth did not answer but stared at Olaf in grim-faced silence.

'Lord Beornoth, this is Kraki Farmanson, jarl of the Tronds.'

'I have heard of you, Beornoth,' said Kraki, curling his lip.

'Whereas I have never heard your name before.' The men around Olaf shifted at the insult.

Olaf laughed. 'Very good, Lord Beornoth. Should I call you that? I burned your hall and killed your people this summer, so perhaps you are not a lord any more. I see you have one of my Norsemen with you?'

'Lord Olaf,' said Brand, inclining his head.

'Have you turned Saxon? Or are you his lover?' The Vikings roared with laughter.

'I took Lord Beornoth from the battle, lord. To repay a blood debt.'

'So, are you a traitor or a man of honour we should respect for saving our greatest enemy to pay a debt? I will think on it, Brand Thorkilsson.'

'This man is Hrodgar, a thegn of King Æthelred.'

'So, why are you here?' said Olaf, ignoring Hrodgar.

'I have come to ask you for my Lord Byrhtnoth's body, Lord Olaf. So that I might take it to his family for a Christian burial.'

'You are an insolent bastard, Beornoth. I'll give you that. We have pissed on that corpse, and laughed at how small your warlord's manhood was. Have you come to beg me for it?'

'No. I have come to ask you as a man of honour. I hoped that you would see a worthy foe in Byrhtnoth, a man who should not be denied the glories of the afterlife after living his earthly life so bravely. He fought like a Northman, and he was ever a man of his word.'

'Kraki?'

'Yes, lord?' said the scarred warrior.

'Did we feed the Saxon jarl's body to the pigs yet?'

'No, lord.'

'Good. But I am not sure if I should let you have it. You killed my White Wolf in the great battle, and before that you killed

Palnatoki. So, I think I hate you, Beornoth, and am not inclined to agree to your request.'

The Jomsvikings rumbled in anger at the mention of their former leader, who Beornoth had killed at Watchet. Palnatoki had raised Olaf, taught him to fight, and helped him rise to power so that he might pursue his slaughtered family's claim to the throne of Norway. Olaf had not achieved that dream yet, but had become one of the most feared and powerful Viking lords.

'Give him nothing,' screeched a high-pitched Norse voice from somewhere behind Olaf. 'He is a thing of Loki, Beornoth Reiði, a curse on our people. A hell-demon. Grab him, deliver him to me.' Two men barged their way through the crowd behind Olaf, and they carried a long timber box, a stained brown container shaped like a horse trough. The men grunted, and stood the box up on its end. Within it was a hollow-cheeked head which rocked from side to side on top of a bloated body with no arms or legs. Wide eyes shone in sunken, dark pits in a face framed by a greasy beard and thin, wet-looking hair. It was Ragnar the Heimnar.

Olaf barely stifled a sigh of disappointment at the arrival of the heimnar. 'Easy, Ragnar. Lord Beornoth comes to us under a truce to talk. He is my guest.'

'Your guest?' spluttered Ragnar, his head thrashing from side to side. For a moment Beornoth thought he would fall out of his box until one of the two men who had carried him tightened a leather strap which ran across his chest and through the back of the wooden casket. 'He is our enemy, hated by the gods, give him to me. Let me have him, Olaf, let me have him!' Ragnar's shrill cut the air like the sound of a fox cry, and men shrank away from its awful rancour.

'Take him away,' said Olaf with a wave of his hand. Ragnar screamed in protest, but there was little he could do as his two handlers carried him away.

'I thought he was Sweyn Forkbeard's man?' asked Beornoth.

'He was, but when King Sweyn left for home, he left Ragnar as a gift to me.'

'A gift?' said Beornoth, and Olaf shrugged with a wry smile. 'Why not throw him into the river? He wasn't a warrior of honour when he was whole. Now he's just a turd with a head.'

'Some men think he has power, that the gods keep him alive in his tortured state to speak their will.'

'If I may, Lord Olaf,' said a voice so quiet it was barely audible. A little man, no higher than Olaf's chest, appeared between the warriors. And Beornoth was surprised, because he was a priest. The man wore a roughly spun brown woollen robe, and his tonsure was freshly shaved. 'Byrhtnoth was a good man, a pious man, and a great benefactor to the church at Ely. He should be allowed to rest in the glory of God.' He spoke in a serious, almost scalding tone, and Beornoth half expected Olaf to backhand the little man across the face. But instead, he scratched his beard thoughtfully and then grinned at Beornoth.

'Very well,' he said wolfishly. 'Winter in this country is a mess of rain and mud, and my men are bored. Your jarl was a great warrior, and perhaps I should let you bury him the way the nailed god demands. So, I will allow you to challenge for his corpse. You know our ways, Lord Beornoth, so you can fight for the headless, piss-stinking offal if you wish.'

Beornoth couldn't contain a long sigh. Every bone, wound, scar and knot in his body pulsed in protest. But he nodded. He would fight for Byrhtnoth's body. If he won, he would return the corpse to Byrhtnoth's wife so that she could bury him with the honour that he deserved. If Beornoth lost, then it would be humiliation or death, or both, and Byrhtnoth's body would remain with Olaf.

7

'He wants you to fight two men?' asked Hrodgar.

'Yes. Olaf has made me fight for sport before, and it would seem that's my fate whenever I come to parlay with him,' said Beornoth. He stretched upwards and backwards, tilting his head and holding a hand to the tender wound still healing in his stomach.

'Could you not ask to wrestle or fight with wooden practice blades or swords dulled with cloth wraps?'

'Olaf wants blood. He wants his men entertained and me dead. It is nothing to him if we take Byrhtnoth's body, but he sees a chance to amuse his gods, himself and his army. Not too hard, boy.' Beornoth frowned at Tata as the boy ran a whetstone along the edge of Beornoth's seax. The lad glanced up at him, then looked across the square at the two men Beornoth would fight. Both were huge, bearded, experienced Viking warriors. The first man's head was bald and covered with black tattoos that depicted writhing dragons and other clawing beasts from legend. He lunged and swung practice strokes with a war axe, long-hafted and heavy. Its blade was oversized and after every stroke he beat it upon the iron rim of his shield. The second man was taller, a head above most of the leering Vikings huddled around the square, which Olaf had laid out carefully with hazel rods. He was of a size with Beornoth himself, but not as broad across the shoulder. He had a long black beard woven into a plait shot through with silver wire. This man had stripped off his armour and waited to fight bare chested, wearing only his trews and boots. He carried a spear in his right hand and a shield in his left, with a seax tucked into his belt. Their shields were iron bossed and covered in dark leather painted with clawed beasts, snarling and bright beneath the rain-soaked buildings of Maldon. They were huge, fearsome killers, experienced Viking warriors who were waiting for their chance to kill Beornoth and burnish their reputations bright with his death.

'Will you fight them one at a time, or both at once?' Hrodgar stood beside Beornoth, staring across at the mighty Viking warriors with a worried look on his face.

Beornoth shrugged. 'I'll fight them as they come. Doesn't matter.'

'Did you see the priest at Olaf's shoulder?'

'I saw him.'

'What business would a Saxon priest have in a nest of heathen vipers?'

'Little bastard probably smells silver. Find me a shield, if you can.' Whilst Beornoth had rediscovered his faith in the Lord during the previous year's troubles, he still held little respect for priests and men of the Church. There were some exceptions, but in Beornoth's experience they were either greedy, power-hungry, or both. Priests and bishops were generally the second or third sons of wealthy men; fathers had their sons take holy vows, and then influenced their promotion to take control of swathes of valuable land owned by the Church. Once in high-ranking positions, concessions were made to families for grazing rights, access to forests for woodcutting, and other important benefits.

Hrodgar nodded, walked two steps one way, looked at a snarl of grim-faced Vikings, and then walked in the other direction. Neither Beornoth, Brand nor Hrodgar carried a shield on their travels, so Hrodgar would need to borrow one from Olaf's men.

'Are you ready?' asked Brand in Norse.

'As I'll ever be,' replied Beornoth.

'I know one of those men. The big one with no jerkin. He is from an island in the far north, close to my home. He is a renowned Holmgang fighter and has killed four men that I know of. The bastard will be as fast as a wolf with that spear, so be careful.'

'He's going to die. They both are. Both fought at Maldon, and I can smell the blood on their stinking hands. They will be the first to suffer for what happened. They cut off my friends' heads and pissed on their corpses and they laughed at Ealdorman Byrhtnoth's body and denied him burial. I'm going to kill them.' Beornoth realised that by the time he had finished speaking, he was shouting. Not just with a raised voice, but bellowing like a madman. His boots stomped in the mud and his teeth gnashed.

There was a ceremonial part to a Viking Holmgang duel; it honoured the gods, and Olaf or his Norse holy men would want to say words to Odin, Thor or Týr. To hell with that. Beornoth wanted blood. He ripped his sword free from his scabbard and the leather grip of the king's sword was as warm and comfortable in his hand as the skin of a lover. Where before he had been afraid to hold it, shirking from the memories it evoked of the slaughter at Maldon, now he welcomed it. He let it wash over him and the faces of his dead friends came before his eyes to give him strength and rage.

Beornoth didn't even wait for Hrodgar to return with a shield. The blood fury was on him, and it could not be contained. He kicked off his boots, because the rain had turned Maldon into a muddy mess, and he didn't want to slip into the swing of that monstrous war axe. He strode forward with his sword raised, and the Vikings gathered about the fighting square, cheered, spat and clashed their weapons at the prospect of the fight to come. The mud squelched cold and mushy between his toes, and Beornoth looked across the faces of his enemies. Men in leather breastplates with gaping maws snarled and spat at him. Men in mail with bright weapons shaking in their fists, brown teeth and scarred faces cursed him, baying for his blood. These were men of the north, who had braved the treacherous Whale Road on their shallow-draughted warships to bring war and death to Beornoth's people. They were adventurers, willing to risk their lives in search of reputation, silver and glory. Death was their trade, and many had suffered and bled because of their lust for more. They could have stayed at home in Norway, or Jutland, the Vik or the lands of Svears, but they had come to England with axe, sword, spear, greed and spite.

Beornoth raised his sword and roared back at them. He stared into their blue, brown and hazel eyes and let them feel his hate and his power. He was Beornoth, killer of Skarde Wartooth and the White Wolf. He was an avenger and a killer, and he was here to punish them. Beornoth strode forwards, his rain-soaked hair slick to his scalp. His bare feet sunk into the wet filth and found purchase on the hard ground beneath. He went slowly at first, cautiously, as though he were wary of his enemies' heavy shields and bright blades. The bald man threw his head back and whooped for joy. He came on with his shield held low and his heavy axe held halfway up the haft. It was a weapon to break a shield wall, its bearded blade designed to hook over an enemy shield and yank it down so that a sharp blade could slice into the space and tear the life from the shield man. Most Vikings

preferred shorter-hafted weapons, with better balance. Beornoth
had wielded such a weapon himself before. It gave the fighter
options for hack, slice, punch and drag, but the heavier weapon
would be clumsy and brutal unless the man had a giant's strength.
Beornoth saw in the man's feral brown eyes, like those of a wood-
land animal hungry for blood, that he was a front ranker, a lover of
battle who prided himself as a shield-wall breaker. Had he broken
Byrhtnoth's own shield wall at Maldon? Was he one of the men
who had formed the swine-head wedge that had punched through
the ealdorman's battle line and swarmed him, hacking him to
death?

Yes, Beornoth decided, he was one of those men. Beornoth told
himself the man was, in fact, the Viking who had cut Byrhtnoth's
head from his body. So, as the axeman picked up his pace and
raised his axe, Beornoth ran at him. The axeman's shield was still
low at his side, he was so confident in his own prowess that he
believed the weight and power of his axe would be enough to
scythe through Beornoth's sword blade in one mighty stroke and
cleave his chest open like a pig on the butcher's block. Beornoth
ran and instead of raising his sword to block the overhand axe
below, he kicked out and his bare foot pinned the man's shield low
and Beornoth stepped into the axe swing. Most men would dart
backwards from the monstrous blade or swerve out of its way. But
Beornoth was not most men. He stepped into it, catching the haft
in his left hand, and pulled the bald warrior across his body off
balance. Beornoth slammed the pommel of his sword on the back
of the Viking's skull with an audible crack. The Viking fell
forwards onto his knees and Beornoth turned, bringing his sword
around overhand to smash its long blade into the Viking's shield
arm. The blade cut deep into the arm above the wrist and
Beornoth sawed it backwards, smiling as the axeman howled in

pain. Beornoth crashed his knee into the kneeling man's face and turned to face the spearman.

The long-bearded man came quickly, and Beornoth only just reacted in time to raise his sword and block the spear point from slicing into his eye. The blow went wide, but the man's shield thudded into Beornoth's shoulder, and he took three steps backwards under its force. The spear came low and Beornoth stepped over it, then the spear butt whipped around and Beornoth ducked under the swing, and the whoosh of its passing sang in his ears. Beornoth grabbed with his left hand but found only the hard iron of the spearman's shield. He swung low with his sword, but the spearman parried with his spear shaft and slashed with its blade so that the point scraped down the front of Beornoth's byrnie. Had he not worn the armour, that blow would have sliced him open from neck to navel. Beornoth growled and set about the Viking with a flurry of sword strikes, he thrust overhand and underhand, but the man caught each blow with his shield, shuffling backwards under the fury of Beornoth's attack. Beornoth stabbed low, and the shield dropped to block it, so Beornoth swung his left fist over the shield rim and punched the spearman full in the face. The Viking tottered backwards, dark blood rushing from his nose.

The crowd howled in anger that two of their champions were bloodied. Three men surged from the crowd to Beornoth's left and he went to meet them. A short man wearing striped trews came at Beornoth, his face bright red and twisted with rage. Beornoth plunged the tip of his sword into the man's belly and a gush of his fetid breath swamped Beornoth's face. The second attacker suddenly fell back, a small knife protruding from his neck. Beornoth turned as Hrodgar threw a second knife underhand, and the blade cut through the air to take the third man in his ribs. Beornoth dragged his sword free of the little man, and a gout of blood came out with it.

Olaf himself charged at the side of the fighting square from which the men had spilled over into the arena. His Jomsvikings followed and shoved the heaving mass of Vikings back with their shields. The Holmgang was ceremonial for Norsemen; they believed battle brought them close to their gods, so any infringement upon it was done so knowing that the Aesir themselves looked upon the fight, and to displease the gods could bring bad luck or punishment. The men shrank back from the Jomsvikings, and Olaf emerged from the crowd with his rain-soaked hair loose and wild about his face. He held up a hand in apology to Beornoth and flashed a murderous scowl at his two champions who had so far struggled against Beornoth.

They restored order in the crowd, and the spearman helped the axeman to his feet. He had dropped his shield and stuffed his shattered, bloody wrist into the side of his breastplate to keep the useless arm out of his way. His face was pale and pulled tight with pain and anger, and the two men came on together, both huddled behind the spearman's shield. They knew now that they faced a dangerous foe and approached the fight cautiously. Beornoth still held only his sword. He turned and nodded his thanks to Hrodgar for dropping the two attackers with his throwing knives. Then Beornoth attacked. His right shoulder burned from the effort of swinging his sword and his breath was short. He tried to disguise his limp, a remnant from a wound to the thigh taken in last year's fighting, but the more exhausted he became, the less easy it was to mask. But he would not wait for these men to kill him. He had come into their lair for Byrhtnoth's body, and he would not leave without it.

As he surged forwards, Beornoth pulled his seax free from the sheath at his back and gripped it in his left hand. He punched his sword forwards and its blade stabbed into the top of the spearman's shield, tilting towards the two Vikings. At the same time,

Beornoth dropped to one knee and stabbed his seax into a booted foot. He twisted the knife and yanked it free, accompanied by a desperate cry of pain. The axeman fell to one knee, and as he fell, he stabbed forward with his mighty weapons, and the top of the axe haft thumped into Beornoth's face. Pain surged beneath Beornoth's left eye and he flung himself away from the Vikings. His vision blurred and pitted with black spots. He shook his head to clear his vision, but had to close his left eye. Just as he focused his right eye, the spearman was upon him. Beornoth parried a spear thrust with his sword and stabbed his seax into the shield to stop it from cannoning into his face. He wrenched at the weapon, but it was stuck fast in the linden wood boards, so he left it there.

Beornoth scrambled and his bare feet found purchase in the slime. He swung his sword at his enemy, but the blade whistled through thin air as the man ducked out of its path. The swing had been wild, and Beornoth was overextended. The spear shaft hit him in the stomach, and now it was Beornoth's turn to gasp in pain. He stumbled backwards and clutched his left hand to the wound in his gut, the Maldon wound which had yet to heal properly. It pulsed and drained his energy, as though the blow had reopened the terrible cut. The spearman smiled at him over the rim of his shield, and he spat a gobbet of blood at Beornoth's feet.

Beornoth straightened, and it was as though he had a blade stuck in his belly again. The spearman came for him, lunging and slashing with his spear, and every time Beornoth swung his sword, pain seared through his insides like a red-hot poker. He missed a parry, and the spear punched Beornoth in the shoulder, but his mail held. Then the butt came around in a whirr and cracked Beornoth across the skull on his left side, where he still couldn't open his eye.

'No,' Beornoth growled. He ingested the pain, swallowed it like a fire-eater at a summer fair. They would not defeat him. He had not yet avenged his dead friends. 'No, no, no,' he said between gritted teeth. The spearman lunged again, and Beornoth danced to his left. The Viking pivoted on his heel, but his boot slid in the muck and his leg kicked out to the side. He fell, caught himself with his shield and looked at Beornoth with the realisation that death had come for him. Beornoth sprang forwards and stepped onto the antler hilt of his seax which was still embedded in the shield's boards. The man tried to lift the shield, but it was stuck fast by Beornoth's muddy foot, so he plunged the butt of his spear into the slime to steady himself and Beornoth rammed the blade of his sword into the man's gullet. It sliced through his plaited beard and into the soft, sunken flesh between his collarbones. Beornoth bellowed and twisted the sword. He pushed it deeper and then dragged the hilt upwards to split the spearman's neck wide open. Dark blood gushed down the man's pale torso and on into the rain-soaked ground inside Maldon's burh.

Beornoth took his foot off the seax and kicked the dying man off his sword blade. The crowd fell silent as their champion slopped into the mud. The wound in his neck was horrific and terrible to look upon. Beornoth held his bloody sword up, and he turned slowly in a circle so that all the crowd could see him. Beornoth was battered and in agony, but he had won. The Vikings stared at him, no longer angered and maddened, but silent and baleful. A thousand cold eyes watched him, hating him, wanting nothing more than to spring forward and cut him down. The only thing that protected Beornoth from their blades was the respect they held for the Holmgang, and the fear of their gods' displeasure. Beornoth limped through the mud towards where the axeman writhed and moaned in the mud. His foot splashed in a pool of blood and his useless arm flapped beside him. He stared at Beornoth, holding his axe close to him, perhaps hoping for another strike at Beornoth before he died.

As Beornoth drew closer, his right foot dragged in the mud and the rain beat down on the increasing swelling at the left side of his face. He thought about cutting the axe away from the Viking. To die without his axe in hand would deny him entry to Valhalla, and that would bring Beornoth pleasure. The man would wander the underworld of his gods' afterlife, forever denied the glory of Odin's Hall. But that might push Olaf over the edge, and though the Viking warlord respected the right of the Holmgang, what was to stop him killing Beornoth before he could leave Maldon? So, Beornoth took three quick steps and swung his sword backhand into the axeman's neck. He wanted to take his head, just as they had taken the heads of Beornoth's friends. But the blade met too much resistance on the man's spine and Beornoth had to wrench it free and chop at him three times before the grizzly head rolled free.

'Now, where is my Lord Byrhtnoth's body, you Viking shit eaters?' Beornoth said with a curled lip, and he kicked the axeman's head so that it rolled in the mud and came to a stop at Olaf Tryggvason's feet.

The rain stopped, and a shaft of warm sunlight broke through the clouds to shine upon the soaked land. Wet thatch steamed under the bright sun, and Beornoth sagged back against the wall behind Maldon's hall. The Viking crowd melted away, seeping back into the snarl of streets and laneways inside the burh. Three broad-shouldered Jomsvikings stood guard in front of where Beornoth allowed Brand to help him slide out of his byrnie. Olaf had set the men to protect Beornoth from the ire of his warriors as Beornoth recovered from the fight.

'The wound is not split, lord,' said Brand, peering beneath the byrnie. 'You must have just hurt the insides again.'

'Put the bloody mail back on then,' Beornoth said. He sucked his teeth as he lowered his arms and the byrnie slinked down over his shoulders.

'But your face is a mess. I hadn't thought it was possible for you to be any uglier, but it is.'

'Norse bastard.'

Hrodgar came around the corner and the Jomsvikings let him pass between their shields. He slid his two knives back into the rear of his belt. His lad, Tata, scampered behind him, his straw-coloured hair dripping fat drops of rain onto his shoulders.

'A glorious victory,' said Hrodgar, inclining his head at Beornoth.

'They almost killed me, but for your well-timed knives I would have been overrun.'

Hrodgar shrugged. 'Glad I could help. I have never seen such a ferocious fight. Tata, take Lord Beornoth's sword and seax and wipe them down.'

The lad bowed his head and stooped to take the weapons from Beornoth's belt, which lay on the ground beside him.

'Well fought, Saxon,' said a familiar Norse voice. The Jomsvikings parted to reveal Olaf, wearing a dry cloak and a sour look. 'You won fair, and I will honour our bargain. I have a wagon prepared, and your Byrhtnoth's corpse is in it. You can leave this place in peace; you have my word.'

'Thank you, lord,' said Beornoth.

'Your face is swelling quicker than a grandfather's bladder. You should slap some cow dung on it. It will bring the swelling down.'

'I will try that,' Beornoth lied.

'You won today, Saxon, just as you have defeated my men in a Holmgang before. This is the last time. Do not return to my presence or request a parlay, for if I see you before me again, I will kill you where you stand. Brand Thorkilsson, you came here today under the protection of guest-friendship, so leave in peace.' Olaf turned on his heel and marched away, but the little priest took his place, smiled nervously. He had buck teeth and pursed lips and wore a wooden cross over his heavy priest's robe.

'A triumph for a warrior of the Lord,' said the priest, and made the sign of the cross.

'Who are you?' asked Hrodgar. 'Any why is a priest tolerated by these heathens? Greater men than you have been tortured and killed for their beliefs by men such as these.'

'I am but a lowly emissary of the bishop come to talk of God to heathens,' said the priest, and he clasped his hands together as though his presence at Maldon were a sort of miracle. 'Forgive me for disturbing you so soon after your... encounter. But I must ask if your intention is to take the late ealdorman's body to the abbey at Ely?'

'I will bring the body to Byrhtnoth's wife, Ælfflæd, and let her decide where her husband is to be buried,' said Beornoth.

'I studied at Ely, when I was a boy, and the ealdorman was ever a great benefactor of the abbey. It is only right and proper that he should be interred there in God's glory.'

'Who are you?' Beornoth took an ale skin from Hrodgar's outstretched hand. He took a long pull and winced as opening his mouth stretched the swelling on his face. He rarely drank ale, not since the drink had become his master during the dark days of his life, and would have preferred water, but after the fight, any sort of liquid was welcome. Beornoth suspected the priest wanted Byrhtnoth's body taken to Ely because he saw some sort of profit in it for the abbey. Perhaps to charge a silver coin to any who wanted to gaze upon the tomb. But he was tired and sore and couldn't summon the energy to bandy words with the little priest.

'I am Wulfhelm. Come to the heathen by the order of Archbishop Sigeric.'

'Why haven't they killed you?' Beornoth avoided cursing the

name of the archbishop who had done so much to keep the king's army from the battlefield. He did not want Wulfhelm to warn Sigeric of his open enmity.

'Because my lord archbishop negotiates the terms of the gafol with Olaf, and as part of that arrangement, he has agreed to hear the word of God. He is an eager listener, the power of our Lord shocks and intrigues him. It is most inspiring.' Wulfhelm clapped his hands together.

'You don't believe you can actually persuade Olaf Tryggvason to become a Christian, do you?' Beornoth was so astounded that he almost dropped the ale skin.

'He wonders why his gods have not allowed him to overrun our entire country. Olaf questions his pagan gods, they do not speak to him, and he has no evidence for their existence other than the rumble of thunder and the flight patterns of ravens. But we have miracles, and we have the words of the Lord Jesus set down in the Bible. I think Olaf will see the light; he will come into the warmth of the Lord.'

'What is this little shit babbling about?' asked Brand, so Beornoth translated for him, and Brand roared with laughter. 'Olaf, become a Christian?' he said, running a hand down his face. 'There is more chance of me humping the king's wife. The Saxon holy men probably demand that Olaf let them wash him before they pay him to go away. That's all it is, ask the pious little bastard.'

'Is Sigeric asking Olaf to be baptised before he gets the gafol payment?' Beornoth asked the priest.

'Yes, he is, and what a miracle it would be if he does! We will have accomplished more with the word of God than you could have with your swords in a hundred battles.'

Beornoth swallowed his anger at the priest's foolishness. 'How much has Sigeric committed to pay?'

'Ten thousand pounds of silver.' Wulfhelm raised a hand and

coughed as Beornoth choked on his ale. 'A small price to pay for peace, and to convert a heathen warlord.'

'Go away,' said Beornoth. Wulfhelm opened his mouth but glanced at the Viking blood still spattered on Beornoth's hand and byrnie, and thought better of it and left.

'Can such a sum even exist?' asked Hrodgar, gaping at the unbelievable size of the payment offered in return for Olaf's peaceful departure.

'It can, but it will cripple the kingdom and build more discontent towards the king,' said Beornoth. 'Olaf will happily let them wash him and crow some holy words over his head for ten thousand pounds of silver. With that, he can win his father's kingdom back and become king of Norway.'

They loaded up the cart and tied Virtus to the rear. Beornoth drove the wagon, led by a large farming horse with shaggy fetlocks and a chestnut coat. Behind him was a large corpse wrapped in an old sailcloth. Beornoth clicked his tongue and led the cart out of the burh and past the line of decayed heads along the roadside. He had recovered Byrhtnoth's body and could return it to his widow, but had taken a severe beating to do it, and not a single traitor had been punished. But Beornoth had felt strong in the fight, just like his old self. So on to Ælfflæd and then vengeance.

8

Beornoth, Brand, Hrodgar and Tata led the wagon containing
Byrhtnoth's body south-west from Maldon towards Ealdorman
Byrhtnoth's Essex estate. Vikings had destroyed Byrhtnoth's horse
stud in the fighting before the Battle of Maldon, so Beornoth
decided they should head for Rettendon, the site of a hall and
village which had formed part of Lady Ælfflæd's marriage portion
and which she favoured.

Every jerk and rattle of the cart hurt Beornoth's stomach
wound, and once they were out of sight of Maldon, he stripped his
byrnie and had Tata clean the armour with sand from a shallow
river, dry it, and rub it with lanolin to protect the iron links. A line
of horsemen shadowed them from Maldon and along the crest of a
forested valley. Once they were satisfied that Beornoth rode away
from Maldon, Olaf's riders turned back towards the burh.
Removing the byrnie gave Beornoth some comfort, but not as
much as dipping his face in the cool river water. His eye was
swollen shut and throbbed every time he moved, and Beornoth
thought he could sleep for a week. He was glad to have recovered
the ealdorman's body, but the fight to get it had been brutal.

They came upon a farm later that day, as the last of the rain clouds fluttered away east towards the sea. It was a roundhouse roofed with turf, surrounded by sheep and goat pastures, and the farmer was a toothless man who offered them a night in his barn. He bowed and scraped when he saw Hrodgar and Brand's byrnies and weapons, but Beornoth wore only his jerkin and trews. The farmer had no room in his roundhouse and his wife was sick inside, so he begged them not to make him yield his home for the night for fear that she might perish. Beornoth gave the man two pieces of the silver and the man wept with relief. They settled into the barn, and Tata made a spluttering fire from the farmer's stack of winter firewood. The toothless man came hirpling into them with a bundle of thick, potent-smelling cheese, a loaf of dark bread and a crock of goat's milk.

'Now that we have the ealdorman's body safe, we move on to the traitors,' said Hrodgar once they had finished the meal. Tata sang softly to the horses as he brushed them down with a handful of dry hay.

'Godric and his brother's lands are in Essex,' said Beornoth. 'They were, after all, Byrhtnoth's oathmen. But we also must also punish the lords of East Anglia, for had they come to battle as they swore they would, then our forces would have equalled the Vikings.' He yawned, and the swollen side of his face pulled and pulsed. The pain in his stomach had all but gone. A rest and meal had helped. Beornoth sat with his legs out straight, and leant back, and that position seemed to help with the pain. The scarring on his gut had held, and Beornoth was sure that after a night's sleep he would have a more comfortable ride. His sword belt and byrnie lay close by and Beornoth opened his mouth wide every so often to stretch the pain in his swollen face.

'So, we either scour Essex for Godric, his brother and the scoundrels who fled the field, or we ride for East Anglia. King

Æthelred wants them all to suffer, every man who had a hand in the defeat.'

'And so, they shall. When I visited his hall, Ealdorman Leofric of East Anglia was dying in his bed. The old bastard has been dying for years, and I have not heard that he has died yet. His son Wictred gave his word to send warriors. But we cannot simply ride in and kill the ealdorman and his son. Their hall lies within a fortified town and is protected by a hearth troop of warriors. Even if we can ride in there and cut them down, we won't get out alive.'

'We must use cunning, then,' said Hrodgar, with a glint in his eye. 'Which is where I come in. You are a fine man for the shield wall and to stand and fight, Beornoth, but the subtler side of war is more suited to my skills.'

'You do not fight in the shield wall?'

'Not with this.' Hrodgar raised his stump. 'I solve problems for the king, here and abroad.'

'You are an assassin, then?'

'Let's just say I make people who offend the king disappear.'

'And you think we can make Wictred and Leofric disappear?'

'Unless you have a better idea? My plan would be to find a way into their stronghold, perhaps at night or during a busy market day. We use stealth to enter their chambers, or at a moment of privacy, and relieve them of their traitorous lives.'

'The king believes that the ealdorman of East Anglia is a traitor?'

'Wictred and Leofric did nothing whilst Forkbeard took control of the mint at Gippeswic. Many say they provided food and succour to the Danish king. So, at best, you could brand them collaborators with the enemy. I took word to them myself that they were to help Lord Byrhtnoth throw out the Vikings and give men to the East Saxons. They feared Forkbeard, and many of the folk in East Anglia are the sons and grandsons of Vikings leftover from when Guthrum, who became Aethelstan, ruled East Anglia. They sympathise with the Vikings, miss their ways and the freedom from the yolk of Church taxes and demands. So much land has been yielded to the Church since King Edgar's day that men resent the abbeys and monasteries. Viking rule is not such a bad thing for the men of East Anglia, or further north in Northumbria. To them, it seems like a perfect world, no taxes, no Church to cede land to every time the family patriarch dies. They remember the Danelaw like a drunkard whose memories are filtered through the fog of ale. They choose not to remember the paganism and the brutality by which the Danes and Norsemen captured that land.'

'If Thered is now ealdorman in Northumbria, then we have an ally there. For though he is from the Danelaw, he fought the Vikings and is certainly not a supporter of the invaders. He fought bravely beside us at Maldon, even though he came as a hostage because of his father's crimes against the crown. And we have Ealdorman Alfgar in Cheshire, and surely the king if it came to open war.'

'The king believes his position is precarious. He must strike at his enemies using the very shadows by which they threaten his rule. Which is where we come in.'

'You are the son of the ealdorman of Defnascir?'

'The third son, and the fifth child that survived childhood. My father's heir will succeed him, my middle brother entered the Church and will no doubt rise to a powerful rank in the shire, where the Church holds much land. Good land. So, I became a warrior.'

'What happened to your hand?' Beornoth had asked the question before and Hrodgar had shaken it off. But sitting by the fire in a barn with little else to do seemed as good a time as any for the tale.

'The king and I are of a similar age, and as you know, he came to the throne early after the unfortunate death of his brother, Edward. When I was young, my father sent me to serve in the new king's retinue and grow into his household troop. I did that. I learned to fight, thought that would be my life. Was barely old enough to grow the finest of beards upon my chin when the king and his mother were attacked whilst on the road between Winchester and Lundenwic. The king's mother ruled the kingdom in those days, and there was still some discontent over the succession. A disgruntled thegn attacked the king and his mother on the road and broke through his guards, and I managed to get my shield in the way of an axe aimed at the royal neck. I closed my eyes when the axe blade came. I don't mind admitting it now. I was but a boy. The axe ripped the shield from my grip and the backswing took my hand. There was so much blood that I thought my body was emptied. The king said that I had saved his life and the Lady Aelffwyn sent her finest healers to care for me. I have been honoured to enjoy the king's favour ever since.'

'You must have a fine reputation in Winchester, for everyone must know you are the man who saved the king's life.'

Hrodgar held up the stump of his left wrist and turned the leather cover around, so that the firelight danced on the finely cut carvings upon it. 'Nobody knows who I am,' he whispered. 'They saved my life, but I died that day on the road. What remained is a husk of what existed before. I saw myself bleed out, and I cowered from the axe blow. I got my shield in front of it, but I was rooted to the ground in terror. What I did was not brave. It was a reaction to overwhelming fear. What is left is not the son of the ealdorman of Defnascir, but a killer. A different man. A king's man.'

'Do you have a wife or any children?'

'No, my duty is my only companion.'

Beornoth pitied Hrodgar in that moment. For though he lifted his chin and puffed out his chest as though that statement was something to be proud of, his eyes told a different story. Their emptiness spoke of loneliness and a sadness, of a man alone. Even though Viking raiders had cruelly ripped it from him, Beornoth had experienced the joy of being a husband and a father. He knew that the true meaning of life was not glory or reputation; it was love. He couldn't put into words the impossible joy of having children, of watching them grow from helpless babes into running, laughing children. Of how their giggles made a man's heart warm, of the pride at watching their accomplishments, and the satisfaction that one's family slept soundly and safely in their beds. A wife made a man whole, a confidant and a wise head to talk through important matters, a mother and a lover. Beornoth thought of Eawynn, and also of Aethelberga, who had been the lady of Branoc's Tree. Both ran complex households, with responsibility for counting and storing the harvest, ensuring weaving and distaff working was maintained, that the house was correctly provisioned. Both helped Beornoth listen to and adjudicate upon the complaints and issues within the hundred farms he had been responsible for. Aethelberga was dead, and so was her lover Wulfhere. Beornoth missed them both deeply, just as he missed Eawynn's soothing presence. Hrodgar had experienced none of that, and so his was a life unfulfilled, a part of his humanity closed off. But such things were not discussed between warriors, and so Beornoth held his pity within, and just nodded to show that he respected Hrodgar's devotion to his king and country.

'How did you come by the lad?' Beornoth asked, jerking his thumb towards Tata.

'He came to me just before I departed from Winchester. The king's steward said that the lad arrived bedraggled, an orphan looking for work, food and shelter. They had no place for him there, and I would need a pair of hands on the road. For preparing food, making fires and such. Only having one hand makes some tasks difficult. I saw your man there talking to the Norseman at Maldon. Are you sure you can trust him?' said Hrodgar, and pointed towards where Brand fed a handful of grains to his horse and stroked the beast's long nose.

'I can trust him. Perhaps more than any man alive. He is one of them. His own kinsmen were in that camp. Men from his home-land with whom he sailed to these shores.'

'I don't like the look of him. He is not a man of God. It would be better if you let him return to his own kind. He can sail away with them and never return. Breaking bread with the likes of him sullies us. He is not a man of honour.'

Beornoth let that comment hang above the fire. He finished his meal and lay flat on the hay. Brand was a man of honour; he had risked his own life to save Beornoth's when it would have been easier to let him die. Brand had protected Beornoth against his own people, and had he let Beornoth die, nobody would ever have questioned his honour or his drengskapr. Brand had saved Beornoth because of the blood debt, and because he would know that he had let a man to whom he owed his life die. Beornoth would die to protect the Northman, and he would not allow an assassin to decide whether Brand could ride with them. If it came to a choice between the two men, it was no choice at all.

They slept close to the fire, surrounding its edges with rocks to keep the barn safe from its flames. Beornoth huddled beneath his woollen cloak against winter's chill. He listened to the horses' snorts and the crackle and spit of the blaze. Darkness fell, and as Brand fell into a deep slumber, he snored. Brand usually snored, but that night it was like the rumble inside a hungry giant's belly. After a time, Hrodgar sat up straight, like a man who had been stung by a bee.

'For the love of God, will someone shut that grunting pig up?' he said.

The boy Tata had his cloak pulled tightly around his head to block out the noise, and Beornoth stifled a laugh at the sheer noise of the Viking's snoring. Hrodgar shuffled around the fire and kicked Brand's boot. Brand grumbled and mumbled, and then continued to snore. Hrodgar reached over and grabbed the crusty remains of the farmer's loaf and tossed it at Brand. It hit the Viking in the face, and he sat up, a half-asleep look of annoyed surprise on his face.

'What was that?' he said in Norse, voice thick from sleep.

'Stop snoring!' shouted Hrodgar.

'What did wolf-joint say?'

'He said your snoring is too loud,' said Beornoth.

'Ha!' Brand laughed. 'Tell the one-handed bastard that I was dreaming of his mother and sister. If he wakes me again, I'll thrash him to within an arse hair of his miserable Saxon life.'

'He says he is sorry,' said Beornoth to Hrodgar in the Saxon tongue.

'He did not say that,' Hrodgar barked, his face a cliff of tired frustration. 'Just tell him to be quiet.'

Moments later Brand's snoring began again, just as loud as before. Hrodgar twisted and turned, trying to find a position where he could block out Brand's rumbling croak. Beornoth found himself in the half-sleep, where he wasn't sure if he was awake or asleep. Strange thoughts and vivid memories mixed with dreams, and his breath steamed above him as the night grew colder. Brand's breath caught in his chest and he rolled over, and the snoring stopped, leaving the barn with only the sounds of the horses, and the gentle sigh of sleeping men. The barn door creaked, and Beornoth's head turned like a night owl. A boot scraped on hay stalks and a timber plank groaned. There were men in the barn, and more sneaking through the door. He could smell garlic and onions, and the acrid stench of sweat.

Beornoth shifted under his cloak and reached for his sword belt. His hand curled around the seax's antler hilt. His sword hilt was outside his reach, and he rolled his leg to kick Brand's boot. The Norseman lay next to him, but he did not wake up, so deep was his slumber. Hrodgar was too far away for Beornoth to alert him to the imminent danger. Steel rasped in a wooden throat, and there was no time for any chance to surprise whoever came upon them in the dark of night with weapons and malice.

Beornoth surged from his cloak, stomach wound stabbing at him and his seax in his fist.

'Enemy blades!' he bellowed at the top of his voice. 'Enemy blades!'

Beornoth jumped backwards and kicked the flaming fire logs with his boot, hoping that the firelight would show him how many enemies had entered the barn. Sparks flew and orange light illuminated dark figures at the barn's walls. Hrodgar scrambled to his feet, a knife in one hand, but Brand still would not stir.

'Who is out there?' Hrodgar shouted.

'Thay your latht prayers, turdth,' said a low, guttural voice with a heavy lisp. 'We hab come to thend your thoulth to hell. Kill them!'

The shapes moved, and light from the flaming logs shone on a long blade. A voice roared, and a shadow raced at Beornoth with a spear outstretched, the blade wickedly sharp. Beornoth side-stepped it and sliced his seax across the attacker's ribs and the man cried out and danced back into the darkness. Hrodgar struggled with a cloaked attacker, fighting for his life in the half-light of the fire's remnants. Beornoth's sword belt lay on the ground by where he had bedded down, and he reached out with his boot and tried to slide his sword belt towards him. Before he could hook the leather under his heel, two men came for him, both armed with short-hafted axes.

'How many of the bastards are there?' said Hrodgar, wrestling with his assailant.

'Too many,' said Beornoth. The two axemen came on cautiously, weapons brandished in front of them, whilst the spearman cursed and spat to their right, with a hand clamped to his injury. There were five men, and possibly more. The axemen came on together, teeth shining in the dark, and they muttered to one another, looking for confidence in words of encouragement. They were no simple robber band; they had come heavily armed and knew who they faced.

An axe came overhand and Beornoth diverted the haft with his left elbow so that it fouled the attack of the second axeman. It knocked him sideways, and he tumbled over Brand's sleeping form. The Norseman roared into wakefulness, swearing in Norse, and immediately tangled with the fallen attacker on the barn's dusty floor.

'Who are you?' Beornoth said to the first axeman, who recovered his feet and came at Beornoth again. He ignored the question and slid his hand up the haft of his axe so that it became a wicked lump of metal in his fist and tried to slice at Beornoth's arm. Beornoth whipped his arm away and punched the man in the jaw. He reeled away and Beornoth kicked him back a further two steps, which bought enough time for Beornoth to bend and pull the king's sword free of its scabbard. He shifted the seax to his left hand and held the sword in his right. Tata leapt from his cloak and ran towards the horses, whimpering as he went. The axeman came back at Beornoth, but he paused as he noticed the long sword in Beornoth's grip. A sword was the weapon of the warrior class, men whose profession was war. Thegns, ealdorman, men who protected the people from the viciousness of the world. To own a sword, a man must either be wealthy enough to have one made, or have one granted to him by a great lord in return for his skill and courage. So, when the axeman saw the sword, he realised he faced a warrior of reputation.

Beornoth lunged at him, feinting with his sword, and the man was so transfixed by its shining blade that he bought the feint and raised his axe to block the blow. Beornoth punched the tip of his seax twice into the man's stomach, once into his thigh, and then hammered the pommel of his sword into the man's face. Hrodgar's attacker fell to the ground, gurgling from an unseen injury, and the Defnascir man came to stand at Beornoth's shoulder.

'I'll go around the edges and force them out,' Brand said, where he knelt over a twitching corpse. The Viking set off in a crouch, axe in one hand, his shape merging with the shadows. Ahead of Beornoth, a glow emerged from beside the barn door. One log he had kicked from the fire had carried its licking flame onto a bale of hay which had crackled into light. As the fire danced into life, three more shapes appeared. They came with axes and knives, thinking they would slaughter the riders in their sleep, but hesitating now that their prey had turned into sword-wielding warriors.

'Who sent you?' called Hrodgar, but the men said nothing. They spread out into a line, and the injured spearman joined them. The horses whinnied and scraped their forelegs, unsettled by the growing flames at the door. Beornoth's heart thumped. He did not know how many men had come to kill him. They kept on coming, and there could have been a dozen more outside the barn waiting to pour in and hack him to pieces. These men were Saxons, not Vikings, and that was a surprise.

A figure rose up behind the attackers, axe in one hand and knife in another. Brand charged them, calling to Odin as he ran, and he descended upon the attackers with Viking fury. They turned, surprised to be attacked from their rear, and as they did, Beornoth set about them. He sliced one man's knee with his sword and shoulder-charged another. Brand chopped his axe into the spearman's skull with a wet slap and it burst like an egg. Hrodgar fought with the leftmost man, punching and jabbing with his knife. The final attacker came at Beornoth, and he was huge. He was taller than Beornoth, and larger by far. The axe was like a wand in his meaty fist, and he lumbered forward, his bulk framed by the roaring flames that had crept up the barn door and now crawled along its roof timbers. The roof creaked and groaned as the fire consumed it; thatch sparked to light and smoke drifted from the rafters like a deadly fog.

'Time to die, thitworm,' said the big man, the words coming in a garbled lisp. Beornoth stabbed his sword, but the giant batted it away contemptuously with his forearm as though it were no more threatening than a wooden spoon. The axe came around at frightening speed, and Beornoth met it with his seax, but such was the strength in the giant that he drove Beornoth backwards, his seax arm pushed towards his face by the axe. A thunderous crash sent sparks and smoke billowing as a section of the barn came down. A heavy boot kicked Beornoth in the chest and he fell sprawling into the remnants of the campfire. Above him, a clump of burning thatch drifted down like a feather and he rolled so that it wouldn't land on his face and burn the flesh from his skull.

The fight raged in the barn, and droplets of fire dripped from the roof, where the fire crept along the thatch. It was hot in the barn; the night's cold replaced with the searing, eye-melting fierceness of fire. The winter air became sucked into the fire's rapid hunger.

Beornoth tried to rise, but a boot larger than his head stood on his sword arm and pinned him to the ground.

'Lord Godric thendth hith greetingth, bathdard,' the giant said. Beornoth struggled but could not rise. The enormous man smiled, and he had a mouth completely empty of teeth, a maw of red gums and a lolling togue like a monstrous baby. The axe came overhand,

and would have killed Beornoth in one strike, but Hrodgar chopped his blade into the giant's back. He bellowed with rage, turned, grabbed Hrodgar by his jerkin and tossed him into the fire as though he were a cut log. Beornoth had to get out of the fight and out of the barn; soon the whole thing would come down about them in a burning mass of old timber and mouldy thatch, and if he had a choice Beornoth would rather die on the end of a blade than feel the unthinkable pain of fire eating the flesh from his bones.

Beornoth cut at the giant with his sword, and it sliced into the meat of his calf. The big man shouted in a mix of pain and rage. He saw Brand slashing into his men, more of them lying dead or writhing in pain on the barn floor. The big man turned back to Beornoth and howled in impotent fury, then turned and ran. He limped because of the cut Beornoth had dealt to his leg, and it was like watching a bear shambling into a forest. He crashed into the barn's wall like a sledgehammer, and its timbers shattered before his bulk. He fell through the hole, stood and lurched into the night.

Beornoth pursued the man, but he noticed Tata struggling with the horses, who were now wide-eyed and panicked from the fire. The flames had reached halfway across the barn, and the heat kissed Beornoth's skin, forcing him backwards. He fought against the instinct to run and dashed to the horses, flanked by Brand and Hrodgar. They shouted to each other, but the words were lost in the roar of the burning barn. Beornoth dragged Virtus towards the barn's centre, stroking his flank and talking to him in soothing tones.

'We can't get out!' shouted Hrodgar above the din. He held one arm above his face to protect his eyes from the unbearable heat.

Beornoth picked up his sword belt and fastened it on. He carried his byrnie and saddle across Virtus' back and sheathed his sword. Smoke billowed out of the giant-sized hole in the wall and

Beornoth dashed to it, grabbing a fallen axe as he went. He hacked at the edges of the jagged timbers, the axe blade chopping chunks of wood free and making the hole larger. Beornoth paused, coughing and retching from the smoke, which poured from the thatch in great, stinking clouds. He turned and beckoned to the others, and they led the horses from the barn. Beornoth ran to Virtus, lifted Tata onto the horse's back and led them both outside.

They collapsed onto the cold grass beyond the barn, each of Beornoth, Hrodgar, Brand and Tata coughing and retching, steam rising from their mouths in the chilly night air. The barn cracked and moaned, and the entire front section collapsed in on itself with a crash of wood and fire. The farmer knelt in the dirt by his roundhouse, hands clasped to his head in despair at his destroyed barn. His winter stores, food for him, his wife and his animals, destroyed. He would starve without it, and Beornoth walked to him and dropped a fistful of silver coins onto the grass before him.

'Who, or what, in all Satan's realms was that?' asked Hrodgar, his voice coming like a croak from the smoke.

'He was Godric's man. The traitor knew we were here and sent men to kill us,' said Beornoth.

'Godric, Byrhtnoth's thegn?'

'Yes. Essex is not safe for us. We need to get the ealdorman's body back to his widow and set about sending these treacherous dogs back to the dirt.'

Beornoth had a new enemy. Men hunted him just as he hunted them. He had Byrhtnoth's body, but the traitors he sought were one step ahead. How had they known he was in Essex and been able to find him on a small farm deep in the Essex countryside? Beornoth thought about those problems as the farmer brought water to wash the smoke from their faces. Word could have come from Olaf's camp at Maldon, or from any of the taverns on the journey south. But Godric had clearly heard that Beornoth rode south, and

Beornoth hoped that in his nightmares, Godric saw Beornoth charging at him, sword in hand. A giant hunted him, but Beornoth was not afraid. Essex had been his home once, but it had become a nest of serpents who had betrayed their lord and now tried to steal his lands and wealth. But Beornoth was coming for them.

9

Snow dusted the frozen pastures of Essex as the riders pushed south. Beornoth rode the cart, bumped and jostled by the frozen ground, and Byrhtnoth's headless corpse rolled in the back, its rotting stink escaping its yellowed sailcloth shroud to taint the air around the cart with the sickly-sweet stench of decay. The land approaching Rettendon was flat and bare, a patchwork of grazing pastures and tilled fields marked by ditch and hedge which in spring and summer would explode with vibrant greens and browns, but now in the depths of winter, was a hard white wasteland. Beornoth held the reins in hands wrapped in cloth to keep out the frost and cuffed at a running nose, which felt like it could snap off if the air grew much colder.

Rettendon itself was a simple village. It was not a fortified burh but merely a collection of turf-topped longhouses, a stable and a small gatehouse. It was ringed by gorse hedging, which served as a sort of natural, low palisade. Beornoth counted a flock of three score sheep and four cattle shivering in a miserable field on the settlement's west side, and then a sty of six pigs close to the dwellings. Smoke billowed from the largest of the longhouses; it

was a hall of sorts, too small to be a feasting hall, but large enough
to hold a dozen people.

Beornoth rode in the cart, and Tata huddled in the back,
swathed in his cloak. The lad had said little since they had left
Mameceaster weeks earlier, and nothing at all since the ambush at
the barn. Beornoth glanced back at him, and the lad looked up
with large, wet eyes. Beornoth guessed he was fourteen years old;
he was thin and sullen but tended to all the warriors' chores with
silent dedication. He kept their weapons oiled and sharp. Tata fed
and brushed the horses each morning and night and filled their
water skins whenever they passed a fast-flowing stream. He bought
food and ale from villagers, made cook fires and baked flatbread.
He was, Beornoth thought, the perfect servant. Hrodgar spoke little
of Tata or where he had come from, and when Beornoth had asked
him, the king's man had brushed off the question, saying only that
Tata had wandered into the king's lands as a beggar, starving and
in need of help. Brand and Hrodgar rode beside the cart, but on
opposite sides. The longer the journey went on, the more they
seemed to rub each other up the wrong way. Saxon and Viking,
Christian and pagan, as different as cat and dog.

As the cart rumbled and rocked along the road, which looked
as though it had once been dark with mud but was now the grey of
an old man's beard, three warriors ambled from the hedge gate.
They wore byrnie coats of mail, helmets and carried stout aesc
spears. The cart's wheels shambled inside ruts in the road, and
Beornoth cursed as the left wheel ran over a stubborn rock and the
entire cart jolted, lifting him from the seat. The bounce sent a stab
of pain through his gut, and he was not sorry that Byrhtnoth's body
was close to its destination.

'Those men are finely armed for such a small village,' said
Brand. 'Maybe there is silver hidden here. Saxons bury their silver
beneath the ground like dogs. Maybe we could dig up a small

horde?' He grinned, and Beornoth rewarded the Viking with a frown. Brand chuckled and said, 'Tell wolf-joint I said that.' Beornoth shook his head and ignored the provocative jest.

Beornoth raised a hand in greeting to the three men and took down the hood of his cloak so that they could see his face. This was Lady Ælfflæd's home, part of her wedding portion, and these were guards allocated to her by Ealdorman Byrhtnoth. They were men of his hearth troop.

The leading warrior was bow-legged and lean, and he nudged the man next to him and jutted his chin towards Beornoth. They exchanged hushed words, which Beornoth could not hear. Beornoth raised a hand in greeting, and the bow-legged warrior raised a nervous hand in reply.

'Is that really you, Lord Beornoth?' the man shouted. He lowered his spear, and his mouth fell open in anticipation.

'It is I,' Beornoth replied. 'Is the Lady Ælfflæd here? For I bring her the body of her husband, who was killed by the Northmen at Maldon.'

'We'd heard you were dead, lord, that all of you were...' The warrior caught himself. He bowed his head to Beornoth and clamped a closed fist to his chest in salute. He whispered something to his men, and the two warriors ran back towards the gate. Beornoth pulled on the reins and soothed the horses to a stop. He clambered down from the cart, stretched his back and stamped his feet to awaken the muscles in his numb arse.

'You served the ealdorman?' Beornoth asked.

'Yes, lord. My name is Wuffa. I saw you fight at Watchet. I rode with the ealdorman that day, but I missed Maldon.' He tore his eyes away from Beornoth and stared at his boots. 'I was ordered to guard the lady. There are ten of us here, lord. And we all... well... we should have been there.'

Beornoth took a step forward and placed his hand on the

warrior's shoulder. He looked up, and there were tears in his eyes despite his grizzled beard and the experience in his lined face.

'They slaughtered all who were there. You honour the ealdorman by protecting his wife. Do not feel shame. You can be of service now, Wuffa. Show me to the lady.'

'Of course, lord. This way, lord.' Wuffa nodded and stood straighter. He turned and led them through the gate, which was little more than two pine squares hinged against posts sunk into the earth between the hedge fences. The houses centred around a circular crop of frozen grass, a meeting area where they would have small market days and celebrations throughout the year. A dog with a missing hind leg limped between two buildings with its ears pinned back, and two skinny chickens pecked hopefully at the frost. Folk came streaming from the houses, wrapped in cloaks, and steam billowed from their mouths in the cold. They stopped and stared at the warriors and clasped hands to their mouths as they watched the cart shamble into the village. Beornoth added that humiliation to his list of degradations against Byrhtnoth. This was no way for the ealdorman's body to return home to his shire. He had been the warlord of all England, the leader of the fight against the Vikings, and a man of honour and reputation. The two warriors must have spread the word that Beornoth had brought their ealdorman's body for burial, and some womenfolk wept, and children with mucky faces gaped at the sailcloth-wrapped mound in the cart, trying to link it with the man whose legends were spoken of at firesides across the shire.

A woman in a fine green gown came from the largest house, flanked by a younger maid with plaited hair. Beornoth had never met the lady, but he assumed by her proud stature she was Byrht-noth's widow. She followed one of Wuffa's warriors, and strode with her head high, though Beornoth noticed a quiver in her bottom lip. A priest shuffled from the same building; he wore a fine robe beneath a dark fur cloak. He was a small, wiry man with tightly curled grey hair sprouting from either side of his otherwise bald head. It was Bishop Nothhelm of Essex. Beornoth had met him before in the ealdorman's company.

'My lady,' said Beornoth. He bowed his head and gestured back towards the cart. 'I am sorry for the dishonourable method of transport, but I have returned Ealdorman Byrhtnoth's body to you for burial.'

Lady Ælfflæd was a tall woman. She was wide at the hip with a strong-boned face. A wisp of grey hair had escaped her headscarf, and she smiled at Beornoth. There was no joy or warmth in that smile. It was a dry, sad thing and melancholy tinged her eyes.

'Thank you, Beornoth. My husband spoke of you often. Please, you and your companions must come inside where it's warm.' She touched Beornoth's arm lightly and led him towards the house. Brand and Hrodgar followed, and Tata set about tending to their horses.

The longhouse was a simple structure. It had a second floor on its western side, which contained a small room where the lady slept. The building was split in two: the larger, communal area to the left with a hearth and roaring fire; and then various smaller chambers to the right where the lady's retinue lived. There were rich tapestries hung on the walls, which seemed out of place in the small longhouse. This was not Byrhtnoth's primary residence, but his shire was vast, and Beornoth had been there on the day Olaf Tryggvason's Viking marauders had burned and sacked the ealdorman's horse farm.

'Please, have a seat,' said Lady Ælfflæd. She gestured to three mead benches huddled around the fire. 'Fetch ale and food for these brave men.' Her maid hitched up her skirts to reveal soft slippers and helped the servants pull together food and drink.

Beornoth sat and Brand leant against the wall on the far side of the fire, keeping a respectful distance from the lady and bishop, all too aware of what he was and how that might offend them. Brand took a bowl of steaming porridge from a servant's tray, along with a mug of steaming hot ale.

'Thank the Lord God that you are alive, Lord Beornoth,' said Nothhelm, taking up a seat opposite Beornoth. The lady sat beside the bishop, and a servant laid out bread, thick porridge and ale for the riders. 'We feared the worst.'

'Your fears were well founded, for I am one of the few survivors of the battle,' said Beornoth.

'Pray, tell us how you managed to retrieve the ealdorman's body from the heathen?'

'I went to Olaf and begged for its return.'

'He had to kill two Vikings in a duel before the entire Viking army,' said Hrodgar. 'And the price of the ealdorman's body was their corpses. They were brutal Viking warriors, and Beornoth killed them both to bring your husband home to rest.'

The lady stared at the purple bruising on Beornoth's face, and his drooping eye where the swelling had pushed it closed. He removed his big hands from the tabletop, conscious of the coarseness of his skinned knuckles. She reached out before he could whip them away, and she held his rough hand in her soft fingers.

'Thank you, Beornoth, from the bottom of my heart. Now I can bury my husband in the light of God and send his soul to heaven.'

'I will take Byrhtnoth to Ely,' said Nothhelm, 'the abbey he so honoured during his life will now house his earthly body for eternity. The monks will pray for his soul every day.'

'Was the battle awful?' asked Ælfflæd.

Beornoth looked at her, and then at the bishop. They had no idea of the horrors of the shield wall, of the terror a snarling Viking warrior strikes into a man's heart. They could not fathom the sight of two thousand Vikings charging with axes, swords and spears, hell-bent on ripping your life away with hacking blades and war savagery. Even he shuddered at its memory.

'Yes,' he said, simply. Unable and unwilling to describe the horrors. 'We were attacked on the road here. I know that Byrhtnoth's warriors perished at Maldon, but the shire should not have descended into lawlessness so quickly. Who will be the new ealdorman, and who could have ambushed us?'

Nothhelm cleared his throat. 'These are dark times, dark indeed. After the battle, those who did not fight returned to the shire with all haste and began to annex land to their existing holdings. The shire is in turmoil, and men rework boundaries and deeds to take woodland, cattle, pastures and rivers from lands which rightfully belong to those who died alongside the ealdorman.'

'Godric?'

'Yes, amongst others.'

'Why does the king not intervene? Why does he not send men to restore order and appoint a new ealdorman?'

'We have sent word to the king,' said the bishop, laying his hands palms up on the table. 'But such things take time. Even if he sends a force of warriors, it is mid-winter. I am surprised to see you on the road. It could be spring before the king can intervene.'

Beornoth sighed at that truth. Winter was a time for huddling around the fire, of short days and long nights. Warriors did not march in the cold months, for there was not enough food and ale to support it. But if the king waited too much longer to act, then Essex would be torn apart by greedy traitors.

'In my experience, the king does not act quickly when faced with dire circumstances,' Beornoth said, shocking those gathered with his critical words.

'King Æthelred faces many dangers,' said Hrodgar defensively. 'You think it is so simple for him to send a force of Wessexmen to restore order in Essex? Do not fool yourselves that being king is so simple. Æthelred sent one hundred warriors of his hearth troop to their deaths at Maldon. There are many threats all over the kingdom, not least a victorious Viking army on the banks of the River Blackwater. There are raids on the west coast by Viking crews from Ireland, and the Welsh raid western shires continuously. The realm is divided between those who would welcome a return to Viking rule and those loyal to the throne. Then there is the cloying embrace of the Church. The archbishops are powerful and wealthy. They administer God's will and can grant or take a man's pathway to heaven. Abbeys own much land and therefore wield a lot of power. If the archbishops advise Æthelred not to march, and he disobeys that advice, there are severe consequences.'

'Who will succeed Byrhtnoth?' asked Beornoth, changing the subject, because the depth of Hrodgar's words kicked at his thought cage like a bucking stallion. Hrodgar had banged the table with his fist to emphasise his point, and Beornoth did not want words spoken against the king to wing their way back to Winchester. Nothhelm was a bishop, and his face reddened as Hrodgar spoke so scathingly about his Church. Beornoth wondered how much power the king actually wielded, how many decisions he made for himself, and how much of what Æthelred did was based on the influence and advice of others.

'Unfortunately, my two brave sons are both dead, killed in the endless wars that plague these lands. And no mother should outlive her children,' said Ælfflæd, and made the sign of the cross across her breast. 'My daughter Leoflaed and her husband Oswig will take over from my husband as soon as we bury him. We will send word to the king to ratify the succession. But there are those who will oppose that; they will make claims and protestations that Leoflaed is not of the male line.' Ælfflæd could no longer hold back her pain, and the lady crumpled into tears. Her shoulders shook, and she hid her face in shame.

Beornoth stood and moved around the table. He sat next to Lady Ælfflæd and put his heavy arm around her slight shoulders. She sank into him, her body shuddering against his chain mail.

'Do not worry, lady,' said Beornoth. 'Your daughter and her husband will inherit Byrhtnoth's titles and estates. Oswig will be ealdorman. I will see to it.'

Ælfflæd cleared her throat, straightened her back and shrugged Beornoth's arm gently from her shoulders. She smiled sadly at him, and then her face became as cold and hard as a slab of rock. 'I won't let these snakes steal my husband's legacy,' she said. Her two hands curled into fists on the tabletop. 'My father was the champion of the East Saxons, back in the time of the great King Edgar, and my husband was the warlord of all England. I am the lady of Essex, and I will not let these turncloaks enrich themselves whilst the heads of brave men adorn the blood-soaked road to Maldon. They must be stopped, Beornoth. I will raise what remains of the bravest fyrd men and have them ready to march and fight if necessary. I will send warriors to the borders of Godric's lands and spoil his plans wherever I can.' She paused and stared hard into each man's face, her mouth a flat slice of grim determination. 'Know this, all of you. These men cannot be allowed to live, for they are rich and powerful and that influence buys them favour at the royal court with powerful bishops and lords. This is a local matter, a thing to be dealt with by us. Godric can be fought, but someone will need to put a stop to Archbishop Sigeric, and he walks with the protection of Christ.'

'I must warn you,' said Nothhelm, wringing his hands. 'Godric's father Odda was wealthy and powerful, and the son now wields his father's might. Outside of Byrhtnoth's estates, he is the largest landowner in Essex. Since Maldon, Godric has gathered dozens of warriors to his banner and has amassed a small army of cut-throats and brigands. Godric sees opportunity in the aftermath of Maldon, a chance to seize power for himself. He rides across the shire, demanding loyalty from the men still alive after the battle, and the Viking raids before it. Essex is in peril, Lord Beornoth. Its defenders are dead, and the shire is unprotected. Godric takes land and I fear he will challenge to become ealdorman. He could make a case to the king if he can establish that Oswig is too weak, and that he alone can restore stability.'

'It was Godric's men who attacked me on the road. There was a big man with them. He had no teeth and was monstrous in size.'

Nothhelm nodded and crossed himself. 'He is Godric's man. The brute was a masterless man who has found service here in Essex. Men say he is from the borderlands with the Welsh, a killer and veteran of the endless border cattle wars, who sells his sword to the highest bidder. His name is Ansgar. A back-stabber and a rogue. He has bullied widows and young heirs into ceding land to Godric. Godric also acts with the blessing of Archbishop Sigeric, and it is he whom you should truly fear. You know Godric as well as I, and he is a braggart and a bully, but not a man capable of deep cunning. He is Sigeric's puppet, and I don't doubt that much of the land taken by Godric is shared between the thegn and the archbishop.'

Beornoth's mail suddenly felt heavier and the bruising on his face ached. His eyes stung, exhausted from the hard journey south in winter. Olaf was an enemy he could meet on the battlefield, who he could strike at with his sword. But this fresh attack on Essex was something else. It was low and dirty. Sigeric and Godric were exploiting a terrible defeat, a slaughter of their own countrymen to enrich themselves, and Byrhtnoth was not even buried. 'Sigeric has a priest with Olaf at Maldon, seeking to convert him to the one true God.'

'There is much afoot there. Sigeric had always pushed to pay off the Vikings, this you know. But if he can convert a powerful Viking like Olaf to baptism, then he moves into a new realm of power. Men have become saints for less. He will claim the baptism as a spiritual victory of Olaf Tryggvason and the Vikings, and that he has achieved that victory with prayer and God's grace, which the king and his warriors could not achieve with the sword. He will push that tale and make of himself a spiritual warlord, the slayer of the pagan gods. Sigeric is like a spider spinning a vast and complex web; we are caught in it, trapped in the wind and waiting for the monster to eat us.'

Lady Ælfflæd pushed gently away from Beornoth and gathered herself, wiping her face dry of tears with a cloth.

'Enough talk of these spineless cowards. I must show you something,' she said, rising from the bench. She led Beornoth to a far wall, where a long, half-finished tapestry hung from a high beam. Its leftmost panel showed Byrhtnoth marching to battle, and then the intricate weaving depicted the ealdorman speaking to gathered warriors before the battlefield. As the pictures moved from the left to right, sleek Viking warships with curved prows cut through waves to land on the Essex coast. Ælfflæd and her hand-maidens had not yet woven the battle itself, and Beornoth wondered how they would depict the death of the great ealdor-man. 'It is a tapestry to honour my husband and all those who fought at Maldon. I will gift it to the abbey at Ely, along with some land, in return for their care and prayer for my husband's soul.' It was a beautiful thing of bright colours, warriors and blades and it would ensure that folk would remember what had happened at Maldon and how bravely men had fought to protect their people.

'You do your husband, and all of us who stood against the heathen horde, a great honour. Our deeds will live on through these pictures even when our names are long forgotten.'

Beornoth marvelled at the detail of the stitched men on the tapestry. Amongst the warriors and riders, he saw Leofsunu of Sturmer, Aelfwine of Foxfield, and other men he missed so much immortalised.

'What will you do?' asked Nothhelm, looking up at Beornoth from his face taut with worry. 'How can you stop this spider, who is also a man of God, and his cruel brutes from stealing a shire?'

'I'll gather warriors, loyal men and hard fighters,' said Beornoth, and he noted the look of fear on Nothhelm's face. Could a man kill Archbishop Sigeric without damning his soul for eternity? 'Then I will kill all our enemies and return Essex to peace. But before there can be peace, there must be blood, and those who try to profit from the glorious dead will suffer. I swear it. They are cowards and traitors to the shire, to the king, and to England.'

10

Beornoth, Hrodgar, Brand and Tata stayed the night at Rettendon. The village was deep in the heart of winter, and the Lady Ælfflæd apologised profusely about the simple fayre her household could offer for the evening meal. Her people took Byrhtnoth's body from its sailcloth wrapping and laid it out on a table to wash, bind and prepare for burial. Nothhelm said solemn prayers at the evening meal in gratitude for the return of the ealdorman's body and that he could now be buried in a godly fashion. He blessed Beornoth and Hrodgar for the fateful tasks which they must complete if Byrhtnoth's family was to succeed to the ealdorman's titles, and if Sigeric and Godric were to be stopped.

They imitated a feasting hall by pushing tables together in the longhouse, and Beornoth strategically placed Brand next to him to prevent the Norseman from losing his temper because of the disrespectful sideways looks from the dinner guests. Brand was a proud Northman and did not hide the hammer pendant around his neck or the large raven tattoo upon his neck. He did, however, make a small concession by not eating, farting or laughing as Nothhelm prayed at length whilst the food was laid out before them.

Ælfflæd's people laid on as fine a feast as they could with what remained of their winter supplies. There was porridge, flatbread, vegetables cooked in garlic and other herbs, and a cured leg of lamb which had to be shared amongst all the guests in the hall so that each person received only a few slices of meat. There was good ale, honey and a soft cheese which spread easily across the warm bread. At Beornoth's request, they provided a pitcher of fresh water, for he would not drink ale unless absolutely necessary.

Once the feasting was over, and they had exchanged thanks and prayers, Beornoth bedded down for the night by the central hearth. Ælfflæd's people pushed the eating benches to the sides of the room so that Beornoth and his companions could lie beside the fire with their cloaks for blankets. Sleep came fitfully, and Beornoth lay upon his side, staring into the hearth's glowing embers. He pondered on where to start and where to go. He had too few men to take on Godric and his band of hired blades. To ride to Godric's lands would be to walk into his hands. Hrodgar had spoken at dinner about his preference to use stealth to enter Godric's hall and slit his throat in the darkness, but he baulked at any talk of killing Archbishop Sigeric; to kill a man of God was to attack God himself, and he would hear no talk of it.

Beornoth pondered on those problems. Hrodgar's plan to kill Godric in his bed made sense given their lack of warriors, but Beornoth wanted to look the traitor in his eyes as he ripped his life from him. A knife in the darkness was not an honourable way to deal with an enemy, even if it was the most practical. Godric's burh at Hareswood was not a full burh, in that it did not meet plans laid out by King Alfred. It had a ditch, and a palisade built of stout timbers, a gatehouse and hall, but was smaller than the traditional burh, which Alfred had built throughout Wessex and beyond to keep out Viking incursions after the Great Heathen Army had come within a hair's breadth of conquering Britain and ending Saxon rule. Hareswood would be well defended, and Beornoth blinked sleeplessly at the orange embers. He wondered how they could sneak in, kill Godric and get out again without his warriors noticing. The notion of an assassination rankled with his warrior's conscience and kept Beornoth awake, until his worries overwhelmed him like an enemy shield wall, and he drifted off to dream of Eawynn and her garden.

'The horses are ready,' said Hrodgar, gently nudging Beornoth's shoulder to wake him. He sat up, groaning at the ache in his belly wound and the stiffness in his ageing joints. Beornoth blinked, and his left eye opened fully for the first time since the fight at Olaf's camp. They left Ælfflæd's home on a windy morning under a low, brooding sky. Leafless trees swayed, their branches reaching towards heaven like the thin, praying hands of those in need of a miracle. Wuffa and three of Ælfflæd's guards waited for them beyond the hedge fence.

'We will escort you to Celmersford, lord,' Wuffa said, and would not be turned away. Celmersford was a slow day's ride away. 'If north is where you plan to ride.'

'We go north,' said Beornoth. 'And your escort is welcome. We might need your blades if Godric's brigands attack again.'

'Hareswood is north-east of here,' said Hrodgar. He spoke tersely, and Beornoth shook his head.

'We need men. So, we go north. We must punish East Anglia for their failure to march to Maldon. For that, we need warriors. Then we go for Godric.'

'Where will we find this magical force of fighting men who will appear from nowhere and march with us to East Anglia?'

'In the north. Thered of Northumbria will give us men, as would Alfgar of Cheshire. We have two powerful ealdormen who will support us. We could go to the king, but he supports only with words, and not with swords.'

Hrodgar opened his mouth to protest at the accusation against Æthelred but thought better of it when he saw the stubborn look of Beornoth's cliff of a face. They rode through the small gate, and Beornoth turned Virtus to wave at Ælfflæd and Nothhelm.

'What's to stop Godric riding to Rettendon and killing the widow and the bishop?' asked Brand in Norse as they cantered along the frost-hardened road.

'Godric might be a shit-stinking coward, and a greedy land-grabbing bastard,' said Beornoth. 'But even he must draw the line at attacking the widow of an ealdorman who so recently and hero-ically died in battle, and no man would kill the bishop of Essex if he wants to keep the blessing of the Church. If Godric has his eye on becoming ealdorman, he can't do it with a widow's and bishop's blood on his hands.'

'But he can do it with a shire washed in blood, as long as he doesn't touch the widow or Bishop Nothhelm?'

Beornoth shrugged, and they rode to Celmersford through a country absent of travellers, the cold roads empty as people stayed indoors to see out the dark season. But riders shadowed the small column, visible on the edges of a windswept bluff to the east of the road. Brand saw them first, emerging from the woodland's edge to cross open ground and climbing to watch them from the high ground.

Wuffa led them to a tavern on the road into Celmersford, a small place called the Fighting Duck, where they found food and lodging. Beornoth asked Hrodgar and Wuffa to find food and talk to the tavern owner about the goings-on in Essex and then slipped out with Brand into the evening chill. They had Tata saddle their horses, which he did without a grumble, even though he had just finished brushing and feeding the animals after the day's ride.

'You want to kill the watchers, lord?' asked Brand as their horses trotted away from the tavern, and its warm fire and food.

'They must be Godric's men, so let's send a message before we leave the lands of the East Saxons.'

Brand grinned and patted the haft of his axe. They rode north and east, keeping a close eye on the low-lying hills and woodland around the road and tavern. It was not a place of deep valleys or ranging cliffs, but of gently rolling hillsides, farmlands and forest. Darkness came early and quickly, but the moon was a sliver from its full glory and lit up the shire in silver so that the frost glistened on grass, branch and hedge like a sea of shattered ice. The two riders circled around the route they had taken towards Celmersford, easing their horses through the darkness, letting the mounts choose their own pace. Men who knew horses better than Beornoth swore the animals could see just as well in the dark as they could in sunlight, and that the real danger of night riding was to the rider.

They rode past a steading of low roundhouses, and Beornoth's head turned as an owl hooted its ghostly cry in a tangle of shadowed trees. Brand laughed for joy as both men noticed a glow in the depths of the forest, as though it were the entrance to the gates of hell. The Viking laughed because they had surely found their prey, for who else would hide out in woodland on a winter's night but hunters who wanted to remain hidden from their prey?

Beornoth tied Virtus' reins to an ash branch on the forest's edge. He stroked the beast's ears and fed him a carrot he had taken from Rettendon.

'If I do not return, I wish you good luck,' he whispered, and Virtus brought his powerful head up so that Beornoth could touch his forehead to the horse's. Beornoth put up the hood of his dark cloak and drew his sword. He crept into the undergrowth, moving slowly and carefully the closer he came to the brightness at the heart of the wood. Brand crept alongside him, axe in one hand and a long knife in the other. Voices laughed and talked in the darkness, growing louder with each step forward. The four men spoke with northern accents, with the slightest tinge of Danish in their Saxon tongue. Men of the Danelaw then, fugitives of some minor war or dispute between thegns or lords in the distant north, masterless men who had found pay in the service of Godric and his ambition.

Brand pointed his axe to the left, and Beornoth nodded. The Viking peeled away and circled around the band of men so that he and Beornoth could attack from opposite sides. The four men Beornoth had seen on the bluff above Celmersford drank ale and told stories by the fire. As Beornoth crept closer, he listened to a man with a Pictish accent boast about how he had killed six men and was a man of great reputation in his homeland. He told a story of how a churl had begged for his life as the Pict tupped his wife and stole his silver. The other three laughed and Beornoth emerged from the darkness.

Beornoth waited there, sword drawn and hood up, staring at the four warriors. They thought they were clever men, spying on Beornoth and sending word to Ansgar the Giant or to Godric himself. One of Beornoth's great joys of war was to surprise men who had planned his death, men who had wrought a cunning scheme to come at him with blades and dark intent, and then to kill them instead. To live when a man who sought Beornoth's life died himself.

'Holy God,' said one of the four men, and he shot up from the log on which he sat. He pointed at Beornoth, his face lit up by the firelight and his mouth curled downwards in fear. The others turned and Beornoth stepped forward.

'Who are you? We are not men to suffer robbery. Be off with

you, before I skin you alive,' said the Pict. He reached for his spear, which rested beside him.

'I am Beornoth, king's thegn,' he said, and strode towards the Pict.

'Holy God,' the rearmost man repeated and took short steps away from the fire. He shrieked and spun around as his back collided with Brand's chest. Brand laughed, and the man stumbled back towards the fire.

The Pict licked his thick lips and ran a hand down his drooping moustaches. He held his spear in his right hand, and he glanced from its point to Beornoth's sword.

'Now is your chance,' said Beornoth. 'You are four, and we are but two. Cut us down and bring our heads to your lord, and he will reward you handsomely.'

'We haven't come to kill you,' said the Pict. He tried to be belligerent, but fear cracked his voice and he swallowed hard. 'Just to watch, that's all. We meant you no harm.'

'No harm? Who asked you to follow us?'

'Lord Godric of Hareswood, lord,' said a wiry man on the Pict's left, and the bigger man shot him a baleful frown.

'And once Godric knew of our destination, he would kill us. Would he not?'

The wiry man looked at his friends and shook his head. Beornoth wasn't sure if he did that because he disagreed with what Beornoth said, or because he couldn't believe the cruel twist of fate about to befall him. Because fate had caught up with these men in an East Saxon forest; Beornoth had come for them, and any man who crossed him did so in full knowledge of his reputation.

Beornoth sprang forwards and struck with his sword, both sudden and brutal. Rather than raise his spear to counter Beornoth's sword, the Pict turned his back with a fearful whimper. Beornoth

snarled in disgust and opened up the Pict's thigh with the point of
his blade. He kept the sword moving and slashed its edge across the
throat of the wiry man as he fumbled for an axe in the undergrowth.

Brand chopped his axe into the rearmost man's chest, ripped it
free and hacked again as the enemy fell screaming into the fire.
Embers flew into the dark, and Beornoth stepped over the Pict. He
had fallen into the rotten, frozen leaf mulch, crawling like a worm,
and he left a trail of gleaming blood behind him. He turned over
and wept like an infant at Beornoth's snarling fury. The Pict
covered his face and howled with fear, and Beornoth caught a waft
of shit where the boasting coward had soiled his trews in terror.
Beornoth stabbed the tip of his sword into the man's guts, twisted it
savagely, and pulled the blade free. As the Pict lowered his hands
to cover the wound, Beornoth ripped out his throat with the
bloody sword point.

'Leave that one,' Beornoth said as Brand advanced on the final
spy, wanting to kill the man. Brand turned to him with a hurt look
on his face, like a child who has been told he cannot accompany
his father on market day. Beornoth stalked across the blood-spat-
tered campfire to where the fourth man sat, stuck to his log seat by
crippling fear. Beornoth pointed his sword at him, leaving the
blade a hand's breadth from his pox-scarred face. The man stared
at the bloody sword blade, mouth open and eyes glassy with shock.

'I am Beornoth, and you can live to run back to your Lord
Godric and tell him I killed his men. Tell him I saw him run from
the battle at Maldon and take the fyrd with him. He left his
oathsworn blood brothers to die. He is an oathbreaker, a traitor
and a coward. Tell him that death stalks him, that I have been sent
back from the jaws of hell to punish him for his crimes. Now, go.'

The man scrambled off his log and ran into the darkness. He
fell over a dead branch, rolled in a clutch of ferns, and fled into the
forest on all fours like a whipped dog.

'Now Godric will live in fear,' said Beornoth in Norse, and Brand nodded, a feral grin splitting his golden beard. 'We will gather a band of fighters, men who will fight to avenge my fallen brothers. We shall return to East Anglia and Essex, and traitors' blood will run through the fields like a river.'

11

___

After a hot meal and a night spent huddled in a small tavern outside Celmersford, the riders started on the hard road north. Wuffa's men returned to Rettendon to protect the Lady Ælfflæd and her household, but Wuffa himself would not return. He asked Beornoth to let him join their war band. Wuffa had loved Ealdorman Byrhtnoth, and begged Beornoth for a chance to be avenged upon those who had betrayed the great lord. Beornoth reluctantly agreed. Wuffa did not seem like much of a fighting man with his narrow, wiry frame and bandy legs, but there was something about him. There was an air about the man, something that stopped him from holding Beornoth's eye for longer than a few seconds. At first, Beornoth thought the man callow, but through talking to him on the road from Rettendon to Celmersford, Beornoth realised it was shame that cast Wuffa's eyes down. The shame of not being there at Maldon when Byrhtnoth and his hearth troop fought to the death whilst Wuffa guarded the Lady Ælfflæd. Beornoth could not imagine having to live with that knowledge, that the men Wuffa had been born and raised alongside, men he had fought and lived with his entire life, had sacrificed their lives to protect the people, and he had not been there. Wuffa lived, and the warriors he knew and loved were dead.

Five riders made the hard journey north, and it took twenty-two long days. There were days where the road was unpassable, gripped as the country was by winter's fury. Rain lashed the roads and bounced on tavern thatches. Beornoth spent ungodly amounts of silver to keep the men and horses fed and lodged at way stations along the well-trodden trading roads leading to Tamworth, and then north-east towards York. They coughed and sneezed with colds, and huddled around fires where the tavern keepers served ever-thinner stews as winter supplies ran out. Luckily, there were few on the road, and so the riders could secure rooms at most stops, though the straw in the pallet beds was often grimy and stinking from the backs of many travellers since that hay had been cut stiff and golden from late summer fields.

York sat at the confluence of two rivers, the Ouse and Fosse, and had been an important city before even the time of the Rome folk. Some men believed the Romans had used giants to lift and place the enormous stones that formed the walls and older buildings around the city, and there were certainly no men alive in England who could cut and dress stone as closely as the Romans. The Rome folk had called the place Eboracum, and then Beornoth's ancestors, Saxon warriors who had braved the Whale Road to wrestle the land from the Britons, had muddled that name in their own tongue so that it became Eoforwich. When Ivar the Boneless and his Great Heathen Army descended on York to kill its King Aelle in revenge for their murdered father, Ragnar Lothbrok, their tongue struggled with the Saxon name, and it became Yovrvik. Over time, men simplified that to York. In the time of Beornoth's father, the kingdom of York had been a mighty state outside the rule of King Alfred and his descendants. It had ruled at the heart of the Danelaw until the death of Eric Bloodaxe just before Beornoth was born.

They rode through the huge south-facing gate on a day where the sun shone without heat, and the clip-clop of Virtus' hooves on the cobbled streets brought back grim memories. Before they had fought together, Thered and Beornoth had been enemies, and Thered's father, the old Ealdorman Oslac, had tried to have Beornoth taken and killed in the city's great hall. It had only been thanks to Byrhtnoth's quick thinking, and the support of Leofsunu, Aelfwine, Wulfhere and the rest of the hearth troop, that he had escaped with his life.

Tata gawped at the looming, magnificent walls of the city's great minster, where the Vikings had once stacked their looted treasure. It was a bustling place of merchants, traders, warriors and folk about their daily business. Men pushed carts loaded with earth-brown pottery, and Beornoth cursed at the driver of a wain stacked with the curved amphorae of expensive wine from across the sea when he let his wheels run over and pin an old woman's ragged cloak.

'I'll never get this stink out of my nose,' grumbled Brand. He wrinkled his nose and gazed up longingly at the sky. For a man used to the open sea, and the hill and fjords of Norway, a city was a foul place. After a day or so, a man became accustomed to the ever-present smell of piss, shit, smoke and cooking food, but upon entering the city it assaulted a man's senses and Beornoth pulled his cloak up around his nose to block out the worst of it.

The great hall sat on a wide, cobbled square close to the minster, and Beornoth approached a warrior who stood guard over the open square where folk sold baskets, charms, bowls, fish, bread and ale.

'I seek Ealdorman Thered,' said Beornoth. He tied his horse to a rail above a stone trough filled with water. The warrior stared up at Beornoth, and took in his byrnie, sword and size.

'Who shall I say seeks the ealdorman, lord?' asked the warrior. He wore a leather breastplate and carried a spear; his beard was clipped short about a small mouth.

'Lord Beornoth...' He wasn't sure where to say he was from. Before Maldon, he would have said of Branoc's Tree, but Olaf's Vikings had destroyed that place. 'King's thegn.' It was his official rank, he supposed, but it was unfamiliar, and the warrior looked surprised. Being a king's thegn put Beornoth at a similar rank to an ealdorman, and no ealdorman would introduce himself to a simple warrior. That would be a job for one of his warriors, or his steward.

'Yes, lord. Please wait here, lord.' The warrior bowed his head and marched towards the great hall.

'Let's see if we can find something to eat,' said Hrodgar, placing his good hand on his empty belly.

'And some fresh ale,' said Wuffa. 'We've been drinking dregs for days.'

Wuffa and Hrodgar set off into the throng of people, carts, wains and stalls whilst Beornoth and Brand waited by the horses. Tata fed the animals with fistfuls of grain from his saddlebag.

'How old are you, boy?' asked Beornoth. He had become increasingly aware of Tata's silence. He didn't seem sad, or happy, or express any emotion at all. Tata just worked all day. He cared for the horses, ground grains for porridge or gruel, he prepared meals, and never spoke unless spoken to.

'Me?' Tata replied. He looked up at Beornoth as though he feared being struck. Then his face flushed red, and he licked his lips. 'I don't rightly know, lord.'

'Can you count beyond ten?'

Tata shrugged.

'Can you speak Norse?'

He shook his head and shrugged again.

'Can you fight?'

Tata looked up at Beornoth with a blank stare.

'You are good with the horses, lad. But do you want to be a servant to Hrodgar, or do something else with your life?'

'Haven't really thought about it, lord.'

'What did your father do?'

'He owned land, lord. But he's dead now. So I went to the ealdorman in Defnascir, because I had nothing.'

'Well, whilst we are on this journey, you might as well learn a few useful things. Brand will teach you Norse, and you will teach him Saxon.'

'But he's a...'

'A Viking, yes. He's a warrior and you can learn about his people and how they fight by learning his words. It might come in useful.'

'Yes, lord.'

'And I will teach you to fight.'

'You will, lord?'

'Yes.'

'What for, lord?'

'So that you can defend yourself. Also, so that you can strike at the enemy when we must fight. We start with spear first, then seax, then axe.'

'Thank you, lord,' said Tata, though he didn't look very thankful. His eyes turned as wide and round as the full moon and he licked again at dry lips. His eyes darted from Beornoth to Brand, and he shifted on his feet as though he wanted to ask questions, to understand why Beornoth was saying these things to him.

'Why is that runt looking at me like that?' said Brand in Norse, staring at Tata with a mix of interest and hostility.

'Because you are going to teach him to speak Norse, and he is going to teach you to speak Saxon.'

'I don't want to learn your foul Saxon words; they sound like pig farts.'

'Well, I'm not translating anything for you until you start to learn, so it's up to you. Here is some silver.' Beornoth handed Brand a handful of hacksilver from a pouch at his belt. 'See if you can buy him a spear, or a seax.'

'Ha!' Brand scoffed, throwing his head back. 'What for? The little piss weasel can't fight. He can barely hold his manhood, never mind a spear.'

'At Maldon, I saw the smallest of farmers fight and kill your people with their teeth and nails once their spears had broken, whilst lords in shining war gear fled the field. So, I will teach the lad to fight.'

Brand stopped laughing once he noticed the serious look on Beornoth's face. He nodded, shrugged, cuffed Tata around the head and led him into the throng. Beornoth smiled a little to himself as Brand pointed to a horse, a woman and the sky and told Tata how to say what they were in Norse.

A clatter of boots on cobblestones caught Beornoth's attention, and he turned to see a group of three warriors approaching. One was the man Beornoth had sent for the ealdorman. The rightmost man was a hulking brute with long blonde hair braided in the Viking style, and Beornoth smiled as he recognised the man in the middle.

'Thered,' Beornoth called, and held up his hand in greeting.

'Beornoth,' Thered said warmly, and he quickened his pace. His face lit up with joy. Beornoth noticed that the young ealdorman limped badly, his left leg stiff and dragging along as he moved. As Thered drew closer, Beornoth also noticed a gruesome scar had cut his face badly, running across his nose and down through his mouth so that the nose was crooked and his mouth pulled down on the left side, with a white bald line through his beard.

The two men came together, not with the usual warrior's grip of the wrist, but with the warm embrace of blood brothers. They held each other, arms tight across one another's back, and the embrace lingered as Beornoth recalled the horrors of Maldon. Memories came back to him of how bravely Thered had fought alongside men who had once been his enemies. He was a hostage, held by Byrhtnoth against the good behaviour of his rebellious father Oslac, but had become one of the blood brothers of Byrhtnoth's hearth troop.

'I thought you were dead,' said Beornoth. 'It does me good to see you alive and well.'

'I thought I was dead,' said Thered. 'Then I realised I was just in the south.'

They laughed together and then pulled away to drink in each other's appearance. Beornoth held up his hand, and the scarred palm where he had made the cut to commit his life to the service of Byrhtnoth and his brothers in arms, and Thered did the same. They stared deep into one another's eyes. No words needed to be said; a knowing passed between them. Each knew what the other had experienced at Maldon, the brutal savagery of the shield wall as they tried against all odds to hold against Olaf Tryggvason and his legendary Jomsvikings. The overwhelming terror as the war-king of Denmark, Sweyn Forkbeard, and his picked Viking champions, came wading from the sea to hack their friends to pieces.

'I am glad you are here,' said Thered, 'but surprised to see you so far north. What brings you to York?'

'Vengeance.'

'Then we had better sit down and talk.'

Thered's servants brought Hrodgar, Brand, Tata and Wuffa to a chamber at the rear of his great hall where they would be fed and brought ale. Thered and Beornoth sat on two carved logs in a garden beyond the ealdorman's living quarters. It was a mild day for winter, still and dry, but cold under a clear sky. A serving girl brought two horn mugs of steaming spiced water and a platter of bread and cheese.

'You were badly wounded,' said Thered. He pointed at Beornoth's stomach. 'I saw it, and you are lucky to have survived that.'

'Maybe God kept us alive for a reason,' said Beornoth. He placed both hands around the cup, and its warmth spread into his fingers, through his hands, and flowed through his body. 'You also sustained severe injuries.'

'Aye.' Thered raised a hand instinctively to his face and caressed the long scar. Two fingers on that left hand were missing from the first knuckle. 'I was afraid in the days following the battle, and I don't mind admitting it. I rolled and screamed in the dark as men dragged me to safety. So much blood came from my wounds that I thought I had none left inside me. This cut blinded me for a week and I feared the wound that does not kill, the one that leaves a man blind or a cripple. Nobody knew who I was, and I sat in a churl's barn as his wife tended to five of us injured warriors. My leg was run through, and the bone broken, and my face cleaved almost in two. Two of the five died within a week of the rotting sickness, festered wounds stinking and sweating them to nothing. Once I had survived that week, then I feared I would not walk again, that I had survived only to be left a cripple who would depend on others for the rest of my life. A warrior useless to all, a maimed, piteous thing.'

'Maybe there is a reason you are still alive. You are the ealdorman now.'

'And you are a king's thegn.'

'And there is a debt owed. The dead demand vengeance.'

'Godric?'

'He fled the field and encouraged the fyrd to rout. He left us all for dead, and most of us died. We two are left to punish those responsible. Godric has hired a small army of masterless men and cut-throats and he tries to steal Byrhtnoth's lands and would stop the ealdorman's daughter from inheriting. Archbishop Sigeric backs him. Forkbeard has returned to Denmark, and Sigeric will pay Olaf a ruinous gafol to persuade him to leave our shores.'

'Do we have men?'

'All my men died at Branoc's Tree or at Maldon. Our blood brothers are all dead. Wulfhere is dead. Alfgar, my friend who is ealdorman of Cheshire, sent us one hundred swords to fight at Maldon and none returned. His captain, Streonwold, who I had known for years, also died.'

'How many warriors has Godric marshalled?'

'Perhaps three hundred, maybe more. And we must punish the East Anglian ealdorman and his son for their broken oath.'

Thered nodded solemnly. 'I am ealdorman here now. My father died whilst we were in the south. I cannot simply raise the fyrd of Northumbria and march an army upon Essex; a war between the shires would rip the kingdom in two.'

'But you will fight?'

'Of course I will fight. I can bring thirty warriors of my hearth troop. We don't need to match Godric's three hundred cut-throats, but a third of that number, stout men with sharp blades, will do the job.'

'So, where do we find sixty warriors to march with us?'

'There are men in Northumbria I can ask to fight, but they are not Saxons, Beo. These are the sons of the kingdom of York. They are the descendants of Danes and Norsemen who have settled here and will fight for silver.'

'They will ride and fight for you?'

'They will if I give them land and we guarantee silver, reputation and battle.'

'Godric is a wealthy man, so there is silver to be had. And we ride to fight, so there is reputation in our war.'

'They won't march until spring, though, Beo. So, you must rest here with us until the white-arsed bird returns and the trees bud.'

To delay gave Godric and Sigeric more time to plunder Essex, and Beornoth feared that each day they would grow stronger. But Thered was right. No army, not even one as small as sixty men, could march in the depths of winter. It had been a long, slow and expensive slog to ride five men from Essex to Northumbria. Beornoth's head hurt as he tried to fathom how they might feed and water a mounted war band across the length of Britain. So, they must rest in York and wait for the season to change, and then try to raise a force of Danes and Norsemen to wreak vengeance on Byrhtnoth's enemies. Beornoth sipped his spiced water and ate a piece of hard cheese. He wondered at the strangeness of the world, of the sheer bloody irony that he would bring a force of Vikings to Essex to fight against one if its thegns, when he had spent much of his life trying to beat back Viking raiders. But all that mattered to Beornoth was revenge, and he did not care who wielded the swords and spears to help him do it.

Each morning, as the sun rose, Beornoth would rise and meet Tata in Thered's garden. Hrodgar did not mind that Beornoth would teach the lad to fight, and some days he would come and watch, and shout advice or encouragement as the young man struggled to parry or skip away from Beornoth's attacks. They began with a simple stave to serve as a spear. For two weeks, each day, Beornoth drilled Tata on how to hold the weapon. The correct form to lunge and stab overhand, how to use the shaft to block an attack. On most days Tata left the garden with a sore head or bloody knuckles from Beornoth's harsh lessons.

'The point isn't the only part of a spear,' Beornoth shouted at him more than once, before clouting him over the head with the stave's butt.

On the third week, Tata improved and lasted ten heartbeats before Beornoth's onslaught. Hrodgar was there that day and he roared with delight to see the lad hold his own until Beornoth sent him flying into a flower bed. After that, Beornoth borrowed a shield from Thered, and taught Tata how to use both shield and spear. After their lesson, Beornoth had Tata hold the shield before him with two hands until his shoulders burned under the weight. Then, he made the lad run around the garden with the shield above his head until both legs and shoulders burned like fire.

Brand took over after the fifth week, and he and Tata could communicate effectively in a melting pot of Norse and Saxon. Brand showed Tata the cuts of an axe, and the wicked stab and slash of the seax. Then, one morning, the sun shone and Beornoth left his cloak indoors. The willow tree in Thered's garden showed small green buds, and a familiar bird twittered a bright song. Spring arrived, and it was time to find warriors.

12

Beornoth rode out of York's ancient walls with Brand, Hrodgar, Tata, Wuffa, Thered and ten of Thered's hearth troop. Thered's men rode with shields and spears, and their spear points wavered above them like wind-shook pines. They headed north-west, into the heartlands of Northumbria's rolling countryside. The north was a place of deep valleys and high crags, of farms marked by river, brook, hedge and wood. Beornoth was born in those harsh lands, across the vast Pennine mountains whose peaks stretched to the sky and scraped heaven itself. He felt at home here, rather than in the flatlands of the South Saxons. Virtus picked her way across the shallow ford of a foaming stream, above which a hillside swept away into a slope of harsh, dark rock. Stories from Beornoth's childhood came back to him as the spring wind whipped his face. Tales of Wicce, thurses and euton, the witches, trolls and giants who lived in those old places and would clamber down in the night to steal away naughty children or steal from the wicked. Those stories carried echoes of the wise woman who had stitched Beornoth's guts together. He pondered over the lost ancient knowledge of the world – the knowledge of paganism and the worship of the sun, trees and rivers – that people knew before Christ came to England and drove it to the high mountains and far corners of the kingdom.

'The first steading we must visit is over that rise,' said Thered. He rode next to Beornoth and pointed his hand across a hill of green ferns and yellow flowers.

'What will we find there?' asked Beornoth.

'Warriors.' Thered flashed a smile, the gesture misshapen by the scars across his face.

'I would remind you, Beo,' said Hrodgar, nudging his mount to come alongside Thered and Beornoth, 'that we are king's thegns. I am not entirely comfortable with us recruiting Danes and Norsemen to our cause.'

'Why not?' asked Beornoth. 'We want to punish traitors and the king cannot give us men. So, we find our own.'

'Yes, but surely not...' Hrodgar paused, glancing over his shoulder at Brand. 'Vikings.'

'These men are only as much Viking as I am,' said Thered, 'or many of your noblemen in East Anglia, or anywhere in the old Danelaw. Vikings settled here and married Saxon women, or the daughters of Viking settlers married Saxon men. But in these high places, they have just continued with the old ways, whereas we have adopted the Saxon way of life.'

'But how can we trust them?' asked Hrodgar.

'Trust?' Thered said through a mocking laugh. 'Our own blood brothers turned their backs on Beornoth and I at Maldon, and they were of Saxon stock. It was thegns and noblemen who led the fyrd away from the battlefield. These men will fight for pay, and for the promise of a chance to burnish their reputations, and that's good enough for me.'

They crested the rise, and in a shallow curve between three hills ran a quick stream alongside a huddle of buildings topped with sprouting turf. Sheep brayed in a meadow, and six horses trotted in a fenced paddock.

'Brand?' Thered called over his shoulder, raising his hand for the riders to halt.

'Yes, lord,' said Brand. He said the words in Saxon and his heavy Norse burr rolled around them. He tried to practise the new tongue whenever he could and spent time each day with Tata, going over unfamiliar words and trying to string together conversations.

'Come up here with us. It will encourage them to see a Norseman with us.'

The riders waited on the hillside, and Beornoth's horse cropped at the wild grass. Below, a woman took a bucket to the stream, bent to fill it with water and strolled back to her house without casting her eyes up at the riders. Children ran between the buildings, shouting and laughing, and somewhere out of sight a baby screamed its little lungs out.

'What are we waiting for?' said Hrodgar, after a time spent sighing and fidgeting in the saddle.

'We wait to show we come in peace,' said Thered. 'And so that they can see us.'

'But we are in plain sight! Everyone in the village can see us.'

Beornoth held up a hand to settle Hrodgar down. He knew Vikings as well as Thered, having fought and lived amongst them in his youth. Three men came from the largest building, which had an ox skull nailed to the gable. They strolled towards the riders, talking and laughing amongst themselves. The man in the middle was big and barrel-chested and carried a long-handled Dane axe over one shoulder. He had a golden beard which had run to grey, and long silver hair tied at the nape of his neck. He had a wide slash of a mouth, in a big, open face. The men on either side of him wore swords in their belts and all three wore

byrnie coats of chain mail. Their arms were thick with Viking
warrior rings.

'Thered Oslacsson,' called the big man in Norse as they drew
close. 'I hear you are the ealdorman now?'

'You heard right, Vigdjarf. You look well. How is your wife?'
replied Thered.

'She nags and complains like a bitter old sea hag. But she still
makes the best lamb stew this side of the Humber.'

'And your daughters?'

'Keep your eyes off my daughters,' Vigdjarf said, and he lifted
his great axe from his shoulder and shook the blade towards the
riders. 'I don't need turds like you lot coming into my house and
making eyes at them. If I see any man within talking distance of
my daughters, I'll cut his bollocks off and feed them to my dogs. If
you've come here to ask me to kneel, you can piss off. I like you,
Thered, even though you used to be a piece of stinking weasel shit.
But I won't bend the knee just because you are an ealdorman
now.'

'That's not why I've come. I'm putting a war band together, but
I only want the fiercest warriors, the reckless ones, the men who
fight in the front line and long for Odin's Hall. I go south to kill the
men who betrayed me when I got these.' Thered gestured towards
his scars. 'There is silver in it for any who ride. We must go deep
into the lands of the East Saxons and kill a man protected by three
hundred warriors. And before that, we must kill the ealdorman of
the East Angles.'

'Thats a lot of killing. How many will ride?' asked Vigdjarf.

'We are only fighting Saxons, so my thirty and another twenty.'

'Two score against three hundred?'

'Aye. But we have Beornoth Reiði, and Brand Thorkilsson,
whom I have fought beside and are worth a hundred men each. So,
we will outnumber our enemies.'

Vigdjarf chuckled and pointed his axe at Beornoth and Brand. 'I have heard of you, Beornoth. You are the Viking killer?'

'I've killed Vikings, yes. But then, I've killed lots of men,' said Beornoth. He met Vigdjarf's belligerent stare and held it until the Viking shifted his gaze to Brand.

'You are Viking?'

'I am Brand Thorkilsson from Hålogaland in the far north. I sailed here with the army of Olaf Tryggvason.'

'Welcome, Brand. I am Vigdjarf Rognvaldsson, and my great-grandfather fought beside Ivar and Halvdan Ragnarsson when they won this country with axe and spear.'

'Then it is my honour to meet you.' Brand dipped his head in respect, to which Vigdjarf puffed his chest out and raised his chin.

'Will you ride with us?' asked Thered.

'I can bring eight warriors to your fight, including two of my daughters who fight like beasts from Niflheim. But the price must be right, Thered. Let's go inside and make a bargain.'

And so they did. Vigdjarf's wife, a small woman so broad across the hips and chest that she was almost as round as the sun, served bowls of thick lamb stew and Thered haggled with Vigdjarf over his price. They finally landed on a complicated mix of silver, sheep and cows, and Thered had to swear an oath that none of his warriors would lay a hand on Vigdjarf's daughters who would ride with the company. They stayed that night with Vigdjarf and ate a hearty evening meal swilled down with ale, whilst Beornoth drank fresh water from the stream. By the fireside, Brand told stories while they ate. He told the lay of Olaf Tryggvason's life, of how Olaf's father, the king of Norway, was murdered and his mother forced to flee their homeland. He spoke of how Olaf's mother and the young Olaf were sold into slavery far to the east, and of how Olaf had fought his way up to become a great Viking warlord. Once the crowd was dizzy from hearth

smoke and ale, Vigdjarf told the story of how Ivar the Boneless
had carved the blood eagle into the back of King Aelle of
Northumbria one hundred years earlier in revenge for his father's
death.

Hrodgar hugged his ale and grumbled at being in the company
of Vikings, and Beornoth too stayed silent. Thered made merry
with Vigdjarf and his people, but darkness lay heavy on Beornoth's
heart. He felt guilty resting whilst the traitors yet lived. They had
wasted too much time waiting for winter to lift, and now he sat
drinking and laughing in Vigdjarf's longhouse whilst his friends'
corpses rotted unavenged. Being around Vikings made Beornoth
uncomfortable. As a people, they had brought so much pain and
suffering to his life. But he needed men, and Vigdjarf introduced
the six men who would ride south, and each one seemed a stout
fighter. Beornoth glanced at their hands and was satisfied when he
saw the nicks and scars of fighting men on knuckles and thumbs.
There were endless raids and cattle wars in the north, and these
men were clearly no strangers to a fight.

They woke early the next morning, and Vigdjarf marched from
his home flanked by two golden-haired women. Brand's jaw fell
open.

'Close your cheese-pipe,' Beornoth hissed.

'But they are... beautiful,' gasped Brand. They were tall, lithe
and dressed in leather breastplates. Both girls had round faces and
bright blue eyes, and Beornoth wondered why the Viking would
expose his daughters to the dangers of the road, and to the hard
fighting ahead. They came armed with long spears, bows and
quivers of arrows.

'These are two of my daughters,' said Vigdjarf, standing in
front of them as the girls checked their horses. 'Hrist, and Sefna.
They do not need my protection, but I warn you again. Any man
touches my daughters and this axe, war-troll, will take your balls.'

He brandished his axe, and growled at every man in Beornoth's company to make sure the message was clear.

'So, we march with women, now?' said Hrodgar. 'This just gets better with every new day.'

Each of Vigdjarf's warriors came mounted, and Thered led them further west, where the land rose towards the slopes of the great mountain range which separated east from west. The land became harder there, less pasture and more hard rock, colder and more like the harsh lands across the sea in the Vikings' homelands. A vast pine forest covered an east-facing slope, and a fast-flowing river curved around its base like a shining worm.

'The river Hverfi,' said Thered as they rode down towards its banks. That meant crook or turn in Norse, and the river was named for its winding meander. That its name was Norse, told of the dense population of Vikings in the area. On the banks of the Hverfi, Thered led them towards piles of golden timber planking, stacked and ready to be shipped along the river. A long barge bobbed in the water, and it would take that timber with the river's flow west towards York, where it would build homes, repair fortifications and be sold at the great market inside the city.

'Do you think Reifnir will fight for you?' asked Vigdjarf as they rode past the stacks of freshly cut wood, which shone like gold. The valley rang with the chop of axe on wood, and the smell of fresh pine filled the riverbank.

'He doesn't need silver, but he needs reputation,' said Thered. 'Wait here.'

Thered rode alone between the stacks of timber and raw pine logs still gnarled with bark and waiting to be trimmed.

'Who is this Reifnir?' asked Brand.

'He owns the land around the pine forest,' said Vigdjarf. 'His family has been caught in a blood feud for three generations with the family in the next valley. They hate each other for reasons nobody can even remember. Reifnir lost two sons in a fight over grazing rights for their cattle. So, Reifnir burned his enemies' hall, with the family sleeping inside. He killed the head of the family, his wife, and their children. Even small children died in the blaze, and Reifnir lost his honour as well as his sons.'

'Doesn't sound like a man we can trust,' said Beornoth. The mention of dead children tugged at his own loss, and he doubted he could ride in the company of a child-killer. Even if it meant the difference between Godric's death or not.

'He didn't know the little ones were inside. They didn't live there but were visiting. Reifnir knows what he did was wrong, and he has never forgiven himself. He lives up here at his mill with his only remaining son. He would do anything to repair his reputation, for he has no place in the glorious afterlife and is surely destined to walk as a wraith in Helheim for eternity.'

Whilst Thered went to find Reifnir, the riders took the chance to rest and water their horses. Beornoth didn't have the stomach to explain to Hrodgar who this Reifnir was, and the crimes he had committed. The company spoke mostly in Norse, which added to Hrodgar's barely hidden frustration and to explain to him the horrors of Reifnir's past would not improve his mood. Tata shared out some baked biscuits from his pack, and he, Wuffa and Hrodgar ate away from the Vikings. Beornoth understood how Hrodgar felt. The Viking was the instinctive enemy of the Englishman, and it felt as though their mission for vengeance was slipping out of control. Beornoth watched Vigdjarf and his warriors eat and laugh, and Thered's men mixed freely with them. When together, they spoke a strange mix of Saxon and Norse. Beornoth ate his meal, hoping that this delay in the north was worth it.

Brand had fallen asleep on the riverbank by the time Thered returned. The Norseman could sleep anywhere, and Beornoth wished he had the same knack. Beornoth's mind was an always churning maelstrom of hate for his enemies, love and sadness at being away from Eawynn, and concern for completing his task. Thered marched with a short man with a bald head and a thin, tired face. Behind them came four warriors clad in leather and armed with axes and spears. Thered introduced Reifnir, and his cold brown eyes passed over each man, as though peering into their thoughts, wondering if they knew of the terrible thing he had done.

'Are there no other warriors we can find besides child-killers?' Beornoth asked as Reifnir's men saddled their horses and joined the company. He wondered if it might have been better to ask Alfgar for some stout Cheshire men to swell their ranks, rather than this ragged band of Viking murderers. But he had already asked too much of his friend and could not ask the ealdorman of Cheshire for another favour.

'Reifnir and his men are seasoned fighters. The one with the dog is his last surviving son, Ornir Hauknefr, and he is the best tracker in Northumbria.' Hauknefr meant Hawknose, and a wolfhound hunting dog loped along beside the young warrior's horse. It was a large, wiry animal with long limbs and short, scruffy hair which seemed almost blue with its black and silver colouring.

The column spent a night in a neighbouring farmer's barn and then rode east to York. Thered had his steward prepare provisions for the journey south, and each warrior carried enough food for horse and rider for seven days. With the rest of Thered's hearth troop, the company swelled to forty warriors. It was not enough men to stand and fight Godric's force in an open battle, but enough to cause Godric and his cut-throats problems.

It was a ragged band of Danelaw Vikings and Saxons who rode from York's south gate under a shifting sky. City cobblestones turned to soft grass and the deep cart ruts of the old Roman road as travellers moved aside from the armed warriors. Those they met

on the road bowed their heads as the warriors passed, a mark of
respect to those who lived their lives by the blade. They reached a
wide bridge across a turn in the River Ouse and met half a dozen
horsemen blocking the road. Their axes, spears, long hair and
beards gave them away as Vikings. Their leader came forward, a
broad-shouldered man with six warriors behind him.

'I heard you were looking for men,' said the man in a gruff
voice. His beard was long and plaited through with pendants. He
wore a shining byrnie coat of mail and a shield emblazoned with a
raven rested upon his saddle. His face was burned the colour of
stained wood and as cracked and split as a fisherman's net.

'Dolgfinnr Amundrsson,' said Thered in greeting. 'I heard that
you had sailed east to Frankia.'

'I did, but we met ill luck there. Bad bargains with weak men
and good friends killed in a meaningless war. I've sailed the Whale
Road for ten years, and this is all that remains of my crew.' He
waved a hand at the warriors behind him. 'My ship is lost, and I
need silver. I seek battle luck and Odin's favour. So, if there's a fight,
I'd join your war band.'

'Your axe is welcome,' said Thered, smiling in his scarred face.
'As are you, Bodil and Anarr.' Two of the six nodded a sullen
greeting to Thered as he mentioned their names.

So, with fifty warriors, Beornoth rode south for revenge. The
company at his back was not to his liking. Hrodgar had soured
further, and he and Brand sniped and cursed at each other every
day. Reifnir and his men maintained a baleful distance from the
rest, whilst Thered, Vigdjarf and Dolgfinnr's men drank ale each
night, laughed, wrestled and snored like they were travelling
towards a yuletide feast. Brand joined in with them, enjoying the
company of like-minded Vikings. They followed the old ways; they
worshipped Odin, Thor, Týr, Njorth and Frey and so rode gleefully
towards what they hoped was a glorious battle worthy of honour

and a song, and which might open the doors of Valhalla if they found a glorious death.

They travelled from York along Earninga Straet, the old Roman road which cut through England from York to Lincoln and then on to its final destination at Lundenwic. The straight, well-built herepath, or road fit for an army, sped their journey. They pushed hard each day, rising early and only stopping to rest horses and either find lodgings at way-taverns or make camp at night. Their large band set tongues wagging, and inquisitive eyes staring, and Beornoth wanted to get to East Anglia before news of their journey could outpace them. For it was to East Anglia where Beornoth led his company, to those who had provided succour and support to the Danish war-king Sweyn Forkbeard, and those who had sworn to fight at Maldon and then broken their oaths. They had left Ealdorman Byrhtnoth to his fate, outnumbered and betrayed. Now Beornoth came for those men, and he would not stop until they were dead.

13

Spring burst into life across East Anglia. Buds burst from the crawling branches of rowan, beech, oak and ash trees. Alder and silver birch leaves added a splash of colour to what had been a bleak, flat landscape in the heart of winter. Instead of waking to water barrels sheeted with ice, and darkness until well after a man wakes from slumber, mornings began with birdsong and cows lowing in the fields. East Anglia took its name from the brave warriors who had crossed the wild northern seas with the Saxons to conquer the fertile, verdant land from the native Britons. The Angles weren't so far removed from the Danes and their curved dragon ships, and Beornoth could almost imagine the men who rode in his war band striding from the seas to bring axe, fire and conquest to Britain's south-east coast. Those raiders had become settlers and rulers, and East Anglia had once been a powerful kingdom in its own right, as mighty as Northumbria and Mercia before it fell under the rule of Wessex.

Beornoth had visited the ealdorman of East Anglia at his home, Ravensbrook, last year, to ask why he had not thrown Sweyn Forkbeard out of Gippeswic and its mint, and so was familiar with the burh and its defences. The company rode hard from their last way station, which was a half-day's ride from Ravensbrook, and came upon the burh as the sun was midway through its daily journey across the heavens. Beornoth called a halt on the edge of a farmer's field. The once frost-hardened soil, which would soon grow thick with crops, was now soft, loose and fertile. The farmers had evenly turned over the rich, deep brown earth into neat furrows, running across the low, flat land. Six men sowed seeds into their deep furrows, and the air was thick with blooming grasses and wildflowers, and the smell of freshly turned soil. The farming churls fled once they saw the riders approach, and Virtus trampled their seeds into the thick clods of earth.

'That's Ravensbrook,' said Beornoth as Thered, Hrodgar, Brand and Vigdjarf came alongside him. The horses snorted, forelegs pawing at the damp earth. Virtus turned in a circle and Beornoth soothed the beast by stroking its powerful neck. A coat of shorn dark grass covered the land around the burh. Sheep wandered around the gentle slopes grazing on the wild grass, and lambs stumbled and jumped playfully after the ewes. Their bleating carried up to the tilled fields, mixed with the sound of a black-smith's hammer from deep inside the burh, and the gentle rumble of voices coming from the village folk about their daily business.

'Looks formidable enough,' said Vigdjarf, stroking his beard thoughtfully. Which it did. A well-kept palisade of stout, spiked timbers ran around a bank above a deep ditch. Its wide gate was open, and people came and went as they pleased, though Beornoth noticed two guards with spears above the gate's fighting platform. That platform ran around the entire palisade, supported on the inside by earth and timber planks. The defenders, when under attack, would amass on that platform and hurl missiles down upon their enemies. To attack a burh, an army must first descend into the ditch, climb its face of slick earth, clamber up the bank under a deathly rain of arrows, spears, rocks and whatever else the defenders could throw down from above to crush skulls and slaughter the attacking force. Once up the bank, the attackers would need to scale the tightly packed, high timber palisade, again under attack from missiles, and clamber over the posts' spiked points as the defenders hacked and slashed at them with spears and axes.

'We can't attack it with fifty men,' said Beornoth.

'How many men do they have inside?' asked Brand.

'Only the ealdorman's hearth troop,' said Thered. 'So maybe twenty warriors, then whatever churls of the fyrd they can arm and add to the defences. So it could be sixty men, maybe a few more. They won't have had time to raise any more than that from the shire thegns. If they knew we were coming, the walls would be heavy with warriors.'

'We can defeat twenty men,' said Vigdjarf, astonished at Thered's resigned tone when talking of fewer numbers. 'These are only Saxon pups, no match for us.'

'What did he say?' asked Hrodgar, noting the scornful look Vigdjarf cast in his direction. 'Speak the tongue of our country. You were born and raised here, just like me. So, speak Saxon.'

Beornoth sighed in frustration. 'From now on, if Hrodgar or Wuffa are present, we speak the Saxon tongue,' he said, and Vigdjarf smiled mockingly at Hrodgar, but the king's thegn ignored him and continued to watch the burh.

'There are gate guards there, but the gate to the burh is open,' said Thered, ignoring the bickering. 'They could put all the people in the burh on the walls and close the gate. Hundreds of hands to throw rocks, stones and buckets of shit at us as we try to scale the palisade. We would never get across.'

'King Alfred was a clever bastard. He learned his lessons well,' said Vigdjarf. Which was true. Alfred had almost lost his kingdom to the Great Heathen Army. They had beaten him back from his capital at Winchester, and Alfred had fled deep into the maze of waterways and islet fens in Athelney. From that bleak position, and with only a handful of loyal retainers, he had marshalled the armies of Britain. Once Alfred had broken out from his watery stronghold, he won his kingdom back and ordered defensive burhs built at strategic locations and to his exact specifications. They sat across the borders of Wessex, into Essex and East Anglia and along any rivers where Vikings might attack. The burhs were a defensive haven for people to flee to in times of attack or Viking raids. Churls from the hundreds around the burh could run to safety inside its walls. If the fyrd was called out, every five hides, or farms, in the vicinity were expected to provide one man to defend the burh's walls.

'You and I should ride in alone,' said Hrodgar, his face like thunder. 'These men live in England, and so should speak Saxon so that I can understand.'

'They will speak Saxon from here on in. You heard me give that order and it shall be so. They want to attack the burh, and Thered explained why it cannot be done. Why just you and I?' asked Beornoth.

'We are king's thegns, and they cannot refuse us entry.'

'They will remember me and know that I have come because they broke their oaths. Last time I was here, the place was riddled with priests like fleas on an addled mutt. So, they will probably close the gate once they recognise me.'

'So put up your hood, and I will announce myself. Once we are inside, we can do as we please.'

'I will kill the ealdorman and his son. I want you to know that before we go in. The king might not be pleased about that.'

'The king wants traitors to feel his wrath, and we are the instruments of that justice. So, we do what we must. I believe in doing things subtly, with less slaughter that you might have planned, but the same outcome.'

'Let's hear it then,' said Beornoth with a raised eyebrow. Hrodgar's plan would be much different to Beornoth's. Beornoth's plan was to say they came in peace to talk with the ealdorman. Then ride through the gate, kill the warriors and the ealdorman, and then leave. It was a simple plan, and Beornoth wanted the fight. He had yearned for it through a long winter. In the months he had spent sweating and moaning in pain from his wounds after Maldon, he had dreamed of vengeance. When he had clung to life on the back of Brand's horse as he dragged him from the battle-field, revenge had kept Beornoth alive. Now it was time to bring down that fury upon those who had sown the seeds of slaughter at Maldon.

'The gate guards will demand to know who we are before we enter the burh,' Hrodgar said, 'or they will close it once they notice fifty armed men approaching. I will announce that I am a king's thegn, come from King Æthelred to talk with the ealdorman, and that this is my hearth troop who require food and shelter. The ealdorman will greet me and will ask me to join him for a meal, as is his duty under the laws of hospitality. You keep yourself hidden, and your face beneath your hood. We feast and make merry, and then afterwards I kill the ealdorman and his traitor son Wictred in their beds. Then, we ride out with only two men dead and no bloody fight to get in or out.' Hrodgar nodded to himself, satisfied with his deep cunning.

'It's a fine plan,' said Beornoth.

'You don't sound convinced.'

'We are going to do it my way. Remember what I said back in Mameceaster when you first came to me?'

'I recall the conversation, but what exactly is your way?'

'We do as you said. Only once we are through the gate, we kill the ealdorman's warriors and the ealdorman and his son. Then, we burn the burh to the ground. I want them to understand that they betrayed warriors, to see the fear in their eyes when the blades fly and brave men fight. We must meet their cowardice with bravery.' Beornoth took his helmet from the leather thong, which fixed it to Virtus' saddle, and pushed it onto his head. The liner smelled of sweat, and the edges of Beornoth's vision blurred. The cheekpieces closed around his face and Beornoth felt darker, stronger, almost like a demon from hell. Wearing the helmet made it harder to fight, because it blocked his full range of vision, but he knew it made him look terrifying and it protected his skull from blows. Beornoth was a huge man, only Byrhtnoth had matched him for height and breadth of shoulder. The helmet shadowed his eyes so that to his enemies he would appear as a metal-clad giant, baleful and fearsome.

'We shall all be killed...' said Hrodgar, but he didn't have to finish because Beornoth clicked his tongue, and nudged Virtus' flanks with his heels. The company followed behind him, and Beornoth called his plan out to Brand, Thered and Vigdjarf on the way towards the gate.

Fifty horses cantered along the road towards Ravensbrook, and the smattering of people fled from their path. Some bowed their heads in respect at the column of armed warriors, and others cursed as carts and wains floundered from the hard-packed earthen road into the soft fields beyond.

'Who goes there?' shouted a guard in a broad East Anglian accent. He peered down from the platform above the open gate and Beornoth ignored him. Beornoth had expected the guards to close the gate once they saw the band riders approaching, but they had not. Fifty armed men should have raised concerns with the guards and Beornoth could only assume that the East Anglians felt no threat. There were no enemies in their shire. Forkbeard had

taken to the Whale Road and left Gippeswic to its former Saxon
lord. Olaf Tryggvason was far to the south and the East Anglians
would have heard of Olaf's approach if ships sailed north, or an
army marched through their shire. So, they believed the armed
column were visitors, an ealdorman or thegn on the march looking
for shelter. What they didn't expect was Beornoth.

Beornoth rode in through the open gate. He didn't halt, nor
identify himself to the guards. He simply rode Virtus beneath its
high lintel and emerged into the burh's courtyard. It was a wide
square, surrounded by wattle buildings topped with grey thatch.
Beyond the gaggle of thatched roofs, the ealdorman's hall reached
high above the other buildings, and next to it, a church with a high
cross on its gable glowered down at the burh's buildings with age-
blackened timber walls.

'You can't just...' shouted the gate guard. The guard next to him
was already clambering down from the platform to warn that the
hearth-troop riders had entered the burh.

'Kill them both,' Beornoth said, and Virtus wheeled as
Beornoth hauled on the reins. Fifty horses filled the courtyard,
their hooves throwing up clods of earth, their snorting and
stomping like thunder rolling in from a wild sea storm. Vigdjarf's
daughters smiled wolfishly and nocked a white goose-feathered
arrow to each of their bows. The bowstrings thrummed, and the
guard climbing down shrieked and tumbled from the ladder with
an arrow in his back, and the guard atop the gate slumped onto his
knees, staring in confusion at the feathered shaft buried into his
stomach.

Two warriors came running from further along the palisade
armed with spears and shouting the alarm. Thered leapt from his
horse and drew his sword, his face twisted in a rictus of hate.

'For Byrhtnoth, and the heroes of Maldon!' Thered shouted,
but it came out more like a frenzied scream, high-pitched, almost

as though some hell-thing had taken possession of the ealdorman of Northumbria. Thered's men clambered down from their horses and Wuffa went with them, racing to keep up with their lord as he charged without fear or hesitation at the two spearmen. Thered attacked them with the brutal efficiency of an expert swordsman, no wild swings or desperate lunges, just controlled powerful strikes with his blade. He moved like a dancer amongst them, his flashing blade cutting and stabbing with ruthless efficiency. The spearmen fell, and Thered hacked at them, screaming and roaring with anger. For a moment, Beornoth thought Thered wept as he struck at the dying warriors. No man could bear the wounds he and Thered had taken at Maldon, wounds of both body and soul, without it leaving a dark stain on their mind.

'People of Ravensbrook. Flee this place,' Beornoth shouted at the wide-eyed faces staring at him from shuttered windows and around walls. 'Go now, for any man left inside this burh shall be killed. I am Beornoth, and I have come to punish traitors and cowards. Run if you want to live, we will not harm you.'

Beornoth climbed down from the saddle and drew his sword from its fleece-lined scabbard. He handed his reins to Tata, who had dismounted to collect the horses whilst each of the warriors jumped to the earth and armed themselves.

'Odin, bring me luck,' Dolgfinnr said. He had both arms stretched wide with his palms facing to the sky. He closed his eyes and whispered a prayer to his Aesir gods. Each of his men followed his lead, touching the iron pendants around their necks, which were shaped into hammers, phalluses, fish or the symbol of whichever Norse god they revered most. Dolgfinnr's men searched for the luck they had lost in Frankia, and Beornoth hoped they would find it inside Ravensbrook's walls: luck and slaughter.

'I don't want the people harmed,' Beornoth called in Norse.

'Any warrior who kills an unarmed Saxon churl will face my blade. We kill the warriors, only. The people can leave.'

A woman came from a doorway with three barefooted children gathered about her skirts. She paused, staring at the warriors in the courtyard, and sobbed.

'You can leave, go, now and you will not be harmed,' Beornoth said, and waved her on. She took a few tentative steps, gaping in horror at Brand, Reifnir and the other Vikings. Once she was sure they would not harm her, the woman ran for the gate, and her children's small white feet whirred like birds' wings. More followed once that first family found safety, and they flowed around Beornoth in a sea of frightened faces, clutching whatever valuables they had to their chests. Women shrieked as they took in the Vikings' fearsome appearance, Brand's tattooed neck, and the long beards and hair of Dolgfinnr, Vigdjarf, and Reifnir's men. Beornoth felt a pang of guilt that he had brought Vikings into Ravensbrook, that Norse axes would soon seek Saxon flesh and blood, but as he closed his fist about the hilt of the king's sword, the soft leather grip and the steel weight of the blade drowned that guilt, for it was nothing compared to the forge-bright flame of his revenge.

Men appeared in the snarl of laneways and streets surrounding the courtyard, one in a hard-baked leather breastplate and armed with a spear, another in a stained jerkin carrying an axe. Then a warrior in a shining byrnie marched down the main street which led from the main square through Ravensbrook's middle towards the ealdorman's hall. That man had his hand on a sword hilt at his waist. His mouth moved as though he called to Beornoth, but his voice was lost beneath the screams of the townspeople and the racket of fifty horses.

Beornoth strode towards the mailed warrior, but the man with the axe stepped into his path. He was thick-chested and shaggy-haired, and he held his axe up in two hands as though to block Beornoth's path. Beornoth lashed out with his boot and kicked the man in the groin. He let out a gasp in surprise and dropped to his knees in wide-eyed pain. Beornoth swung his sword overhand with two hands on the hilt and the blade crunched into the kneeling axeman's skull with a sickening crack. The blade cleaved the man's head in two like it was a piece of rotten wood. Blood and grey filth poured from the ruined head and Beornoth yanked his blade free. He held the sword aloft, his heart racing now that he was finally striking a blow for his slaughtered friends. He realised he was bellowing at the sky, but he didn't care. His company let out a feral howl, and Brand charged past Beornoth to attack the spearman.

More warriors poured into the courtyard, and Reifnir ducked beneath a wild spear lunge to drag his axe blade across the guts of a sandy-haired Saxon warrior. The mailed warrior drew his sword and set his feet. He carried no shield nor helmet, and his long brown hair was cropped close to his head.

'I am come for Leofric and Wictred,' said Beornoth as he entered the space between two buildings.

'How dare you kill my men! Leofric is my father, and Wictred is my brother. You are one of us, a Saxon?' said the warrior, his brows knitted together in confusion.

'No, not one of you. I am a loyal Saxon, oathsworn to Ealdorman Byrhtnoth. I am Beornoth, survivor of the Battle of Maldon. You are the son of a coward and a friend to the Danes.'

Realisation dawned on the man's face, and his mouth set in a grim line. He knew who Beornoth was and must have heard of the events of last summer. He wore a byrnie and carried a sword, so was likely the ealdorman's second or third son, a thegn, or a high-ranking warrior within the ealdorman's household. The warrior shouted his challenge and darted forward, chopping the edge of his blade at Beornoth. Beornoth parried the blow, and the East

Anglian tried to hit him in the face with the pommel of his sword, and then chopped again. He attacked with strong wrists and kept the edge of his blade before him, no wild swings to send him off balance or leave his body open to attack. The man was a warrior, both skilled and strong. Beornoth sprang backwards, and the two men circled one another. Beornoth was taller and wider than the East Anglian, and they eyed each other carefully, swords held before them and poised to strike.

An arrow whipped past Beornoth and slammed into the East Anglian's thigh. He grunted and clutched at the wound. Another missile flew across Beornoth's shoulder and missed the warrior's face by a finger's breadth.

'No,' Beornoth said in a whisper. He wanted to fight the man fairly, to make the warrior understand that he should have used his war skill when it was needed against Olaf Tryggvason and Sweyn Forkbeard. 'Where were you?' Beornoth said, louder this time. 'Why didn't you fight beside us at Maldon?'

The warrior snapped the arrow so that only a thumb of wood stuck from his bloody thigh, and his face twisted in pain.

'I do my lord father's bidding,' he said through gritted teeth.

'When I was last here, your father lay abed, dying. It was the black crows who ruled this place, priests who cowered in the shadows counting Danish coin.'

Beornoth lunged at the East Anglian, but he swayed away from the blow and Beornoth turned on his heel, bringing his blade around, but just as he was about to strike, a figure with flowing golden hair burst past him, keening a high-pitched scream. It was Sefna Vigdjarfsdottir, and she cut at the East Anglian's sword hand with a long knife, and hacked her axe blade into his face with a sound like a chopped log. Blood sprayed bright on the spring morning; Beornoth had unleashed his vicious company upon Ravensbrook. Vikings had killed Saxons, but

Beornoth was bringing vengeance down upon those who had betrayed him. Sefna turned to Beornoth and grinned, blood spattered across her pretty face. She dragged her knife across the dying East Anglian's throat and dipped her forehead into the wound so that she came up sheeted in crimson. She tipped her head back and cried out to Odin, her tongue undulating a terrible war cry. More East Anglian warriors joined the fight in the courtyard, but Beornoth left them to his warriors, and strode towards Ravensbrook's main hall.

'Those women are feral,' said Hrodgar, running to come alongside Beornoth, his sword tip dark with blood.

'Vikings let their women fight, if they so wish. They can be every bit as savage as their fathers and brothers. Let them fight, let them punish the warriors here for the pain they have caused, for the peace enjoyed through their friendship with the Vikings when others suffered,' said Beornoth.

They marched down the main street, and people continued to flee from single-storey houses, with sacks over their shoulders bulging with wool, dark pots or iron spits. They ran, desperate to flee the carnage with whatever they could carry. A group of ten warriors stood guard before the hall, armed with shields and spears. All wore shining helmets and three wore byrnies. The rest went clad in leather, with patches of iron and mail here and there to provide protection over their chests, necks or hanging from the backs of their helmets to protect vulnerable necks.

Ealdorman Leofric's hall was high and wide with bright, fresh thatch, so that it seemed to be topped with gold. An elk's skull hung above the door, antlers huge and sprawling. A well-built man forced his way between the line of warriors and pointed his sword at Beornoth. He wore a chain-mail byrnie and a thick silver chain about his neck. Beornoth recognised him, and Wictred, the son of Ealdorman Leofric, was within reach of his sword.

'How dare you attack the burh of the ealdorman of East Anglia?' said Wictred coldly.

'You shall be excommunicated! This is an assault against God and the king!' howled a high-pitched voice. Beornoth peered over the shoulders of the East Anglian warriors to where a priest in a black robe capered before the hall doors. 'You have brought heathens into a royal burh!'

'You are friends to King Sweyn Forkbeard,' called Hrodgar. 'And enemies of King Æthelred. I am a king's thegn, as is Beornoth. You gave succour to the king of the Danes, and then he brought his warriors to kill the king's men and Ealdorman Byrhtnoth of Essex.' Hrodgar held up a closed fist to show his ring; the dragon set in gold shone and showed the king's seal. Beornoth did the same so that defenders knew they faced the dragon banner of Wessex.

The priest spluttered and made the sign of the cross before disappearing into a crack between the two oak doors.

'We did what we had to do to keep our people safe,' said Wictred.

'You gave me your word that you would send men, that you would fight the invaders and support Essex. You are a betrayer, an oathbreaker, and a coward. Prepare to die,' said Beornoth, and the words gave him strength. He imagined the harsh face of Ealdorman Byrhtnoth, and Aelfwine, Leofsunu and Wulfhere looking down upon him from heaven, urging his sword on to avenge their deaths.

Boots pounded on the ground. Brand and Dolgfinnr filled the street with their bulk and their weapons. Behind them came Dolgfinnr's men, and from a side street came the malevolent presence of Reifnir and Ornir. Their arms and armour were slick with blood and their eyes bright and filled with a thirst for more. Ornir Hauknefr roared his war cry and attacked the East Anglians with an axe in each hand. He hooked one over the edge of an East

Anglian shield and dragged it low and then smacked his other axe into the chest of the exposed warrior. His hunting dog barked and snarled and leapt at another warrior, teeth bared. The dog's vicious teeth sunk into a warrior's arm, and he cried out as a Viking spear pierced his armpit.

'You cannot do this,' said Wictred, shaking his head. 'We are East Anglia...'

'I told you I would come back, and I warned you not to take Forkbeard's coin,' said Beornoth. 'I said that if you did not honour your word to join us last year that I would return and kill you all. So, here I am.'

Beornoth charged, and his Vikings charged with him. They crashed into the East Anglian shields in a fury of axes and swords. Linden wood boards splintered and cracked beneath chopping blades. Men bellowed their war fury and screamed in pain as cold steel hacked into soft flesh. Wictred stumbled backwards through his men and turned to watch as they fought whilst he cowered. The East Anglians brought their shields together, and each man overlapped the left side of his shield with that of the warrior next to him. Their spears rested on the iron-rimmed tops of each shield, and they glowered through conical helmets. But when the blades came with full force, when snarls and stabbing iron ripped at them, those firm jaws turned to surprised and terrified rictuses of fear. These men were the ealdorman's hearth troop, and like warriors up and down the land, they practised each day with their weapons, but there was a difference between a practice drill and the force and savagery of battle. They were warriors who had not fought. Their masters had kept them at bay when they should have been fighting and harrying Sweyn Forkbeard's fleet of Danish invaders. Now, they faced hard men, warriors experienced in battle with scars and knowledge of what it took to face a man with a blade, to fight him so close that you could smell the ale on his breath and hear the last gasp of his life as you ripped it from him forever.

Beornoth kicked a shield savagely so that its upper edge smashed into the face of the man crouched behind it. Eyes appeared over the iron rim, green and full of fear, staring into the horrifying darkness behind Beornoth's helmet. Beornoth growled and grabbed the shield in his left hand. He hauled it towards him, ripping it from the frightened warrior's hands. When the man stumbled forwards, scrambling for the shield's handle, Beornoth stabbed down with the point of his sword, and it drove through the man's leather armour behind his collarbone and punched through his chest. Beornoth pulled it free, and blood surged from the terrible wound to dung the earth. Beornoth stepped over the dying man's twitching body and stalked through the hole in the East Anglian battle line.

Reifnir's men attacked from the flank, howling and stabbing, and the East Anglians crumbled in the face of so savage an onslaught. Brand howled with delight as he killed a warrior with his axe, snarling into the dying man's face. An arrow slapped into the ground at Beornoth's feet, and another thumped into one of Vigdjarf's men, tearing through his throat. One of Dolgfinnr's men fell with an arrow through his eye before Sefna and Hrist fell back from the fighting and loosed arrows of their own at the East Anglian archer on the hall roof. They each loosed three shafts before the man toppled from the rooftop and crashed to the ground like a sack of grain, spilling his quiver of arrows.

Wictred stared at Beornoth, and his face was as white as a fetch. He shook his head and turned to flee into the hall. Beornoth followed. He marched to the heavy doors and pushed them open. He strode inside, helmeted and clad in his heavy chain-mail byrnie. His sword dripped warm blood on the threshold, and it was time for oathbreakers to suffer.

14

The hall was dark inside, lit only by the central hearth fire which sent a column of smoke through the smoke hole in the roof thatch. Wictred stood before that fire, flanked by two warriors wearing byrnies with swords drawn. He heard gasps from the sides of the hall where a gaggle of priests cowered in the shadows. They peered at Beornoth from the smoky gloom, white-faced with beady eyes, wondering why God had sent such a beast to punish them. They clutched the crucifixes and beads around their necks, praying to the Lord and the mother of Christ to help them, to answer their prayers and stop the metal-clad avenger from slaughtering them.

Beornoth's boots crunched on the floor rushes, and he pointed his sword at the priests and smiled as they gasped at its bloody blade. He let the sword fall to his side, so that its tip dragged across the ground, the sound echoing around the high rafters. Candles flickered on holders behind supporting timbers. The two warriors came forward, swords held in two hands. They came between Beornoth and his prey, and he enjoyed the worry on their bearded faces as the hall doors were pushed wider and Beornoth's war-band men entered the hall.

'There must be treasure in here,' Vigdjarf said in Norse, his voice loud in the hall's silence. The priests gasped again at the sound of Viking words, and they sounded like washerwomen scandalised by some piece of gossip.

'Where there are priests, there is silver,' said Brand. 'Let me kill those two turds, lord.' He pointed his axe at the warriors before Wictred.

'No,' said Beornoth, holding up a hand to keep Brand back. 'I'll do them both.'

Beornoth reached to the small of his back and slowly slid his seax free of his sheath. He showed it to the warriors, and then held his sword and seax out wide, challenging them, daring them to attack. They shuffled forwards, proud men; their armour and swords made them wealthy, and they had lived their lives basking in the respect of the simple folk as a warrior elite. Now, they faced a true warrior, a veteran of countless fights and shield walls. Their eyes took in the wealth of his helmet, byrnie, sword and seax, and they knew they faced a warlord.

Beornoth swung his sword before him, to the left and right so that its sharp edge sang through the air and the patterns on its forged blade shone in the fire's glow. As the sword made its arcs, he took two long strides forward and brought the blade down with full force towards the warrior on his right. The man parried the blow with his sword, but Beornoth's strength drove him backwards, and at the same time he flashed his seax at the left warrior's face, and the man jerked his sword up to block the attack. Beornoth went for them both again and weapons clanged, filling the hall with sword song.

After a brief exchange, Beornoth stepped backwards. He feigned heavy breathing and let his shoulders sag. There was pain in his stomach, and his old thigh injury ached, but it was nothing compared to the joy of battle. They both came on, imbued with confidence. They had met his assault, and it hadn't been so bad. He was one, and they were two. They had trained their whole lives for moments such as this.

'For God, and Ealdorman Leofric,' shouted the leftmost warrior, a barrel-chested man with a pudgy face and a snub nose. He had found his courage and surged at Beornoth with the point of his sword. Beornoth swerved the attack, and smiled inside the darkness of his helmet, because they should have attacked him together, as one, and hacked him to pieces with their swords. But only snub nose was brave enough to attack, and he was unprepared for Beornoth's savagery. Beornoth let the sword point pass him and he raked his heavy boot down the warrior's instep and crashed the antler hilt of his seax into the side of the man's head. He stumbled and grunted in pain. Beornoth slashed the edge of the king's sword across the warrior's hamstrings and swung his blade around in a wide arc so that the second warrior had to dart backwards or lose his head.

The snub-nosed warrior grimaced and turned to face Beornoth, but the wounds to his legs had crippled him and as he tried to raise his sword, Beornoth hammered the edge of his sword into the man's wrist. Its blade crunched through bone and severed flesh and muscle. The warrior's sword clattered to the hard-packed earth and a severed hand flopped onto the floor rushes. The warrior fell to his knees, staring in horror at his missing hand, and Beornoth stabbed the wicked point of his seax into the warrior's eye. He twisted the seax and slid it free, turning to face the remaining warrior as the snub-nosed man died behind him.

'Kill him!' roared Wictred, and he pushed the second warrior towards Beornoth. Beornoth batted the man's sword aside and stabbed the seax underhand so that it jabbed into the warrior's hip.

Beornoth kept moving forward and crashed his helmeted forehead into the warrior's face, crushing his nose with a loud crunch. He let go of his seax and held his sword in two hands, stepped back and drove the point hard into the man's guts. The sword smashed through the chain-mail links and punched deep. Beornoth pulled the blade free, and the warrior slumped to the ground. He gasped in short, shallow breaths and clutched at his stomach, trying to hold in the purple-blue coils of his insides.

Wictred held his sword before him, but the blade trembled and Beornoth ran his own sword along the blade, his brawny arm forcing Wictred's sword wide. The ealdorman's son swung a punch at Beornoth, but he simply dipped his head so that Wictred's hand broke against his metal-covered forehead. Wictred cried out in pain and Beornoth let his sword go. Wictred was no fighter, which explained the lack of resistance to Forkbeard's presence in Gippeswic.

'You broke your oath,' Beornoth snarled. 'And my friends died.' He grabbed Wictred's throat with his right hand and squeezed. Wictred tried to peel Beornoth's fingers away from his crunching windpipe, but he did not have the strength. The broken left hand flapped at Beornoth, but merely slapped his muscled shoulder. Beornoth dragged him close and stared deep into Wictred's pitiful soul, waiting for him to die.

'Demon!' a voice screeched from the back of the hall. 'Devil's puppet! Release that man.'

Beornoth moved Wictred's choking red face to one side. A little man in a faded black robe strode towards him, holding forth a jewel-encrusted cross, and his left hand shone with a huge ruby ring. Beornoth remembered the priest from his last visit. He had baulked at Beornoth's request for East Anglia to rise against Fork-beard and had argued that he was in charge of what went on in East Anglia. Beornoth dragged Wictred to the hearth and tossed him into the flames. The ealdorman's son howled in pain as the flaming logs burned him, and he tried to crawl out of the fire, but Beornoth kicked him back in. Beornoth picked up his sword and slashed at Wictred until he fell back into the flames, screaming and burning to death. The stench of his burning flesh filled the hall, and a priest vomited.

'Brand,' said Beornoth, pointing to the priest with the ruby ring. 'That man you can kill.' Despite the betrayal and horror he had witnessed at Maldon, Beornoth could not bring himself to kill the priest. His daughters, he hoped, were in heaven waiting for him. He dreamed of greeting them there when he died, of seeing their little faces again and holding them close. There would be no entry to heaven for a man who killed a priest.

The priest dropped his crucifix and ran to the edge of the hall, but his holy colleagues pushed away, crying out as Brand approached with his blood-soaked axe. Brand laughed and followed the fleeing priest, dodging around feasting tables. Vigdjarf roared with delight and urged his daughters to fetch their bows to add to the sport.

'The warriors inside the burh are all dead,' said Hrodgar. 'Where is the ealdorman?' He made the sign of the cross over his chest and wrinkled his nose at the stench of Wictred's burning corpse.

'Last time I came here, he was in his bed, taking years to die and allowing these silver-hungry priests to run his shire.' Beornoth beckoned for Hrodgar to follow, and he led him through a small door at the rear of the hall. They walked along a narrow corridor until they came to the ealdorman's bedchamber. Beornoth pushed the door open, and inside Ealdorman Leofric lay in a wide bed, swathed in rich furs and with a fire crackling in a wall hearth. A priest knelt beside him, head buried in clasped hands as he whispered a prayer over the ealdorman.

'Run if you want to live,' said Hrodgar.

The priest turned to them and made the sign of the cross. His cheeks were wet with tears, and he shook his head. 'The Vikings are almost gone,' he sobbed. 'You warriors and your dull-headed violence. Forkbeard has gone, he has sailed across the sea and East Anglia is free without bloodshed, and Olaf is about to be baptised. The death of Ealdorman Byrhtnoth and the slaughter at Maldon was all for nothing. All we had to do was to pay them to leave. No God-fearing people had to die.'

Beornoth lunged at the priest, furious at his disrespectful words, but Hrodgar caught him.

'Wait,' Hrodgar said. 'What do you mean Olaf is about to be baptised?'

'It's been arranged; Olaf has become a man of God and will be baptised a week from now in Andeferas, close to Winchester.'

'And he will receive his gafol of silver?'

'Ten thousand pounds of silver,' the priest nodded fervently, 'and in return, he will sail away and never come back.'

'The Vikings will always return,' said Beornoth. 'That ruinous payment your bishops have arranged will bring the kingdom to its knees. It will cripple shires for a generation to raise that sum. Killers and pirates in Sjælland, Jutland and Vik will hear of ten thousand pounds of silver and will flock here like ravens to a battlefield to pick over our impoverished bones. You say that East Anglia was spared bloodshed? I saw with my own eyes Sweyn's man, Ragnar, slaughter your people. He flayed the skins from their bones and used them to cover his men's shields. They enslaved your people and sold them at slave markets in Dublin and Hedeby. You bowed and scraped to Sweyn Forkbeard and took his coin to leave him in peace, whilst he used the king's mint in Gippeswic to press silver coins for himself, and then used that base to launch his attack on Ealdorman Byrhtnoth and his men at Maldon. I was there that day, and I saw many hundreds of men butchered by Forkbeard. So how dare you say Forkbeard left without bloodshed? God sees all. He must see the pain you caused by keeping your warriors behind these walls. God will judge you at the end, and when the souls of the innocents you let die because you would not fight meet you on the path to heaven, what will you say to the fathers and mothers of raped daughters and enslaved sons?'

The priest opened his mouth, but Hrodgar raised a finger to warn him off. The priest scowled at Beornoth and scuttled off out of the doorway, his soft slippers scuffing on the ground.

'He looks dead,' said Hrodgar, peering over the lying ealdorman, whose ancient, pale face was so gaunt that his skin was like the skin on a crock of milk. His lips curled back from a handful of long yellow teeth and his cheekbones stood out like plough blades. Furs were piled over his body and up to his neck, and Hrodgar bent low to see if he could feel the ealdorman's breath on his cheek. 'But he is alive.'

'He hasn't been alive for years,' said Beornoth. 'The old bastard has been trying to die, but the priests keep him alive. They ruled while he shrivelled away to nothing in his bed. His son Wictred was too weak to throw the black crows out of his hall and so they grew rich and powerful. The Church rules East Anglia, and Forkbeard paid them to leave him alone.'

'So, what do we do with the old man? It doesn't seem right to kill him.'

'He's already dead, and so are his sons.' Beornoth turned and stalked from the bedroom. His stomach soured at the sight of the frail ealdorman, and though Beornoth had dreamed of killing Leofric, he could not bring himself to do it. Leofric had no part in the betrayal of Byrhtnoth. He was a drooling corpse-man, incapable of giving orders or understanding why Beornoth had come. Byrhtnoth had told Beornoth that Leofric had once been a great man, a fierce warrior who had fought beside Byrhtnoth at the time of King Edgar's death. It had been the priests and Wictred who were responsible for East Anglia's betrayal. The only crimes Leofric had committed were failing to die and rearing weak sons. Beornoth barged through the door into the hall and found his Vikings using Ravensbrook's priests as playthings. Sefna chased a naked priest around the fire, his white body jerking when she stabbed at his arse with her spear. All the little man wore was his fat ruby ring, and Beornoth was glad to see the belligerent priest suffer. Reifnir and his son dug at the floor with knives searching for buried silver whilst Anarr Holtaskalli, which meant wood skull, held a priest upside down by his ankles, shaking him as though he were a purse that would empty silver coins.

'We're done here,' Beornoth said. 'Take what you will and burn the hall.'

Beornoth walked back to the burh's courtyard. He took his helmet off and ran his fingers through sweat-soaked hair. The East Anglians had paid the price for their oathbreaking, and they left the house of Leofric in ruins. Behind him, the Vikings whooped for joy as flames bit into the hall's thatch, and they skipped along Ravensbrook's streets with armfuls of silver plate, jewelled cruci-fixes and leather bags of silver coin. Beornoth noticed Thered sat against a stone wall. He clutched his bloody sword by the blade, holding the weapon upside down so that it looked like a cross. The ealdorman of Northumbria shook and stared wide-eyed at noth-ing. Beornoth knew that look, had seen it on many warriors after a fierce battle, a haunted stare that spoke of a troubled mind, hard memories that scarred a man's mind. The men he had killed, and seen killed, haunted Beornoth too, coming to him in the dark of night with torn bodies and ripped-out throats.

'Olaf is to be baptised,' said Hrodgar. He came up behind Beornoth and stared back at the burning building. 'The king will be pleased that East Anglia is purged. He will appoint a new ealdorman, a man loyal to him.'

'We should go to that baptism and see if there is any truth that Olaf has forsaken Odin for God. Archbishop Sigeric will be there, and he is surely one of the cowards who wove the threads of Byrhtnoth's death.'

'Andeferas is in the heart of Wessex. The king has a hunting lodge and a church there. We cannot ride fifty warriors into Wessex. The king would prefer that we perform our task without attracting attention.' Hrodgar glanced back at the burning hall and ran a hand down his face. 'Killing men of God does not sit well. Are we condemning our immortal souls?'

Beornoth waved to Tata to fetch his horse. He climbed into the saddle and stared down at Hrodgar. 'We won't bring the entire company to Andeferas. You and I will ride, along with Brand, Tata and one other. The rest can wait for us further north of here. They are rich with what they have plundered here. Let them spend it on ale, food and women somewhere in the old Danelaw. After Andeferas we ride for Godric. Genuine men of God are kind and administer to the people's souls. They help the poor and spread the word of God. The men we strike down wear the vestments of holy men, but they are not good men. They are schemers, cowards, and do not walk in the ways of the Lord.'

Beornoth rode Virtus out of Ravensbrook with a pillar of smoke at his back and a burh full of dead oathbreakers. Beornoth had thought he would feel satisfaction once he brought vengeance down upon those who contributed to the treachery of Maldon, but there was only emptiness. Wictred had fought like a mewling pup, and Leofric burned in his sickbed. Beornoth had recovered Byrhtnoth's body, and it comforted him to know they would lay the ealdorman to rest at Ely amongst holy men who would pray for his

soul. East Anglia was purged, and all that remained were the trai-
tors in Essex.

Beornoth looked west, because before riding to Essex, he must
go to see a Viking warlord convert to the word of the Lord. He
doubted it was true. Any Viking daring and hungry enough to sail
a fleet across the wildly dangerous Whale Road would let a fat
priest wash his head fifty times if it brought him ten thousand
pounds of silver. How the Vikings must laugh at the English king
and black crow priests. Beornoth arched his back and frowned at
the aches in his body. They protested and pulsed at him, pain
jabbing and constant. He was a battered, scarred old warrior, well
past the time when he should be spending his days in front of a fire
with his wife. But if that was to be his destiny, it was not yet time,
for there were still traitors to kill.

15

Beornoth and his company spent a night at a tavern on Earninga Straet, a small grey thatched wattle building on the edges of East Anglia. It had stables for the horses, ale, beef and a tavern keeper who was not unfriendly to Viking travellers. Beornoth paid the swarthy tavern keeper a fistful of silver to close the tavern to other guests to avoid any trouble, and the company drank tankards of frothing ale and celebrated their victory at Ravensbrook. Dolgfinnr and his men laughed and sang sea shanties and the weathered Viking proclaimed that his luck was returned, and that he was already on the way to building a silver horde large enough to buy a new ship.

Beornoth sat by the fire with Hrodgar, Wuffa and Thered. He ate a plate full of roasted beef and drank cool milk. Tata had cleaned their weapons and sat beside them, sipping on a mug of ale and watching the Vikings sing and drink themselves stupid.

'Have you been practising with your shield?' Beornoth asked Tata. The lad looked up through the sheet of hair which covered his hooded eyes and nodded his head. Beornoth had given Tata a shield and told him to practise with it whenever they paused their journey to rest the horses. He would lift the heavy linden wood shield in front of him and hold it steady until his arms and shoulders burned. 'Good, it will strengthen you. I have something for you.'

Beornoth reached beneath the table and handed Tata a seax sheathed in a leather scabbard. Its hilt was white bone, and Tata smiled nervously as he took the gift and turned it over in his hands.

'Thank you, lord,' he said.

'You've earned it. I took it from a fallen warrior at Ravensbrook. Now you carry seax and shield, and if you keep up your weapon practice, you will have the skill of a warrior in no time.'

Hrodgar reached over and ruffled Tata's hair and the lad smiled bashfully. Beornoth used his eating knife to push a slice of beef into his mouth and shook his head as one of Reifnir's men stood on a table and drank a full tankard of ale. The liquid ran into his beard and down his chest. When he had finished, he belched and turned the empty cup upside down upon his head, and the room erupted into raucous cheers.

Thered ate in sullen silence and had not spoken since the fight at Ravensbrook. On the journey, he had ridden amongst his own warriors and did not celebrate the victory.

'East Anglia has paid the price for its betrayal,' said Beornoth. The words were clumsy, but he and Thered shared the bond of Maldon, and Beornoth wanted the ealdorman to know that he understood his pain. Feelings and such things were not spoken of between warriors, and Beornoth struggled to search his thought cage for a way to tell Thered that he too lived in a fog, in a mire of desire for vengeance and sadness for what they had lost, and what they had suffered.

'Aye,' said Thered. He rolled the ale in his tankard and stared at the swirling liquid. 'And yet there is no joy in it.'

'No joy at all,' admitted Beornoth. 'But it had to be done. For those who fell.'

Thered shrugged and nodded. There had been no joy in the burning of Ealdorman Leofric's hall, Wictred's death, or the suffering of the conspiring priests. Beornoth had hoped that he would feel relief as he killed those he blamed for the defeat at Maldon. That a burden would lift from his shoulders, or the pain of his wounds would lessen in some way. But there was nothing. He still missed his slaughtered brothers of the sword.

'I hope they can see us, though,' said Thered. 'I pray they are looking down upon us, and they know what we do in their name.'

Beornoth placed his hand on Thered's arm, and the ealdorman turned to look at him. The scars on his face drew his features downwards so that his eyes, ruined nose and mouth looked perpetually sad. Thered glanced at Beornoth's hand and met his gaze. They exchanged a silent understanding, a knowing that is only possible between men who have balanced together on the edge of death, who have killed and protected each other with weapons and ferocious violence.

Brand stumbled across the tavern and plonked himself down next to Beornoth. His beard was damp from ale and littered with scraps of his meal.

'That daughter of Vigdjarf's is a fine-looking woman,' he said, draping a heavy arm around Beornoth's shoulder. 'Don't you think?'

Beornoth glanced at Sefna, the tall, blonde-haired warrior-maiden. She stood with her sister and the two laughed at the drinker on the tabletop.

'She has pretty eyes and golden hair,' Beornoth allowed, 'but she's as vicious and deadly as a she-wolf. She'd scratch your eyes out in the night or open your belly with a knife the minute you fell into an argument.'

'A fine-looking, brave Viking shield maiden.'

'Why don't you tell her that, then? It's about time you found yourself a wife.'

'A wife?' Brand choked and coughed on a mouthful of ale and banged the table. 'I have not yet finished my adventures. When we have finished your revenge saga, then I will find a wife.'

'You are afraid to talk to her,' Beornoth said, leaning back and grinning at Brand. 'You who have killed mighty warriors and broken shield walls.'

'I'm not scared.' Brand frowned with indignation.

'Go and tell her how beautiful she is, then.'

'All right, I will.' Brand left his tankard on the table and sauntered across the tavern to where Sefna and Hrist stood. He tapped her on the shoulder and whispered something into her ear. Sefna shouted something, which Beornoth couldn't make out amongst the din inside the tavern. She pivoted at the hip and punched Brand in the stomach. He doubled over and stumbled back towards Beornoth. Hrodgar howled with laughter and even Beornoth chuckled. Sefna laughed behind her hand, and she and Hrist sat down, talking and glancing at Brand as he slumped into his seat next to Beornoth.

'That went well,' said Beornoth.

'Piss off,' Brand moaned. 'I'm going to be sick.' He got up and stumbled out of the tavern door, clutching his stomach and nursing his wounded pride.

'Lord Beornoth,' said a booming voice, and Beornoth turned to see Vigdjarf standing before his table on steady legs.

'Vigdjarf,' said Beornoth, inclining his head in respect. 'You and your men fought bravely at Ravensbrook.'

'Thank you, lord. You have filled our purses with silver, and there was reputation in defeating those warriors at the burh. I am thankful to be part of this journey. To show my trust, I would ask you to take one of my daughters with you to see Olaf Tryggvason be washed by the priests. Men will talk of it for generations, a great Viking warlord receiving so much silver and becoming a Christian, and I would have one of my girls witness it. I trust she will come to no harm, for you are a man of honour.'

'Thank you, Vigdjarf.' Beornoth smiled, because he doubted any man could harm Sefna or Hrist even if they wanted to. 'I will bring your daughter Sefna to witness the spectacle, and we shall meet here afterwards in ten days' time.'

Beornoth, Brand, Hrodgar, Tata, Thered and Sefna rode west, keeping to the Roman roads. Wuffa and Thered's ten warriors had grumbled about waiting at the tavern with the Northumbrian Vikings, but Thered left them well provisioned with a leather pouch of hacksilver to spend on the tavern's ale, salted pork and cheese. The travellers skirted south of Lundenwic, and the roads led them to Andeferas in five warm spring days. They rode through the luscious fields and farms of Wessex, close enough to see the tall buildings of the king's capital at Winchester, and Brand marvelled at the richness of the countryside.

'No wonder our people have longed for Wessex for a hundred years,' he said one day as the horses rested by the River Itchen. He grabbed a handful of thick, wet soil and sniffed its richness. 'A man who owns these fields will never go hungry, and will always have surplus to sell. He can keep many warriors, fast horses, and marry beautiful women.'

Wessex was a flat land of rustling water meadows, deep woodlands and curling streams which marked the ancient borders between landowners' holdings. Shallow valleys sheltered villages with bright thatch and fat herds and the spring sun warmed Beornoth's neck. Andeferas lay north-west of Winchester, and travellers thronged the roads approaching the town. Priests and bishops rode on carts or wains, and thegns and noblemen from across the kingdom flocked to Andeferas to see a famous Viking pagan convert to the one true God. Andeferas was famous for being the location of the king's hunting lodge, and it held a beautiful church with a high roof topped with a finely carved cross. The walls of the church were furnished with wood carvings of the crucifixion, and of the tales of saints and apostles. The town nestled in a low valley of the River Anton, and like Winchester, lush farmland surrounded it, separated by thick hedgerows, and pastures busy with grazing sheep and cattle.

Travellers on the road spoke effusively about Olaf's baptism as though it were a triumph, a glorious victory for King Æthelred and the Church over the pagan Vikings. Beornoth spoke little and left the pleasantries to Hrodgar. Such talk angered Beornoth, but he kept his own counsel, for his quarrel was not with the men who came to witness the portentous event. Andeferas was full to bursting with noblemen, priests, bishops and warriors. Leather and sailcloth tents littered the fields around the small town, and the air was thick with the smells of roasting meat and paddocked horses.

On the day of the great event, King Æthelred's warriors lined the road into Andeferas as it wound around the valley, around the small collection of thatched buildings to where the church rose magnificently between leafy alder and oak trees on the banks of the river. Those warriors each carried a shield covered with leather daubed with the grasping dragon of Wessex. Every so often, a glinting spear pointed towards the pale blue sky, and that same dragon fluttered on green banners in a gentle breeze. They had built a platform of freshly cut wood where grass met the river, and people were already thronging the town behind the king's warriors to catch a glimpse of the famous Viking warlord.

'You would think a king was being crowned today,' said Hrodgar, as they took their place close to the riverbank. Beornoth's size was enough to move most people out of their way, and despite the warm spring sun, Beornoth and Brand kept the hoods of their cloaks up to hide their faces. Sefna did not care that she was so obviously a pagan with her hammer amulet and Viking clothes, but there were many such people come from the old Danelaw to see Olaf turn his back on the Aesir, so she was not alone.

'That must be the fortune Olaf will use to make himself king of Norway,' said Brand, and he pointed to a wain covered with sail-cloth. Its contents bulged above its sides, and five of the king's warriors guarded it.

'You think he will go to Norway?' asked Beornoth.

'His father was king until he was murdered. What is the point of all this if Olaf won't try to win back what they stole from him?'

A horn blared, long and loud. The rolling rumble of chatter stopped instantly, and heads turned to peer down the road leading out of Andeferas. A roar went up from beyond the town and around a bend. It rolled down the road and washed over the town like a fearsome fog. Beornoth shivered. He had heard that same thunder before. It was the clipped roar of a Viking army, and sure enough just as the horn sang out again, two columns of Jomsvikings in shining byrnies and brightly painted shields marched down the road, their boots stomping in unison, each foot stamping into the earth at the same time. Their spears all pointed straight, as though they were one mighty serpent slithering along the road. Their helmets glinted beneath the sun, and the professional warriors of Jomsburg stunned the gathered Saxons. Amid the two columns pranced a magnificent white horse, its bright mane glimmered, and its tracings were of bright silver and gold. On that horse sat a man wearing a byrnie polished so brightly that he shone like the north star. It was Olaf Tryggvason, and he wore a thick white bear's-fur cloak draped around his shoulders and a golden-hilted sword at his hip. The sharp planes of his clever face were as hard as rock, chiselled and strong.

'Forgive me for saying it,' said Sefna, touching the amulet at her neck, 'but he looks like Týr or Thor.'

And so he did. Olaf rode into Andeferas like a god of war. He let his horse trot slowly, and stared at the faces in the crowd, letting them drink in his magnificence. The Saxon people marvelled at him, talking in hushed voices, pointing and in awe of the barbarian warlord who had reduced the kingdom to a quivering, fearful state of hiding and terror. Mothers told their children that Olaf would come for them in the night if they did not behave. Men feared he would strike in their shire, and they would be called out to join the fyrd and forced to fight his fearsome warriors. Olaf was a conqueror and a warlord, a man who had risen from a slave pen in the distant and mysterious east to serve the emperor in Miklagard as his *dux bellorum*. Olaf was what common people feared. He was a man of daring and adventure. He did not work the land and was subject to no man. A warrior who had raised an army with the strength and luck of his own hand and had brought a fleet of warships to England to make his legend. He had scoured the south coast, both west and east, and now rode into the heart of the English countryside, into what had once been the heart of coveted Wessex, like a king, to receive a fortune in silver.

Olaf's marching column reached the dais by the river, and Olaf raised his hand in greeting to the king of the Saxons. He bowed his head as a mark of respect, and King Æthelred did the same. The king had long auburn hair and wore a circlet of gold upon his brow. His long, lantern-jawed face was solemn, and he wore a large crucifix over his finely woven green tunic. There were no warriors gathered about the king as the vicious Viking warlord approached, only men of the Church who stood close, little men with soft faces and gentle hands. Most wore the black cloth of the priesthood, and they clucked and chirped around Æthelred like a murder of crows. Others wore the vestments of higher office: greens, whites and reds, heavy cloaks and soft scarves. Olaf's cunning eyes drank in the king's appearance, and though he was too far away to hear what words were exchanged between the two great men, Beornoth swore he saw a smirk play on Olaf's face as he realised Æthelred was thin and slight of build.

'What are they saying?' whispered Brand in Norse. He leant into Beornoth and Sefna so that the surrounding crowd wouldn't hear that he spoke the enemy language.

'We can't hear,' said Sefna, speaking loudly and not caring who heard her Norse words. She spoke both Saxon and Norse, as did most folk in the Danelaw, and Beornoth knew that anyone who challenged her for the way she spoke would meet a swift, and most likely violent, response. 'But it looks like he is going to be baptised.'

'They are going to wash him, and then Olaf can leave with ten thousand pounds of silver?'

Sefna nodded, and Brand laughed at his leader's success. Brand had been part of Olaf's army, had sailed from the distant north in search of wealth and reputation. Olaf had achieved both, and it was not lost on Beornoth that Brand would now lose his share in those spoils because he had saved Beornoth's life. He glanced at Brand, but there was no sign of regret on his broad face. He was a simple man, and an honourable man, and Beornoth would make sure that the Viking would not grow to resent the decision he had made that day at Maldon.

Hrodgar and Tata crossed themselves as Archbishop Sigeric stepped forward with his high, ornately carved staff, and bright green and white robes. He wore a mitre upon his head and a jewelled crucifix strained at the silver chain around his neck. The archbishop made the sign of the cross, and the entire crowd followed his lead before bowing their heads in prayer. Beornoth did not. He had forsaken God after the deaths of his daughters and only rediscovered his faith when Olaf destroyed Branoc's Tree He had prayed and begged that Eawynn's life be spared, and after that day, had returned to his beliefs. But Sigeric was not the instrument of God in England, at least not as far as Beornoth was concerned. He was a snake and a piece of goose shit who had conspired with the pagans, and who had held the king in holy bindings, so that the army of Wessex had not marched to support Essex in the fight against the Norsemen. Sigeric had instead preached in favour of the gafol payment, and Beornoth had no doubt that the slimy, slippery bastard had snaffled some of that vast sum for his own personal coffers.

Olaf dismounted from his pale horse and strode up to the dais. Two huge warriors went with him, Beornoth recognised one from the camp where he had fought for Byrhtnoth's body. More words were exchanged, and then Æthelred and Olaf bowed to each other again. Sigeric spoke a sermon then, and it went on for so long that the crowd began to murmur and talk amongst themselves. Men drifted away to piss or find ale and Æthelred's soldiers had to turn and glower at groups who talked too loudly. Eventually, Olaf slipped off his fur cloak and handed it to one of his warriors. He descended the steps from the dais and let Sigeric lead him into the lapping river water. Sigeric spoke again, hands raised to the heavens, then dipped Olaf's head beneath the brown, rippling waters. Olaf emerged and clasped his hands together in prayer, and the crowd erupted into raucous cheers.

'Though I cannot hear them,' said Thered, 'I do not think there has been any mention of Ealdorman Byrhtnoth and the sacrifice at Maldon.' Thered no longer looked towards the events by the river. He stared up and away, at something unseen and distant in the clouds. His eyes had turned glassy, and his mouth open and slack.

'I wonder how many of Olaf's men died that day on the River

Blackwater,' Beornoth growled. 'How many of his men did we kill as we fought for the lives of our people, for our ealdorman and our king? I wonder if we had fought so hard, or if Olaf had not paid so fiercely in dead warriors, if he would so readily let that little bastard wash him in front of his picked champions.'

Beornoth's stomach turned at the sight of the Saxon crowd cheering to support Olaf, a man who had slaughtered their fellow countrymen.

'Where are you going?' asked Hrodgar, grabbing Beornoth's arm.

'I've had enough of this mummer's farce. It's time to go.'

'We must talk with the king and tell him of what unfolded in East Anglia.'

Beornoth nodded and sighed. He turned away from the river and stared down the road to where more of Olaf's Vikings watched their leader turn away from Odin and Valhalla. A smile split Beornoth's face then, because within the mass of bearded faces he saw a box, and within that box the snarling, spitting face of Ragnar the Heimnar. So, Beornoth settled in to listen to the rest of Sigeric's loathsome preaching and contented himself with the opportunity to kill the thing he had made of Ragnar the Flayer.

16

Stewards brought in wagons filled with bread, and distributed loaves to the crowds who witnessed the miracle of Olaf Tryggvason's baptism. Ale flowed, and the people rejoiced at what they perceived to be a victory of the soul, rather than one won by sword and spear points. It was their reward for prayer and honouring God, men exclaimed as they swilled ale and slapped one another on the back.

'It is the greatest sign of God's power over the heathen gods since Guthrum became King Aethelstan a century ago,' proclaimed one fat priest holding court on the fence of a pigsty. Beornoth pushed his way through the crowd and resisted the urge to push the pious bastard into the pig shit. Guthrum had been part of the Great Heathen Army and had come so close to taking Wessex for himself before he had suffered defeat in the bloody battle of Ethandun. Faced with that defeat, Guthrum had accepted King Alfred's offer to be baptised, changed his name to Aethelstan and became king of East Anglia. That baptism created the Danelaw, and all Vikings brave enough to make the journey, and wealthy enough to crew a ship, knew that the Saxons were soft and gentle and would gladly pay a crew of warriors to leave rather than throw them out by force. So more Vikings had flocked to England, and Beornoth had no doubt that history was about to repeat itself.

Beornoth took small steps through a field behind Andeferas, where hundreds of boots had turned its grass to mud. Beornoth stepped carefully after a man coming in the opposite direction slipped and sprawled on his face in the filth. Ahead was King Æthelred's tent, guarded by two Wessex warriors with bright spears.

'Let me do the talking,' said Hrodgar at Beornoth's elbow. 'The king will be in fine mood after the baptism, and we must be discreet. Our task is not common knowledge, and it must remain that way.'

Beornoth nodded, and as they reached the tent, the two guards crossed their spears to bar entry to the sheets of sailcloth propped up by oak timbers. Laughter crackled inside, and Beornoth winced. There had been no laughter when the Vikings had cut off Ealdorman Byrhtnoth's head, or when they had hacked Wulfhere to death on the causeway as he held back an army of Norsemen single-handedly.

'Hrodgar and Beornoth, king's thegns,' said Hrodgar. He flashed his Wessex ring and Beornoth did the same. The leftmost guard looked at Beornoth, his blue eyes alive with recognition at his name.

'Lord Beornoth,' he said. 'You fought beside Wighelm and Wigstan of Wessex at Maldon?'

'I had that honour. They fought like proud Wessex men and killed many Vikings that day,' said Beornoth. Wighelm and Wigstan were twin captains of the hundred warriors King Æthelred had sent to aid the fight against Olaf. It had been a token force, and though the twins had indeed fought like bears, another five hundred men would have won the battle and the Saxons could have thrown Olaf and Sweyn back into the sea forever.

'I served with the twins and mourn their deaths. Men talk of the Battle of Maldon across the country, already you, Ealdorman Byrhtnoth and the rest are legends. I will let the king know you are here.' The guard ducked his head inside the tent, and the laughter stopped. Archbishop Sigeric came striding from the open flap and shot Beornoth a sly smirk. Beornoth held his rage and fought to keep his face straight.

'You may enter,' said the returning guard. Beornoth waited for Hrodgar to go in first and then followed him. The tent was large enough to hold ten men. Chairs and a table were arranged at one end, and a brazier burned at the centre beside which King Æthelred stood alone, waiting for his thegns.

'Lord Beornoth,' Æthelred said gravely. He took a step towards Beornoth with an outstretched hand and then checked himself. 'I was deeply saddened by the defeat at Maldon, and by my friend Ealdorman Byrhtnoth's death. You all fought so bravely that day, and it was only by your stoic sacrifice we find ourselves able to make peace with the Vikings.'

'Thank you, lord,' said Beornoth. He wanted to say more, to ask why the king let the bishops rule him, why he had not sent more men to the battle. But he held his tongue. He was just a simple warrior, and his words would be wasted on the king. Beornoth knew his place and what he was, but even being in the king's presence angered him. The king was callow and thin, his eyes wet and his skin soft.

'Olaf will take his fleet and sail to Norway within the week,' said the king brightly. 'He will be our ally and has agreed to come to our aid if other Vikings attack our lands again. Olaf will try his hand at becoming king there, as his father was before him.'

'That is good news, lord king,' said Hrodgar. Olaf Tryggvason was a warrior, hard and ruthless, and Beornoth had no doubt that the young warlord would meet his destiny and become the king of Norway. Sweyn Forkbeard had been the same, and Beornoth clenched his teeth as he remembered the Danish war-king emerging from the river snarling and wide-eyed with his blood-soaked axe, bringing death and doom to the East Saxons. He wondered how Æthelred would fare in a fight against fellow kings, if he, Olaf and Sweyn faced off with swords, shields and axes. Beornoth glanced at the king's arms. They were puny, barely as thick around as an old woman's.

'I have commissioned a bard to write the tale of the battle. He will make a mighty song of Byrhtnoth's noble sacrifice, and all men shall know how my *dux bellorum* and his men suffered so that we might have peace.'

'Let us hope the news of the mighty gafol we have paid to Olaf does not wing its way north across the sea,' said Beornoth, unable to hold his tongue any longer. 'Perhaps God will send us protection now that Archbishop Sigeric has wrung every silver coin from your shires to pay off the Vikings. Maybe Holy Mary will stifle the rumours across the fjords and forts of Norway, and the talk amongst the hard men of Jutland and the Vik. Let us pray that Lord Jesus Christ holds back the fleets of dragon ships moored in Frankia, Dublin and the Braethraborg. All places where glory-hungry Vikings linger like wolves, waiting for word of coastlines where they can sail their ships and use their axes to make themselves rich. Let us pray that the archbishops and priests across the land can soothe the already bitter nobles in the Danelaw who are crippled by the taxes and tithes they must pay to the crown and the Church, by the swathes of land they must cede to the abbeys and monasteries whenever a man inherits. Perhaps this new gafol tax will sway the minds of those in the Danelaw who welcomed Forkbeard and his Christian Vikings at

Gippeswic, and they will now become loyal supporters of the throne.'

'Lord king,' said Hrodgar through tight lips. Æthelred's face dropped at Beornoth's harsh words. He seemed surprised to hear his thegn utter anything but praise for his policy of paying off the Vikings. Which, Beornoth assumed, was the problem all along. No strong men to tell the king the truth, nobody brave enough to stand up to the archbishop and explain to the king the potential repercussions of his deal with Olaf. Hrodgar looked around the tent to make sure they were truly alone with the king and stepped forward so that he could lower his voice. 'Word may not have reached you yet, but we return to you from East Anglia, where Ealdorman Leofric and his sons have met a most unfortunate end.'

Æthelred clasped his hands behind his back and nodded gravely. 'Word had not reached me, and whilst I am saddened by the news, let us hope their deaths can usher in a change in that shire. I will look to appoint a new ealdorman now that Leofric's house has no heir.'

'We also managed to successfully retrieve Ealdorman Byrhtnoth's body from the Vikings, lord king. He will now be buried with honour and under the eyes of God at the abbey of Ely, to which Byrhtnoth was ever a generous and pious patron.'

'I will go to Ely once this is over and pay my respects to the ealdorman. You have done well, my king's thegns. I am pleased with your work.'

'Now we must return to Essex, for that is where the most egregious traitors are. The men who fled the battle and left Beornoth here and his warriors to die.'

'Just so, be discreet though, Hrodgar. Once those foul men in Essex are punished, this is over, and we will not hear of it again.'

'There is the other traitor we spoke of, lord king,' Hrodgar said carefully. He paused, waiting for the king to respond and save him from uttering so dangerous a name where sharp ears outside the tent might overhear.

'Let it be done here, tonight. Although it does not sit well.' Æthelred raised his hand and pressed a long finger to his lips. 'But he grows too powerful, and his influence may have led to... regrettable decisions.'

'Yes, lord king.'

'Those traitors in Essex look to steal Ealdorman Byrhtnoth's land, my king,' said Beornoth He felt the heat of Hrodgar's angered stare but kept his own eyes on the king. 'They will come to you, lord, to say that Ealdorman Byrhtnoth has left no heirs to inherit the shire. But his daughter Leoflaed and her husband Oswig are capable of taking his mantle. Oswig is a thegn and from a good family and can become ealdorman. Will you support their claim, lord, if Godric comes to you before I can get to him?'

'I give you my word as king, Lord Beornoth, that I will support Byrhtnoth's widow's wishes in this matter. Oswig shall be ealdorman of Essex.'

'Thank you, lord king.'

Beornoth and Hrodgar bowed low to the king, and he handed them each a leather pouch of silver to aid their quest. They marched from the tent, and across the muddy field towards where the gifted ale and bread had turned Andeferas into a boisterous town full of laughter and song.

'I must see to my business,' said Hrodgar, stopping where the field ended and the town began. He wiped a hand down his face and shook his head. 'The other traitor I spoke of with the king is Archbishop Sigeric. It doesn't sit well, killing a man of the cloth. I hope Christ sees the justice in my deeds, and some right in it. Sigeric will be drunk and in his bed before long, and he will never wake from that slumber.'

'Sigeric? So, the king has finally woken up to the archbishop's ill advice?'

'Aye, but too late for it to do any good I fear.'

Beornoth nodded. 'I will meet you outside the town, where the oak tree marks a fork in the road. Brand and the others will also be there, and we will ride for Essex.'

Hrodgar strode into the heaving mass of revellers and Beornoth did not pity him the task of taking the archbishop's life. He had the king's blessing, which was one thing, but Hrodgar was a pious man and Beornoth knew that killing a man of God would haunt Hrodgar for the rest of his days. He did not pity the archbishop; the man's poor advice had cost many good men their lives and emboldened the Vikings. Beornoth had business of his own to attend to, and he met Brand, Sefna and Thered by their horses.

'Olaf's men are camped to the west,' said Brand, 'away from the town and the drunken Saxons.'

'Wise to keep the two peoples apart,' said Sefna. 'Mixing drunken Vikings and Saxons together is not a good idea. Olaf's men have barrels of ale of their own and are currently feasting and discussing how to divide their silver.'

'I'm going into Olaf's camp to kill the heimnar,' said Beornoth. 'You three wait for me where the oak tree splits the road. Hrodgar will meet us there. Tata, fetch the horses and wait for us at the tree.'

The lad nodded and scampered off to retrieve their mounts.

'You can't go into Olaf's camp alone,' said Brand. 'Leave the heimnar. The crippled bastard can't do anyone any harm.'

'I made him, and I must end him. Forkbeard left him behind with Olaf's men, and he wanted my head at Maldon. You saw that. He would have presided over the beheading of Wulfhere, Leofsunu and Aelfwine. I can't leave him alive.'

'Then I will come with you,' said Brand.

'And I,' said Sefna.

'I will meet you at the oak,' said Thered. 'I cannot remain in this place any longer. These people celebrate and drink to a victory, but I see no glory. I see only the horror at the Blackwater, and I must get away from their leering faces.'

Beornoth nodded, understanding Thered's anger. The ealdorman of Northumbria stalked away with his head bowed, and Beornoth led Sefna and Brand towards the Viking camp.

'Keep your hoods up,' said Beornoth as they marched along the rutted road away from Andeferas towards where the Viking camp curled along a gentle hill. Leather and sailcloth tents covered the pasture like so many sheep, cook fires lit up the camp like stars in the sky and, just as in Andeferas itself, laughter and the rumble of chatter drifted from the fires like smoke. 'Men might recognise you, Brand, or me, for that matter.'

All three lifted the hoods of their cloaks so that their faces were cast in darkness. The sun had reached the low horizon and cast the sky in an orange hue, and as Beornoth reached the Viking camp, he let his anger with the king, the Church and all of his enemies take over his being. It was always there, bubbling beneath the surface of his consciousness like a cauldron, simmering, waiting to boil over into an all-out fury if he allowed it. He hated the peace between Olaf and Æthelred; there could be no peace between fox and hen.

Beornoth stalked through the Vikings, hundreds of the bearded growlers he had fought against at Maldon and countless times before. Big men with windburned faces, scarred fists and long hair. Ale slopped into their beards, and in every face he saw mockery. They laughed at the Saxon king and at those who had given their lives to defend his country. Beornoth met any eye who looked in his direction with his own belligerent anger. He hated them, and it was not lost on him that he exacted his vengeful quest with the help of the very people he hated. That paradox made Beornoth even angrier, because respect and even admiration complicated that hate. They were daring sailors and warriors, their gods encouraged them to war and battle, and Beornoth often wondered if a man like him would not have fared better had he been born to a Viking father. He fought like they did, thought like they did, and enjoyed being in their company. That line of thought rattled Beornoth's thought cage, and he purposefully did not move aside as a gang of five Vikings walked towards them, coming in the opposite direction. Beornoth walked through the middle of them, slamming his shoulder into the biggest man, who turned and shoved Beornoth in the chest. Beornoth pushed him back, and Thered shoved another. There was snarling and curses exchanged before Beornoth went on his way, allowing his anger and his warrior's pride to bloom.

Blood pounded in Beornoth's ears, his heart quickened, and his rage given its head. He walked towards a gang of warriors standing around a fire, drinking ale and sharing a meal.

'Where can I find the heimnar?' he asked them in Norse, and a bald man with one eye pointed east, towards where the River Anton wound down the low valley towards the town. Beornoth followed the river, past smaller tents and a crowd of Vikings gathered to watch two men wrestle bare chested inside a square of hazel rods. The larger tents stretched away to the west, and Beornoth could make out the Jomsviking banner above the largest of them. They were on the opposite side of the camp, and Beornoth was glad that he had not come face to face with Olaf's professional warriors of Jomsburg, for he doubted he could hold his temper amongst the warriors who had killed his ealdorman.

'Where is the heimnar?' Beornoth barked at a big-bellied man who swayed on the river's edge, pissing into the water.

'The cripple is that way.' He pointed towards where three

warriors stood outside a high but narrow tent further along the river. 'But if you want him to tell your fortune, you are out of luck. The stumpy bastard is done for the night.'

Beornoth kicked the man in the arse so that he went sprawling into the gently flowing river. Brand laughed at the sheer belligerence of it, but Beornoth was all anger and clenched fists. One of the pissing man's friends reared up at Beornoth with stinking breath and mottled skin. Beornoth punched him hard in the guts, and as he doubled over to vomit ale on the grass, Beornoth threw him into the river as well.

'Be calm,' hissed Sefna, 'or the entire camp could turn on us.'

Beornoth quickened his pace, his breathing seething between clenched teeth. That Ragnar had been reduced to telling fortunes for scraps of silver or food was more than he deserved. Ragnar had become a bile-filled thing of hate and pity, grotesque to look at and grating to listen to. Sweyn had probably left the heimnar with Olaf to be rid of his presence, and Ragnar would have wanted to remain, to see Saxons suffer, and to preach his bitter words of hate to men of war. What would Ragnar do back in Denmark? Who would care for him, wash him, feed him? He was a burden, an abomination, and Beornoth remembered well how Ragnar had bellowed at the Viking warriors at Maldon, urging them on to slaughter Byrhtnoth's force.

'Is this the heimnar's tent?' he shouted at the three warriors who guarded the tent. The leftmost man turned to Beornoth. He carried an axe in his belt and wore a thick leather breastplate.

'Piss off, he's not...'

Beornoth was upon the man before he formed the rest of his words. He grabbed the man's breastplate and dragged him close. Beornoth leant back, and then thrust his forehead forwards with all the power in his muscled shoulders. The gristle in the Viking's nose crushed and mangled against Beornoth's skull and Beornoth

butted him again. He gurgled in surprise, and Beornoth threw him
to one side like a sack of grain and into Sefna's path. The second
guard reached out to Beornoth, shouting in anger, but Brand
stabbed him in the groin with his knife.

'Bastards,' Beornoth spat, and he pushed past where Brand
fought with his man and heard Sefna's axe chop into the first
guard. The last guard was a big man with a bushy red beard and
wild eyebrows. His maw snarled at Beornoth, and he already had
his axe free of its belt loop. Beornoth jumped into him before he
used the weapon, and they crashed to the earth. They rolled,
punching and grasping at one another. Beornoth drove his
knuckles into the Viking's throat, and he gagged, but drove his
knee into Beornoth's stomach. The pain was a blade slicing into his
innards and Beornoth roared in agony. He pushed away from the
red-bearded foe and curled into a ball to protect his vulnerable
midriff. Red beard leapt on him, punched Beornoth in the face and
drove his axe toward Beornoth's neck, bright and deadly. Red beard
had slid his hand up the haft so that he held it just below the
bearded blade. He tried to press the edge into Beornoth's throat
and face to cut and slice him open. Beornoth managed to force his
elbow beneath red beard's wrist and the axe blade stopped so close
to his face that he could smell the tang of steel.

Sefna came at the red-bearded warrior with a shriek and
kicked him in the ribs, but the warrior growled and grabbed her
standing leg. She fell to the ground, landing heavily on her back,
winded and gasping for breath. Red beard leaned over his axe,
putting his body weight behind it, and the blade pressed closer. It
was all Beornoth could do to keep it from cutting his throat. Brand
struggled with the second guard, and if Beornoth waited for Sefna
to recover and save him, he could be dead.

'No,' Beornoth spat, refusing to die. He twisted his hip and did
his best to roll before letting red beard fall upon him. The axe

sliced the edge of Beornoth's neck and ear, hot like fire, but red beard's head came low with it as he bent his bulk over the weapon, and Beornoth snapped his teeth and bit the man's nose. He gnashed and ripped at it as though it were a piece of tough pork, and red beard screamed in horror and pain. He tried to wrench himself away, and Beornoth let him. Beornoth rolled over and grabbed the seax at the small of his back. He spat and snarled at red beard and drove the point of his seax into the man's gullet. Red beard thrashed, grasping at the terrible wound in his throat. He coughed dark blood and his heels scraped desperately at the ground until life escaped him and he lay dead.

Beornoth stood and bent double, gasping at the pain in his stomach. A small crowd of Vikings had gathered, unsure of what they saw. Vikings often fought each other, and they could not understand that Beornoth was their enemy. He looked like a Viking in his byrnie and being so large, and there was no mistaking Brand and Sefna. Beornoth ignored them and ducked into the tent. It was dark and an empty box stood on the far side.

'It's you,' said a spiteful voice, and Beornoth looked down. Ragnar lay on a pillow, thin and wasted. Long hair and beard around a skull-like face, his torso without arms and legs that looked grotesquely large and misshapen. He had once been a Viking jarl, a leader of many warriors, and Beornoth had fought him beside a river when Ragnar had been strong and dangerous. 'I've cursed you, Beornoth Reiði. The gods hate you. Worms will crawl in your belly and corpse ripper will gnaw on your face for eternity.'

'You were there, weren't you? When they cut the heads from my ealdorman and my friends?'

'I was there. We took their heads and offered their souls to our gods. Some of them weren't dead, and we made them suffer. I had one man's belly slit open and his guts tied to a post, then we drove him around the post with a blade until he ripped his own insides out. You Saxons are dogs and deserve to suffer. I nearly had you but you ran away.' Ragnar twitched and frothed at the mouth, his eyes bulging and furious. 'Oh, if we could have got hold of you how you would have suffered.'

'You should not have lived,' Beornoth said, and he grabbed a fistful of Ragnar's greasy beard. Beornoth dragged Ragnar out of the tent by his beard, and the cripple screamed and roared, unable to do anything to stop the humiliation. Beornoth didn't break stride and tossed the heimnar into the river, where he bobbed for a moment like a piece of flotsam, his screams gurgling in the cold water. He cried out, and then his head dipped beneath the water, then another stifled cry and then nothing. Beornoth left the heimnar to drown, for he could not save himself without arms or legs.

'Stop him,' said one Norseman as Beornoth barged through the crowd that had gathered to watch the violence. He wanted to stride away from the heimnar's tent and away from Olaf's camp as quickly as possible. The pain in his stomach burned and clawed at him, and it was all Beornoth could do to stop himself from collapsing.

'The crippled bastard wanted putting out of his misery,' called another.

'We've done you a favour, lad,' said Brand, grinning. He clapped one man on the shoulder and winked at another. 'I heard Olaf is about to talk. Maybe we shall find out what share we will have of the Saxon horde.'

The crowd peeled away, shuffling off towards Olaf's tent and leaving Ragnar's pitiful corpse to the riverbed. Beornoth limped, holding one hand to his stomach, blood on his neck and face where red beard had cut him. The wound Beornoth had taken at Maldon clawed at him. It was agony and Beornoth dropped to one knee. Sefna ducked under his arm and helped him to his feet, and they stumbled away from the tent and the dead guards.

'They've killed Gylfi,' shouted a man, and Beornoth heard a blade scrape on the wood lip of its scabbard. 'Stop them.'

A powerful hand grabbed Beornoth's shoulder, but he shrugged it off. Sefna stopped and kicked out at a man who tried to pull at her arm. A dull thud cracked across Beornoth's back, and he would have fallen, but Sefna propped him up. Heat rose in Beornoth's belly, the burning of fear which rises quickly and makes a man's face burn. Beornoth expected a knife in his back or a spear in his gut. He tried to quicken his pace, but the pain from his old wounds was too much. He could hardly put one foot in front of the other and he grunted as a boot connected with the back of his left knee and this time Beornoth fell to his knees. Shouting around him, lost in the fog of his pain, Beornoth felt dizzy and shook his head to clear his blurred vision. A man reared up in front of him, hatchet-faced with piercing eyes.

'Cousin Brand, you piece of stinking seal shit,' said a bright Norse voice, 'is that you?'

'Hrafn Horseface!' called Brand with delight and relief in his voice. 'It is me, you ugly bastard. How are your mother and father?'

A huge Viking with a broad face and a thick neck gently pushed the hatchet-faced man out of the way and clasped Brand's forearm in the warrior's grip.

'They are well. We looked for you after the battle at the river, but could not find you?'

'I had a debt to this turd here,' Brand said brightly, and he helped Beornoth to his feet. 'So, I had to honour that, or the gods would see my shame.'

'Just so,' said Hrafn. He looked at Beornoth and Sefna, and there were questions in his eyes, and a knowing in his pursed lips. He gave an understanding nod. 'What is a man who doesn't honour his debts? On your way, cousin, no one will trouble you here.'

'Thank you, Hrafn.' Brand smiled, and glanced around the increasing crowd of Viking warriors who'd come to see what the disturbance was about.

'Olaf will leave this place soon, and I will return to our island home. We are rich, Brand, and I think I will buy a new farm and a new ship. You should come with us; we sail in a month when summer arrives.'

'I will find you, if I can,' said Brand. Hrafn glanced at Beornoth again, and then clapped Brand on the shoulder. He turned and joined his crew as they made a ring around Brand, Beornoth and Sefna, allowing them to hobble away from Olaf's camp.

They found Hrodgar and Tata waiting at the oak tree with their horses. The one-handed Saxon knelt in prayer by a gnarled, ancient oak tree, a string of beads in his hands as he moved through a set of prayers.

'What news?' Beornoth said, squeezing the words out through his pain.

'Archbishop Sigeric lies dead in his tent. He won't be found until morning,' Hrodgar whispered.

'That was a good deed well done, then,' said Beornoth. But Hrodgar just stared at him. His eyes seemed strangely hollow. Hrodgar offered no further explanation of how he had killed the archbishop, and Beornoth did not ask. Whatever his crimes against the people of England, Sigeric was still a man ordained as God's representative in the world of men. That killing would haunt Hrodgar for the rest of his life, and perhaps beyond. Beornoth wanted to tell Hrodgar that he had struck Sigeric down in the name of those innocent people who had suffered at the hands of the Vikings, whilst Sigeric pushed his desire to pay the Vikings to leave, and no doubt enriched himself in the process. Sigeric was a wicked man, and surely no true representative of God's will. He had hoped to build his fame through Olaf's baptism and cared little or nothing for those who had died under Viking axes. But Beornoth did not offer any of that to Hrodgar, because it wouldn't make any difference. A man must make his own peace for the men he has killed. It is a solitary journey in one's own thought cage, and Beornoth knew the truth of that more than most.

'So on to East Anglia?' said Sefna. 'Back to my father?'

'And so, to East Anglia,' said Beornoth. 'To Godric and his army of cut-throats and bastards.' Sefna and Brand helped him into the saddle, and it was all Beornoth could do to stay upon it. Every step Virtus took shot his body through with agony, and Beornoth wondered how he could fight his way through Godric's hired army in this state. But it must be done, it had to be done, and he would force his body to do it.

17

Beornoth and his small party returned to the borders of East Anglia and Essex with all haste, and they pushed the horses hard. They spoke little, and even though his path of vengeance was almost complete, the journey was solemn and quiet. Thered rode apart from Beornoth, keeping his own men about him, and when they spent evenings camped on the road, or at tavern firesides, conversation from the Saxons was few and far between. Hrodgar and Thered prayed together, following the liturgy of the hours as much as they could on the road. Neither warrior had done so on the ride south, but since Ravensbrook and Andeferas, it had become of the utmost importance. Whilst Beornoth thought himself a godly man in those days, he did not follow the regular requirement for prayer each day. He would say thanks to God before he slept, and ask Christ to keep Eawynn safe, but he was not given to praying all day.

Thered had not been so pious when he was a hostage in Byrhtnoth's hearth troop, or not that Beornoth could recall. Thered had spent the last year riding and fighting beside Beornoth and his men, and Beornoth did not force his men to follow the Christian prayer rituals. However, on the journey east from Andeferas, the sounds of Hrodgar, Thered and his men making their matins prayers before dawn woke Beornoth each morning, just as horses were being saddled and readied to ride; they would thank God for the day in the lauds prayers, and so it went on throughout the day until vespers and compline at the day's end. Brand and Sefna cursed at the Christians each morning and laughed at how often they prayed to their nailed God. But it worried Beornoth. Thered was a different man. Maldon had changed him, shaken the war fury out of him and replaced it with a detached hollowness like a rotten tree.

Killing a bishop had left Hrodgar scarred, and though Beornoth did not ask him about it, he knew the king's thegn worried for his immortal soul. Was it a sin to kill a churchman who was himself a sinner? Beornoth had neither the inclination nor the depth of understanding of God's will to talk to Hrodgar about it, but he doubted Christ looked with favour upon men who saw simple folk slaughtered by pagans for their own benefit. There were good men in the Church, godly men who helped the poor and provided comfort for the souls of those troubled by loss or sick with disease. Sigeric had not been such a man. He was a greedy, self-serving coward, and the kingdom was a better place without him.

As they rode through the lush meadows and along the babbling streams of Wessex and into the lands of the East Saxons, birdsong accompanied their hoofbeats and the scent of blooming wildflowers made Beornoth sneeze and his eyes stream. Amongst the depths of the grim task the company had undertaken, the killing quest of vengeance that had already seen traitors dead in East Anglia, Essex and Wessex, there was a sliver of joy, because Brand had fallen in love. He and Sefna rode beside each other all day and camped beside each other each night whenever they slept in the open. They talked in Norse, giggled and teased each other, whilst Vigdjarf tolerated their blossoming relationship through frowns, growls and warnings whenever he felt Brand and Sefna drew too close. They went off to forage for food together and would return with Sefna's long hair dishevelled and a grin stuck to Brand's face as though he were drunk. Further east they rode through Wessex, past gently undulating farmland with rolling fields of green-tinged wheat, and emerald pastures where cattle and sheep grazed, lazy and content under a warm, late spring sun.

They found the rest of the company where they had left them, at the crossroads tavern, and the tavern keeper was relieved when Beornoth announced they were leaving and filled his hand with silver. He mumbled that his tavern had been ruined by the nightly drinking bouts, and tables broken by raucous wrestling and drunken brawls. The battlefield traitors were the last foe to be punished, and then it would be over.

'Kill Godric and those who led the retreat, kill those few thegns and we avenge Byrhtnoth,' Beornoth said to Thered on the road.

'Then I shall return to Northumbria,' said the young ealdorman, 'and this will all be over.' He smiled wanly, the scars on his face twisting and crawling so that the smile was more like a grimace.

'You have earned some peace. So, when this is over and you are home in Northumbria, you should marry, have children, find happiness.'

'Just so.' Thered looked at the sky and took a large breath of fresh air. 'My fighting days are over.' That prospect pushed and prodded at Beornoth, it planted a seed within his thought cage which had grown before but had always died in the storm of duty and necessity. He had often longed of a life of peace with Eawynn, and began to wonder again if it were a thing he could ever enjoy, if the violent world would ever allow him any peace.

They pushed south towards the vast holdings Godric had inherited from his wealthy father. The estate was called Hareswood, and its hall and burh sat deep in a land surrounded by old forests. They reached that woodland after three days riding, which would have been two but for the driving spring rain which came in showers, and the company huddled inside farmers' barns to keep out of the wet. When the iron-grey clouds cleared, Beornoth led the company into a valley of towering trees with thick canopies of sea green and earth brown. Branches reached upwards, grasping towards the sunlight as oak and beech trees held hidden birds' nests and perches. The agony in Beornoth's stomach lessened with each day following the fight at Andeferas. At first, he had thought his insides would burst from the scar tissue, but it had settled into a lingering press of discomfort, rather than constant, searing pain.

Rather than skirt around the woodland, Beornoth led them through the dense forest in a direct line towards Hareswood. The woods creaked and swayed in the breeze, and the gentle trill of robins, the chirp of sparrows, and the haunting calls of wood pigeons made for pleasant riding. Beornoth called the halt at a clearing cut through by a shallow brook and ringed with dark rock and thick roots. A rabbit hopped through a patch of wild grass bluebells and Tata went off hunting for their supper. Brand swore he saw a deer dart between the leafy boughs, and Vigdjarf reluctantly agreed that Sefna could take her bow and join him to see if they could bring it down.

'I have turned a blind eye to their courtship thus far. But if that bastard touches my daughter, I'll feed his corpse to the ravens,' Vigdjarf said, scowling after them.

'Brand is a good man and a fine warrior,' said Beornoth. 'Sefna could do worse.'

'I know it, but I don't have to like it.' Vigdjarf kicked at a rotting branch in the undergrowth and Hrist laughed. She linked her arm under her father's and took him off to look for firewood.

Ornir Hauknefr followed his dog, sniffing beyond the clearing, and Reifnir sat on a log and ran a whetstone along the edge of his axe. Dolgfinnr and his men prepared a fire in anticipation of whatever meat the hunters would bring back for the pot.

'Tell us of this Godric, then,' said Dolgfinnr who, Beornoth noted, wore a new green cloak of the finest wool purchased from one of the many traders who had passed through the tavern whilst he had waited there for Beornoth. They spoke in Saxon, so as not to further irk Hrodgar, even though the king's thegn was not in earshot. He rested with Thered's hearth troop, sipping at a skin of ale.

'He's the son of Odda, who was a powerful East Saxon nobleman and close friend of Ealdorman Byrhtnoth,' said Beornoth. 'He is probably the second-largest landowner after the ealdorman's family. Odda died, and Godric inherited his vast estates. Godric was a thegn and warrior of Byrhtnoth's hearth troop, but he and his brother fled the field at Maldon and took most of the fyrd with him.'

'So, you fought beside this Godric; is he a brave man?' asked Bodil Balti, which meant the pounder, so named for the war hammer he carried into battle.

'He is a coward and a braggart, and a filthy piece of toad shit and I will rip the life from him to avenge my fallen brothers.'

Dolgfinnr laughed at that. 'So, you are saying that you don't like the man?'

Beornoth frowned at the jest. 'He is a coward, but he has silver and men. We can expect his burh to be stout and well defended, and the lands around it crawling with the masterless men he has hired. Godric and his brother Godwig led the fyrd from the field at Maldon, but they were not alone. There were other Essex thegns amongst them, and those pieces of shit will also rally to Godric once he knows we are coming.'

'Why has he paid these men to fight for him?' asked Anarr Holtaskalli.

'Because he wants to steal Byrhtnoth's land from his widow, stop the ealdorman's daughter from inheriting, and become ealdorman himself.'

'And we are going to kill the bastard?' said Dolgfinnr.

'Yes. He and his men led the rout at the battle, even though he swore an oath in blood to fight for Byrhtnoth until his last breath. Once Godric and the remaining traitors are dead, our quest is over.'

'Will there be silver in Hareswood?' asked Dolgfinnr, and then shrugged in indignation as Reifnir frowned at him. 'What? There must be treasures there if the bastard is as wealthy as Beornoth says.'

'This Godric has his own hearth troop, like all Saxon thegns. So perhaps ten men?' said Reifnir, running a hand across his bald head.

'Seems likely,' said Beornoth.

'Then he has the three hundred cut-throats roaming the shire, stealing land and generally making bastards of themselves. These are the men who attacked you in the barn?'

'They are.' Beornoth had recounted the tale of the night attack in the barn to Reifnir and the rest of the company on the road south from Northumbria.

'We are just over two score strong, and we shall attack a fortress held by three hundred hired fighters and a dozen well-armed warriors, if we include this Godric and his brother.'

'We must get to the place first. Hareswood is just beyond this forest, maybe a half-day's ride from here, if we travel through the forest, and we don't know if Godric's three hundred are close or out in the shire.'

'I like these odds,' said Reifnir. He touched the hammer amulet at his neck and stared upwards, where shafts of light broke through the trees. 'Few will stand against many, and we shall fight with honour. If we fight bravely enough, Odin will see our deeds. Perhaps we can amuse him and catch his eye.'

'You seek the gods' pleasure, Reifnir?' asked Dolgfinnr.

Reifnir stood and stared into each man's eyes. 'Don't we all? I have done things I am not proud of in the name of the blood feud. My enemies killed my sons, the things most dearest to me in all Midgard, and in my wrath I took the lives of innocents. Such deeds would stop a man from joining the einherjar after his death. They would curse him to an eternity as wandering Niflheim. My sons died in battle, and they wait for me in Valhalla. If I can stand and fight with honour, blade against blade, in the clash of arms where heroes fight, I can redeem myself before the All-Father. If I die, let it be amongst the brave men I have slain, and with an axe in my hand.'

'And take your place in Valhalla,' said Anarr, rapping a fist on his leather breastplate.

'I will drink ale from curved horns with my ancestors, and my two dead sons. I will fight all day and feast all night on the benches of Odin's Hall, beneath the roof of shields, and take my place amongst Odin's einherjar.'

'Then let us hope we find the fight you are looking for,' said Anarr, and both he and Reifnir's eyes blazed at the prospect of Valhalla and a glorious death. Beornoth sighed as he listened to the warriors talk of their glorious afterlife. It was so different to heaven, and when Beornoth was a child growing up around Cheshire and the kingdom of York, the Norse gods had appealed to him. The tales of Odin, Thor, Njorth and Týr were so much more attractive to a boy who was obsessed with fighting, riding and hunting. The Norse gods loved and drank and fought like people. Beornoth could imagine them in the crags, brooks, copses and hollows of the land, not like God and Christ who were ethereal and majestic in their heaven of purity and prayer. Beornoth wondered in that moment, as he saw the belief and inspiration in Reifnir and Anarr, if that was the reason that the Vikings had been so successful in their wars against the Christ worshippers of England and Frankia. Their gods encouraged war and savagery; it was the pathway to heaven. The Vikings were like hungry, savage wolves and the Christians were gentle sheep hiding behind a fragile pen of rotting wood as the predators howled in the darkness.

'Just not too glorious,' said Dolgfinnr, shaking his head at how the two warriors stirred each other's hearts. 'And not too outnumbered. I might have lost my harminger, my luck, at sea, but I am not quite ready to join my ancestors.'

The others chuckled, and Beornoth stretched the aches in his stomach and thighs. He pressed his stomach wound gingerly and twisted his body left and right. There was no pain, unless he forced his fingers into the scar, and then there was sharp, severe discomfort. He feared as the fire crackled into life, warm and inviting, that he might fall asleep. So weary were his bones that Beornoth thought he could sleep for a week. It was close now, the end of his search for vengeance, and Beornoth hoped his old body wouldn't let him down now that it was almost over. Hrodgar came striding across the clearing, stepping lightly around a rock dotted with yellow lichen.

'The boy has been gone awhile,' said the one-armed Saxon. He jerked his head in the direction which Tata had gone after the rabbit. 'I'll go and see what keeps him.'

Beornoth rolled his shoulder, another old wound which added

to the stiffness in his legs, stomach and back. He went to the stream to wash his face in the cool water. It was fresh on his skin, and he took another handful and splashed it through his beard. Beornoth wondered what Eawynn was doing in that moment, as a robin hopped along a tree branch across the water. She would be busy with her garden in Cheshire, with the flowers and the bees. Beornoth hoped he would be with her soon, and then perhaps it would be time for him to put down his sword and byrnie, and find a different life, a quiet way for him and Eawynn to see out their remaining years together.

A cry split the woodland like a woodcutter's axe. Ornir's dog raced through the wood, leaping over fallen logs. It stopped and turned, barking into the forest's gloom, and behind it came Ornir himself, running with his axe in his hand and shouting a warning to the warriors around the campfire.

'Arm yourselves!' Beornoth shouted, and he drew the king's sword from its scabbard. A great roar went up from the trees, many voices joined as one to make a sound like the crashing of waves on a storm-ravaged shore. The sound shook the forest. It was a wild, fearsome thing, the cry of bloodthirsty men who came to kill. Desperate men who believed they attacked an unsuspecting and unprepared enemy, they saw a chance to kill men and steal the pouches of silver and coin from their purses, their knives and spears. Wild men without honour, Godric's cut-throats shifting through the trees to murder and enrich themselves.

An arrow thumped into a tree five paces away from Beornoth, and another whipped through the air to his left. Arrows made even the bravest man flinch when he had no shield to protect himself. The lowliest archer could kill the greatest champion with a swift shaft through the throat. Wuffa threw himself to the ground as an arrow flew through the camp.

'Archers,' Beornoth shouted, and dived behind the closest rock to crouch behind its cold stone. Voices from the murky boughs shouted instruction and encouragement to each other, and boots crunched on rotten twigs and fallen branches. An iron arrowhead clinked off the stone, and another plunged into the leaf mulch beside Beornoth's foot. An arrow flew from behind Beornoth, white feathers flying between the trees as Hrist loosed missiles of her own towards the attackers. She keened her war cry, and another arrow sang from her bow, seeking the enemy. A voice cried out in pain from deep in the woods. Hrist had struck back, and Ornir crouched behind a tree close to Beornoth, red-faced and sucking in gulps of air.

'There are fifty men out there at least,' said Ornir, cursing as an arrow thudded into the tree behind him. 'They are all around us. It's an ambush.'

Beornoth shook his head, refusing to allow Godric the traitor and his vagabond army to come between him and his vengeance. He snarled and ran back towards the camp. His boots sloshed into the babbling brook and another missile soared past him to disappear into the distant trees. Thered acted quickly and his ten men unslung shields from their horses and formed a wall behind which the rest of them could shelter. They moved quickly, forming a half-circle, and crouched behind the stout boards as arrows thumped into linden wood instead of flesh. More arrows whipped through the camp, and two of Thered's men lay on the rotting forest floor, one with an arrow in his eye and another gasping in horror at one buried deep in his chest.

'We must charge them,' said Beornoth, finding Thered amongst his milling warriors. 'It's the only way to survive an ambush. We could be surrounded, and they'll cut us to pieces with their bastard arrows.' Thered nodded, and his face was long and pale. He knew as well as Beornoth what must be done, but the

young ealdorman just stared vacantly. Beornoth clapped him on
the shoulder. 'You stay here with your men and the horses.'

'Bastards!' Vigdjarf bellowed into the forest.

'Form a wedge on me; we make the boar's snout and charge
them,' said Beornoth, aches, pain and age swept away in the heart-
pounding desperation. Soon, the enemy would close their circle
around the camp, they would pour arrows into Beornoth's men
and then attack with axes, spears and clubs until they were all
dead. He would never see Eawynn again, and Godric would be free
to pursue his ambition.

'Yes,' said Reifnir, pale eyes gleaming. The Vikings formed up
behind Beornoth, in a spear formation, with Beornoth at the tip.
Thered's men spread out and made a circle of shields around the
horses, and Beornoth turned once and felt saddened as Thered
peered over the shoulders of his warriors. A year ago, Thered
would have stood shoulder to shoulder with Beornoth in the front
line, swinging his sword with bravery and daring. But the once
brave and noble warrior had been reduced to a ghost-faced husk
by the horrors of war.

'Stay on me,' Beornoth barked, and he took a shield from a
Northumbrian and marched forward. An arrow thudded into the
linden wood boards, jolting Beornoth's arm, and Beornoth pushed
his tongue through the tooth he had lost when an arrow had torn
through his cheek in a long-ago battle. He caught the glint of steel
behind a tree to his right, and a man shouted to his left. 'We punch
through their line, and then roll them up,' Beornoth ordered. It
had to be Godric's army of masterless men; not all of them, but
enough to surround and massacre Beornoth's company unless they
acted decisively. If Beornoth's boar's snout could punch through
their surrounding ambush, they could turn and roll up the line,
and the ambush would backfire, and it would be a slaughter in an
East Saxon forest, warriors against a rabble.

Beornoth tripped on a rock beneath the leaf mulch, and Vigd-jarf grabbed his belt to stop him from falling. They huddled together to make the boar's snout compact, and another arrow glanced off the iron rim of Beornoth's shield to twang off into the treetops. Hrist popped up from the centre of their formation and loosed an arrow of her own and an enemy bowman fell out of a high branch to crunch into the forest floor. More men ahead, emerging from the trees; they wore jerkins, wool, fur and leather. Beornoth glimpsed an axe, a cudgel and a long knife in filthy fists. They were not warriors, and they saw an organised force of well-armed, armoured fighters coming towards them.

'Charge them!' roared a voice deep enough to shake the very ground, and five of the enemy charged at Beornoth. He snarled and picked up the pace, meeting the charge with his shield. He didn't pause to strike with his sword, but just burst through them, leaving the Viking blades behind him to carve up the charging cut-throats. Beornoth's size and strength surged him forwards, his shield crashing into one enemy to send him hurtling through the air. A man with a harelip cried out as the iron shield boss slammed him into a tree trunk with a loud crack. They fell away before Beornoth's shield like mice from a cat.

'We are through,' Beornoth said. 'Split up and attack.' He veered to his left, and a stocky man armed with a rusty spear staggered backwards as he drank in Beornoth's fearsome appearance, a huge warrior clad in shining mail and armed with sword and shield. Beornoth was like a thing from a nightmare, a professional warrior, a thegn from the warrior's caste whom the man, and all like him, had been taught to respect and honour from when they were children. A flash of steel from behind a bush, and a short man with a grizzled beard swung at Beornoth with a wood axe. Beornoth parried the blow with his sword and smashed the iron shield rim into the man's face with such force that his neck

snapped like a breaking twig. Bodil Balti roared in anger and his
war hammer smashed into the head of the man with the rusty
spear, and there was blood in the forest. Men who had come to
surround and kill Beornoth found they faced not villagers or
farmers who they could bully and steal from, but organised and
brutal killers.

Beornoth crashed through the undergrowth, moving along the
ambush line, killing with his sword. A man tried to flee from him,
and Beornoth stabbed his sword point into the small of the master-
less man's back, snapping his spine before driving his skull into the
ground with his shield. Reifnir moved amongst the trees across
from Beornoth, cutting with his axe and calling to Odin. The
ambush had failed and Vigdjarf raised his axe and shouted for the
victory, which all in Beornoth's company took up with a single roar
in response.

Suddenly, the forest around Beornoth erupted, and a
monstrous man came at him with an axe in each hand. Beornoth
raised his shield to catch one axe blade and then ducked as
another sang over his head. The attacker towered over Beornoth,
and spittle flew from his toothless mouth. It was Godric's man,
Ansgar the Giant, and he ripped his axe free of Beornoth's shield
with such force that it tore the shield from his grip. Beornoth
slashed his sword at Ansgar, but the bigger man batted it aside
with an axe. He swung again and Beornoth swayed away from the
bright blade, but Ansgar lashed out with his boot and caught
Beornoth in the knee. He was off balance and toppled backwards
into a clutch of ferns, rolling and swinging his sword desperately at
the giant.

'Die, turd of thatan,' Ansgar lisped through his gums. Beornoth
rolled away from an axe strike, down into a shallow ravine and into
a nest of exposed roots. Ansgar grinned and held his two axes high,
showing Beornoth the weapons that would chop and hack his life

to ruin. Ansgar wielded the weapons like they were twigs. He was the biggest man Beornoth had ever seen, untrained and fighting with pure brutal savagery and strength. Just before the giant could strike, Hrodgar burst from the trees and chopped his sword into Ansgar's shoulder and the giant spun away, his blood spattering on dark green leaves as he ran from the fight.

Beornoth scrambled in the roots, their foul dampness cloying and rotten in his nose. By the time he got to his feet, ready to fight, the giant had disappeared with his men, and the clearing was once again a place of silent tranquillity, broken only by the groans of Thered's men who had taken arrow wounds.

'The bastards almost caught us,' said Hrodgar, sheathing his sword so that he could reach out with his good hand and help Beornoth climb out of the ditch.

'We must move out of the forest before they come back,' said Beornoth. The boar's snout had worked, but if the attackers had got closer before their trap was sprung, it could have been a different story. Beornoth and his company would now be corpses rotting in the forest's depths. The giant was formidable, and Beornoth would have died with an axe in his skull if Hrodgar hadn't arrived when he did.

'What's going on?' shouted Brand, running into the clearing with his axe drawn, Sefna at his side with a white-feathered arrow nocked to her bowstring. Dolgfinnr laughed at Brand's red face, and the leaves caught in Sefna's hair, and then laughed harder at the fury on Vigdjarf's face as he came to the same conclusion as why Brand and Sefna had missed the fight. Tata walked sheepishly from the trees, with the shame of someone who had hidden from the fighting. He had a brace of rabbits in his hand, and he looked away from Hrodgar when the king's thegn asked him where he had been.

'We'll have to leave the forest and ride to Hareswood through open ground,' said Beornoth. 'Godric's men are in the woods; they outnumber us, and we can't reach Godric's burh with them in front. We have a half-day's ride left, and they can harry us at every step. Every tree could have a bowman hidden behind it, and every place we rest the horses could be an ambush.'

'So, we go back the way we came?' asked Hrodgar.

'We do, and then ride hard for Godric's burh.'

'We can't take a fortress with so few men?'

'No, but if most of Godric's forces are out in the field searching for us, then maybe we have a chance. Or we can at least scout the burh and search for a way to kill the traitor. He must die, and we must find a way.'

Hrodgar agreed, although Beornoth knew it was no plan at all. They were retreating and had been forced backwards by Ansgar and his men. The ambush had failed, but it had been enough to force Beornoth's company out of the forest and into open ground. Whilst it removed the risk of ambush, travelling across farmland towards Hareswood afforded Godric's fighters the opportunity to track Beornoth's company across the countryside. Taking the route through the forest would have given Beornoth the chance to approach Hareswood unseen, and perhaps to spring a surprise attack on Godric, but that opportunity had died in the forest with two of Thered's men. Godric knew Beornoth was close, and he hoped the traitor was afraid.

18

Twilight came with a hateful rain, a blowing damp harr which swirled and bled in the falling darkness. The wet seeped into every gap in Beornoth's clothing, cold and cloying against his skin. The leather lining of his byrnie became even heavier, pulling at his neck and shoulders and weighing him down. Once the company had left the forest following Ansgar's ambush, Hrodgar and Wuffa had ranged ahead in search of the burh. Wuffa was an East Saxon and knew where to find Hareswood, but the two had scouted for enemy riders or any force which might wait for them over a hill or in a wood. They had found the burh nestled in the bend of a narrow river on a plain of flatland which stretched to the horizon. There were no enemy forces in the field, and after darkness had fallen, Wuffa led them to a farm hidden from the burh by a line of trees which bordered the farm's fields and marked it from the next plot over. Beornoth's company had led their mounts into the barn under cover of beech and elm trees, unseen by Godric's men. The farmer was a squat man with a shiny, swollen goitre on his neck. He had gaped at the warriors when they appeared at his gate, squinting and unable to object to their request for hospitality.

'Are they patrolling the land around the burh?' asked Vigdjarf
as they huddled in the farmhouse, lit by two sputtering rushlights.

'Not that I saw,' said Hrodgar. 'The bulk of Godric's men are
probably still in the forest, waiting in case we come back that way.
They would expect us to come at them from cover, not across open
land.'

'But they know we are coming now. And they forced us to
retreat in the forest,' said Vigdjarf, 'and how do we know they
aren't all packed into that burh like pigs in a sty? Just waiting there
to slaughter us.'

The farmer's wife, a scrawny woman with quick eyes and wrin-
kled lips, brought a spare meal of goat's milk and a loaf of dark
bread. Vigdjarf tore a piece from the loaf and then winced as he
fished pieces of grit from between his teeth. The woman tutted at
him and marched to the back of the room, mumbling under her
breath. There were twenty men packed into the small space that
was the farmer's hovel, the rest were in the barn with the animals.
It was little more than a table with rickety chairs set upon the
hard-packed earthen floor, with a cot on the far side where the
farmer and his wife slept. A fire burned at the rear, where the
farmer's wife cooked something in a cauldron which smelled like
cabbage boiled in piss, and Beornoth passed up a share of the grit-
filled bread.

'We attack anyway, whether Godric's army of bandits is in there
or not,' said Beornoth.

'There could be three hundred men inside the place,' said
Dolgfinnr, speaking slowly and struggling to roll his tongue
around the Saxon words, which they all tried to speak whenever
Hrodgar and Wuffa were present. 'You already told us of the hard-
ships awaiting us if we assault the place. Ditch, bank, palisade,
arrows, rocks, boiling water, axes and spears.'

'We won't attack during the day. We march tonight under cover of darkness and sneak over the walls like shadow walkers from legend. Before they know it, we shall be inside, and our warriors are more than a match for twice their number of thieves and grave robbers.'

'They will have torches and guards on the walls, Beo,' said Hrodgar, pinching the bridge of his nose between the two fingers of his only hand. 'We can't simply march up the walls in the dark and clamber over. There are too many of us. They will see us, and will simply slaughter us from above.'

'We go tonight,' growled Beornoth. The rushlights flickered and Beornoth felt each of their eyes upon him. Some men nodded at his belligerent determination, but others looked away from his wild stare. Beornoth knew some of them thought he was mad, that he allowed hate and rage to cloud his judgement. He recognised that in himself, but Beornoth didn't care. He had never been a cunning man. There were men who could plan and wait in the shadows like a spider spinning a web, setting a trap, and waiting for the right time to strike. Archbishop Sigeric had been such a man before Hrodgar had sent him to hell. Beornoth was more bull than spider, and his only plan was to take his sword, his chain-mail byrnie, his helmet and his seax and go out into the darkness. He would clamber down the ditch and up the bank, he would drag his weapons and his broken-down body over the spiked timber walls, and he would kill any man who got in his way.

'There is another way,' said Hrodgar. He sat upon a three-legged milking stool and stood, holding up the stump of his lost hand for all to see. 'I cannot stand and fight in the shield wall like you men, but I do not shirk from what must be done. The king set me on this path to punish men who allowed his enemies to destroy an army of loyal Saxons, and though I might not be a warrior, I can accomplish this task whilst you men sleep in your beds.'

'What are you saying, Saxon?' asked Vigdjarf, his moustaches turned white with goat's milk.

'That I will go to the burh alone. One man can approach unde-tected, where forty men would raise the alarm before we even reached the ditch. I can find the gaps where their torches do not light, the patches of deep dark, and there I will slip over the palisade like a wraith and be amongst Godric's defenders whilst they peer into the gloom for signs of your bright spears. I can cut the traitor's throat and those of his closest retainers and slip away again. By the time the men inside the burh discover their master's fate, we can be halfway across Essex.'

'What if you fail?' asked Sefna. She stood behind her sister, tugging at Hrist's long hair, platting it into a golden braid.

'Then I will be dead, and you can try Beornoth's plan.'

'So, we lose the chance to attack at night, and a wolf-jointed fool is dead,' said Brand in Norse, and the Vikings chuckled. 'If your attack fails,' he said in the Saxon tongue. His Saxon had improved, but he still spoke slowly and struggled around some words. 'We lost the chance to attack by surprise this night. How, then, can we kill this bastard once his army knows we are here?'

'They already know you are here,' said Hrodgar. 'If they are still in the forest, it is only because they guard its edges against your attack. If I go in there and die, you are in no worse position. So, let me go. If I have not returned by morning, then you can seek another way to kill Godric and his men. But I would counsel against attacking the burh. Wait, bide your time. He cannot feed his grubby little army for long; spring is not yet over, and Godric surely cannot have enough food and ale to supply three hundred men. So, if I die, wait a week or two, and once his men have disbanded, then kill him on the road, or on market day, when he is unprotected and vulnerable.'

'We will not strike thieves in the night,' said Beornoth. 'Or with a knife in the back whilst Godric sells lambs at market.'

'He will still be dead.'

'Men must know that Godric and his brother died by the sword because they are traitors. We are warriors, and this is the life we have chosen. To live or die by the sword. Men who swear oaths and break them because they fear to fight, or have deep cunning and treacherous plans must be punished, and men must know that punishment was swift and brutal. All that separates us from beasts are our oaths and our honour. We must uphold our warrior code. There must be consequences for oathbreakers. So, we will not sneak into Hareswood and kill Godric, we will do it in plain sight where men can see and tell the tale of his death across the kingdom. People must know that we have avenged Ealdorman Byrhtnoth.'

'What say you, Lord Thered?' said Hrodgar, after holding Beornoth's stare. The king's thegn could see plainly enough that there would be no deviating Beornoth from his warpath. 'You were there at Maldon, just like Lord Beornoth. Can you agree I should kill Godric tonight and save us a slaughter?'

Beornoth closed his eyes and sighed. Hrodgar was wrong to ask Thered that question in his current state, but Beornoth did not wish to speak up for Thered now that Hrodgar had formally asked him before the gathered warriors.

'I just...' said Thered. He swallowed and looked at Beornoth, and then down at the farmer's chipped table. 'I just want it all to be over. I will leave tomorrow and return to Northumbria. I have done my share for King Æthelred, I have atoned for my sins and those of my father. My work in the south is done.' He spoke so quietly that those gathered in the farmers' home had to lean in to hear his words.

'You cannot leave,' said Beornoth without thinking.

'I am the ealdorman of Northumbria, and I can do as I please,' said Thered, and for the first time in days, Beornoth saw the old spark return to Thered's eyes. 'Byrhtnoth brought me south after he had defeated my father in the king's name. Byrhtnoth held me as a hostage, and I did everything that was asked of me and more. I have atoned. Did I not fight beside you, Lord Beornoth? Did I not battle as hard as any in Byrhtnoth's hearth troop, even though he laid my father low? I fought at Maldon, in the blood and the screaming. I killed so many men that day that I cannot count their souls. Their faces howl at me in the deep of night. Viking blades hacked my face and body to bloody ruin, and when my sword was lost, I fought with my teeth and nails until they, too, became shattered. I stood ankle deep in blood and innards and I drowned a man in a pool of other men's offal. Godric must die, so let Hrodgar do what he must, but whether or not Godric dies, I ride north with my men.'

Thered set his jaw and did not look away from Beornoth's rueful stare. The paleness fled from his face like a fox before hounds, and the spark of life in his eyes kindled into defiance. Everything Thered said was true. He had fought at Maldon even though he was a hostage in Byrhtnoth's retinue. Thered's father had sided with the king's malevolent mother and was ever an ally of the Danes and Norsemen. He was the ealdorman of Northumbria and descended from Viking stock.

'You are right in what you say, Lord Thered,' said Beornoth. He stood from the table and filled the room with his bulk. The rushlights cast his broad shoulders in a shadow to darken the world. 'No man can deny either your courage, or your right to march your warriors wherever you please. You have more than atoned for your father's deeds, and I remember the day we first met at Loidis when we fought against each other, and how much you have changed since then. I was proud to fight beside you at Maldon and would have died gladly to protect you from Viking blades just as our brothers died fulfilling their oaths.'

Beornoth raised his hand, palm open, and passed it slowly across the room. 'The cut that made this scar was an oath I took in blood. I swore with the blood in my veins that I would fight for Ealdorman Byrhtnoth and my fellow thegns until my last breath. I took that oath with brave men like Leofsunu of Sturmer, Aelfwine of Foxfield and Wulfhere, my oathman who fought like a giant at Maldon. Those men would turn in their graves at this talk of back-stabbing and sneaking. I fight where my enemy can see me, and Godric of Hareswood will die looking into my eyes. He led his band of treacherous thegns from the battlefield and encouraged the simple men of the fyrd to leave with him. He left us to die. I cannot abide him to live any longer whilst brave men died because of his actions. Each day we delay allows him to steal more of Byrhtnoth's land and sully his memory. You bear the same scar as I on your hand, do you not my brother of the sword?' Beornoth held his open palm towards Thered, who stood and raised his in return.

'I do, and I remember swearing the oath as well as you, Beornoth.'

'So let us fulfil it together. Let us honour the brave men who died beside us on that riverbank of horror. Olaf Tryggvason will leave England with ten thousand pounds of silver and make himself king of Norway. Sweyn Forkbeard took his fleet draped in glory and awash with the blood of our friends and ealdorman and his reputation shines like the brightest star. What do we have but the nightmare of defeat, and the memories of our slaughtered friends whose heads adorn the road to Maldon with their eyes and lips torn away by ravens? Are there any here who wish to fight beside me this night?'

'Yes!' roared the Vikings, and Reifnir the Bald banged his fist on the farmers' table.

'What say you, my brother of the sword, shall we fight together once more in honour of the noble dead?' Beornoth held his hand out to Thered, who snatched it in his own powerful fist.

'We shall do this together, my brother,' Thered said. There were tears on his scarred face, and the ealdorman pulled Beornoth into a firm embrace. They clapped each other on the back and a great roar went up inside the farmers' house as warriors felt their hearts stir at Beornoth's words.

'We kill these traitors even if we all must die to do it,' Beornoth said in Thered's ear. 'I will piss on Godric's bloody corpse and send his soul screaming to hell.'

Beornoth felt Thered nod against his body, and so they would march. Hrodgar sat on his chair and shook his head at Beornoth; he couldn't understand the way they thought, why the Vikings and Saxon warriors went to each other in that lice-ridden farmers' hovel clasping forearms and shouting words of bravery into each other's faces. This was the way of the warrior, of men who stood in the shield wall together and trusted the man next to him to defend his left side with his shield, just as he protected the next man. They were all warriors who had taken lives, and to kill a man with a knife in the darkness was not the same as to trade blows on the battlefield where you looked into a man's eyes as you took his life before he could take yours. The warriors who roared and stamped their feet and swore to kill Godric and his men would face sharp blades and snarling faces. Beornoth's war band would risk losing the most valuable thing a man possesses, something that cannot be recovered once lost. They would do all of that to help Beornoth achieve his ruthless quest for vengeance. They would risk their lives.

19

Beornoth led forty warriors across night-blackened flatlands deep inside Essex. They marched slowly, careful to watch where their boots tramped in the wild grasses and furrowed fields. The moon was but a sliver, and so the darkness was as deep and thick as a quagmire. Beornoth wore his helmet with the cheekpieces and boar-shaped nasal, his byrnie, and went swathed in a dark cloak so that his shining mail wouldn't glint in the meagre moonlight. He carried a heavy shield taken from one of Thered's men who had died in the forest ambush. The king's sword was belted at his waist and his seax hung from its sheath at his back. Beside him marched Thered, the haunted battle-sickness now washed from him like mud from a boot. Brand was at Beornoth's left shoulder, moving like a cat across the uneven ground, ever hungry for war and the chance to burnish his reputation bright with his enemies' blood.

The eight remaining men of Thered's hearth troop and Wuffa took up the rear of the column, with Vigdjarf, Reifnir, and Dolgfinnr's men at the centre. Thered's men carried shields, and the Vikings had taken what timber they could find in the farm, such as the cracked and pitted tabletop, broken-up sections of timber wall or fencing, and all would come in useful if they faced a hail of missiles from the burh's high palisade. The farmer's wife had wept and beat her chest as Beornoth's warriors chopped her hovel to pieces to use as makeshift shields, but had then become struck with dumbfounded joy when Beornoth filled her hands with hacksilver. Sefna and Hrist carried their bows and quivers hooked to their belts and full of white feathered arrows. They were a war band of warriors and killers moving through the darkness like hell-spirits, bringing death and destruction to Godric the traitor.

The burh rose from the night-shadowed land like a black slab, all jagged edges and sharp foreboding. Torches or braziers flickered at regular intervals across the walls, their fires like beacons in the darkness, and in that half-light Beornoth could make out three spears resting near the torches where the guards huddled for warmth. An owl cried out from the forest to their left, and the leaves of the great trees sighed in the breeze like the sound of the sea. The rain had stopped, leaving the earth smelling damp and heavy. Night insects clicked and chattered in the wild grass and the warriors' weapons clinked as they tried their best to move silently towards the foe.

Beornoth made for a gap between the torchlight, where the arcs spread from the burning braziers on the walls did not overlap, and where Beornoth hoped he and his small band of fighters could slip over the walls undetected, much as Hrodgar planned to do in his assassination attempt. They skirted around the burh to the west towards the forest, because Beornoth hoped they would assume there was little threat from that side. Ansgar and his men were in the forest, he thought, and so the defenders inside the burh would think it unlikely that an attack could come from that side, or so Beornoth hoped.

A man coughed on the walls, and Beornoth dropped into a

crouch. The warriors behind followed his lead, but their spears banged accidentally on shields and axes, and the noise was like a merchant's cart rocking and bouncing along a rutted road, amplified by the darkness. Beornoth wondered if they should not have ripped up their cloaks and wrapped their weapons in the cloth to quieten them, but it was too late for that now. On the wall, a spear point ambled from the glow of one torch into the darkness, and then emerged ten heartbeats later in the light of the next torch. The warrior whistled a sad tune, slow and melancholy, as he trudged slowly across the fighting platform which ringed the inside of the palisade.

Burhs were usually constructed around the land's natural defences, such as rivers and hills, and sometimes used existing fortifications, especially the grass-covered hill forts of the Britons, the folk who had lived in England before the Saxons came and now lived only in the far west in Wales or Cornwall. As he crouched in the silvery dark, Beornoth thought Hareswood was built on one of those ancient hill forts; the ditch was deeper than a usual burh, and after the rainfall he dreaded clambering up the rain-slick sides of its steep walls.

Beornoth searched the palisade wall, peering into the dark and looking for some weakness between the arcs of torchlight which might make the attack less daunting. Often, burh palisade timbers would rot and push out over time and the bank would collapse, but Hareswood's palisade was reinforced with stone and its staves as high and sharp as bears' teeth.

'What are we waiting for?' hissed Brand. He looked from Beornoth to the fortress.

'Nothing,' said Beornoth. 'Forward.' Beornoth pushed himself into a run and closed the distance between the open field and the ditch, all the while keeping his eyes on the walls for a sign of any guards approaching along its length. He reached the edges of the

ditch and slid down its sides on his arse, and then cursed as his
boots splashed into an ankle-deep pool of rain at its bottom. The
darkness in the ditch was cloying, its earth walls close and the
water at its bottom stinking and putrid. Beornoth grabbed a fistful
of grass from the bank and hauled himself up, but his hand
slipped on the wet and he slid back down to splash into the ditch.
He tried again, and this time found a secure handhold, driving his
boot into the soil to heave himself upwards. Beornoth reached
again with his left hand and found a handful of earth, pressed his
chest against the bank and tried to move upwards, but lost his grip
and slid down the bank back into the ditch. Thick mud coated
Beornoth's byrnie, and his hands and trews caked in slick sods and
soaking wet.

Along the line of warriors, only Brand and Sefna had made it
to the top, and she lay on her belly and reached down with her
bow to pull Hrist up after her. Hrodgar sat back against the ditch.
He raised his missing hand and shook his head at Beornoth. There
was no way that the king's thegn could climb the muddy bank with
only one hand, and even if Sefna or Hrist pulled him up with their
bowstaves, how would Hrodgar climb the palisade?

'Come on, quickly,' Brand whispered from above. He reached
down, holding his axe behind its bearded blade so that Beornoth
could grab the leather-crossed haft. Brand pulled him up, grunting
under the weight of man, mail, weapons and shield. Beornoth
grabbed at the grass and tried to walk up the bank, but it was hard
with the missing tops of two fingers on his left hand. He slipped
half a dozen times before he crawled over the summit and rolled
gasping onto his back. Two of Thered's men hauled Hrodgar up,
one with a spear which Hrodgar held on to with his good hand,
and the other with a fistful of his byrnie. After what seemed like an
age, and with more noise than Beornoth would have liked, the
entire company was at the summit. Beornoth placed his hand on

the rough, gnarled palisade timbers and looked upwards. Each sharpened post was ten feet high, and from below they seemed to reach to the stars, high and impossible to climb.

'Axes and knives,' Beornoth said, and he drew his seax from the small of his back. 'We must go quickly now.' He reached up, ignoring the protests from his stomach scar, and stabbed his seax into the wood. He reached out and took an axe from Ornir, leapt as high as he could and chopped the axe into the post. Beornoth dropped to his feet, crouching with his ear tilted towards the wall. No sound of alarm. Along the line, warriors chopped blades into the wood and the sound in the night's still air was like an army of woodsmen chopping a forest into firewood. Beornoth reached up, grabbed the hilt of his seax and the haft of the axe and pulled. Ornir put his shoulder behind Beornoth's rump and pushed him upwards. Beornoth yanked the seax free and sank it into the wood again higher, and he was almost at the summit when a cough barked from the walls, and a bearded face peered out over the sharpened stakes. The man spat a glob of phlegm into the ditch and stared open-mouthed into Beornoth's eyes.

'We are under attack!' the man roared at the top of his voice. Beornoth reached up and grabbed the guard by the scruff of his tunic and hauled him over the top. He fell, screaming into the ditch, and the sound of that scream might as well have been a church bell ringing on a saint's feast day, because suddenly Hareswood erupted into a storm of shouted orders and sparking torchlight. Beornoth grasped the top of a wall timber and pulled himself upwards. He was halfway over when a roaring guard ran at him across the fighting platform inside the wall. He was bellowing for help, red-faced and fearful, and he cracked the shaft of his spear across Beornoth's skull.

Beornoth fell, and for a moment it was as though he flew like a crow through the night sky, until he crashed into the ditch below

and the air whooshed from his lungs. He scrambled, splashing in
the filth, unable to breathe and his vision blinded by the blow and
the fall. Beornoth's helmet was askew, and he righted it. He rolled
onto his knees and jumped as one of Reifnir's men landed dead
next to him with a spear in his chest.

'Kill the bastards, kill them!' came the order from above, and
then the rain of missiles began. Beornoth surged to his feet, his
boot slid in the filthy water, and he tipped forward just as an arrow
flashed from above to slap into the mud next to his hand. A man
screamed, and a body fell upon Beornoth's back, driving him down
again. He shrugged it off and staggered, unsure of his footing.
Blackness pitted with flashing stars clouded his vision, and next to
him there was a wet thud, followed by the crack of bone as a rock
crushed another warrior in the ditch.

'Shields,' shouted Thered, and his men slid down into the ditch
and made a roof of linden wood with their shields held above
them. Beornoth shuffled through the water, still dazed and trying
to focus. He raised his own shield to join it to the Northumbrians',
and he tried desperately to regain his senses.

'Beornoth, Beornoth,' said Hrodgar. He pushed Beornoth's
shoulder to get his attention. 'We must act quickly, or we will all
die in this ditch.' Beornoth glanced down at Hrodgar, and his face
was drawn, teeth bared in a look of utter desperation. Beornoth
wanted to attack. He wanted the bank to be dry and sure under-
foot and for the palisade to open before him so that he could
burst inside and kill Godric and his men with his mighty sword.
But all he saw was earth, mud, blood, and death. One of
Dolgfinnr's men fell to the ground with two arrows in his face and
his blood trickled down the bank to churn into the rainwater pool.
A huge man appeared over the jagged timber wall, and he had a
rock above his head; it was as big as a wheel of cheese and he
threw it down into the ditch. The rock crushed a Viking skull,

driving one of Vigdjarf's men into the earth to soak the ditch with his brains.

'Hold the shields steady,' Sefna said, staring down at the warrior from the top of the ditch. The warriors clamped their shields together, and she ran across their tops to leap to the other side, and in one swift movement she turned, grabbed an arrow from her quiver and loosed it at the walls. Hrist followed her lead, and the two Vikings released shaft after shaft at the wall's defenders. More torches came to illuminate the wall, and a man threw a burning bale of hay into the ditch to bathe Beornoth's company in firelight. The glare from the burning bale stung Beornoth's eyes, but it also snapped him from the fog and suddenly his thought cage rattled into life.

'Out of the ditch or we are all going to die,' he roared. 'There's no way in. Fall back, fall back.' He hated to retreat, but he also couldn't allow himself to die before Godric the traitor. Beornoth scrambled up the ditch, back towards the fields, turned and hauled Hrodgar up after him. 'Make a shield wall, and retreat behind it.'

Thered appeared, face slick with mud, and two arrows jutted from his shield. They overlapped their shields, and others followed so that they could back away from the fortress, shuffling away from the hail of death from above. Sefna and Hrist moved behind the shield wall, ducking away when an arrow whistled from the rampart, and then rose to loose a deadly shaft of their own at the attackers lit by torchlight. They moved into the darkness, panting and desperate, drawing and loosing arrows at the faces upon the walls.

'They're coming over the walls,' said Hrodgar, pointing to where Godric's men slithered over the palisade like demons crawling from the pit of hell. They dropped into the ditch, men in dark leather armour or woollen tunics, blades shining in the firelight. The gate creaked and grated as they dragged it open on the burh's east side and more men poured out of its mouth, some with torches, all with weapons and every man baying for blood. They smelled a slaughter, a chance to kill men of reputation and take their weapons and silver. Any man who killed Beornoth, Hrodgar, Thered, Brand or any of the men in mail would become instantly wealthy. He could sell that armour, a sword, or helmet and have enough wealth to drink and whore for the rest of his days.

'Odin's balls, but there must be a hundred of the bastards,' said Vigdjarf.

'Stand and fight,' growled Beornoth. 'If we retreat all the way to the farm, they'll pick us off one by one before we can get there.'

'We can't fight that many warriors,' said Hrodgar. 'There's bravery, but this is suicide.'

'We don't have to fight them all. We are warriors, veterans of countless battles. We just have to kill the bastards in the front. Most of them will lurk at the rear, waiting for us to break and run, or until there are so few of us, they can surround us and hack us to pieces. They don't want to trade blows with true warriors.' Beornoth planted his feet and clasped his hand around his sword hilt. The familiar feel of the leather wrappings was soft and comforting, and he dragged it free of the scabbard to hold the blade aloft. 'Stand and fight for your lives,' he called, and the warriors responded with a clipped, guttural roar.

Godric's men came on in a ragged line. They shouted and roared like a band of churls chasing a witch from their village. Beornoth's shield wall was too small to hold them all back, and the attackers did not have shields themselves. Time was against him. If he allowed Godric's men to attack him, they could hang back and wait for more to surge from the burh to swell their ranks, and then, in daylight, Beornoth's war band would be surrounded and peppered with arrows and spears. He had to attack, to kill the bravest amongst them, and so he did.

A broad-shouldered man with wild eyes and a bright spear ran at the head of Godric's men. He looked furious and confident, waving to his fellows with his left hand and his spear held before him in his right. He wore only a simple tunic, no armour, and carried no shield. Beornoth broke from the shield wall and charged him. He took five long strides in his sodden boots and the man's fury turned to panic as he realised a huge warrior in a shining helmet, bright mail, a heavy shield and a bright sword came for him. His spear came up instinctively, and he tried to slow his run, but it was too late. Beornoth drove his sword forward, past the spear so that the point punched into the man's body. Beornoth was running, and his sword pierced deep into the man's chest and punched through his back. Hot blood spattered on Beornoth's hand and face, and he turned, twisting and wrenching the blade free of the dying man. It made a crunching, sucking sound as the sword ripped away and Beornoth spun, and he swung the sword again; this time the edge chopped into the shins of another brave man, and he fell screaming to the mud where Reifnir's axe met his skull.

Beornoth kept moving, smashing his shield into one man's face, gutting another with his sharp sword. The attack slowed, and Godric's men fell back in a baying pack. Brand, Dolgfinnr, Thered and Vigdjarf cut and hacked into the ragged force, Bodil Balti lumbered past Beornoth and his war hammer stove in a man's chest like it was made of rotten firewood. Hrodgar moved like a nimble dancer, jabbing and cutting efficiently with his thegn's sword. A monstrous figure came at Beornoth with an axe, and Beornoth caught the blow on his shield, but the force of it drove him backwards. The toothless face of Ansgar the Giant leered at him across the shield's rim, and Beornoth kicked him in the groin, and then drove his iron shield boss into Ansgar's face. The big man staggered backwards into the mass of Godric's warriors.

'Beornoth must die, kill him,' shrieked a familiar voice, and the sound of it set a fire in Beornoth's belly. It was Godric, and Beornoth searched for the traitor in the gloom but could see no sign of his hated face. 'Kill them all. What are you waiting for?'

'Godric, you treacherous son of a pig-rutting whore,' Beornoth called. 'I've come for you, bastard.'

'And you will die. You were ever a clumsy, belligerent oaf. I will dance on your bones and piss on your grave, and then I will become ealdorman of Essex.' Godric pushed through the front line of his men; he held his sword with hilt wrapped around with gold wire. His brother Godwig stood beside him, long-faced and wild-eyed. There was triumph on Godric's lopsided face, his eyes burning with desire for Beornoth's death. They had clashed often whilst in the service of Ealdorman Byrhtnoth, and that dislike had turned to mutual hatred.

Men pushed through Godric's ragged band, and these new enemies were clad in byrnies and leather and carried shields. It was Godric's hearth troop, and the thegns who had rallied to his banner, men who had shirked battle at Maldon but now came to stand with their lord, warriors come to fight and kill, and they knew their business for they came on slowly, with spears levelled atop their shields in a line of wood and steel.

'Hrodgar,' said Beornoth. 'Go to the farm, find Tata, and get the horses ready. They must be saddled and ready for us to leave.' He could not win this fight, and if he attacked Godric's warriors, he would surely die. So, Beornoth backed away, Godric's words cutting him like the brightest axe blade.

'Fire, fire,' came a shout from deep in Godric's ranks, and sure enough, behind the ruddy faces and shining torches, the palisade had caught fire. Perhaps it was another flaming hay bale, or a spilled brazier, but Godric's burh was aflame. The orange-red monster ate at his walls, spreading and burning his precious fortress, and Beornoth whispered thanks to God and Christ.

'Back, put out the flames,' Godric said, and his men edged backwards. Beornoth pointed his sword towards the mass of men, still unable to pick out his mortal enemy. Sefna strode forward, loosing the last of her arrows at the retreating force. They had survived, but the attack on Hareswood had failed. Men had died, and all they had to show for it was a fire on Godric's palisade. Beornoth slumped to his knees in the mud and watched the silhouettes of Godric's men as they raced to put out the fire before it consumed the entire burh. He glanced around at his company, faces mired with dirt and blood. They had barely escaped with their lives, and some had not, and they were not clear yet. Beornoth stood and trudged back to the farm, and his company followed him under the terrible blanket of defeat and death.

20

'We must leave now,' said Thered, marching beside Beornoth with his shield slung across his back. 'Once they have quelled the fire, and the sun rises, they will send riders after us.'

Beornoth nodded, unable to speak with the shame and failure of their attack balled in his throat. He sheathed his sword and turned to look at what remained of his company. They trudged across the fields in a jagged line, heads bowed, and shoulders weary from the fight. They were beaten, too easily thrown back by Godric's men. It had been a poor plan, hopeful at best. Men had died and Beornoth wondered if it would not have been better to let Hrodgar kill Godric his way. Perhaps the king's thegn had been right. Godric would still be dead, whether it was a knife in the dark or a sword strike on the field of battle.

The shame was suddenly overwhelming, growing like a plant which has remained dormant in the earth, a bulb just waiting for the right time to push its way free of the soil and grow into something bigger and stronger above the surface. The realisation of it was like a slap across Beornoth's face. It was the shame of the defeat at Maldon which had haunted him, which had brought the mangled faces of his dead friends to fill his nights with sleepless visions and half-dreams. Now, he had suffered another defeat, and it shamed him before those he sought to avenge. Beornoth's boots were wet and heavy, clumps of earth stuck to their soles and the leather lining of his byrnie sopped with wet, making it feel like he dragged an ox across his chest and back. Everything weighed down upon him, misery, shame, hate, and longing for Eawynn, so that Beornoth felt so bowed by it that he must crawl back to the miserable farm and flee from his enemy.

Brand, Sefna and Hrist bounded ahead of Beornoth towards the farm, beyond which a sliver of sickly, pallid sunrise had crept across the distant horizon. Hrist pulled up, a hand clutched to her mouth in horror, and Brand grabbed his axe from its belt loop, crouched and ready for trouble.

'What is it?' asked Beornoth, dragging himself towards them.

'Look,' said Hrist, and she pointed to the pigsty, where the farmer's wife lay between two grunting, pink pigs who nudged and probed her with their filthy snouts. Her belly was ripped open, and her guts shone and glistened in the starlight.

'Someone has killed her,' said Thered. 'Spread out, look for signs of the enemy.' His men drew their blades and moved cautiously around the farm's fence, staring into the darkness for any sign of Godric's men who may have come from the forest to cut off their escape.

'Stay here,' Beornoth said to Brand, Hrist and Sefna. 'I'll check the horses.' He marched around the side of the farmhouse towards the small barn, and stepped over the corpse of the farmer, who lay face up in his own farmyard, staring up with his dead eyes at the heavens. Beornoth rounded the barn's front post, and he stopped dead two paces inside. The horses were skittish, scraping at the ground and snorting at the blood-stink of iron in the air. Tata crouched over something, and Beornoth stepped forward, squinting into the darkness to see what had happened.

'What is it, boy?' he asked.

Tata turned, surprised. He leapt away from a dark mass, which at first Beornoth thought was a sack of grain, but as he drew closer realised was in fact Hrodgar. He lay on his back with his throat cut, the wound wide and gaping so that it looked like a huge, grizzly mouth. Dark blood pulsed from it and pooled on the hay-strewn floor.

'I am sorry, lad,' said Beornoth, reaching out his hand to comfort Tata, whom he thought had been crying over Hrodgar's corpse. But Tata was not crying, he was snarling, crouched like a feral animal. His hand whipped at Beornoth, and he held a wicked blade like an animal's claw. It was the bone-handled knife, a gift from Beornoth. The blade missed Beornoth's fingers by a hair's breadth and it would surely have sliced away his digits had he not recoiled so quickly. Tata came at him, slicing and jabbing with his knife. Blood spattered his hands and face, and Beornoth realised it had been Tata who had killed Hrodgar, the farmer and his wife. He had murdered them whilst the fight beneath Hareswood's walls unfolded, and Beornoth just gaped, unable to understand why.

'Turd of Satan,' Tata hissed like a serpent, and he came too close to Beornoth, too drunk on murder to be cautious of what Beornoth was. Beornoth grabbed his wrist and broke it with a crushing twist. His left hand closed about Tata's throat, and he lifted him from his feet, so that his legs kicked and bucked in the air, his angry eyes bulging. Beornoth threw him backwards into a post, and Tata fell to his knees, cradling his broken wrist. He spat at Beornoth, and tried to run, but Beornoth tripped him, and picked Tata up again, this time by the scruff of his neck.

'Why did you do this?' Beornoth said in disbelief.

'I serve Lord Godric of Hareswood,' Tata said, glaring at Beornoth through eyes brimming with hate.

'You are a spy for Godric the traitor?'

'I am the son of Aethelric of Bocking. A thegn, whom you hanged from the gate of his own hall.'

Beornoth let him go and staggered under the grim warp and weft of the boy's words. Aethelric had been the thegn of Bocking in Essex, and he had sided with the Vikings, one of many who had invited them to England's shores in search of a new king, and to break away from the Church's crippling grip upon the land. Men such as Aethelric had been sick of ceding land to abbeys and monasteries, and tired of Æthelred's rule. The king had sent Beornoth to punish Aethelric for siding with the Vikings, and so he had.

'How could you do this? After the kindness we have shown you?' Beornoth asked, glancing again at Hrodgar's corpse.

'After you killed my father, Godric took me in, said he would help me and my mother recover our lands. He helped us. Godric is a good man, kind and generous. He sent me to Winchester, to watch and send him word of what the king's response to Maldon would be. Godric needed ears close to the king, and there are few closer than Hrodgar the Assassin. Hrodgar took me in and brought me to you, and now you are here, burning and killing another good man, just as you did my father. You are evil, and this land will never be just whilst men like you live.'

Beornoth sighed. People viewed the world through many different eyes, sight tainted by each person's experience. To some, a hero was a villain; to others, the villain was the greatest of heroes. To Tata, Beornoth was an evil man because he could not see the right of things through the fog of his own suffering. Beornoth had spent time with the lad, teaching him to fight, trying to offer him something better than life as a servant. But the lad was the son of a thegn whom Beornoth had killed. Tata was a soul burned up with hate and a thirst for vengeance, just like Beornoth himself.

'Go,' Beornoth said, rubbing at his exhausted, stinging eyes. 'Go to your lord.' Tata stood and edged away, then spat at Beornoth and kicked a clump of hay at him before running off into the darkness.

'God in heaven,' said Thered. He walked into the barn and made the sign of the cross above his chest. 'The boy did this?'

'Aye,' said Beornoth. 'He was Godric's spy.' He didn't have the strength to explain the entire sorry tale. Violence begets violence, and Tata hated Beornoth with the same bright fury with which he too hated. It was like a miller's wheel, turning under the force of a river, endlessly moving, driven by the water's churning strength. That was the world in which Beornoth lived: violence, vengeance, battle and blood. It would never end, he realised. His eyes became fixed on Hrodgar's opened throat, unable to look away from the horror. There would always be men who wanted to take from the weak, there would always be swords and axes and spears, and men who must stand up to them. War made orphans and bitter warriors who lived for vengeance. Men craved wealth and power, and so it would be until the end of days.

'Why doesn't God stop it?' Beornoth said.

'Stop what?' asked Thered.

Beornoth didn't answer. Nobody could answer his question about God's mystery, not even the greatest and most holy priest, monk or bishop. Beornoth rose and wiped his face on the back of his hand.

'We must leave this place,' Beornoth said. He quickly saddled his horse, and the company rushed in behind him, each one gasping at Hrodgar's corpse before making their horses ready to ride. Saving his burh from the flames had pulled Godric and his forces away from the fight, but it would not be long before he sent men after Beornoth, to finish him and remove the last threat and barrier to him seizing Essex and becoming ealdorman. Beornoth knelt and stripped Hrodgar's byrnie. He tugged and pulled at the strings at its rear and struggled to pull the heavy chain-mail coat over the dead man's arms and shoulders.

'We don't have time to give him the honour he deserves,' said Thered. He held his horse's reins at the entrance to the barn, and Beornoth realised they were all watching him as he grunted and heaved at the dead body.

'The mail and weapons are his heriot. They must be returned to the king,' said Beornoth. 'They are what made Hrodgar a king's thegn. We must return them.' He drew the sword from Hrodgar's scabbard and showed it to the company, and they looked away from its blade, which was still crusted with blood from the fight at Hareswood. Thered turned away and mounted his horse, and the rest of the company hurried to lead their mounts from the barn and make ready to ride. Beornoth pulled again at the byrnie, but could not pull it free from Hrodgar's body. He sagged, resting his forehead against the cold iron rings on Hrodgar's chest. It was not the heriot which made Hrodgar a king's thegn, it was the man himself and the blessing of the king.

'I am sorry, lord thegn,' he said, and turned away from Hrodgar's body. Beornoth had to go. He slipped the royal ring from Hrodgar's finger and tucked it beneath his own byrnie. The lives of his company were more important than the heriot, as was his quest for vengeance. Beornoth had fought to recover his own lost heriot, and that was how he had first come into the service of Ealdorman Byrhtnoth. It was important, woven into his understanding of what his rank was and how king, ealdorman, thegn and churl maintained order and stability in the kingdom. But he left Hrodgar's body there, dishonoured and killed by a vengeful boy, and it was another death to turn the never-ending wheel of revenge and feud.

21

They rode away from the farm as a red sun crept over the lowlands. A column of smoke twisted from Godric's burh to stain the sky with grey, and Beornoth led his company west, away from the traitor, leaving his hopes of vengeance in a blood-soaked ditch with the corpses of too many men. Nobody spoke on that morning, as they rode under the shame of defeat, and Beornoth did not know where to go or what to do. They needed food, rest and to find some deep cunning if he was to kill Godric. The traitor was much smarter than Beornoth gave him credit for, for he had embedded a boy-killer close to the king, a lad whose soul was bitter and twisted because Beornoth had killed his father, and Tata had got close enough to become servant to a king's thegn. Godric had thwarted Beornoth's attack, he had too many men, and his burh was well defended. It seemed like an impossible task, as Beornoth let Virtus pick his way along the rutted roads and hedge-lined paths of Essex. There had been so much blood and suffering both at Maldon and now also in the killing in its name. So, Beornoth rode west and searched his soul for a sign of what to do next, of how to avenge the fallen.

'We are close to Branoc's Tree,' said Brand, breaking the silence. 'Or what used to be Branoc's Tree.'

Beornoth looked up from his defeat-induced stupor and recognised the slope of a treeline to the north, and a clutch of silver birch trees where a thicket ran between two fields.

'It's just over that rise,' Beornoth said, nodding towards the trees.

'We can rest the horses there and take a rest ourselves.'

Beornoth patted Virtus' neck; the horses needed a rest after the long ride away from Hareswood. Godric would have men pursuing them, and there were probably scouts watching Beornoth even now, but there was little he could do about that. They had not tried to conceal themselves as they rode aimlessly away from the farm. But somehow, Beornoth had led his broken war band to the familiar lands which had once been his responsibility as thegn of Branoc's Tree. There was old Wicca's farm to the south, a man with ten children who bred hunting dogs, and across a babbling brook were Ceol's fields of barley.

At midday, they arrived at what used to be Beornoth's burh and were surprised to find people inside its damaged walls and burned buildings. Smoke rose from what had been Beornoth's hall, a section of it repaired and roofed with earth rather than the thatch which had covered it in his day. Whoever occupied the place had gathered fencing from around the burh to make a grazing pasture for a handful of sheep and goats. The fence cornered a piece of land which had once held a much larger flock, and Beornoth had fond memories of lambing season and how happy that new burst of life had made the people of Branoc's Tree. That was before Olaf Tryggvason had come with his Vikings and hung their corpses from the mighty oak tree which gave the place its name. The tree stood high and proud even now within the repaired structures, and Beornoth winced at the memories woven into its bark and roots, the laughter of children, joyous feasts and good friends, and the howl and cry of the slaughtered.

'Who are those people?' asked Thered, sitting upright in the saddle and shielding his eyes from the sun to peer down at the activity in the ruins. Only they weren't ruins any more: as well as the repaired hall, other buildings had been covered in grassy earth to keep the new occupants warm and dry, and as he rode closer, Beornoth noticed that most of the people in the place were women in long tunics of undyed wool, belted with knotted rope, and white hoods over their heads.

'They look like nuns,' said Beornoth. He was as surprised as Brand and Thered, who had both spent time at Branoc's Tree, to see people inhabiting it again, and that those people were nuns. 'And children.' For a dozen barefooted children ran about the place, and the sound of their laughter brought a welcome lightness to Beornoth's heart.

Three of the nuns strode from the gate, which wasn't really a gate any more because the actual gate was missing, so that all remained were the former posts and lintel. Beornoth approached the women with his hand raised to show that he came in peace. A band of armed riders would strike fear into the nuns' hearts, with every person in England fearful of Viking raids or the wrath of masterless men.

'I am Beornoth, and we come only to rest our horses,' Beornoth said. 'We mean you no harm.'

'I am Abbess Agatha, and are you the same Beornoth who was thegn in this place?'

'Yes.' Her eyes flicked to his byrnie, and then across Beornoth's companions. They had not had time to clean the mud, blood and filth of battle from their weapons, armour, faces and hair, and so looked like a desperate war band, hollow-eyed and crusted with other men's blood.

'The Lady Ælfflæd gave us permission to build on this place,' said the abbess. She had a strong, broad face with a thin-lipped mouth, and she did not shy away from Beornoth in his soiled war glory, but held his gaze.

'Then you are welcome to it. I hope you have better luck here than I did. We will stay awhile and water our horses, if you do not object?'

'Of course not. You are Beornoth, the hero of Watchet, Rivers Bend and Maldon. Please, come inside.'

Beornoth dismounted and led Virtus through the gate. Agatha led them to a trough full of glistening water. A gaggle of barefooted children ran to the horses but stopped short of stroking their flanks. They were warhorses, each beast over fourteen hands, muscled and frightening. One small boy with tousled hair darted forward and touched Virtus' tail, and they all laughed and ran away.

'Why do you have so many children here?' Beornoth asked, as a nun approached with a bowl of water for Beornoth to drink.

'We are building a nunnery and a home here for the orphans of war. These are the children of those who have died during the Viking attacks this last year. Without our care, they would be without home, food, warmth and love.'

'And who pays for that food and warmth?'

The abbess frowned at the awkward question and fussed at the wooden crucifix hanging around her neck. 'The Lady Ælfflæd has granted us this land, to use its hides to fund the work we do in God's name.'

'Then she has been very generous.' Beornoth took a drink of the cool water and passed it to Thered. The old burh was busy not only with nuns and children but also with chickens and geese, and four pigs snorted and foraged in a hay-filled pen. 'Do you have any food?'

'Yes, please follow me.' She led Beornoth and Thered towards what the nuns had salvaged from Beornoth's hall. The earth roof was roughly done, clods of cut grass packed on top of the old with the fire blackened timbers still showing beneath.

'Do you mind if I wait out here?' Beornoth asked. Inside that door were memories best left where they lay. Old friends had died inside the feasting hall, which had been Beornoth's home, a place of happiness and safety. His mind was already torn and ragged, hurting from so much loss, too much pain. He did not care to have another reminder of those horrors brought to life.

'Of course not. Please, sit.' She gestured towards a half-circle of logs which someone had trimmed of bark. 'We have little, but I should be able to spare a bowl of broth for you and your men.'

Abbess Agatha called four of her nuns, and they disappeared inside the hall. Brand and Sefna approached, followed by the rest of the company; the last nun through the door almost fell as she noticed that most of Beornoth's warriors were Vikings.

'They have done fine work here,' said Thered generously, taking in the crooked planks and rough workmanship of the new buildings pieced together from the old. Beornoth could imagine how leaky and cold the structures were in the winter.

'They could do with a carpenter,' said Brand. 'A blind sailor could have made better joints.'

'They are providing a home for the children of folk murdered by your people,' Beornoth said. 'This is the cost of your reputation and the real cost of Olaf's ten thousand pounds of silver. This is what happens after the warriors have left, when the glory has been taken and the skalds have written their songs of shining weapons and brave deeds.'

Brand shrugged, and Beornoth ground his teeth. A man like Brand simply didn't care about the fate of the weak. He was a Norseman, a worshipper of Odin, and Thor, who cared only for war, reputation and silver. The plight of these orphans was not his concern, and if Beornoth pushed him – or Vigdjarf, Sefna or Dolgfinnr – on it, they would answer that the Saxon warriors should have protected them.

'So, what now?' asked Vigdjarf, sighing as he sat down heavily on a log.

Beornoth felt all their eyes upon him, and he could not meet their stares. He looked ahead, past them towards a distant hill. A bird soared there, floating on the wind, and Beornoth watched it, wondering at the simplicity of its life. They had all lost men, Vigdjarf, Dolgfinnr, Reifnir and Thered. Of the fifty who had made the journey south from Northumbria, only thirty remained. They had lost eight men in the ditch at Hareswood. Thered's hearth troop, which had been ten strong, had seen five good warriors perish in Beornoth's search for vengeance. Many of those who stared at him were wounded. They were tired and cowed by defeat.

'I came south with you, Lord Beornoth,' said Thered, 'but this journey is over for me now. We have recovered Byrhtnoth's body, and he will now lie with honour in Ely. We have punished many of those responsible for Maldon. But I will return north with my men. My days of war are over.'

Beornoth nodded without taking his eyes from the bird. It was too far away for him to be sure if it was a falcon, but he thought so. Thered was a brave man, an ealdorman, and he had more than played his part in the war against Olaf's Vikings and in the search for revenge, and Beornoth understood his desire to go. Thered was a changed man, made wise by the horrors of battle, and he had earned some time by his fire with good hounds and strong ale.

'Go then, Lord Thered,' said Beornoth, and he smiled for the first time in so long that he had almost forgotten how to. 'Return to your shire with honour, and I thank you and your brave men for what you have done, and what you have lost.'

'So, it's over then?' said Thered.

'Even with you and your men, we fight against a force ten times our number. Their scouts will know we are here, and by tomorrow, Godric's men will come for us.'

Thered passed a hand over the scars on his face and looked at his men. They were brave, stalwart warriors, and they offered no reaction. Those warriors would fight, or ride, just as their lord commanded. They were his oathmen and would die fighting beside him if necessary.

'What are you saying?' said Brand. 'That we are beaten?'

Beornoth yawned and rolled his stiff shoulder. 'We cannot win here, Brand. There might still be time for you to find your people before they set sail. Go back to Olaf, find your cousin, Hrafn. You have more than repaid the blood debt, which I never held over you anyway. You saved my life, and we will always be brothers.'

Brand stood and kicked at a loose stone. He strode one way and then the other, looking from Beornoth to Sefna, and hiding a quick glance at Vigdjarf. 'I do not think we should give up so easily. We can kill the Saxon bastard. We can't attack the fort, but we can draw the turd out into the open and fight him on ground of our choosing.'

'Just over two dozen against three hundred?'

'What a song that would make,' said Reifnir. 'We would have the gods' attention, and even if we were to die, we would live on in glory until the day of Ragnarök.'

'There won't be another fight,' said Beornoth. 'Go north with Thered and return to your lands in Northumbria as brave men; your reputations are sealed for the deeds you have performed on this quest.'

'Shit on the quest,' said Brand. 'I don't want to take to the Whale Road and live out my days knowing that Godric, the snivelling piece of seal offal, has bested me.'

'It's over, Brand.' Beornoth held out his hand to Brand, but the Viking slapped it away. Beornoth was not mad at the insult. He understood. He felt the same way, bitter and shamed at the defeat, but he could not see any way to kill Godric. He had become too powerful, and Beornoth simply did not have enough men.

'Maybe I will stay in England, take a wife, and then come back and kill the bastard years from now when he is not expecting it.'

'Take a wife?' said Sefna, her face turning from pretty to anger in a heartbeat.

'I hope you aren't referring to one of my daughters?' said Vigdjarf, and he rose from the log, with his chest puffed out and his hand dangerously close to his axe.

Brand waved a hand at them both and stormed off towards the horses. The abbess and her nuns came from the hall with bowls of steaming broth and cups of ale. Beornoth refused the ale, and his cup was filled with fresh milk instead. The company ate in an awkward silence, and Beornoth felt lighter now that he had relinquished his vengeful desires. Godric would live and would more than likely become the ealdorman of Essex.

'Your men seem full of sorrow,' said Abbess Agatha, sitting next to Beornoth and taking a sip of milk from her own cup. 'Shall we pray for you? Though I note that some of your companions are pagans.'

'You do not mind feeding pagans?'

'Even the Viking warlord has now become a man of God, so there is hope for all of them. I believe Christ would want me to treat each man the same, and to extend love and care to all travellers.'

That surprised Beornoth, for most priests hated pagans. They preached against them in sermons and cursed them to the pit of hell. Any man who did not worship God and Christ was an enemy to be killed or turned to the true faith. Beornoth was more tolerant than that,

mainly because he had been raised amongst men who worshipped
God and the Vikings' gods. But he also understood why people hated
the Vikings. They had brought nothing but violence and suffering to
the Saxon people across the country, a land they craved to take for
themselves. So, there was no love lost between Saxon, Norse or Dane.

'We are defeated, lady. Rogues and traitors prosper, and good,
honest men are cast down. We came to punish a man who
betrayed the old ealdorman, and we have failed.'

'You hunt for Godric, son of Odda?'

'Aye, we did.'

'And does the Lady Ælfflæd know you are here?'

'She does. I recovered her husband's body from the Vikings
and returned it to her for burial.'

'Men flock to her home at Rettendon,' said the abbess. 'A man
came here yesterday to request food to help them cope with the
arrivals.'

Beornoth stared at her over the lip of his bowl and then set it
down on the log.

'What men?'

'Warriors, like you. The news that you have come to avenge
Ealdorman Byrhtnoth has spread throughout the shire and
survivors of the battle. What few there were have come to help you.
Other men of the fyrd, or old warriors who had fought beside
Byrhtnoth, arrive in ones and twos. The man who came spoke of
grandfathers with rusty seaxes and spears, and men with scarred
faces and healing wounds gather in the fields around Rettendon.'

'Are you sure?' Beornoth's heart soared like the falcon above
the field, but he checked himself. He still bore the muck on his face
and hands from the fight in the ditch, and his head throbbed from
where he had been cast down from the palisade. A small fire
kindled in his being, like the tiniest ember in a snowstorm, but he

clung to it, hope igniting where it had seemed like continuing on was impossible.

'Send a rider to see for yourselves if you won't take my word for it, but I'm busy and I won't repeat myself. There is work to be done here, Lord Beornoth. You are welcome to spend the night with us whilst you wait for your man to return. We have meat, eggs, milk, bread, cheese and butter.'

'Thank you, lady,' Beornoth said, wanting to grab Abbess Agatha in a tight embrace of joy, but holding himself back from scandalising her.

'What is it?' asked Reifnir, scratching his bald head in confusion.

'There are men at Rettendon, men who might help us in the fight against Godric. Good men, loyal men.'

'So, it is not over?' asked Vigdjarf. He and Reifnir exchanged shrugs.

'Not if there are enough men there who can fight. Thered, will you ride to Rettendon with your men?'

Thered swallowed hard, and his fingers flicked over the hilt of his sword. 'I'll ride to Rettendon and send whatever men are there this way. But I won't join the fight, Beornoth. I return to York tomorrow.'

'I will go with you, Lord Thered,' said Wuffa. 'Rettendon is my home, and I would tell the Lady Ælfflæd of all that we have done in her dead husband's name.'

'We have a day to prepare then,' said Beornoth, suddenly feeling strong and light, as though he had slept for a week in a bed of goose feathers.

'Prepare for what?' asked Hrist, leaning on her bowstave and just as lost as the rest of the warriors gathered about Beornoth. They had thought their campaign was over and could not understand how Beornoth had shifted from shamed defeat to talk of preparation.

'To fight and kill Godric of the East Saxons. Men will come, and I can feel the strength of Byrhtnoth's spirit in my bones. He looks down upon us, as do Wulfhere, Leofsunu and Aelfwine. They have sent us a gift, the gift of luck. Men will come. East Saxon fighters and men of honour have roused to avenge their slaughtered ealdorman. We will stand and fight and Godric will die. Then we can go home.'

22

Thered led his men away from Branoc's Tree that afternoon. His warhorses cantered across green fields trailed by a gaggle of orphans who whooped and cheered until the horses rode out of sight. Godric would come for Beornoth, that was certain. He had always hated Beornoth and could not resist the chance to bring his army to Branoc's Tree and lay him low. Godric saw a chance to take a shire for himself and to become one of the most powerful men in all England. Godric faced an outnumbered foe, bloody and beaten, and with one more fight, he could end it all. Beornoth and Thered were the last of Byrhtnoth's hearth troop, the only warriors in England who had fought beside the mighty ealdorman and who could spread the word of Godric's cowardice and betrayal. So, he would come with every warrior, ruffian and masterless man he could muster.

'You should go to the forest,' Beornoth said to Abbess Agatha as he organised the defence of Branoc's Tree. 'My coming here has brought danger to you and your sisters, and the children.'

'We will not leave,' she said firmly, scowling at him as she would if she were scolding a child for stealing honey. 'We have worked hard to turn this place into what you see today. It was a ruin when we arrived, and I won't let you warrior-brutes hack it to pieces again.'

'Then perhaps I should lead my men away, and we can make our stand elsewhere, so that you are not in danger.'

'Danger?' She laughed and cast her eyes up to heaven. 'You warriors think you bear all the danger in your shield walls, that the pain and suffering of war is at the end of a blade. But I assure you, Lord Beornoth, that the real pain and suffering of war is borne by women and children. When the Vikings come, we are the ones who are raped or enslaved. My own cousin was taken by the Vikings two years ago, and the Lord God only knows where she is now, in some pagan land living as a slave, or dead in a ditch. So, we will not run, and neither will you. We shall stand up to these men. The Lady Ælfflæd granted us this land, and by God, we shall protect it. Show us how, Beornoth, and you will see that we can cut wood, build ramparts and do as much as your warriors to help protect this place.'

'Very well, lady,' said Beornoth, and he bowed his head in respect. 'Reifnir,' Beornoth called, and the bald Viking looked up from where he carved at a wooden stake with his axe.

'Yes, lord?'

'The nuns will help us prepare the defences. Show them how.'

Reifnir nodded. He was a woodcutter and a carpenter, as were his men, and they had started work immediately, repairing what remained of the palisade. They could never repair the entire ring of fortifications in time for Godric's attack. The nuns had pulled timbers free to help construct their dwellings. More had been scorched by Viking fire, and entire sections had bowed outwards towards the bank and ditch or collapsed completely. There was, however, a half-circle around the hall, which was in good repair, and Reifnir reckoned they could build enough of a ring inside the old burh to mount a stout defence. It would not be a proper palisade, but they could build a defendable barrier inside the settlement, running between the houses and around the hall.

'I have to say, Lord Beornoth,' said the abbess, making the sign of the cross as she watched Reifnir and Ornir cut wood. 'I am surprised to see you in the company of Vikings. Are you not the most famous Viking killer in the kingdom?'

'These men were all born in Northumbria, sons, grandsons and granddaughters of Viking settlers. They are people, just like us, and they came when I asked. They are as English as you and me now, lady. For a hundred years we have been a country of two peoples, Saxon and Viking. The Danes and Norsemen who settled the Danelaw are here to stay and, over time, it will become as normal as when our ancestors took the land from the Britons. Maybe someone will come and take it from us one day. They are brave and follow a code of honour, and I would rather share a meal, or stand in the shield with one of them than any warrior in Godric's force.'

'Let us hope we can return to times of peace now that this Olaf Tryggvason has become a man of God and will leave our shores. We need time to heal, to dig furrows and sow the seeds of healing and growth.'

'We shall see,' said Beornoth. He didn't want to ruin her hopes of peace, but in his heart, Beornoth knew that there would never be peace in the world. Men would always want more and had always wanted more. He imagined that in the times stretching back before man's memory, men fought because they wanted more cows, or better water for their horses and sheep. Now, they fought for silver, reputation and new lands to settle their people. They came from places where farming was hard, and where they served other men. With a ship of spear warriors, a man could make himself a lord, rather than serve one. So, as long as violence and greed lived in men's hearts, there would never be peace.

Abbess Agatha rubbed her hands together and took a wood axe from Reifnir. She called her sisters together and Reifnir showed them how to chop the old palisade timbers in half, and then how to sharpen them with four strikes of his axe. There would be no fighting platform on the hastily prepared defences, so the stakes needed only to be high enough so that the defenders could reach and fight across their tops. Dolgfinnr and his men dug holes for the stakes to be planted into, whilst Sefna and Hrist took the orphans to make as many arrows as possible to fill their quivers. Vigdjarf walked the perimeter, pulling at his beard, pointing and barking orders at points which needed to be shored up, or where they should make piles of missiles. His men worked with some of the damaged palisade timbers to cut makeshift wooden spears, which were little more than sharpened staves, but they could still kill a man.

Beornoth and Brand made piles of rocks and stones inside the new defences and between the old dwellings, which the defenders could use as missiles once the enemy came close enough to the walls. They paced the ruined burh, trying to foresee how the attack might go, and how they might best defend it. They talked of an all-out attack, or of Godric sending his best men at the weak side of the burh, which was the hastily erected new, shorter palisade. It was not a complicated problem to solve. Godric's scouts would already have reported that Beornoth and his company were in the ruins of Branoc's Tree. At the time when Olaf brought fire and death to Branoc's Tree, Godric and Beornoth were blood brothers in Byrhtnoth's hearth troop, so he knew its fate and condition. Godric would see the broken buildings and crumbling palisade and send his fighters around the perimeter. They would charge the walls and overwhelm Beornoth with their greater numbers. They would probe and stretch the defenders too thin, like too little butter over too much bread. Godric's fighters would cut and hack with their weapons and find a way in. Once they were inside, the fighting would become desperate. A bloody brawl amongst the buildings and lanes where many would die until the greater numbers put down the fewer, and Godric could boast that he had killed Beornoth, king's thegn and Viking killer.

'We can start on the old walls,' said Brand. He walked to a section where the timber palisade had pushed outwards like a set of claws, and he kicked a splayed post. 'On the old palisade. Let them think we will stand on the broken timbers, lure them in and retreat to the new defences.'

'Godric is belligerent. He's a bloated bag of piss full of his own self-importance. When we retreat, they will swarm after us. That will give us a chance. Kill some on the outer wall, and then as we retreat, hammer them with arrows and rocks; once we fall back to the new wall, we can make a stand.'

'If we have enough men.'

'If we have enough men who will stand and fight,' Beornoth agreed. 'What we have here is not enough, but with another thirty or forty warriors, we can make a fight of it.'

'We need at least another three score to have any chance. Even then, each man would have to kill three of the enemy. Our best hope is that we can hurt them enough so that they fall back.'

'Which is what we shall do. We have luck on our side today. I feel it.'

'Few fight against many.' Brand shrugged. 'Sefna says the Valkyrie are already swirling above us, unseen and looking for fallen heroes, ready to whisk them away to join Odin's einherjar.'

'Sefna says that, does she?' Beornoth smirked and Brand bridled.

'What of it?'

'Everyone can see the two of you are in love. You are like youngsters stealing kisses behind the hay bales.'

'Do you think Vigdjarf knows?'

Beornoth laughed. 'Of course he knows. It's a miracle he hasn't split your head open with his axe.'

'The sun rises and sets with her, Beo. She fills my every thought. Her eyes seem to cast a seiðr spell upon me and turn me into a gibbering fool. Her hair is...'

'That's enough. I don't need to hear any more of your lover's chatter. She is fierce and beautiful, and you should ask Vigdjarf if you can marry his daughter. If we survive this fight.'

'If we survive, maybe I will.' Brand stopped and tucked his fingers in his belt. 'I have little to offer her. No land, no wealth.'

'She would be honoured to have a warrior of reputation like you. You have silver, and either of Thered or Alfgar would take you into their service as a warrior. In Northumbria you would even be amongst your own people.'

'Or she might return to Norway with me. I will have land from my father there one day.'

'So, you will ask Vigdjarf then?'

'If we live. But that doesn't seem likely, lord. You seem confident, and I don't want to take the shine off that blade, but we can't defeat three hundred men with our small company, some Christ women and a handful of orphans. Wait, who is that?'

Brand pointed to the eastern fields, where a man marched towards Branoc's Tree. Beornoth shielded his eyes from the bright sky and stared at the striding man. More figures appeared behind him, emerging over the slope until ten men strode across the field, and they carried bows, mattocks and hoes. One carried a wood axe, and another a spear.

'Let's find out,' said Beornoth, and he clapped Brand on the shoulder. They walked through a missing section of the old palisade and the line of men waved a greeting.

'We are from the next valley,' said a thick-chested man with broad shoulders. He carried a long staff, and he was almost as tall as Beornoth himself. 'My name is Dudda, and I was in the fyrd at Maldon. These men are from the farms close to mine. You were seen, Lord Beornoth, riding towards Hareswood, and then we heard you were here. Word travels fast around these parts.'

'You fought at Maldon?' asked Beornoth.

'No, lord.' Dudda tore his eyes away from Beornoth's and cast them down to the earth. 'We ran. We let Godric lead us away. And I haven't been able to live with myself since. So, we have come to make amends, for Ealdorman Byrhtnoth, and to you, lord.'

Bile rose in Beornoth's throat and stung as he swallowed it down. The men were traitors, fyrd men who should have fought for Lord Byrhtnoth at Maldon, but who had fled and saved themselves as their ealdorman perished. Beornoth's heart told him to strike them down, to punish them for fleeing the battlefield. But his head told him he needed them. Beornoth needed every man he could get, and perhaps a chance at redemption would spur them on to brave deeds.

'Is that a staff or a bow?' Beornoth said, gesturing to the length of wood in the man's fist, noting the curved taper at each end.

'It's a war bow, lord. My father taught me how to use it. It's a stag killer.'

'Welcome, Dudda, and to the rest of you. Godric led you away from the field at Maldon, and good men died. Now is your chance to redeem yourselves. So, fight with us here against Godric the coward and regain the respect of your wives and children. Running from battle is a stain that would have haunted you all for the rest of your days. After this fight, men will look upon you and know that you stood with me and fought for honour and vengeance, that you are brave men worthy of respect.' Beornoth walked to them, and each man stared at him in awe. They were churls and farmers, and he was a thegn clad in mail and with a sword at his hip. He clapped their backs and took their wrists in the warrior's grip. They were shamed for running and leaving their ealdorman to die on the battlefield and saw a chance to regain their honour.

Beornoth ordered the defenders to take their makeshift spears and pile some with the rocks behind the broken buildings beyond the new defences, and others inside the new timber wall. The nuns were eager to help, and Beornoth had them dig pits in between the old buildings outside of the new wall. They covered them with alder branches to hide the pits and stuck markers into the ground so the defenders would not fall into them during the retreat. Against men in mail or hardened leather armour, holding shields, rocks and wood spears would not slow an organised advance, nor kill any of the enemy. They could simply allow the crude weapons to bounce off their shields as they approached behind a wall of linden wood, with their bodies protected by armour. But, from what Beornoth had seen of Godric's men in the forest and at Hareswood, most of the men in Godric's war band were not armoured and nor did they carry shields. The men who did were Godric's retainers, his hearth troop of warriors sworn to serve and protect him. Rocks and sticks would not slow those men, but Beornoth had enough warriors of his own to deal with them.

The work continued until the sun dimmed to cast the heavens in a red hue, and before dark, more men came to join the fight. They drifted in, in twos and threes, more shamefaced men of the Essex fyrd who had fled the field at Maldon. A man with an old shield with a rusty boss and his squint-eyed brother, a small man with a two-handed wood axe over his shoulder and a sack full of food; three brothers with an old seax, a mattock and a hoe for weapons; and a thegn from the border of Essex and East Anglia named Cyneric arrived on a dappled mare with three retainers. Cyneric had been shown kindness by Aelfwine of Foxfield years earlier and came to repay that debt with his sword. The men were all put to work, cutting old palisade logs or digging holes to sink them into. As darkness overcame the land, the defenders' numbers had swelled to fifty fighters, and the abbess made sure everybody had a simple evening meal of bread, honey and cheese.

The defenders made a fire outside the new walls, and folk gathered around it to take that evening meal. The Saxons were wary of the Vikings with their pagan amulets, long hair and tattoos, but Vigdjarf, Reifnir and Dolgfinnr's men all spoke Saxon with a Northumbrian accent and, once the Saxons realised that, there was no hostility between the defenders. Cyneric asked for the tale of Maldon, but Beornoth was reluctant to give it; he was a warrior not a skald or a skop and he had no desire to relive the pain of the battle, which took up so much of his thoughts already, without giving voice to it. Then, Dudda told what he knew, up to where he had run from the fight, and the fyrd men all listened to that tale and stared into the night, pondering the shame of their cowardice. So, Beornoth told them what had happened next. How he had fought beside the ealdorman against the dread Vikings and their vicious axes. He told them of the shield wall, and how the river-bank had run red with blood, and how the thegns of Essex had fought and died to the last man. Beornoth told them how the Jomsvikings had formed a wedge and killed Byrhtnoth. He spoke of when Sweyn Forkbeard, the war-king of the Danes, had come from the river dripping with water and savagery, and with wrath and fury had killed the Wessex men King Æthelred had sent to the fight.

'Tomorrow we will face the man who led you away from the glorious field of battle,' Beornoth told them, repeating what he had said to Dudda earlier. 'When I rode to Maldon to retrieve

Ealdorman Byrhtnoth's body from the Vikings, they had cut off his
head, and the heads of my friends, the thegns and warriors you left
to die. They mounted those heads on the road to Maldon, with
their eyes pecked out by crows and their naked bodies thrown in a
midden heap, and not given a Christian burial. So, think on their
fate this night, and let that anger give you strength when Godric
and his ruffians arrive tomorrow. They have scoured your shire,
and Godric has done his best to steal the dead ealdorman's land
and snatch Byrhtnoth's daughter's inheritance for himself. Byrht-
noth died for you, so that you would be protected from Viking
blades, so that your wives and daughters would not be taken and
turned into slaves. So, fight for him, and fight for me, and let us
send Godric to hell where his stinking soul belongs.'

Beornoth slept well that night, even though he knew Godric
would arrive the next day with his war band. He felt no fear, even
though he was outnumbered. Beornoth was at Branoc's Tree,
which though it was not the place it had once been, still felt like
home. He lay in the repaired hall, finally braving the ghosts of
dead friends, and the smells of old feasts and roaring fires which
still clung to the surviving rafters. Fresh rushes covered the floor,
and Beornoth stood on the spot where Aethelberga, the one-time
lady of Branoc's Tree, had been killed by the Vikings. The ghosts
left him alone that night, and visions of walking with Eawynn in
her garden and of peace filled his dreams.

Morning came with a warm sun and a clear sky; a cock crowed
the start of the day and Beornoth woke to the sound of birdsong.
He walked the new walls and tested their strength. The timbers
were well sunk into the earth, and the new makeshift palisade
would serve well enough against Godric's men, or so Beornoth
hoped. The wall would not hold back an army of Vikings, but it
would do. He stretched his stomach wound and kneaded away the
stiffness in his leg and shoulder. His body owed him one more

battle. The scars and knotted muscle would hold for one more day, he hoped. His hands were strong, and his heart was full, not just of vengeance and hate for Godric, but with pride. For people had come, and perhaps the world was not so bleak a place after all.

The defenders woke, and they continued their work, so that Branoc's Tree rang with the sounds of axes and shovels, and the smell of freshly cut wood filled the air. Something strange happened that morning. People seemed to enjoy their work even though they knew enemies would come with blades and violence and that the day was to be filled with pain and death. They worked together, remembering what Essex had been like before the Vikings came and tore it apart with their sleek warships and brutal war skill. The people cheered when a fresh post was sunk into the earth and laughed when one fell, and three men sprawled in the mud. The orphans ran about the busy defenders, and Brand chased them around the walls barking like a dog, and everybody laughed loud and hearty. Beornoth smiled to see it, and the sense of being a people, of accomplishing something together, lifted the melancholy from his heart, but his eyes were on the distant tree-lined hills. He watched west for signs of the enemy and east for the signs of the warriors Thered had gone to fetch from Rettendon. If Godric came before Thered's force, then there would be a great slaughter again at Branoc's Tree, and as the joy of togetherness rang around the old burh, the sparks of fear glowed again like embers in Beornoth's belly. He watched the abbess and her nuns and the barefooted children and wondered if his coming had condemned them all to death.

23

Riders appeared to the west mid-morning, three men on ponies who watched Branoc's Tree until Brand and Sefna chased them off. They were Godric's scouts, come to count the number of defenders and report back to their Lord Godric. Brand and Sefna returned on lathered horses flecked with white sweat and reported that Godric's war band was on the march. Three hundred men crossed the shire, some on horseback and most on foot. They tramped through grazing pastures and furrowed fields, and a warm wind caressed the land from the west. Godric had the ten men of his hearth troop in mail and well-armed, along with a handful of thegns, and the rest were his masterless men, who came with their clubs, spears, axes and malice. Brand reckoned they would be at Branoc's Tree by midday.

The defenders took a meal of salted pork and cheese, and Beornoth watched the western fields and hills waiting for Godric's ragged war band to approach. Spear points wavered and their weapons clunked and clanked, attracting curious glances from the sheep and cows, but the first fighters to arrive came instead from the east and the folk inside Branoc's Tree whooped for joy as a column of riders picked their way through the high pastures. Beornoth allowed his own heart to soar as a hunting horn blared from the column, loud and confident. At the head of those riders came Lady Ælfflæd, her hair whipped by the breeze and her chin held high and proud. Wuffa rode beside her with his spear held straight. Though he was surprised to see the lady riding with the warriors who had flocked to Rettendon, Beornoth was glad to see she had brought forty riders with good spears. Thered rode with the lady at the head of the column and raised his fist in salute. Forty spears to add to the numbers inside Branoc's Tree. They were still vastly outnumbered, but Beornoth let his hand fall to the hilt of his sword. He clutched the leather bindings and let hope build, for with these new men they could make a stand, and with luck it would be enough to wreak vengeance for the glorious dead of Maldon.

Lady Ælfflæd led the horses into a canter, and their hooves thundered the ground so that it felt as if an army of horsemen approached Branoc's Tree. She took the fluttering red banner of Essex from one of her spearmen and held it high and proud, leading the riders in a wide arc towards Branoc's Tree and the people inside the burh cheered and cried out with joy as though it were the greatest host in all England.

'I told you I would raise warriors, Lord Beornoth,' called Lady Ælfflæd as she brought her mare to a snorting, stomping halt. 'And warriors I have brought.'

'So, you have, my lady. And we are most thankful, but it is not safe here for you. There will be a fight today.'

'I have been fighting my whole life. At least today I will see my enemy before me, rather than fearing the sharp tongue of a courtier at Winchester.'

Beornoth smiled at that truth, and he held her bridle as Lady Ælfflæd dismounted. But some of Beornoth's hope died as her riders drew closer. Of the forty, ten at least were greybeards with veined hands clasped around their spears, another twenty were fyrd men on farm ponies or shaggy-hocked labour nags. But there were also the ten men of the lady's personal guard, men who had served Byrhtnoth, and those men were warriors, well-armed with shields, spears and seaxes, and would be a strong addition to the defences. Beornoth smiled to see Thered returned, for he had been sure that the young ealdorman would have left for Northumbria in search of peace.

'Thank you, Lady Ælfflæd,' said Beornoth, and he bowed his head in respect. 'Your husband would be proud.'

She smiled and walked to greet Abbess Agatha. The two women embraced warmly and Beornoth shook forearms with Thered as he climbed down from his horse.

'They aren't the sturdy band of warriors we had hoped for,' said Thered. He shrugged as one of the old riders coughed and wheezed. 'But many of the old ones were warriors once, and the fyrd men are eager to strike a blow for their dead ealdorman.'

'They will do fine,' lied Beornoth. 'I thought you were returning to Northumbria?'

'It's not good riding weather,' Thered said, and peered up at the clear blue sky with a wry grin. 'So, I think I'll go tomorrow.'

Beornoth laughed and pulled the young ealdorman into a bear hug. They slapped each other's backs. He was glad that Thered would stay and fight. He might have had the spirit shaken out of him by the horrors at Maldon, but Thered was a stout fighter, and they would need his sword if the people at Branoc's Tree were to survive the day.

'What shall we do with the horses? There are too many here now to keep inside the new walls.'

'We can use them, fetch your men and five of Lady Ælfflæd's warriors,' said Beornoth, and he called to Brand, Vigdjarf, Reifnir and Dolgfinnr. 'Leave most of the men here, but get twenty on horses and armed with spears.'

'It's not the right time to go on a hunting trip, Beo?' said Vigdarf, and the others laughed.

'It is if our prey is the enemy. We will ride out and attack their scouts. Harry as many as we can before they form a column.'

'These are not warhorses, they won't charge an enemy,' said Thered. Which was true; it was an expensive business to breed and train a horse for war. Beornoth had owned such animals in his time, and they were magnificently brave beasts, huge and terrifying. But most horses would not charge a line of spears or a compact group of men. Beornoth's horse Virtus would, but she was not a savage warhorse like his old horse Ealdorbana had been.

'We don't need to charge them. Just thin them out and get them angry before they get here. We go to pick a fight and kill as many of the bastards as we can before they reach Branoc's Tree. I want Godric's pride hurt. He fancies himself an ealdorman, picking at the bones of Maldon like a carrion bird. So, let's make the bastard fight for it.'

'Let's go kill some Saxons, then,' said Reifnir, and then shrugged apologetically at Beornoth and Thered.

Beornoth rode with his helmet on, not because he intended to be fighting at close quarters, but because with the cheekpieces it made him look more fearsome. He carried an ash-shafted aesc spear with a lead shaped blade, and Virtus cantered him across the green East Saxon fields. Each rider carried a spear and Beornoth led them towards where Brand and Sefna had last seen Godric's scouts. Ornir's great dog bounded along with them, and after the defeat at Hareswood, it felt good to take the fight to the enemy again. Beornoth rode with Brand and Thered whilst the rest of the riders peeled off in two companies, one skirting around to the north, and one to the south. Beornoth knew this land like the

contours of Eawynn's face. The land to the west of Branoc's Tree
formed a shallow valley, where two hills rose on either side of a
meandering river. Those hills were topped with elm, oak, birch
ash, pine and hazel. The forests were thick enough to offer cover
on the high ground, and so Beornoth sent riders there to wait
hidden from the enemy.

Six riders on hardy ponies rode alongside the river, and they
kicked their mounts up the valley when they saw Beornoth's three
riders approaching. Their horses were the small, thick-haired
animals common throughout Britain, less than fourteen hands,
durable and useful for both riding and farm work. The riders
spread out into a line; legs splayed over their mounts' tubby bellies
so that their heels stuck out like rudders on a ship. One man
carried a bow, which to use whilst riding was a trick which took a
lifetime to master and was the reason Sefna and Hrist had
remained at Branoc's Tree. Vigdjarf had worked through the night
cutting and fletching arrows to fill their quivers, but neither could
draw and loose effectively whilst riding so their arrows would be
better loosed from the walls rather than wasted on horseback.

The riders came on, and Beornoth dug his heels into Virtus'
flanks and hauled on the reins so that the horse turned and
bucked as though something spooked her.

'What are you doing? You ride like you have never ridden a
horse before,' asked Brand. He crossed his arms and leaned over
his horse's neck, shaking his head at Beornoth.

'Let them think we're panicked. Do it,' Beornoth said, and
Brand laughed. He and Thered followed Beornoth's example and
brought their horses about in a circle whilst the six riders
approached slowly. Beornoth, Thered and Brand shouted at one
another as though in argument about what to do, whether to fight
or flee, and the scouts spread out wider, grim-faced men with griz-
zled beards and hard eyes. The scouts let their horses amble across

the field, and the animals' rolling gate gave the scouts a menacing swagger. They wore woollen hoods and travel-stained jerkins with fur around collar and chest. They licked their lips like wolves, taking in the three warriors in their byrnies, with swords and Brand's Viking axe. Beornoth, Brand and Thered looked like warriors in their fine war gear, and the scouts knew who Godric fought, so they would be wary. But they also knew the warrior caste, just as all common folk did. They knew that most lords and thegns were born to that position and inherited their fine byrnies and beautiful swords. On such men, expensive war gear was a decoration, a symbol of their status. On a Viking they were a signal of war glory and battle prowess, worn proudly by a man who had the strength to win his mail and weapons, and to keep them from those who would tear them away. The scouts scratched their chins and cocked their heads, wondering if the three men were gentle lords with soft hands and pudgy midriffs. A few thegns, and some lords, however, were lovers of battle and men to fear. The type of man who pushed his way to the front of the shield wall to trade blows with the dangerous men, someone who gloried in his reputation as a fighter and sought the biggest, most fierce warriors to fight and kill.

One scout said something which Beornoth couldn't hear, and then spat contemptuously. The rest of the scouts laughed, and the bowman dragged a dirty feathered arrow from a quiver in his saddle and nocked it to his bow. The scouts had decided that the three inept riders were easy prey for expert horsemen such as themselves, and if they could kill Beornoth, Thered and Brand, they would become rich men with byrnies, a fine helmet and weapons fit for a lord. The scouts made a wide half-circle around Beornoth, and he shouted curses at Thered and Brand for them to run, and they shouted at their mounts in turn so that they looked like fools in panic on the hillside.

Beornoth swore and shouted at Virtus until Godric's scouts
were close enough downwind for him to smell the stench of old ale
and garlic upon them. Then, Beornoth let Virtus steady herself
and she surged forward, and as her flanks rose, Beornoth levelled
his spear, leant forwards and launched the leaf-bladed weapon at
the bowman. Beornoth shouted with the effort of throwing the
heavy spear. He pivoted at the waist, using his powerful back
muscles to launch the weapon with as much power as possible. It
happened too quickly for the scout to react in time. What the
enemy thought was a fool who could not control his horse had
suddenly become a vicious warrior, and the spear flashed through
the air like a darting swallow. Its shaft quivered in the air as it flew
flat and true. He raised his bow but was too slow and Beornoth's
spear hit him in the chest with horrifying force. The leaf-shaped
blade carved through the bowman's chest bones with a crack and
threw the man from the saddle as though ropes yanked him back-
wards. His pony whinnied and shook as it smelled blood and the
enemy scouts gaped at the fallen man, who was dead before he hit
the grass. It was sudden, brutal violence. The spearhead was as big
as Beornoth's hand and the wound in the dead scout's chest pulsed
blood through his jerkin; the shaft stuck straight up into the air
like a fence post, and the scouts' dream of easy prey and riches had
turned to blood and death.

'Kill the bastards,' Beornoth growled, and Brand charged the
scout closest to him and drove the point of his spear into the neck
of the man's pony. The beast screamed and reared and tossed its
rider to the ground. He scrambled on the earth on all fours like a
pig, head darting from side to side to see where his attacker had
gone and Brand brought his spear around and drove the point into
the man's neck and kicked his horse so that the scout was pushed
forward, jerking on the end of the spear like a landed trout. Brand
yanked his spear free and aimed the point to the sky, calling to

Odin with his blood-soaked weapon. Thered chased a scout who had wheeled his horse around, and Thered had the momentum, so his spear point drove through the fleeing man's back and broke his spine.

The three remaining riders turned their horses and raced away towards the river, the ponies' little legs racing and throwing up clods of earth. The surviving scouts glanced back over their shoulders in wide-eyed terror to see if Beornoth pursued them. Beornoth slowed Virtus and reached down to yank his spear from the man he had killed. The two columns of hidden riders burst from the trees on either side of the valley and galloped down the slopes to cut off the fleeing scouts. The three men reined their ponies in, heads snapping about them, panicked and unsure where to flee. They had mounted enemies on bigger, faster horses on all sides, and so they did the only thing they could, which was to throw down their weapons and beg for mercy.

After the brief skirmish, Beornoth scratched Virtus' ear and told her she was a brave and strong horse. He fed her a carrot from his saddlebag and stroked her neck and flank. Ahead of him, three hundred men approached across a swaying sea of wheat and barley fields. Godric's army trudged through the crops in small groups, not in any sort of marching formation and without discipline. Behind him, Beornoth dragged the three scouts naked and tied to his saddle. They wept and groaned as their bare feet split on stones and were stung by nettles. They scrambled to stand as Virtus' strength dragged them on their backs whenever they fell. Godric's advancing force did not know of Beornoth's approach without their scouts, so there was a chance for surprise, a few moments to strike at Godric before his men had a chance to react or prepare for an attack. Beornoth held his spear in one hand and his breath echoed inside the helmet's close iron cage. Any army relied on scouts for news of what lay ahead in the next valley, across a river or behind a steep hill. No commander wanted to march his men straight into an organised enemy deployed for battle, and the ability to have eyes on an enemy was vital.

'There are a lot of them,' said Thered, stating the obvious.

'More of the dogs for us to kill,' said Brand cheerfully.

The enemy came through the crops in poor order, like a crowd of men marching to market. They carried their crude weapons over their shoulders and the sun glinted off iron and steel. Amongst the walking enemy, there were twelve riders, Godric's hearth troop, with the traitor himself in their midst. Beornoth paused beside a blackberry thicket and held his spear aloft, knowing that Godric would see him. With his left hand, he untied the hemp rope from his saddle and let the three scouts scarper towards their own men. They ran across the fields, and Brand laughed at their white bodies wobbling through the grass, and Thered couldn't help but laugh himself as one of their feet slipped on a cow turd and he tumbled to the ground with indignity, any sense of honour or pride stripped away. Beornoth wanted Godric's men to see that it was him they faced, a warrior and thegn. They would know of Beornoth, of his deeds in battle, and he rode along the field with the spear held high and his helmet glinting in the sun. He wanted them to see how he had treated their scouts. Three were dead and three humiliated. That would anger the braver men amongst Godric's force and terrify the meeker amongst them. The advancing men stopped in the fields and stared at the riders who had appeared before them without warning, men on large horses armed with spears.

'Charge them,' Beornoth said, and he clicked his tongue and dug his heels into Virtus' flanks. Brand gave a whoop and followed him, as did Thered, and moments later seventeen more horsemen came behind Beornoth in a long line of spear-armed horsemen. Beornoth had heard tales of great companies of warhorses in

Frankia who would charge into an enemy with devastating force, huge warhorses bred for fighting and riders trained to fight from horseback with lances and long swords. But the warriors of England did not possess trained horses in such numbers, and so a charge on horseback was rare. But he did not charge Virtus towards an organised shield wall; Beornoth led her at a straggled bunch of masterless men, and he clenched his jaw with a heady mix of anger and joy as the leading men of that cut-throat army saw twenty horses galloping towards them, their hooves thundering the ground, and riders with levelled, sharp spear points to stab and rip.

Bearded faces stared and fingers came up, pointing at Beornoth. Taut, terrified lips mouthed, shouted panic, but the sound of their voices was lost amidst the ear-shaking thunder of hoofbeats. Beornoth rode past the three naked scouts who dropped to the grass and curled into little balls as the riders surged past them. What Godric's men should have done was clamour together in a tight bunch or column with their weapons ready to strike a horse or rider. The horses would not charge a dense force of men. But Godric's men were not warriors, and nor did they have an experienced warlord to lead them, so they turned and ran. Beornoth found Godric amongst his men. He was easy to pick out with gold on his sword hilt and at his neck, and his horsemen hefted spears and urged their men forwards. The sight of the traitor made Beornoth roar with anger and he thanked God in heaven for the chance to bring the bastard low.

Beornoth killed the first of Godric's men with his spear held overhand and couched in the crook of his elbow. The blade tore through the running man's head as though it were a rotten pumpkin, and the left side of his skull ripped apart to spatter blood and gore into the golden ears of wheat. Another man fell beneath Virtus' charge, and the animal's powerful legs crushed his ribs with monstrous force. Brand threw his spear into the man's back and whipped his axe free to smash the bearded blade into a second man's shoulder. Godric's army ran from the riders and the thegn himself was too far back to do anything to halt the attack. Beornoth drew his sword and slashed her point across the back of a man's neck and Virtus raced on as the men tumbled to die in the wheat. The line of horsemen shouted for joy as they crashed into the enemy, and Godric's army cried out in panic and desperation as twenty horses hammered into them like a landslide.

Godric's warriors rode amongst their army, urging them to come together, bellowing at stragglers to run to the quickly forming circle of fighters. There were only moments left for Beornoth and his riders to injure, maim or kill as many men as they could, and Beornoth rode Virtus hard to where Godric sat astride a huge black horse. Beornoth's stomach soured with bitter anger. The black horse had belonged to Ealdorman Byrhtnoth, and Godric had stolen it at the Battle of Maldon and used the ealdorman's horse to fool the fyrd into thinking it was their lord who urged them to flee the battle. Suddenly, in the shock and tumult of his attack, Beornoth found himself close to the treacherous thegn. His mounted attack had driven through the closest of Godric's army, washing over his men like a murderous tidal wave. Reifnir rode amongst a clutch of them, chopping down left and right with his spear whilst Ornir herded three men away from Godric's main force, using the threat of horse and blade to drive them like sheep onto the blades of Dolgfinnr's men.

The enemy gathered thicker as Beornoth rode closer to Godric; they became braver in numbers and a man lost his hand as he grabbed Virtus' bridle and Beornoth swung downward, and the edge of the king's sword cut through the wrist, bone and all, in one savage blow. The man spun away screaming and spraying dark, arterial blood onto his fellow fighters and Beornoth rode past them, so close to Godric now that he could hear him roaring at his men to strike Beornoth down.

'Traitor!' Beornoth bellowed, his bloody sword pointed at Godric. 'Coward!'

'Kill him,' Godric urged his men, and he pulled his golden-hilted sword free. Two men on big warhorses and armed in mail pushed their mounts forward to get between Beornoth and Godric, and Beornoth snarled as he pressed Virtus forward. He wanted to drive her into the two warriors, kill them, and then cut Godric down and leave him bleeding in the fields. If he could do that, then there would be no attack on Branoc's Tree, Byrhtnoth and the dead of Maldon would be avenged, and Byrhtnoth's daughter and her husband would inherit the shire. It would be so simple and could all be possible with one swing of Beornoth's sword. But for all that Beornoth loved Virtus, she did not have the savagery of a true warhorse and shied away from the bigger beasts, pulling up on stiff forelegs so that Beornoth was almost thrown from the saddle. He tightened his knees on instinct and rocked backwards, almost dropping his sword with the sudden stop in momentum. One of the mounted warriors grinned through a black, wild, tangled beard. He lunged forward with his spear, and it sliced past Beornoth's shoulder, so the man dragged it back and lunged again. Beornoth managed to bring his blade around in time to push the spear shaft towards him so that the point whipped between his shoulder and his helmet. Beornoth sliced the edge of his sword down the spear shaft, and it cut two of the man's fingers off so that black beard howled in pain and let go of his weapon. His warhorse snapped its teeth at Virtus, and Beornoth's horse's ears were pinned back, and her lips curled away from her teeth. The horse tensed, trembling beneath Beornoth. He tried to pull Virtus away, but two men on foot grabbed at her bridle and saddle with meaty hands and snarling faces. Beornoth kicked one of those men in the nose, and then turned Virtus so that her hindquarters forced the other man away.

'You should never have come here, Beornoth,' said Godric in his shrill whine. 'This is my shire now, and I will be ealdorman. have won, and your churlish bravery has lost. I will piss on your corpse and use your scalp for an arsewipe.'

'You'll be dead,' Beornoth yelled, and he swung wildly with his sword, suddenly aware that Godric's men swarmed about him, grabbing his legs and trying to hold on to his horse. Godric's brother Godwig was amongst them, urging them on towards the kill. 'I will kill you, traitor, and your corpse will burn in the fires of hell for eternity, you turd of a coward. I have come for you, and you will die.'

Something sharp dug into Beornoth's side, but his byrnie took the blow, and a brawny hand pulled at his right boot. Beornoth brought the pommel of his sword down on a man's head, and it cracked like an egg to send the man falling into the press of warriors about his horse. Men cried out, and Beornoth turned to see Vigdjarf and Anarr Holtaskalli hacking into the press of men with their axes and suddenly there was space and Beornoth drove Virtus free of his enemies.

'Away, away,' Thered shouted, whirling his sword about his head, and the riders peeled away from the attack like a flock of birds veering across the sky. To Beornoth's right, Bjarki, one of Vigdjarf's men, roared as Godric's men caught his horse and trapped him. Bjarki swung his axe to the left and right, blood flew, and enemies screamed, but he could not break free. One of Godric's warriors rode alongside Bjarki and plunged his sword into the Viking's neck. Bowstrings twanged and arrows flew from the main bulk of Godric's forces and Thered's horse took one in the flank, causing the beast to shift in pain.

'We must have killed a dozen or more,' called Reifnir, wide-eyed and spattered with crimson. Brand veered his horse towards where the three scouts ran across the hill beyond the wheat, their nakedness stark against the green grass. Brand hung low in the saddle, leaning with one hand on the pommel and one with his axe outstretched. The scouts screamed in terror, Brand swept his weapon, and a head flew into the air. Brand wheeled his horse around and ran down a second man who died weeping like a child as Brand hacked him to death. There was no honour in those deaths, no drengskapr as the Vikings called their warriors' code, but there was little point in saying that to Brand, for he was a vicious Viking in his war savagery and he would stab, slash, cut and kill any man who stood against him. His gods wanted him to do it, and he revelled in it, and they had stung Godric's pride and his army. Beornoth led them back to Branoc's Tree, to where he would make a stand even though he was outnumbered by over-whelming numbers. Beornoth felt no fear, his heart pounded, and he cast his eyes up to heaven and hoped that his dead blood brothers looked down upon him and rejoiced in the vengeance he wrought in their name. There would be a last stand now, at Beornoth's old burh. The place had seen so much death and suffering and would now surely see more. But no matter how many men died that day, Beornoth would kill Godric, even if he had to kill fifty men and wade through their blood to do it.

24

The first men appeared to the west of Branoc's Tree mid-afternoon, and Beornoth watched them from a section of the old fighting platform which had survived last summer's Viking ravages. He slaked his thirst with fresh milk from a wooden cup, and Beornoth rolled his stiff shoulder and stretched at his more recent wounds. The damage deep inside his belly scar stabbed as Beornoth arched his back, and he sighed as the first two enemy warriors crested the high ground. Another group quickly followed the two men until Godric's men were as thick in the fields as flies on shit. Others inside the fortification spotted the enemy. A murmur ran through the defenders like the sigh of the sea as the fight they had prepared for and worried about suddenly became real.

'Here they come. We should send the nuns away,' said Thered. He handed Beornoth a piece of cheese, which he ate hungrily.

'You can try if you like,' said Beornoth, 'but the abbess won't leave. She has a fiercer bite than Ornir's dog, that one. She's probably right, for where would they go? If Godric's men overwhelm us, there won't be a place safe for a group of undefended women within half a day's ride from here.'

'True. They can still throw rocks, I suppose. And pray to Christ for our victory.'

'Those women will defend the children as bravely as any warrior.'

'Can we win though, Beo? I wanted to lead my few remaining men north. I thought I was done with battle, that my sword was ready to leave its scabbard and take its place on display above my hearth. But once I saw the Lady Ælfflæd prepared to ride, and the steel in her eyes, I could not bring myself to do it.'

'One more fight, then, old friend. We will need your sword today, so I am glad that you decided to stay. We don't need to win, we just need to kill Godric. Once he dies, his men will melt away. We fight for vengeance, the honour of our slain friends, and to defend the nuns and orphans of this place from Godric's masterless men. They fight only for silver. Kill him and we can win.'

Thered nodded. He lifted his hand so that both men could see the scar on his palm, the cut which marked the oath taken in blood in a smoke-filled hall deep into the war with Olaf Tryggvason. Beornoth remembered that night as though it were yesterday, Aelfwine of Foxfield rousing Byrhtnoth's warriors into a war frenzy as they faced a terrifying enemy. Each man had made the cut across his palm and clasped the hands of his blood brothers of the sword as they swore to fight to the end. Which most of them had. 'Strange that you call me friend, given how we met.'

'You were an insolent pup, back then,' Beornoth said, smiling at the memory. 'When we came for you at Loidis, you were your father's son, belligerent and loyal only to York.'

'And you waded across the river at Loidis and gave me and my men a beating that hurt for a month.'

'Look at what you have become, Ealdorman Thered of Northumbria. A famous warrior, veteran of countless battles, and a noble lord.' Beornoth bowed his head in respect.

'Do you believe it was worth it?' asked Thered. He stared at a shifting cloud in the bright sky, watching as its shape changed forged and altered by the breeze. More of the enemy dotted the fields now, their weapons propped on their shoulders and shifting with their gait like a leafy bough in a gale.

'Do I believe what was worth it?'

'How hard we fought against the Vikings? All that we risked? The brothers we lost, the suffering and pain?'

'Of course it was worth it. We are thegns and warriors, and it is our duty to protect our lord and the people we are responsible for. If we had not fought as hard as we did, Olaf Tryggvason could be king here now and England a land under Norse rule. If we had not stopped them, how many more people would Skarde Wartooth, Ragnar the Flayer, the White Wolf, or any of the other Viking bastards we sent to the mud have killed? We are what we are so that we can protect the folk in our shires.'

'I sometimes wonder if the man who fishes the river or the churl who tills the earth cares if his lord is King Æthelred, Ealdorman Thered, or Olaf Tryggvason. He still must render up part of his catch, or part of his crop to his lord, so that great man can, in turn, feed his household and his warriors. What difference does it make to him who that lord is? What difference did the deaths of our brothers truly make?'

'We stopped Ragnar from peeling the skin from innocent Saxons, and before he could capture women and children and send them to the slave markets into a life of living hell. We stopped Skarde from burning and raping his way across England, and Olaf Tryggvason from unleashing his warriors upon our people until his reputation shone like gold and his ships were too heavy with Saxon silver to sail north. Sweyn Forkbeard would surely have set his gaze on the throne at Winchester if we had not fought him on that terrible riverbank. We made a difference, and we still do.'

'The Church and a divided kingdom ties our king in knots, so much so that we must fight the battles to keep his kingdom in order. You are a good man, Beo,' said Thered, and he smiled wanly. The scars across his nose, mouth and cheeks twisted his face and Beornoth saw the pain in the ealdorman of Northumbria's eyes. He suffered a living nightmare. The horrors of Maldon plagued his every moment. Beornoth understood that, and he felt some of that pain himself. He was just able to lock it away in a chest within his thought cage, though the dead and maimed rattled at the locks and tried to burst free to haunt him. Beornoth had no choice, and neither did Thered. They had to fight. They were oathsworn to do it, and Beornoth could not simply put down his vengeance like an old cloak. Much of what Thered said could be true, but Beornoth didn't have time to ponder the warp and weft of such deep thinking. He was a thegn, and he fought against anyone who brought violence to the people he was sworn to protect. The right or wrong of it was not his concern. Beornoth was certain that he had made a difference, that people had lived because he had risked his life and sent other men to hell with his sword.

'How can I help?' said Lady Ælfflæd, climbing up to the fighting platform and brushing a loose strand of hair behind her ear, the sleeves of her riding gown rolled up to the elbow.

'You have brought men, lady,' said Beornoth, 'that is enough.'

'Don't brush me off, Lord Beornoth. I know the face of war as well as you. I will find whatever cloth I can, and buckets of water. Send any injured men to the hall and I will treat their wounds. I might not be able to wield a sword, but I'll be damned to hell if I'll allow the cowardly cur who turned his back on my lord husband on the field of battle to win this day. Send your men to me and I will send them back to you to fight some more. Fight hard today, Beornoth, be the man my husband knew you to be. You are the Viking killer, the hero of Watchet, Rivers Bend and survivor of

Maldon. So, kill a traitor for me today so that my husband can rest in peace. He wants Godric's soul; Byrhtnoth twists and turns in his grave and he yearns for retribution against the oathbreaker. Soak the ground with traitors' blood and let us be avenged.' Lady Ælfflæd placed a wiry hand on each of Beornoth's shoulders and leaned into him. She fixed him with her pale blue eyes and there was a steel there that flowed through Beornoth's bones. 'Ealdorman Thered, we thank you for bringing your men south to Essex, and many of those brave warriors have already given their lives. The shire thanks you, and so do I. Be sure that you fight today on the side of God, that you wield your sword for justice and honour. You fight for the king, and for the people of England. This Godric is a foul beast, a man who swore an oath and turned his back when the need was greatest. When my daughter's husband is ealdorman here, Essex will always be a friend to Northumbria, and we shall respond to your call if it is ever required.'

Thered stood straighter, and he bowed to the Lady Ælfflæd. At the same moment, Godric's black horse pranced in the distance, and the sun flashed off his gold-hilted sword. Lifted by the Lady Ælfflæd's words, Beornoth pulled his own blade free of its scabbard, turned to face the folk who busied themselves inside the old burh.

'People of Branoc's Tree,' he called, and he levelled his sword and passed the blade slowly across the crowd of Saxon warriors, Vikings, fyrd men, nuns and orphaned children. 'We are all the children of this land. We are Saxon and Viking, two peoples who have learned to live as one in this fine and beautiful land. We are women of Christ and children of parents lost to the sword. We make a stand here today in the name of all who have given their lives for this country and our way of life. A traitor comes to take this place with violence, a man who swore an oath to the noble Ealdorman Byrhtnoth, and when his time came to fight the

Vikings, he turned and ran. He sees a shire weakened, its best and fiercest warriors slain by Sweyn Forkbeard and Olaf Tryggvason at the Battle of Maldon. There are men amongst you who followed Godric's retreat from the battlefield. Men of the fyrd, East Saxon men who Byrhtnoth supported with food in hard winters. Men whom he provided with grain when your crops failed, or the blight took your barley. How many of you looked to Byrhtnoth when you fell on hard times and received succour? He died for you, and the Vikings cut off his head and pissed on his dead corpse. They mocked and dishonoured the great man, and Godric sowed the seeds of that humiliation when he turned and ran from a battle in which he was oathsworn to fight. Godric eyes an opportunity to make himself ealdorman. He picks on the bones of the dead to enrich himself, and we are all that stands between Godric and his cunning plan. I am Beornoth, thegn, and I will bleed every drop of my blood to defend you this day. So, fight now with honour and the valour of East Saxons. Byrhtnoth looks down upon us, and I feel his strength in my sword arm. He sees your deeds, so repay your lord's kindness and bravery. Fight for him today and grant him vengeance with the blood of our enemies. There are Vikings amongst us who fight for reputation, warriors of the Danelaw. Odin looks upon you and respects your drengskapr. He sends you harminger, battle luck, and will glory in the cuts of your axes as so few stand against so many. Defenders of Branoc's Tree, warriors of England, are you ready to fight? Who is with me?'

Fists punched the air, weapons shook, eyes burned wide with fury, and every person inside the hastily constructed defences roared their defiance. Beornoth held his sword aloft, and they cheered even louder.

'For God and Ealdorman Byrhtnoth!' he bellowed, and they sent up a cheer which Beornoth hoped would chill Godric to the bone. Beornoth closed his eyes, and he conjured the faces of

Wulfhere, Leofsunu of Sturmer, Aelfwine of Foxfield, Offa,
Wighelm and Wiglaf and all who had died because Godric turned
his cloak when he was needed most.

Beornoth looked upon the new defences. On the freshly sharp-
ened stakes they had sunk into the ground to make a new wall, the
rocks and timber spears, and the holes they had dug to trap
Godric's warriors. He hoped it would be enough, and he cast his
eyes to heaven and whispered a prayer to Christ, and to his dead
friends, he asked for them to grant him the strength he needed to
fight, to endure the axes, swords, spears and cudgels men brought
to hack and cut at him. Beornoth closed his eyes and sucked in a
deep breath of East Saxon air, and he prayed that his battered,
scarred body would hold up for one more fight, one last clash of
arms to wreak vengeance for the men he had loved like brothers.

'A fine speech,' said Vigdjarf, lumbering up the steps to the
fighting platform. Brand trailed behind him whilst the folk below
hurried to complete their preparations. Sefna and Hrist took up
positions on the hall roof with sheaves of the arrows they had
worked through the night to trim and fletch. The geese of Branoc's
Tree had been plucked almost bald to provide their feathers, and
when those were gone they had plucked the chickens. The
orphans gathered a dozen horses behind the main hall, and the
rest were driven away across the fields. Beornoth ordered some be
kept in case all was lost, so that Lady Ælfflæd and the nuns could
escape with an orphan in their lap, for Beornoth doubted Godric
would stop his men from ravaging any woman found alive inside
the defences.

'Here comes the traitor,' said Lady Ælfflæd. Godric rode
towards Branoc's Tree trailed by his hearth troop in their shining
mail and tall spears. His men trailed behind him, their numbers
spreading out to encircle Branoc's Tree.

'Let's see what he has to say,' said Beornoth. 'Make ready and push the warriors out to the old walls.' Vigdjarf and Brand nodded their understanding and went to make the defenders ready. Beornoth stood at the old, high palisade with Lady Ælfflæd, and from that side Godric would not notice that they had constructed a new wall inside the old fortifications. He would see one side of the burh scorched but still standing with Beornoth and Ælfflæd on its top, and then a ring of burned and collapsed fortifications which his men could probe and swarm with their greater numbers.

'Lord Godric,' Lady Ælfflæd said when he was close enough to hear. 'Why have you assembled so many men? Do you come to do harm to the folk of Essex?'

'Lady Ælfflæd,' Godric said, reining his horse in. There was no disguising the surprise in his voice as he saw Byrhtnoth's widow on the walls. 'There are brigands behind those walls, and I come to restore order to the shire. I am surprised to see you standing with Beornoth, who is not even a man born of this shire. He is a known killer, and I will bring him to justice.'

'It is you who breaks the king's peace.' She pointed down at him. 'My lord husband is still warm in the ground, and you seek to usurp his title? Riding here on my husband's horse, do you have no shame? Your father was a great man, and how could the apple have fallen so far from the tree?'

Godric stiffened at the accusation. 'Beornoth, throw down your weapons and surrender to me, or every soul inside those walls will suffer for it. I give you my word that no quarter will be offered to any who fight against me today.'

'Your word?' said Lady Ælfflæd. 'Is that word the same as the oath you swore to fight and die for my husband?'

'You have my terms.'

'We can settle this now, you and I,' Beornoth said, and he rested his sword across his shoulder. 'I, Beornoth, king's thegn, and I outrank you here, Godric of Essex. As did Hrodgar, who you sent a child to kill. An innocent boy whom you corrupted and turned into a murderer. Hell beckons to you, Godric-traitor, its mouth gapes and yawns to suck you into the fires for eternity. Remove your men from the field and we shall pardon them. But you and I will fight, and one of us will die. We can settle this without further bloodshed. I only come for your head, and for your traitor's soul.'

'Why would I fight you when I have more men? I will enjoy watching you die, Beornoth. You are a fool with your belligerent talk of combat and honour. Always you tried to belittle me, thinking yourself the great warrior and sucking up all the glory, leaving none for the rest of us who fought just as bravely as you. You are no king's thegn; this was your heriot, and you lost it. You are nothing, a man of nowhere with no lord. A masterless man worth less than a sliver of wet pig shit.'

'Come and die, then,' said Beornoth. He raised his sword to his lips and kissed the cold blade, and Godric rode back to his men. They spread around Branoc's Tree with leering faces, weapons clutched in dirty fists, hungry for murder and plunder. But Beornoth was ready, and if this was to be his last battle, then he would die with honour.

25

Beornoth left the fighting platform and strode amongst the defenders. He clasped wrists with the fyrd men who had come to reclaim their honour and with the Vikings, who would stand and fight to defend a scrap of Essex with their lives. Lady Ælfflæd, Abbess Agatha and the nuns ushered the orphans inside Beornoth's old hall. The lady had them gather as much cloth or wool as they could find, and the abbess boiled water in a cauldron over the hall hearth. They made ready to treat the injured, and Beornoth touched a hand to his own scars, hoping to God that he wouldn't be one of the men writhing in pain in the floor rushes as the nuns staunched his wounds. For men would die today, women too, perhaps, and that thought led Beornoth to the outskirts of the fortification. He checked the piles of rocks and wooden spears and was careful not to tread on the branch-marked pits. The defenders followed him, the chink of chain mail and the creak of leather and the heavy footsteps of boots loud as they gathered around Beornoth in the moments before the fight.

'Take the north outer wall,' Beornoth said to Thered, and the ealdorman took his own warriors, and ten of the men the lady had

brought from Rettendon. They went armed with shields and
spears and would hold that side of the burh for as long as they
could. 'Dolgfinnr and Vigdjarf, take the south.' The Vikings took
their warriors with their sharp axes and long beards, and as they
marched, they sang a battle hymn to Odin in Norse, a song of great
heroes and brave warriors sailing across wild seas. Hrist and Sefna,
along with Dudda and his long war bow, waited on the hall roof,
strings hooked on to the horn nocks at either end of their staves.

Beornoth took the eastern defences, and he stood within a hole
in the old palisade, where the defenders had removed an entire
section of wall and cut into the shorter timbers which now formed
the inner wall. Beornoth stood tall and broad-shouldered in that
space. He wore his helmet, his byrnie coat of chain mail and
carried a heavy shield ringed and bossed with iron. Beornoth wore
the king's sword belted at his waist and his seax rested in its sheath,
which hung at the small of his back. He held an aesc spear, and he
stood high and proud. Beornoth stared at Godric's army, and he
wanted them to know they faced a lord of war.

'Bastards are drinking themselves stupid,' said Brand. Sefna
had braided his golden beard into a rope which hung over his
byrnie, and he had left his long hair loose about his shoulders.
Brand held a shield in his left hand and his Viking axe in his right.

'They seek the courage to fight in the bottom of ale skins. Let
them come to us drunk. It makes them easier to kill,' said
Beornoth. Godric had stayed on the western side of Branoc's Tree
with his hearth troop, and Beornoth had put most of the fyrd men
on that side of the wall where the palisade's inner fighting plat-
form would allow them to defend the wall easily against any
attack. Godric and his men remained mounted, and Beornoth
thought the traitor would ride around the defences and look for a
weak point, and then drive his hearth troop, and the few thegns
who had rallied to his cause, into that gap like rats. They were

Godric's best troops, his true warriors, and Godric would depend on them to carry the day. Just as Beornoth knew that Godric's death would end the battle, so Godric would assume that Beornoth's death would cause the defenders to panic and crumble.

'There's that big, toothless bastard,' said Brand, and he pointed his axe to where a colossal figure stalked amongst Godric's war band. It was Ansgar the Giant, unmistakable as he towered over the rest of the attackers, hulking and lumbering amongst them. He carried two axes, one in each fist, just as he had at Hareswood, and Beornoth shuddered at the thought of fighting that monster again.

Godric's men drank and shouted insults. They huddled in small bands and urged each other forward. A pack would dash forwards and then halt, waving their weapons and roaring at the burh, but would then shrink away as none could find the courage to attack the walls. It was no easy thing to risk one's life, knowing that sharp blades awaited. To risk death, or perhaps worse, to suffer the terrible wound that does not kill. To lose an arm, a leg, or to be blinded. Such a man might live after weeks of mind-bending pain and infection, only to spend the rest of his life as a beggar, reliant on the kindness and charity of others for food and shelter. That was the fate the men in Godric's army faced, and they saw Beornoth and knew of his reputation and they would not come.

The afternoon drew on with no attack, and the abbess and her nuns went amongst the defenders with ale, water, cheese and honey. Beornoth and Brand ate together and leaned against the broken wall. The afternoon drew on, and still the enemy could not find the will to attack.

'Here we go,' said Brand. Godric rode amongst his warriors, prancing on his black horse, and he shouted at them, waving his hands and pointing at Branoc's Tree. The giant strode forwards, pushing and dragging at those around him, and a line of men went

reluctantly with him. It was not a solid line of warriors with inter
locked shields like Beornoth would expect to see on a battlefield
but a ragged line of men with squinting eyes, grizzled beards and
crooked grins. These were the bravest of Godric's band of killers
and thieves, and the giant roared at their centre, waving his two
axes and urging them to bravery. The rest came behind, the not so
brave, the ones who would hang back until there was an opportu-
nity to strike a blow against an injured man, or until the defences
broke and they could run into the burh and kill the meek or
ransack buildings for plunder.

Godric rode around the walls to the south, to urge his men on
that side to attack at the same time. A concerted attack on each
side of the fort would allow Godric to stretch the defenders and
make the best use of his far greater numbers. Beornoth was ready
for them. The weight of his shield was comforting, and he closed
his eyes for a moment. He remembered his dead daughters and the
sight of his beloved Eawynn, brutalised and lying with her throat
cut on a day when violence had come to his home, and he had not
been there to defend them. That made his chest heave, and his
teeth grind in anger, cheek muscles working beneath his beard.
Hate and anger fuelled a warrior. They were what gave a man the
savagery and cruelty he needed to kill, stab and slaughter other
men. Beornoth let his memories wander to Maldon then, to his
dead friends and their rotting heads outside Olaf Tryggvason's
camp. That set a fire in his belly and Beornoth's eyes popped open.
He bared his teeth and raised his spear and bellowed like a
madman. The men behind him took up that call, and it spread
around the walls of Branoc's Tree like a brush fire, igniting the
defenders and stoking their hearts to courage.

Beornoth could not contain himself. The longing for revenge
had burned him inside for so long that finally having an enemy in
front of him to fight was a relief, like a dammed stream being let

loose to flood a dry riverbed. Then, Beornoth did what he shouldn't have. He strode out from the defences, leaving his men behind him. Brand shouted at him to get back, but the sound was like a voice heard underwater, drowned out by Beornoth's war fury. Beornoth was shouting the names of his dead friends, and spittle flew from his mouth like a madman. He was a huge warrior clad in chain mail and armed for war, and he begged for his enemies to come and die. The plan was to hold the outer walls for as long as possible, to hammer the enemy with rocks and then retreat ten paces and do it again. But Beornoth could not wait for that. He wanted to kill and hurt Godric's men, and he went to do it.

The enemy saw a man alone, striding towards their greater numbers as though he wished for death. Godric's men found courage together against a single man, and six of them ran at him, waving wooden clubs, axes and spears. Beornoth threw his spear at the biggest man, and the weapon slammed into his stomach, throwing him backwards with an ear-splitting cry. The others slowed then, shocked at Beornoth's monstrous strength, and he laughed as he gripped his sword and ripped it free. The blade sang through the air, its steel shone bright and deadly, and it was glorious. Beornoth threw his head back and laughed like a drunk in a tavern, and he slammed his shield into a man who came at full tilt with his axe held above his head. The shield crushed the little man, the iron boss snapping his collarbone and forearm as though they were dry branches. The man screamed and Beornoth kept his shield moving, letting it swing upwards, and he drove it forwards, punching the iron rim into the face of the next man. That man died instantly, his head thrust backwards so violently that skull separated from spine, and as he crumpled to the ground Beornoth stamped on his dead face with the heel of his boot.

Beornoth let a wooden club hit him in the chest, strangely enjoying the dull pain and force of the blow. He raised his sword

and ripped out the club-wielding attacker's guts and kicked him
into the rest of the attackers. They leapt back from his ferocious
and terrible violence, but Beornoth swung his sword and took a
man's eyes in a spray of bright blood. Brand appeared beside him,
shoving the attackers back with his shield and urging Beornoth to
pull back to the wall. He did so but kept his front to the enemy and
raised his bloody shield and sword to show Godric's men what
awaited them on the walls of Branoc's Tree.

'You're a bloody fool,' said Brand.

'Kill them all,' Beornoth roared, maddened, and lifted into a
higher level of consciousness, his senses heightened by the risk of
death and the suffering of his enemies.

The giant pushed his men forwards, eyes fixed on Beornoth
but possessing the sense to hold back and wait for the first men to
suffer under the defenders' missiles. A rock thrown from the walls
crushed an attacker's nose, and the masterless men roared in anger
as more rocks rained down upon them, hurting some, but many
missing their target to fall harmlessly to the ground. The enemy
clambered up what was once a deep ditch before the palisade, but
in most places the collapse of the bank and wall had filled it in so
that they came on fast and leering. They scrambled up and the first
of the attackers died, screaming in agony as Brand's axe and
Beornoth's sword tore at their flesh and bones.

'Fall back,' Beornoth ordered, and drove a snarling man back-
wards with his sword. 'Fall back to the first marker.' There were too
many of Godric's men for the defenders to hold, but Beornoth had
expected that. He snapped himself out of the fog of fury and he
and Brand stood in front of the fyrd men as they backed away from
Godric's fighters, who slunk through the gaps in the old walls like
monsters from a nightmare, with yellowed teeth and hungry eyes.

An arrow whistled above the heads of the first line of Godric's
men, and Beornoth raised his shield. The arrowhead tonked off

the boss and spun into the air like a crazed bird. More arrows soared over the attackers, and three of Beornoth's defenders cried out in pain. The sounds of battle rang out now from every side of the burh. Godric's men had found their will to attack, and Branoc's Tree was suddenly a pulsing mass of striking weapons, blood and the desperate fight for survival.

Brand tore out the throat of a bald man with a stroke of his axe, and the attackers pushed back as that man fell into them, spraying dark, iron-stinking blood across their faces and chests.

'Now!' Beornoth called, and the defenders unleashed more rocks, thrown from the piles set at this point in the defences. Four wooden spears flew across the space between attackers and defenders, one hit a man in the thigh and the rest fell amongst his comrades. Ansgar batted another spear away contemptuously with his axe and the other two missed their mark. The attackers raised their arms to defend themselves as hard rocks cracked their skulls and bruised their bodies. Yet more of Godric's men came on until Beornoth could see nothing but hate-twisted faces and sharp iron coming towards him.

'So many,' said Brand, heaving them back with his shield. 'We must fall back again.'

'Back,' Beornoth ordered, and the defenders shifted back another ten paces. Beornoth was careful to leap over a pit covered with leafy branches. The attackers came on, sensing victory in the defenders' retreat. Beornoth stopped them at the next marker, and the front line of attackers stepped onto the carefully placed boughs and cried out as they fell into the pits dug deep into the earth. The fyrd men pelted rocks at Godric's men as they tried to climb out of the pits, and Beornoth lunged forward to stab his sword through the chest of a one-eyed man who fell back to die in his already dug grave.

Yet more of the enemy came on, and Ansgar the Giant struck at the fyrd men with his axes. He chopped and hacked into two, carving terrible wounds that made the rest of the men about Beornoth gasp and leap away in fear. Ansgar cracked bones and split bodies so that dark blood and bluish-purple innards slopped onto the floor. Beornoth tried to get to the huge attacker, but the press of Godric's men shoved him backwards. He pushed back, a wash of stale ale and old mutton breath washing across his shield. The enemy surged at him, their sheer numbers driving Beornoth backwards. He dug his heels into the earth and heaved back at them, the heat of fear suddenly flushing his face. If Godric's men kept up that pressure, then the defenders would retreat inside the walls at an all-out run, and the attackers would pour in after them and all would be lost. Branoc's Tree would be overrun, and the fight would descend in a series of single-combat fights until the defenders were finally overwhelmed.

Beornoth struck with his sword below his shield, slicing the edge across the shins of two men who opposed him. They fell away, and he stepped forward, making a space he could fight in. Brand came alongside Beornoth, and they overlapped their shields and struck around the linden wood, and Godric's cut-throats leapt away from their war skill. A great roar went up, like a bull bellowing on a high mountainside, and Ansgar crashed into the shields at a dead run. His bulk smashed Beornoth and Brand backwards, and Beornoth almost fell under the crushing weight of the attack. He lashed out with his sword, but a small man who grabbed Beornoth around the waist fouled the blow. Grasping hands grabbed his sword arm and Beornoth bucked and struggled to stay on his feet because to fall was to die. Brand came at them; his axe chopped into the arm holding Beornoth and his shield rim crushed the skull of the man who gripped Beornoth's waist. The fight had become desperate. Men slipped in the blood of the dead and wounded, and others screamed at the horror of their injuries.

The giant urged his men on towards the inner fortifications, glimpsing his chance to claim victory for his lord.

'Back to the new walls,' Beornoth ordered, and those around him fled towards the new fortification. Brand turned and waved his axe towards the inside of the burh, and one man who heaved at Beornoth's shield died with a goose-feathered arrow in his eye. Another took an arrow in the shoulders, and then Dudda must have loosed from his stag killer, because one of Godric's fighters was hit by an arrow that flung him backwards as though he were made of wool. The attackers fell back from the archers' wrath, and even Ansgar paused, his ugly face spattered with crimson and his ratty beard matted with other men's blood. The man beside Ansgar took one of Dudda's arrows in his knee, and the bottom half of his leg shattered as though it was made of clay. They fell back like a seething horde, baying and snarling at Beornoth and Brand.

Beornoth dragged the makeshift gate they had made from brambles and thorns across the entrance to the new walls, and then he dropped his shield to grab his knees, sucking big mouthfuls of air, muscles burning from the fight.

'There's so many of the bastards,' said Brand. He stalked before the walls, peering over the new sharpened stakes which came to chest height. The enemy huddled there, snarling and wary. Any time they pushed forwards, Sefna, Hrist or Dudda would sink an arrow into a man and the rest would fall back, wary of the iron-tipped missiles.

'I have to kill Godric,' was all Beornoth could say. He stood and peered over the heads of the enemy, but could see no sign of Godric and his black horse.

'Beornoth, Brand,' came a woman's voice, shouting from above. Beornoth looked up to see Sefna waving at him from the hall roof. She waved her bow, and once she knew the two warriors saw her, she pointed her bow at each side of the burh, where the battle unfolded in a similar vein to the fight on Beornoth's side. The defenders fell back, overwhelmed. Vigdjarf waved his small band of fighters back, and his byrnie was torn and bloody at the shoulder. Reifnir and his men had already taken up a position on the inside of the new wall. Bodil Balti was hard-pressed, swinging his mighty war hammer over the newly carved timbers, and the attackers shrank back from deadly arcs.

Men limped and were carried towards the hall, and Abbess Agatha caught Beornoth's eye as she helped carry a fyrd man with a wounded leg. Her clothes were stained with blood, and she held Beornoth's gaze for a moment, nodding in recognition that a fierce battle raged both outside and within Branoc's Tree.

'We can't hold the entire wall,' said Thered, running to Beornoth. His sword dripped black gore and his scarred face was taut. 'We might have to make a stand before the hall.'

'We'll hold them as long as we can,' said Beornoth. 'We just need to hold long enough for Godric himself to come close, and then whichever of us comes within striking distance must kill the bastard and send his soul to hell.'

26

Blood dripped down golden timber as men fought and died across the newly carved palisade stakes. Godric appeared again. He rode behind his warriors, urging them on to kill Beornoth and Thered, shouting that there were Vikings inside the burh and that any man who brought him Beornoth's head would receive its weight in silver. There were no more rocks to throw, and no more wood spears to cast. The defenders fought across the chest-high palisade with whatever weapons they had brought to the fight, which meant the warriors amongst them wielded swords and axes, but the fyrd men swung wood axes, mattocks and reaping hooks to cut at the mass of enemy fighters.

The enemy grew wiser. Godric rode around the walls, directing his forces with his golden sword. They fell back where they found Beornoth, Brand, Thered, or a Viking blade behind the palisade, and instead pressed their numbers where they found a defender clad in a simple jerkin and with only a farming tool to defend himself. More than once, the enemy breached the walls, and ale-stinking men burst through into the main courtyard before the hall. Beornoth would surge to that point with Brand, or Vigdjarf or

Dolgfinnr, and they would beat the enemy back with shields, axe
and swords. The afternoon waned, and if the Viking gods watched
that fight, they would have seen more than enough bravery to spur
Odin's Valkyrie to carry the dead Vikings' souls to Valhalla. Reifnir
and Dolgfinnr both lost men, and two of Vigdjarf's warriors lay
slumped inside the hall, where the Lady Ælfflæd and the abbess
treated their wounds. Beornoth wiped the sweat from his eyes, and
he thought God must have turned his eyes away from Branoc's
Tree; there were holy nuns inside the hall, and small children who
needed his protection, but the Almighty did not send aid and
Godric's men kept up their relentless attack.

A pull on his shoulder turned Beornoth to his left, where
Brand pointed his axe to a struggle on the northern wall. The
fighting had grown fiercer there, where Wuffa and the Lady
Ælfflæd's warriors were hard-pressed by Godric's hearth troop who
hacked across the walls from horseback. Dudda loosed one of his
mighty arrows from the hall roof, and it snatched a byrnie-clad
warrior from the saddle, but more of Godric's warriors replaced
him, heaving and hacking at the walls. Beornoth and Brand ran to
that section of wall, and Dolgfinnr joined them, as did Thered and
Anarr Holtaskalli.

'Let us through,' Thered called, pulling at the fyrd men in front
of them to make way. The new palisade creaked and there was a
loud crack, like the sound of a mighty tree trunk creaking and
snapping, and an entire length of the new palisade collapsed. A
horse fell with it, the whites of its eyes wide and its teeth bared in
terror. The defenders groaned with fear and fell back before the
gaping hole in their defences, pushing Beornoth backwards, and
Godric's men poured in through the broken stakes, weapons
flashing and faces snarling.

Beornoth took a blow on his shield, and another on his helmet
and it rang his head like a bell. Darkness took him, and he dragged

the helmet off to help clear his vision. Thered killed a man with a sword cut to the belly, and Anarr Holtaskalli fell as three of Godric's men hacked him to death with seaxes. Then, the sound of thunder rumbled across the field of battle, and Beornoth felt the ground beneath his feet shake and tremble. The blow had fogged his head, but Beornoth turned, and just dove out of the way as the herd horses the defenders had kept inside the inner burh came charging towards the gap. Hrist led them and Vigdjarf's daughter rode the first horse in the galloping herd. She swung her axe like one of Odin's Valkyrie and she wrought chaos inside Branoc's Tree.

The charging horses split the attacking force, and their sheer size and power forced Godric's men away from the breach as the horses squeezed and pushed through it. Beornoth roared in delight at Hrist's cunning bravery, and he drove into the enemy, clubbing at them with his shield and stabbing with his sword.

A cry of sorrow, harrowing and blood-curdling enough to dim the sun, tore through the battle, and Vigdjarf, a Viking warrior and loving father, sank to his knees and tore at his own beard. Ansgar had dragged Hrist from the saddle, and as she dropped to the horse-churned ground, the giant chopped one of his axes into her skull, killing Hrist instantly. Vigdjarf howled and surged to his feet. He charged the giant and swung his axe, but Vigdjarf attacked with grief-fuelled anger and Ansgar easily parried the blow. Time slowed, and Beornoth could not move fast enough to get to Vigdjarf's aid. Ansgar's axe tore Vigdjarf's chest open in a wash of blood so he dropped dead next to his daughter, and just as the horse charge seemed to have driven the attackers into chaos, the giant brought them back within a hair's breadth of victory. The sheer brutal horror of Hrist and Vigdjarf's deaths sent the defenders reeling, and they fell back from Hrist's mangled skull and Vigdjarf's terrible wound. Blood soaked the ground and men turned away from the terrible wounds.

Sefna screamed with sorrow and leapt down from the hall roof. She rolled and came up with an arrow nocked to her bow and loosed it at Ansgar. The shaft took him in the arm, and he snarled at her, but the giant kept on coming. Beornoth moved to get between Ansgar and Sefna, but the Lady Ælfflæd shouted his name from the hall. He paused, unsure what to do or where he was needed most. Dolgfinnr rushed past him, and Thered fought like a lord of war, striking at the enemy with his sword, so Beornoth turned and dashed towards the hall. Some of Godric's men had climbed up on the roof and torn at the earth covering. They dropped into the hall's main chamber and were amongst the wounded and the vulnerable.

'They are inside,' Lady Ælfflæd cried out above the carnage. 'Help the nuns.'

Beornoth nodded and surged past her. He ducked under the door lintel and into the inside gloom. Beornoth ran to where a pair of legs dangled through a hole in the roof and he stabbed upwards into the man's groin and blood splattered onto the hard-packed earthen floor. There were already four men inside the hall. One had a nun pinned to the ground, and the others hungrily searched tables and furniture for treasure. Beornoth swung his shield into the man who knelt over the nun, and as he rolled away, Beornoth stabbed down with his sword and opened the man's throat. He helped the nun to her feet and Abbess Agatha led a gaggle of orphans outside of the hall. Godric's men had scattered the flaming logs from the hearth, and the fire filled the hall with smoke.

Beornoth followed them outside, and the fight had turned against the defenders. They fought ten paces in front of the hall doors; a few exhausted survivors held back hundreds of Godric's men. He sagged, because it seemed in that moment that victory had slipped away and that his dead blood brothers would go unavenged. All the fight seeped away from him, and Beornoth suddenly felt old again. His scarred wounds ached, and he wondered what a fool he had been to let Godric trap him inside the ruined walls of Branoc's Tree. There seemed no way to win. He could not fight through hundreds of Godric's warriors to kill the traitor.

The children screamed and wept as they witnessed cruel-faced men cutting and slashing at one another. Reifnir stood before the crying children, and he fought alone against five of Godric's warriors. Reifnir stood with an axe in his right hand and a knife in his left, and the children cowered behind him. The Viking chanted a battle prayer to Odin, and he killed two of the enemy before a club struck him in his face. Reifnir fell to one knee and chopped his axe into the club-wielding man's guts. A seax stabbed Reifnir in the chest and he roared to Odin, so loud that it woke Beornoth from his defeated stupor. Reifnir rose, and a knife ripped his arm open so that he dropped his axe. He killed that man with his knife and then a spear opened Reifnir's shoulder like a side of beef. Reifnir clawed at them with his fingernails and beat at them with his fist, and he gave his life to protect those small children. Beornoth ran to him and put his shoulder behind his shield, driving the bastards away from Reifnir, who fell to the earth, bleeding from his many wounds. But the Viking was smiling through bloody teeth and his hand searched the ground and his bloody fingers curled around the haft of his fallen axe. He had found redemption for his past sins in the slaughter at Branoc's Tree, and though his son Ornir howled like a wounded wolf at the death of his father, Reifnir soared to take his place amongst Odin's einherjar.

'It's not over,' Beornoth growled. Reifnir's heroism brought him back to the fight like a slap across the face. And he drove the enemy back with sword and shield. Bodil Balti crushed a man's head with his war hammer and one of Godric's mailed warriors ran him through with a sword. Beornoth charged that warrior and he died with Beornoth's sword in his armpit. Bodil died and joined the slashed and torn corpses who dunged the earth with their lifeblood. A snarling face appeared before Beornoth, a man in a shining byrnie who swung a sword. Beornoth parried the blow and he roared in triumph because the man who attacked him was Godric's brother Godwig, one of the thegns who had led the retreat at Maldon. Godwig spat at Beornoth, his teeth bared in hate and desperation. He stabbed at Beornoth's midriff and Beornoth sidestepped the attack and punched the hilt of his sword into Godwig's face. The hard iron crushed the small bones in Godwig's nose, and he shuddered and gasped in pain. Beornoth kicked Godwig in the groin and, as the thegn doubled over, Beornoth placed his sword on Godwig's neck.

'Die, traitor,' Beornoth growled, and he cut Godwig's throat with a slice of his sharp sword.

Sefna fought with her axe, and tears streamed down her face. She tried to cut her way to Ansgar, who had killed her father and sister, and the giant turned to her, shoving his own men out of the way to meet her challenge. She swung at him, but the giant caught her wrist and kicked her savagely to the ground. Beornoth tried to reach her, but there were too many of the enemy in his path, and his heart leapt with fearful terror as Ansgar's axe rose high above the melee. The blade arced towards Sefna, and it would surely have taken her life, but Brand hurtled through the press of battle like a demon and he caught the giant's axe blow on his shield. The blade hit Brand's shield boss, and it rang out like a church bell above the din of battle. Sefna lay stricken on the battlefield and Brand stood between the woman he loved and the fearsome giant. Brand swayed on the balls of his feet, crouched low like an animal with his axe poised to strike, facing the enormous, baleful killer.

Ansgar waved his two axes in the air like a maddened bull, and Brand set himself, one foot behind the other, axe and shield ready. Ansgar swung an axe with enough force to carve a man in two, but Brand was snake-fast, and he darted under the blow. He cut his own axe across the giant's thigh and punched his shield into the big man's belly. Ansgar hacked an axe into Brand's shield, but Brand let go of the handle and whipped a knife from his belt. He leapt into the air and stabbed the roaring giant in the eye and jumped back as Ansgar flailed. The giant had one axe trapped in Brand's shield, which dangled from its blade, and the other swung wildly as he howled in pain, the hilt of a knife embedded into his skull. Ansgar's mouth gaped like a dark cave, a toothless maw, and Brand snaked forwards and sliced his axe blade across the giant's throat. Ansgar fell to his knees and Brand cut the giant's head free with two chops of his axe. The attackers fell back at the shock of seeing their monstrous champion fall, and Brand picked up the head by its hair and held it aloft for all to see.

The severed head worked like evil war-seiðr. Brand swung it at Godric's men, and they baulked at the gore-dripping horror of it. They fell back and, sensing the collapse of his army with the fall of his champion, Godric appeared, roaring at his men from the back of his black horse. Godric's panicked eyes came to rest on Beornoth, and the treacherous thegn came on, seeing his chance to kill Beornoth and win for himself a shire. Godric had no choice. He had risked so much in his grasp for power and had spilled so much blood at the altar of his ambition. Just kill an old thegn and his path would be clear to become an ealdorman. So, Godric charged, and Beornoth threw his shield. He took two great steps and twisted at the hip, putting all of his strength into the swing. His shield spun through the air, the linden wood and iron arcing across the fallen warriors like a swooping falcon. Godric shrieked as the shield hit him. The force of the throw and the weight of the shield thrust him from the saddle to land amongst his men.

Beornoth dropped to one knee as pain stabbed through his stomach like a hot knife. It was as though throwing the shield had torn open his wound from Maldon and he gasped at the sharpness of it. Beornoth clasped his left hand to his belly but could feel no blood from the old wound. The damage was inside of him. He tried to rise but retched as the pain increased beyond anything he had felt before. His body wanted to curl up and cradle the wound, but Beornoth had to stand and fight. He vomited as he forced himself to stand, and just as the injury was about to overwhelm him, two of the orphans caught Beornoth's eye. Two small girls with long hair and beautiful eyes. Lady Ælfflæd gathered them to her breast and she and Abbess Agatha fought to get the children away from the violence. The two innocent orphans reminded Beornoth of his own girls, Ashwig and Cwen, long dead to Viking blades. Beornoth gripped his sword tight and pulled his seax free from the sheath at his back. He coughed and blood spattered his byrnie, but Beornoth forced the pain away, pushing it down, allowing his overwhelming need for vengeance to eat his pain like a ravenous monster.

'Byrhtnoth, Wulfhere, Leofsunu, and Aelfwine,' he whispered, mastering his suffering and striding to where Godric was amongst his men. Thered and Dolgfinnr drove Godric's men back, and they ran in terror from the grizzly head in Brand's fist. Ornir Hauknefr killed a man with an axe to the chest, and his hunting dog tore out the falling man's throat, and that was enough. Godric's men were not seasoned warriors oathsworn to die for their lord, and though they still possessed the greater numbers, they ran away like the cut-throats and masterless men they were. First two men ran, pushing through the others, calling for an end to the slaughter, then the rest followed like water retreating on the ebb tide. Godric had scrambled to his feet, and he screamed at them to stand. He promised them the world and all the silver in Essex. Godric's face became twisted and glowed red, and his golden sword swung about his head as though to rally his troops. But they fled from the blood and pain, from the screams of the wounded and the severed head and torn-out throat.

Godric turned and shuddered as Beornoth advanced on him. His mouth flapped as he searched for words that would not come. Beornoth limped, each step like a spear point jabbing at his innards and he had to clutch his left elbow against the Maldon wound to cope with the pain. Godric searched about him, but his ragged army of masterless men were gone, leaving him to face the survivors of Beornoth's defenders. He licked at dry lips and held his sword out to Beornoth, and the blade trembled in his hand. Godric's eyes filled with tears as he realised his dream of power was dead. He glanced at his dead brother's corpse and winced, and then he lunged at Beornoth, all hate and malice in the blow. But it was weak and clumsy and Beornoth hammered it aside easily with his sword. The golden-hilted blade fell from Godric's hand, and he covered his face with his hands, stricken with terror and unable to look up into Beornoth's wrathful face.

The fight fled from Beornoth at that moment. His warpath of vengeance was complete. He had avenged the slain of Maldon. Traitors were dead, and Byrhtnoth was at peace at Ely. Godric's men had deserted him, just as Godric had led the rout at Maldon.

'Kill him,' Beornoth said simply, and he turned his back as his surviving fyrd men fell upon Godric like animals. They hacked and stabbed at Godric with their scythes and mattocks, battering and roaring at him, cursing him for the shame he had hung about their necks in the retreat from Maldon. Their blades rang against the links of his byrnie and chopped into his traitor's flesh. Godric died screaming like a dog.

Beornoth fell to his knees and sighed. He coughed and tasted blood in his mouth, the iron of it bitter and thick on his tongue. So many had died, but it was finally over. He glanced across the mass of writhing, injured warriors and the still corpses and his eyes met Thered's. They shared a look, an understanding that they had wrought vengeance for their dead blood brothers. Thered nodded his face pale and drawn and the horrors of war as scarred on his mind as they were on his face and body. The Lady Ælfflæd ran to Beornoth and helped him stand; she spoke but he could not hear her words. Beornoth thought only of Eawynn and of peace, and an end to his days of blood and vengeance, at last.

It rained for two days after the battle at Branoc's Tree. A hard summer rain which pounded the earth with enough water to wash the blood from the ground and send it drifting away in pale crimson rivulets. On the third day, thick, grey, malevolent clouds gave way to a shy sun which peeped from the gloom to cast a warm golden glow on the fields. Long golden beams of light shone on the wheat and barley fields through which Godric's army had marched and then fled.

'So, you will stay in Northumbria?' said Beornoth. He shifted his position slightly in the saddle to relieve the pressure of the wrappings around his midriff. Virtus whinnied, and Beornoth stroked her neck. Abbess Agatha had bound his injured stomach herself, with a poultice of honey and herbs, and he had left Branoc's Tree in her capable hands. The wound still pulsed and throbbed, and all the places on Beornoth's body where blades had cut and stabbed over the years had made their presence known in the battle's aftermath. Beornoth felt twice his age, and his body was a stiff, groaning thing, like a leather boot which has seen too much use and its stitching has frayed away at the seams. The abbess would continue to rebuild and turn the burh into a holy place of kindness for those who needed it most. That seemed fitting, for all the suffering the burh had seen.

'Thered says he will make me a thegn,' said Brand, 'and there is good land in Northumbria. A place to start a family.' He smiled and turned to Sefna, so that the raven tattoo on his neck stretched as though the bird took flight.

'Are you sure you want to settle down with this ruffian?' Beornoth said to Sefna.

'No, but I don't have any better offers, and besides, he is rich now,' she said, smiling. 'Brand is a fine man, and a drengr, and we shall make a life together on my father's land. There are many good Viking folk there. You should come and visit us.'

Sefna's golden hair shone beneath a warm sun, and she was beautiful. The day after the battle, the Christians had buried their dead with honour and said prayers for the souls. But the evening after that solemn ceremony, Beornoth had dragged his tired body to a riverbank to witness a different funeral. A pagan Viking send-off for the brave Northumbrian Vikings who had fallen in battle. Brand had purchased a small fishing boat, but one with a mast and wide enough in the hull to take a pyre of wood. Dolgfinnr, Ornir Hauknefr and the surviving Vikings had brought wood from Branoc's Tree and set deep pyres in the bilge. They had called to Odin and Thor and prayed that the dead warriors were already in Valhalla drinking ale from curved horns with the warriors of Odin's einherjar. Sefna wanted her father Vigdjarf and her sister Hrist sent off in the old way. So, they had lain Vigdjarf, Hrist, Reifnir, Bodil and Anarr on the carefully piled wood inside the boat. Then Brand waded into the river and pushed the ship into the current. Sefna loosed a flaming arrow from her bow, and the shot flew high and true to land in the oil-soaked wood. The ship

:aught fire, and they sent the Vikings to the afterlife with honour, n the old way.

'I wish you both well, and I cannot thank you enough for what you have sacrificed and done for my fallen brothers.' Beornoth :lasped his fist to his breast and bowed his head.

The Lady Ælfflæd had taken the survivors from Branoc's Tree :o Godric's burh at Hareswood and stripped the place of wealth; she had passed most of it to Beornoth's men and Dolgfinnr had departed to Lundenwic to buy himself a new ship and men to crew her. Godric had amassed a fortune in his raids across Essex, and Brand left for Northumbria with saddlebags full of silver.

'You should come with us,' said Brand. 'There will always be a place for you beside my fire, lord.'

'I have a home in Cheshire, and my lady waits for me there. But I will come and visit you both, I promise.'

Brand nudged his horse closer to Beornoth and leaned in. Beornoth fought back the pain in his stomach and pulled Brand into a warm embrace. He held the Viking warrior there for ten heartbeats, pressing him close. He wanted to tell Brand that he loved him like a brother, and that he would miss him now that their days of war were over, but he said none of those things, for that was not the way between warriors. So, they held one another and then parted and Beornoth watched Brand and Sefna ride away until their horses disappeared into the rolling hills.

Beornoth tugged gently on the leather reins, and Virtus wheeled around slowly. He led the horse westwards, although his heart told him to ride hard to the north. There was one last thing Beornoth had to do before he returned home. Three days' hard riding later he stood in a bright courtyard whose walls were hung with bright flowers of blue and yellow. He waited for the king, in the same court-yard where he had met Æthelred two summers ago with Ealdorman

Byrhtnoth inside the royal palace at Winchester. Beornoth wore his
byrnie but had left his weapons with a palace guard, as none were
allowed inside the palace save those carried by the king's guard.

A steward welcomed Beornoth, and upon noticing his Wessex
ring the steward ushered him through the winding palace corri-
dors to wait for the king. After a short time, a heavy door creaked
open on dry hinges and King Æthelred entered the courtyard and
his soft slippers sighed across the cold stone. His thin, callow face
brightened when he saw Beornoth, and he strode forwards.
Æthelred extended his arms and grabbed Beornoth's broad shoul-
ders; it was a warm and genuine gesture which did Beornoth great
honour. He was surprised by the king's warmth and could not hold
back a smile.

'It is good to see you, Beo,' Æthelred said. 'Only this last week I
had the pleasure of confirming Byrhtnoth's daughter's husband as
the new ealdorman of Essex. Oswig seems like a good man, and I
am sure he will serve me well.'

'That is good, lord king,' said Beornoth. After Branoc's Tree,
Thered had taken news of Godric's death to King Æthelred, and
Byrhtnoth's daughter Leoflaed and her husband Oswig had trav-
elled with him. Beornoth had remained to pay his respects at the
Vikings' funerals and so was glad to hear that Essex would remain
within Byrhtnoth's bloodline. 'I came to give you this.' Beornoth
handed Æthelred the Wessex ring he had taken from Hrodgar's
finger.

Æthelred took the ring and turned it over in his hand, exam-
ining it and seeming to reflect on the death of its owner. 'Hrodgar
died doing his duty, but I will miss him, and the kingdom is less
safe without his sword.'

'I could not recover his byrnie or his weapons, lord king. But
please take the ring as a token of Hrodgar's heriot.'

'You have served me well, Beo. The traitors are gone, as is the bishop whose advice I fear has led us along an ill-wrought path. I think Nothhelm is a good candidate for archbishop. A few friendly faces in the Church would be a welcome change. The task you and Hrodgar undertook was a sour business but one which secured the safety of the realm.'

'Yes, lord. Now that it is over, I would return north to my wife.' Beornoth slipped the king's ring from his own finger and handed it to the king. 'I don't...'

'No, Lord Beornoth,' said the king, and he reached out to stay Beornoth's hand. 'You shall remain a king's thegn, and you may return north for now. See your wife and heal your wounds. But I will send for you in the spring, for there is always a need for a sharp sword and a strong arm to wield it. You are my thegn, Beornoth, my sword and shield, and my enemies will fear to cross the throne when they know your blade protects me.'

The king rewarded Beornoth with a pouch of silver and his thanks, and once Beornoth gave his word that he would return to do the king's bidding whenever he called, he left Winchester provisioned for the journey north. Beornoth spent the night in a tavern on the north road and then left the town on a grey morning soaked by a blustery rain. Winchester and the south disappeared behind him as the grey clouds dissipated into long white streaks and as Beornoth rode across the lush greenery of Wessex they faded into a clear sky and a warm southerly wind warmed his neck. Beornoth clicked his tongue, and Virtus set off at a canter. He rode north-west, towards Cheshire. His byrnie and weapons were rolled and tied to the saddle behind him, and Beornoth travelled in a simple leather jerkin and a warm cloak. He closed his eyes and enjoyed the sun's warmth on his face. The fight was over and Beornoth rode to Eawynn where she waited for him in her garden. He smiled, taking comfort because his brothers of the sword were now at peace in heaven. Their souls were avenged, and they could rest for eternity knowing that they had given their lives so that the people of England could live safe and free. Sweyn Forkbeard was back in Denmark, and Olaf Tryggvason had sailed for Norway with a crucifix on the prow of his ship instead of a pagan dragon. Olaf carried away ten thousand pounds of silver to win himself a kingdom. England was at peace, and Beornoth went home to put up his sword, at least for a while. Until the king called when trouble or war reared its ugly head, and Beornoth would ride again to England's aid.

HISTORICAL NOTE

The *Saxon Warrior Series* deals with the events up to and following the historic Battle of Maldon. In *Brothers of the Sword* we saw the events of the battle unfold, and the death of Ealdorman Byrhtnoth. The battle itself is well-documented in the poem of the same name, as I have summarised in the historical notes of the previous three novels in this series. The aftermath, however, is a little harder to piece together. A number of different historical texts exist to help try and build a picture of those events, which include the account of the battle in the *Anglo-Saxon Chronicle, the Lives of St Oswald and St Ecgwine* written by the monk Byrhtferth, and the *Book of Ely.*

The *Book of Ely* is a collection of documents and charters which recorded the conveyances and landholdings along with some historical anecdotes and facts. It was written in the twelfth century, but records a large number of charters and details from the time of Maldon. It is significant because Ealdorman Byrhtnoth was a patron of the Abbey of Ely, and after his death his body was taken there for burial as we have seen in this novel. In the *Book of Ely*, we learn that the Vikings killed Byrhtnoth by forming their spear and shield phalanx, charging the Saxon ranks and decapitating the ealdorman. The book states that the body was recovered and brought to Ely for burial, and I thought it only fitting that Beornoth be the man to wrestle the corpse from the victorious Vikings. The decapitation of Byrhtnoth was confirmed in the eighteenth century when Byrhtnoth's tomb was opened to reveal a tall headless skeleton.

Also in the *Book of Ely* is the reference to a Northumbrian hostage fighting on the side of the East Saxons. Throughout the eleventh century, Northumbria maintained a level of autonomy from the West Saxon south, and earlier in this series I have Byrhtnoth engaged in a peacekeeping mission to that troublesome shire, which led to the fictional character of Thered taking up his role as the historical Northumbrian hostage.

The *Book of Ely* also contains a reference to Byrhtnoth's widow and her actions following the ealdorman's death. The book referred to Byrhtnoth being killed and buried, and that Ælfflæd gave to the church at Ely an estate at Rettendon which had formed part of her marriage portion. At this time the lady also gave to the church land at Soham, a golden torque, and a tapestry embroidered with the deeds of her husband. In this novel I have described that tapestry imagined as a sort of Bayeux Tapestry-type work depicting the events at Maldon. The lady continued to live at Rettendon, as I have described in this novel, and it was Byrhtnoth's daughter and her husband who inherited the shire after Byrhtnoth's death.

In the *Anglo-Saxon Chronicle* are the details of Olaf Tryggvason's conversion to Christianity. The general tone of the chronicle is that the battle at Maldon was a sort of pyrrhic victory for the Vikings, who may have won the battle but in doing so lost the war and retreated back to their homeland. The writer of the chronicle viewed the battle as a spiritual success, in that Olaf was converted

o Christianity and vowed to become an ally of the Saxon king-
dom. Olaf never returned to England once he had left with his
huge gafol payment, and he went on to become king of Norway
and attempted to convert that country to Christianity. It is in the
Chronicle that we also see criticism of the advice given to King
Æthelred by the writer who looks back on the gafol as a thing
which is loathed by the people.

The payment to the Vikings in 991 was ten thousand pounds of
silver, but when they returned again a few years later the payment
rose to sixteen thousand, and then twenty-three thousand pounds
of silver. The *Chronicle* implies that the policy of payment was a
failure and that King Æthelred was badly advised by Archbishop
Sigeric. It is here where we first see the use of the epithet of
Unready, or Unraed, 'badly advised' in Old English. The ultimate
fallout of the gafol is the return of Sweyn Forkbeard, the Danish
king who returned again to England with fire and sword and
whose son, Cnut, would ultimately conquer and become king of
England in 1016.

'The Battle of Maldon' poem is clear that Godric son of Odda is
the traitor who leads the fyrd away from the battle. In the opening
scene of the poem all of the horses are driven away from the battle-
field, but Byrhtnoth stays mounted in order to inspect and
organise his warriors and he only dismounts when the fighting is
about to begin. Godric then steals that horse in the poem,
including its trappings and harness, and Godric and his brothers
are referred to in the poem as the cowards who fled the battle, and
that the men of the fyrd, seeing Byrhtnoth's horse, believed that it
was in fact the ealdorman who ordered the retreat.

In this novel, Beornoth exacts vengeance for his dead brothers
and whilst Beornoth is a fictional character, the events around him
are historical fact, and any inaccuracies are my own. The bind the
king finds himself in was real, and whilst some will question why

Æthelred did not just descend upon Godric with the forces of th
English crown, there is no evidence to say that he did. Æthelre
was at the mercy of the Church and his advisors and so Beornot
is the instrument of his retribution.

Beornoth hopes that he returns to Eawynn for a life of peac
and rest, but the Vikings will return to England in force and, as
king's thegn, Beornoth will need to take up his sword again to
defend the kingdom.

ACKNOWLEDGEMENTS

Thanks to Caroline, Nia, Claire, Jenna, Candida and all the team at Boldwood Books for their belief in Beornoth's story, and for their unwavering support along the way. Special thanks to Ross and the editing team at Boldwood for all their effort and amazing eye for detail.

ABOUT THE AUTHOR

Peter Gibbons is a financial advisor and author of the highly acclaimed Viking Blood and Blade trilogy. He comes to Boldwood with his new Saxon Warrior series, set around the 900 AD Viking invasion during the reign of King Athelred the Unready. He lives with his family in County Kildare.

Sign up to Peter Gibbons' mailing list for news, competitions and updates on future books.

Visit Peter's website: https://petermgibbons.com/

Follow Peter on social media here:

 facebook.com/petergibbonsauthor

 x.com/AuthorGibbons

instagram.com/petermgibbons

bookbub.com/authors/peter-gibbons

ALSO BY PETER GIBBONS

The Saxon Warrior Series

Warrior and Protector

Storm of War

Brothers of the Sword

Sword of Vengeance

WARRIOR CHRONICLES

WELCOME TO THE CLAN ✕

THE HOME OF
BESTSELLING HISTORICAL
ADVENTURE FICTION!

WARNING:
MAY CONTAIN VIKINGS!

SIGN UP TO OUR
NEWSLETTER

BIT.LY/WARRIORCHRONICLES

Boldwood

Boldwood Books is an award-winning fiction publishing company seeking out the best stories from around the world.

Find out more at www.boldwoodbooks.com

Join our reader community for brilliant books, competitions and offers!

Follow us
@BoldwoodBooks
@TheBoldBookClub

Sign up to our weekly deals newsletter

https://bit.ly/BoldwoodBNewsletter

Made in the USA
Columbia, SC
08 February 2024

31742677R00176